Author's

The minute the referee put an end to the added time at the end of Liverpool's semi-final against Chelsea, my thoughts turned to the same place as umpteen thousands of others: Istanbul.

Thought number one. I'm going. Come hell or high water, I'm going to get there. Thought number two. It's not just me. There are my two sons as well. Every flight and room will be booked already. It's going to cost an arm and a leg and I'm flat broke. Thought number three. All the once in a lifetime stuff. To miss it wouldn't be fair on the two lads. I had already had four European Cups. This might be their only chance.

So like the umpteen thousands of others I started to try and justify to myself why it was OK to fill the credit card up to bursting point. This is where I am somewhat different to most, and maybe why I was able to come up with one of the more exotic justifications for spending money I didn't have.

As a writer of thrillers, I came up with what I felt was a pretty sound theory. We are at a point in history where the East and the West are once again at loggerheads. The Christian and Muslim worlds haven't been at each others throats to this extent since Richard the Lionheart and Saladin. For three thousand years the East has met the West in a particular place. Byzantium. Constantinople. Istanbul. And it seemed like the prospect of dropping forty five thousand Scousers into the middle of it all was a case of fact becoming far stranger than fiction. So it was that I made it seem OK to spend the money and to make the pilgrimage because it seemed like there simply had to be a book in the whole thing somewhere.

Little did I know!

What happened down there both on and off the pitch was a complete and utter one off. The fantastic hospitality of the Bulgarians and the Turks, the unbelievable procession of all the yellow taxis, the human wave of reds yomping to the stadium past snipers and old boys herding goats, the stadium in the middle of a Dr Who set, the bedlam in the food and drink free 'Fan Zone', the sight of four-fifths of the stadium all red.

THE LONG AND WINDING
ROAD TO ISTANBUL

And then of course there was the game.

When it was all over and we fell into our hire car which doubled up as a hotel room, I sat and watched the crowd drain away into the night. That was when I realised that this was going to be more than a book. It was a whole lot more. It was the greatest night any father could ever have had with his sons. It was a city that had been kicked in the teeth ever since Thatcher, getting back to its feet to do an Ali against Foreman. It was forty-five thousand Scousers coming to one of the great Muslim cities and learning all about the hospitality of Islam and realising what a pack of lies we have been sold by Bush and Blair. It had been the greatest comeback of all time. And not just by eleven guys on the pitch, but also by all the ones on the terraces who drowned out Italian celebrations at half-time with the 'You'll Never Walk Alone' to end all 'You'll Never Walk Alones'. A comeback by a city that the rest of the country had got used to laughing about. It had been a night where for once history and tradition and sheer undiluted belief had managed to overcome smug piles of cash.

And as they finally switched off the floodlights, it was really clear that nothing would ever be quite like it again. The road to Istanbul had led to a piece of ultimate sporting theatre. And yes, there just had to be a book in it.

When I got home and started thinking about it, one thing was really clear. The whole event had been drenched in history. The road to Istanbul started a long time before the lads took on AZ Graz in August 2005. It probably started on the day that Bill Shankly started his new job. For me, it was a road that had started in 1977. The mind numbing game against St Etienne and the 'Joey eats Frogs Legs' banner and the great invasion of Rome. There seemed so many similarities to the Rome final and Istanbul. Both were long trips made by hook or by crook by thousands of fans. Rome was the first victory. Istanbul was the fifth, which meant that the trophy would come back to Anfield for keeps. A start and an end. Symmetry.

To reflect this longer road to Istanbul, I decided to start the book in 1977 and take snapshots of the lives of the characters through five European Cup Finals As the story evolved, it took me completely by surprise in that it became a love story. It seemed strange that a book about nearly thirty years of Liverpool in European Cup Finals should turn into a romance. But maybe it isn't so strange after all. We Brits

AUTHOR'S NOTE

aren't the market leaders when it comes to being romantic. Our women never tire of telling us what a lousy second we come to the great Latin purveyors of passion from Italy and France. And yet when it comes to showing passion on a football terrace, they don't even get close. About fifteen thousand made it from Milan to Istanbul and it was a thousand miles nearer. Forty-five thousand of us got there. They like their football team. We love ours. There lies the difference. Maybe that was why 'The Long and Winding Road to Istanbul' turned into a love story.

The other great theme of the story is all about going down and down and then being given one last chance. The story of Liverpool Football Club from the eighties has been so similar to that of the city. The framework of the story gave the opportunity for me to travel back in time to when I was a young man in the days of Thatcher and Scargill and the Toxteth riots and those dark, dark days of the eighties when Yosser Hughes took the pain of Merseyside to the living rooms of Britain. It was a decade that started badly, got worse with Heysel, and ended in the utter nightmare of Hillsborough. Mickey's life is a tale of decline and fall, that mirrors that of the city where he lives and the team that he loves. Getting to Istanbul becomes his last chance of turning it all around.

In many ways, the stakes in Istanbul were the highest any team has ever played for. Winning meant the chance to compete in this year's tournament, of the captain staying, of Carlsberg hanging on in there. More than that, it was the icing on the cake on the city's long road back to self respect to go along with becoming the European City of Culture.

The book is also a thriller. This is basically what I do. So far I have written and published six books, which have now gone through the 50,000 sales mark. There is no league table for self-published authors, but I guess I would be higher than mid-table if there was one. I have had a tonne of feedback from readers who tell me that my books keep them up until two and three in the morning when they have to be up for work the next day. I make no claims to great literature. I try to be a storyteller, and entertainer, to give value for money to the punter. I have never, ever enjoyed writing a story as much as this one. Hopefully that comes out on every page.

A few minutes after the last penalty was taken and missed and the whole place went crazy, we all started a chant that seemed to say it all.

THE LONG AND WINDING ROAD TO ISTANBUL

It was a chant that we have all had to suffer from the fans from the likes of Middlesborough and Birmingham City for the last year or two. It was a chant that they would start up as Liverpool huffed and puffed to yet another miserable defeat or draw. "Champions League, you're having a laugh" meant one thing when they sang it. It meant something quite different when we all sang it in the Ataturk Stadium.

The sheer undiluted pent up passion of that chant is what this book is all about.

Mark Frankland
July 2005

The Long and
Winding Road
to Istanbul

MARK FRANKLAND

A Glenmill Publication

© Mark Frankland, 2005

The moral right of the author has been asserted.

First published in 2005

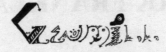

Glenmill Publishing
Dumfries
Scotland
DG2 8PX

tel: 07770 443 483

http://www.thecull.com

British Library Cataloguing in Publication Data.
A catalogue record of this book
is available from the British Library.

ISBN 0 9551057 0 6

Glenmill logo: Andrew Carroll AKA 'Gizmo'

Printed and bound in Great Britain

Dedication

Just about every football fan in the world will tell you that there is something uniquely special about following their team. Those of us who follow Liverpool like to think for us it is something that is extra special. We are the 'Twelfth Man' who broke the world record for human sound as the lads toppled the supposedly invincible Chelsea to make the final. We are the ones who filled the Turkish night with the sound of 'You'll Never Walk Alone' when we were three down and dead and buried.

From 1971 to 1989, being a season ticket holder at Anfield meant league and cup triumph and European glory. And of course it was special.

But on April 15 1989 being a Liverpool fan became something else altogether. None of us who lived through those nightmare minutes on the Leppings Lane End at Hillsborough will ever forget what we saw. Before that day I was a Blackburn lad who had a Liverpool season ticket. After that day I felt that Liverpool was forever a part of me.

I suppose that 15th April 1989 was the turning point of my life. At three o'clock that afternoon I was just seconds away from being crushed to death. If that had happened, I would never have got to take either of my boys to Anfield. But I was one of the lucky ones and so all three of us were there that night in Istanbul.

Ninety-six were not so lucky.

So I dedicate these efforts to the ninety-six who never made it home from Sheffield and all their families and loved ones. And all those who still fight for justice after so many years of lies and cover-up. And all those who still refuse to buy The Sun.

I'll leave the last word to Ian Prowse and Amsterdam and their fantastic 'Does This Train Stop on Merseyside'.

> *'Yorkshire policemen chat with folded arms
> while people try and save their fellow fans'*

Contents

Contents

Chapter 1
Rome – May 1977

It was just after five o'clock in the afternoon and the plan was falling apart fast. A plan that only a few hours earlier had seemed like a really good plan. Almost a perfect plan. Perfect for the day.

The day.

25th May 1977.

A red-letter day. A red day.

The playground at St. Mary's Comprehensive School was split down the usual lines. Red and Blue. Koppite and Toffee. Liverpool and Everton. Of course the split was nothing new. The split was eighty years old and it ran like a great fault line through the whole of the city. It ran through workplaces and schools and households and families. It was a divide that spawned a billion arguments a year. Every minute of every hour of every day, somewhere in the city there was red arguing the toss with a blue. Some days were quieter than others. Lazy summer days with the football season weeks away. Or chilly days of autumn where the next Derby match was still a few months in the future. And then there were days when the whole thing hit fever pitch as the city breathlessly counted down the hours to a clash of the Mersey neighbours.

May 25 1977 was slightly different, but utterly massive all the same. The reds were gearing up for the greatest night in their history. The Holy Grail was just a few hours away. The European Cup. It was more than a heavy piece of silverware. It was the culmination of the dream that Bill Shankly had sold to the red half of the city for eighteen years. Winning would be a culmination. The end of an epic journey. A place at football's high table. For days the city had been emptying out as thousands took the road to the Olympic Stadium in Rome.

Emotions were always going to run high during the final lunch break before the night of nights. The reds were counting down the hours to kick off and every second crawled by like a crippled snail. The blues were sick of the whole thing. Everton had completed a season of grinding mediocrity and bragging rights were all but non-existent. For months they had suffered a more or less continual onslaught of red gloating and now they had just about had enough. Watching their neighbours claim the league title and then miss the FA Cup by a whisker had been bad enough. But now the crowing had hit a new peak. Time to fight back.

It was plainly obvious that the eleven donkeys in blue shirts who turned out at Goodison Park every other Saturday were utterly incapable of doing the fighting on behalf of their followers. So it was that a group of Evertonians threw down the gauntlet ten minutes before the end of a lunch break that had felt like it would never end. The park at the back of Ondurman Street at five o'clock. Six a side. Liverpool versus Everton. Except for the one match it wouldn't be Everton. For one night the Evertonians were going to turn into Germans. They would wear white T-shirts and they would be Burussia Munchengladbach, the champions of West Germany who stood between Liverpool and a lifetime of crowing from their fans.

The game was every bit as intriguing as the main event to be played out in the Olympic Stadium a few hours later. The reds might have ruled the roost in terms of the city, but as far as the second year at St. Mary's Comprehensive was concerned, it was the blues who held most of the cards. The two star players of the year were both diehard Everton and both were signed up for a one-day transfer to the Rhineland. The odds favoured a bet on blue, but as pundits never tired of telling their public, you could never, ever tell with a derby match . . . .

By five past five the plan lay in tatters and the arguments had started. Donny Sanderson was an unusually large boy for his age and he was the centre forward for the school team. There had been talk that he might even make the squad for the region, and from there the road to a Goodison apprenticeship would lie open. He was going to be the prime threat for the blue Germans. The problem was that before leaving for school that morning he had lifted a fifty pence piece from his dad's pocket and the coin had been missed. It was a tough break. He took a coin or two from his dad's pocket most mornings and their loss was never noticed. His dad was a bus driver who liked a pint or ten after his shift and when he woke his brain was never in any kind of state to recall how much change he had finished the night with. But the fates were against the Evertonians and their star striker. Donny's dad was as blue as his son and for that reason he had avoided the pub the night before. He had been in no mood to suffer several hours of gloating reds. Instead he had gone to help a workmate who was re-spraying his car. They had downed a couple of cans of Long Life, but mostly they had stuck with mugs of tea. As a result Donny's dad had woken to the sound of a chaffinch chirping outside and a head that was as clear as a mountain stream. And he knew exactly what he had left in his pocket; change from the pound that he had given to the bus conductor on his way home.

Donny's brother was the messenger.

"He's not coming. No chance. Grounded for ages mi' dad says. Not even allowed to watch the match. I'll play though, if you like . . ."

The five one-day Germans looked down at Donny's kid brother with undisguised contempt. The boy took after his petite Irish mother rather than his six-foot-plus dad. He was an eight-year-old who would have been on the small side for a six-year-old and there was no chance in a million years that he was about to be given the nod.

The next shattering team news was that Alan Boston had taken a fall from his bike on his way to the park. Mrs Henshaw had gone for his mum and his mum had said that the cut looked nasty even though Alan claimed it was not. He had last been seen being marched back to the house. A major argument between mother and son was causing the curtains to twitch all down the street. Mother's view was that it was a nasty cut and muck would probably have got in and that it would have to be seen to properly. And that meant a bus ride to the casualty department. Alan knew all about the casualty department. He had been there a year earlier when he had fallen fifteen feet from a tree in Stanley Park whilst climbing for a magpie nest. That day he had found levels of boredom he had never believed possible as he had sat for four-and-three-quarter hours trying to amuse himself with dog-eared copies of the National Geographic. He wasn't the best maths student in the school, but his sums were more than good enough to work out that a similar delay would mean missing the match and that wasn't even close to being acceptable. In the end he was saved by his dad's arrival home from work. His dad took a look at the cut and declared it to be "summat and nowt" and duly told his wife not to be so daft. This led to a major parental row and his mum spent the night upstairs in the bedroom whilst dad went down the road for chips and father and son watched the match together. Time was to prove dad right as the wound healed with no trace of gangrene, though a small scar remained which for the rest of his life would remind Alan of crowing reds and the last days of childhood before his parents' bitter divorce in 1979.

The news of Alan Baxter's injury threw the whole game into question. If it had been six against five then it might just have been a goer. Even with five, the blue Germans still had three key school teamers and every chance of victory. In fact they were even sensing a 'no-lose scenario'. Were they to win, then it could be painted as a true triumph in the face of adversity. Clear proof of the innate superiority of the men in blue from the Goodison 'School of Science'. Were they to lose, then it wouldn't really count because it was six against five, which meant it wasn't a proper match at all. Even a draw could be turned into a moral victory.

But six against four wasn't on. Not a chance. Which meant there were only two choices. Option one was to call the whole thing off and go home. Nobody much fancied option one. Home meant homework or taking the rubbish out or tidying rooms. Which meant that option two was given long and careful consideration. Option two was based on a simple mathematical solution to the problem. Liverpool had six players. Burussia Everton had four. Were Liverpool to make one of their players available it would be five a side and the game would once again be on. The principle was clear enough but the detail was never going to be easy. The burning issue was which player would take the walk from red to blue. The Germans demanded that it should be their choice whilst Liverpool dug in their heels and said there was no chance.

This was the kind of impasse that the city had come to know on a daily basis. Usually the impasse would be between unions and management over grievances that the national press never tired of featuring. In any other city, a disagreement over the duration of a tea break would generally be resolved fairly easily. Not so in Liverpool. An argument over five minutes of break time could easily lead to a five week strike. The players from both teams were well used to hearing these kinds of disputes being discussed by their dads and their mates and they knew how to argue a point. By twenty past five there was no give on either side and a dog-walker was summoned to arbitrate. As luck would have it the dog-walker was a shop steward himself and he was able to bring a resolution to the conflict.

A coin was tossed, but only when it had been agreed in advance that there was no question of it being best of three. The reds called heads and heads it was. The principle was thus agreed. Liverpool had won the right to chose which of their players would take the walk. Five were delighted with the outcome. One was distraught. Mickey McGuire was the one who was distraught because he didn't need anyone to tell him who would be expected to take the walk. It would be him.

Football in general and Liverpool in particular had occupied the centre of Mickey's world from the age of four. His bedroom was a living shrine to the men in red. There was not a single square inch of wall space that wasn't covered by a poster or pennant or scarf. His bed lay under the gaze of the gods who stared down from all sides. Kevin Keegan. Tommy Smith. Steve Heighway. Arms folded for their pre season photos. Mickey's life revolved around Liverpool. He collected the cards. He devoured the magazines. During the holidays he got up early to take three buses to the training ground at Melwood where he would wait with other fellow disciples for the chance of an autograph. Most of the time there was no chance but he didn't care because he would still get a glimpse as they sped away through the gates after training. Every other Saturday it was the journey to his Mecca. The gates of the Kop end opened at one o'clock and by five past he would have claimed a place at the front of the boys pen.

When it came to football banter Mickey had talent bordering on world class. The problem was that when it came to actually playing football he was not even good enough to be called bad. He was hopeless. At school he was good at English and exceptional at music but a place in the school football team was about as near as a seat on an Apollo rocket headed out to the moon. Unlike his brother Frank, he never seemed to grow. Frank was fifteen-and-a-half and he was already closing in on six foot. More to the point he was the cock of the fifth form and widely acknowledged to be hard as nails. Only two weeks earlier he had dropped Kevin Findlay in a playground fight that had already passed into legend. Mickey on the other hand was not only small, but he was skinny and small. At thirteen he had yet to tip the scales over seven stones and his school uniform still came from the 10/11-year-old rack. If you were big and hard you could get by on the football pitch without much talent. But if you had no talent and you were small and skinny then you were all but out of options. Mickey had no talent and he was small and skinny and everyone knew it. He knew it. It had been what the toss of the coin had really been all about. If Liverpool won then Mickey McGuire would be handed the short straw and sent packing to the hated blues.

But what Mickey lacked in physical stature and football ability he more than made up for in mouth. In a city that was world famous for its lip, Mickey McGuire had more than his share of it. No way was he going to accept his fate without a big fight and he was giving it the verbal equivalent of a Tommy Smith two-footed tackle when his brother's voice stopped him in full flow.

"Mickey! Come here will you."

All heads turned to the undisputed cock of the fifth year and possible cock of the whole school who waited at the edge of the field. Frank McGuire's arrival on the scene potentially changed everything. If Frank decided that his little brother was going to take up a place in the Liverpool starting line-up then that was exactly what would happen. Nobody was ever going to argue that particular toss. Not in a thousand months of Sundays. As Mickey jogged over to his bother the five remaining reds fell into a huddle to start to develop a contingency plan in anticipation of an edict from Frank McGuire.

"Y'alright Frank."

"Yeah. Great."

"They're making me play for Everton Frank. Well not really Everton. It's Borussia Munchengladbach really. Well it's both like. But they's are two short coz Donny Sanderson nicked ten bob off his dad and Alan Boston fell off his bike so that means it's six against four so they said we's got to give them one of ours and they reckon it's got to me but I say that's not on like 'cos I go to loads more games than any of that lot and . . . "

"But you're crap Mickey."

"You wha'?"

"You're crap. Just cos you've got a load of autographs doesn't mean you're any use. You're not. You're rubbish."

"Come off it Frank, you're supposed to…"

"I'm supposed to nothing. Anyway you're not playing. You're coming with me."

"I'm bloody well not, I'm . . . "

"Mickey. I said you're coming with me. And I said it in English."

Mickey had grown up with this tone in his brother's voice. It was that all too familiar thirty seconds before getting battered tone. It was a tone that he had long learnt to listen to. He just couldn't believe it. The greatest day of his life was falling around him like a pack of cards. First they had tried to make him play for Everton and now he wasn't even going to play at all. Now he was going to have to go with his Frank and the thought of it put a shiver through him. For most of his life there had been nothing he had wanted to do more than to go with his brother Frank. Frank had always been a god to him. Hard as nails. Harder than anyone. Going with Frank meant going with the bigger lads who never messed with him. Trips into the city centre or the arcades at New Brighton. Magic days where he always felt a foot taller. But things were different now. They had been different ever since Frank had taken to hanging around with Eddie Tate.

From just about the very moment that Mickey had started to understand the English language there had been a single, consistent fact drummed into him by both his mum and his dad. Stay clear of the Tate family. Not just clear, but about a million miles clear. The Tate family were trouble. The mum was trouble. The dad was trouble. The uncles were trouble. The cousins were trouble. And every one of the seven children who were packed into a house two streets down from where the McGuires lived were trouble. The patriarch of the clan, Gerry Tate was seldom seen anywhere but Walton Prison, in fact there were many who wondered how he had managed to sire such a brood during his always brief tastes of freedom. This time he was down for serious time having been caught attempting a woefully planned armed robbery on a post office in Ormskirk. This left his embattled wife Sheila to bring up the seven children as well as she could. Eddie was the oldest and at seventeen he was already up to enough for neighbours to have 'like father, like son' conversations over the back fence. Yet he wasn't really much like his father at all. Of course they were similar in one key area. Both were more than happy to build and enhance their reputations on the threat of blind, unthinking violence. Eddie had followed his father's lead in this regard and even shared the Stanley knife as a favoured weapon.

Had Eddie stayed on at St. Mary's to sit his A-levels there would have been no question of Frank McGuire even getting close to being cock of the school. This was a role that Eddie had assumed during his third year and had held without a single challenge until he had left at the age of sixteen. Already there were three who walked about their neighbourhood with the trademark neat scar of his blade on their cheeks. However, the similarities between father and son ended with their shared ability for applied violence. The fact was that Eddie could easily have stayed on for the sixth year had the fancy taken him because unlike his dad he was smart. In another life, the path he would have walked would have taken him on to three or four A levels, a good degree and a highly lucrative career in the law or business. The violence would still have been there of course but it would have found a legal home on the rugby field. It was of course a world that Eddie Tate was never going to get a sniff at. His accent and family name were always going to be enough to ensure that would never happen. Not that such a life held any attraction for him. He had grown up with crime and it was always going to become his chosen career. Now at seventeen he was already moving steadily up the ladder.

It wasn't just his brains that set Eddie apart from his father. He also had the happy knack of managing not to get caught which of course was largely down to his ability to think through and plan what he did. His growing number of activities were common knowledge to the neighbourhood and the police who were tasked to keep control. He had been a number one target at the local nick from the age of fourteen but they had never got close to catching him for anything. Eddie didn't hide away his success. He cruised his patch in a gleaming black Ford Capri which he had purchased perfectly legally from a second-hand car dealer in Maghull. To start with the police had stopped him at least twice a day until they had grown tired of his smug smile and impeccable documentation. Whenever they demanded sight of his licence and insurance he made a point of opening his wallet in such a way that they would get a good look at the wedge of tenners that made the stitching on the leather look likely to burst.

The key to Eddie's success was an innate ability to delegate. He did the thinking and negotiating part of the work. But the criminal part was always sub-contracted out to a growing band of foot soldiers. His cannabis trading was typical. He had taken a train over to visit a flat in Moss Side one day to agree supply terms with a Rastafarian trio who sold some of the best grass in the North of England. Once terms and protocols were agreed he never saw them again. Instead he sent youngsters on the round trip to Manchester to buy and collect. In fact it was very rare that Eddie even laid eyes on the product. He merely arranged his various sub-contractors to collect and sell the goods on his behalf. Two of them had strayed from the path and they now wore the trademark cheek scar of someone who had tried it on with the Tates. The last instance of internal corruption had been well over a year ago and the message had been heard loud and clear. Now at the age of seventeen-and-a-half, Eddie Tate was already one of the richest individuals in the neighbourhood and he was a young man in a hurry. His shiny Capri was a magnet for the prettier girls who came into his life and left it like takeaway food, usually departing with a piece of jewelry as a consolation prize. Eddie was wary of attachment, which his instincts told him would easily become baggage to hold him back. He wasn't in a hurry to take on more baggage. Six brothers and sisters and a mother who was fond of the gin were quite enough.

However, as his empire expanded it became clear that he couldn't do everything himself. He was going to need a lieutenant at some stage and finding one became something of a priority. Frank McGuire was a clear candidate for the role. He had known Frank from an early age having shared playgrounds at two schools. He had seen at first hand how easily Frank had always held the position of cock of every year he had been in. As far as Eddie was concerned, it was the way that Frank carried the mantle that interested him more that the fact that he carried it. He liked the way that Frank fought his battles. He did what was needed to put his opponent on the deck and no more. Once they were down he would quietly ask his opponent if they agreed that hostilities were over and that was that. He didn't bother carrying on with a fight once it was over and Eddie was impressed with that. It meant that Frank had never been suspended from school. It meant that he was respected as well as feared and that was something that Eddie knew would be a key asset for his business. He had been quietly cultivating his second in command for over a year and Frank had done nothing to disappoint.

The day had brought a problem that Eddie hadn't seen coming and it had to be dealt with in a big hurry. A sequence of events had unfolded which had left him feeling agitated and annoyed. Things had started a couple of months earlier when he had met up with his Rasta Ganja men in a pub on Claremont Road. They had told him that they had a big demand for blue Valium and that they would always be in the market if Eddie could come up with something. He had sat back into the threadbare wall seat and given them the confident smile of the up-and-coming executive. No problem lads. Give me a couple of weeks. And they had looked like they were proper impressed and they had got the next round in. Eddie's confidence had not seemed at all misplaced at the time. He had learned fast that the most valuable commodity in his game was intelligence. He had developed a knack of cultivating sources of any intelligence that might turn into profit at a later date. One such snippet had come from one of the girls who had once upon a time ridden in state in the black Capri before being moved along with a hot bracelet from Samuel's which Eddie had traded for a quarter of Moroccan black.

The one time gangster's mol had left school and won herself a job as a cleaner at the university. One day she waved Eddie down with a new nugget of information that won her a Chinese takeaway, twenty Rothmans and a fiver for her purse. A second year medical student had been working late one night and had been much taken by the voluptuous curves that stretched the young cleaner's T-shirt to the limit. One thing had led to another and they had gone out. The nugget came out after a fortnight of unbridled passion. The medical student had a fondness for the horses. A very considerable fondness which had taken away every penny of his grant and left him not only skint, but also owing money to the kind of guys who it was a very good idea not to be in debt to. So it was that he wondered aloud one night over a third joint whether or not his new girlfriend maybe had any friends who might be able to shift certain medicines which he was in a position to acquire. Three days later the girlfriend returned with £40 in her purse and an order for 100 blue Valium. All went smoothly.

Eddie instructed the cleaner to drop the pills off on one of his runners who duly split the haul five ways and within a few hours Eddie had turned his £40 stake into £80

The trade had steadily grown and the student had felt sufficiently confident to ask for a £100 advance on future sales to clear away the threat of having his legs broken by one of his creditors. Eddie had decided that it was an investment worth making in order to tie up future supplies.

On his way back from Manchester he had given himself a pat on the back for his far-sighted approach. Now his source was about to come good in a big way and the blues for weed trade would be a serious earner. Then came the hitch. He met his ex-moll off the bus from the city centre to find her love sick and distraught. Her white-coated beau hadn't used the £100 to clear debts. He had put the whole wedge on the 2.30 at Haydock Park and the whole wedge had stayed put in the Ladbrokes' tills. The student's medical training made him more aware than most of the long term implications of having his legs broken with a lump hammer and so he had skipped town and returned to his parents in Hull. Eddie was seething. Of course he could call his Rasta suppliers and tell them that things hadn't worked out. But that would have meant losing both face and credibility and he wasn't ready to risk either. Not unless he had to. What was needed was a plan B. Thanks to his carefully assembled database of intelligence he had exactly such a plan.

At school Mary Rogerson had always been one who sat at the front of the class. Her dad worked in the Job Centre and the family drank wine with their dinner. She had achieved a triumphant seven O-levels and was on route to Keele University when she had got pregnant and had to settle for a job in Harris Pharmacy instead. Despite her official teacher's pet status Mary had always harboured dreams of being an Eddie Tate moll and she achieved that ambition in a very small way when she told him that Mr Harris hadn't fixed the lock on the window in the storeroom, and that even though it looked secure from the outside, it wasn't actually even on the catch. Eddie had rewarded her with £20 to spend on the little one, but more important to Mary was the fact that for the first time ever he had actually noticed her existence. He had taken a stroll along the alleyway at the back of the chemist shop one night and clocked the fact that although the window in question was small it was by no means unbreachable. He had decided that the window could be kept on ice for a rainy day and now thanks to the 2.30 at Haydock Park the rain was splashing in the gutters.

The problem with plan B was that it was not all that well formed. In fact it wasn't really formed at all. The sum of the components was that the chemist window was insecure and that a small boy could wriggle through without too much trouble. Mary had also mentioned that there was no alarm fitted. Now Eddie had just one evening to turn what he had into a result, as he was meeting the Rastas at a service station the next day. It became clear very quickly that he would not be able to stay as far away from the operation as usual. Harris Chemists was a good three miles away from his heartland and there would be a transport element required which he would have to cover with the Capri. That gave him a start. Find a small lad. Get him down to the back alley. Then what? Lookout. There would have to be a lookout, maybe even a second lad to give the climber a bunk up if required. OK. Two needed. Drop off. Park up a safe distance away. One to go in. One to keep watch. Get the Vallies and go. No other way.

The next task was to decide on who to get on board for the job. He had plenty of candidates who would be up for it for twenty quid or so but time was against him, especially as the whole of the city was consumed in anticipation of the big match. It didn't take him long to work out that here was the moment to throw the biggest test yet to his trainee lieutenant. Frank McGuire had a little brother. An undergrown skinny little brother called Mickey who would fit through the window as easily as a ferret slipping down a rabbit hole. Mickey was a mouthy little sod but as far as Eddie knew he wasn't one for getting himself into bother. Well that would be down to his brother to sort out. If he wanted his place at the high table it was the kind of thing Frank would have to be able to deal with.

Eddie parked up the Capri a couple of streets away from the school on the route he knew Frank took to walk home. His suspicions were confirmed by the shadow that passed over Frank's face when he brought him up to speed with the situation.

"When's it need to be done by?"

"Got to be tonight sometime. I'm meeting them tomorrow dinnertime."

Frank stared out at the small groups of school children making their way home.

"It'll need to be done soon."

"How come?"

"You know our Mickey. Liverpool mad isn't he. No way I'll get him along if he thinks he's going to miss the game."

"Stuff that Frank. Get the little shite told. Just sort it."

Frank turned his head and looked Eddie full in the face. It was one of the things that Eddie liked about him. The lad had just about no fear in him.

"Seriously Eddie. I could kick him into next week and he wouldn't come if it meant missing the game. It's the European Cup Final for Christ's sake."

Now it was Eddie's turn to stare ahead and drum his fingers on the steering wheel. Frank wasn't the only one with younger sibling issues to overcome. Number four out of the Tate seven was Lucy and she was the self appointed madam of the household. Tonight was her dancing class and taxiing her to and from was one of the jobs that Eddie undertook as the head of the family in the absence of his father. He doubted that there was anything Mickey McGuire could do that would come close to the tantrum he would have to deal with if he told Lucy that he couldn't take her. When it came to tantrums his Lucy was in a class of her own and it didn't matter if Eddie Tate was hard enough to slice up cheeks with his Stanley knife, he still shuddered at the thought of his little sister going off on one. He was beginning to wish he'd never had anything to do with coming up with a tub of Vallies. But life was all about choices and decisions and Eddie pressed on with honing the plan to meet the needs of the moment.

"OK. Let's have a look at it. You need to tell your Mickey we'll be all done and dusted and back for the game in time. That means we need to do the thing right now. I need to run our Lucy to her dance class so the only way is to kill two birds with one stone. Where's your Mickey now?"

"He's off down the park for a match with some of the lads."

"Right. I'll drop you there and go for Lucy. You bring him to the bus stop on the main road. We do the chemist, drop Lucy and back for the match. Good enough?"

Frank nodded. He didn't like it much. He knew how his mum and dad felt about him and Eddie Tate hanging around with each other and it didn't bother him much. He wasn't going to get any O-levels and he knew what was waiting for him once he left school. All over Merseyside lads left school for the dole queue. Well, the ones with no exams did. Eddie Tate was his ticket to something much better than lying in bed until lunchtime and eking out a living on eighteen quid a week. But Mickey was different. Mickey was smart and even though his head was always up in the clouds there was no reason why he shouldn't be one of the ones to do alright for himself. Frank was forever lecturing his younger brother about staying out of bother. He was worse than their dad on that front.

But now his two worlds had collided and there was no getting away from it. He could open the passenger door and walk. It was an option. But he knew Eddie well enough to know for a stone cold fact that the door would be forever closed on him if he took the hike. If he went along with the plan he would somehow have to make absolutely sure that Mickey knew that this was an absolute one off. Not easy, but the thought of the empty weeks on the dole pushed him into the decision.

"OK. Good enough. Give me twenty minutes and we'll be there."

Eddie slapped the dashboard in satisfaction. "Top man Franko. I knew you'd come through. Let's get it on then."

Frank found it hard to maintain a stone face as he marched Mickey away from the challenge match in the park. He suddenly hated himself more than ever before. Maybe if he'd worked a bit harder at school he might heading for a job now and could soon be treating his little brother to an LP or a new Liverpool scarf rather than press-ganging him into climbing through a chemist window to nick a tub of blues.

"Come on Frank! What's going on? Where are we going . . . "

"Look Mickey. Just shut it will yous! We're going, OK. Just leave it at that."

"That's not on . . . "

Frank spun on his heels and clamped his hands on his brother's bony shoulders. "Mickey. Don't get me pissed off. You know what happens when I get pissed off."

Despite giving it everything he had, Mickey couldn't stop the two tears that burst from his lids and started their way down his cheeks. Frank gritted his teeth as the rancid taste of self-disgust made him feel sick to the stomach.

"Come on. We'll be late."

Mickey wiped at his eyes with his sleeve and walked in silence at his brother's side. They turned a corner and the sight of the black Capri with the engine idling made Mickey stiffen.

"We're not going with Eddie Tate are we Frank?"

"Just shut it OK Mickey."

"But you know what dad says Frank, he'll kill us if . . . "

"Dad's not here Mickey. Dad will never know about any of this. We're going somewhere and we'll come back and that will be it."

Mickey was about to argue more but the look on Frank's face was horrible. Instead he climbed into the back of the car whilst his brother joined Eddie Tate in the front. As soon as he saw the car his brain had started to run at triple speed as he tried to work out was about to happen. Of course he knew that Frank was up to no good with Eddie Tate. But Frank was forever giving him loads of grief about not getting into trouble and that. So what was going on now? As he plonked himself moodily down on the back seat he was in for another shock, for sitting just a few inches away was Lucy Tate.

It was the first time in his life that he had ever sat just a few inches away from Lucy Tate although he had spend many an idle hour thinking about it. In the classroom he sat near the front whilst Lucy occupied a desk at the back. In the playground he knocked about with the other lads from the third form whilst Lucy Tate was rumoured to spend her breaks snogging fourth and fifth formers. As far as Mickey was concerned, Lucy Tate was to womankind what Liverpool was to the world of football. She was perfection. An icon. A living, breathing, walking, pouting fantasy, and all of a sudden his mouth was as dry as a bar in Iran.

"All right Mickey?" Big saucer eyes and a small mocking smile. Was she taking the piss? Of course she was taking the piss. The idea of saying a word was out of the question so he stared fiercely at the back of the front passenger seat whilst his face mirrored the colour of his team.

Lucy was used to making boys blush and she was instantly delighted by the effect she was having. Her and Mickey had been all the way through primary school together and now they had almost completed their third year in secondary. She had always liked him. There was something dead cool about him, especially when he was cracking the jokes. But in all that time he had never so much spoken a word to her. There was nothing unusual about that. Most of the kids at both of her schools had been told to have nothing to do with her for the very simple and obvious reason that her name was Tate and nobody wanted their kids to have anything to do with the Tate family because the Tate family were the scum of the earth. When Frank had started knocking about with Eddie she had rather hoped that Mickey might at least acknowledge the fact that she existed, but he hadn't. Not once. And now here he was blushing like the best of them and looking like he wanted the ground to open up and swallow him. Then another thought occurred to her. What the hell was he doing in Eddie's car at all?

Eddie leaned round and gave Mickey a big we're all mates kind of smile.

"Looking forward to the big match then are you Mickey?"

Mickey kept focused on the seat back. "Yeah."

"Gonna win then are we?"

"Yeah."

Now Lucy was getting more than a little rattled. She realised she was being kept in the dark and that was something she really hated.

"What's going on Eddie?"

Eddie rolled his eyes at the tone of voice. For a good three square miles around the place he had grown up, his name was spoken with fear. Eddie Tate son of Gerry. Eddie Tate who cut you if you messed him about. But none of it washed with his little sister who gave him more lip than the rest of the world put together. Even the police were more respectful.

"We've just got somewhere to go, that's all."

"Well I'd best not miss my dance class or there's bloody war on."

"Calm bloody down. You're not missing anything. We'll do what we need to do and you'll be there in loads of time."

"So what do you have to do then?"

Eddie sighed. This wasn't going to be good. Lucy was happy enough for him to pay for dance classes and pay for fancy clothes but she insisted on pretending that he earned the cash through good old-fashioned honest endeavour. Bloody fantasy island. But there was no way round it today. He would have to explain to Mickey what was about to happen and Lucy was going to have to hear it whether she liked it or not.

He leaned round a little more so that he could fix Mickey with a full on stare.

"OK Mickey. This is what's happening. There's something I need like. Something I've promised to a couple of guys and I need to keep the promise. So me and you and Frank are going to get it. Simple as that. In. Out. Back for the match and £20 in your pocket."

Mickey was looking up now with real fear in his eyes. In? Out? What did they want him to do? He was about to ask but Lucy beat him to the punch.

"Stop talking in riddles. What kind of something are you on about Eddie?"

Eddie took a slow breath and gathered in his growing temper. He was just about sick of beating about the bush.

"I promised some guys a big order of blue Valium. This lad was supposed to get them for me but he's pissed off. So we're going to Harris Chemists and Mickey here is going in through the back window to get them whilst Frank keeps watch. Piece of cake. Five minutes and we'll be done."

The words nailed into Mickey like rubber bullets. He couldn't believe it. Only a few minutes before he had been looking forward to a game of football and then getting home for the match of matches and now he was in a car with Eddie and Lucy Tate and they were expecting him to rob a chemist shop.

"I'm not going." He grabbed at the door handle only to find that it was on child lock. "Let me out. I'm not going. I . . ."

His brother's voice hit him like a real bullet fired from a high velocity rifle.

"Shut it Mickey. You're going and that's that."

"I'm bloody not. Why don't you? Why doesn't he go?"

"Because the window's too small. We need someone small."

"Well get her to go then. She can do it."

This caused a frisson of shock among the other passengers. Eddie immediately felt the gathering of the red mist of temper that was a twenty-second trigger to violence. The little shite. As if he would send his Lucy through a window to nick Vallies . . .

Frank sensed Eddie was about to blow and started to reach back for his brother. He needed to shut his big trap before he joined the list of scar cheeks. But it was Lucy who was the first to respond. Like Frank she had seen the flash of rage in her brother's eyes and she knew exactly what that meant.

"Excuse me Mickey McGuire, but didn't you hear what he said?"

This stopped Mickey in his tracks somewhat. On the one hand he was scared witless and drowning in a sea of rising panic but it still didn't completely dull the fact that Lucy Tate was actually talking to him.

"What."

Again the smile. Taking the piss? Of course she was taking the piss.

"He said someone small, didn't he?"

"So?"

"So you might not have noticed but I happen to have these on my chest. They're called tits and these are big ones." She thrust her chest out in his direction and he jammed himself back into the door. Hadn't noticed? Was she kidding? There wasn't a lad in St. Mary's who hadn't noticed the spectacular and growing bulge under Lucy's shirt. Her tits were the object of endless playground banter and they had been likened to Raquel Welsh's stone age, animal skin clad tits in One Million years BC. "So there are two things here Mickey. Number one, these tits don't go through windows. Number two, no decent sort of lad would ask a lass to do something because he was too scared."

"Who said I was too scared!"

"Me."

"Well that's just a load of crap."

"Temper, temper . . . ."

Eddie now noticed the scarlet hue of the boy's face and realised with great certainty that the thing was in the bag. The red mist slowly began to clear on a soft breeze. He turned back round and dropped into first gear. He decided to leave the lovebirds to it and get the show on the road. Mickey was infuriated at being accused of being chicken by the girl of his dreams and he was about to give vent to his humiliation when she once again stopped him dead in his tracks with a wink. A wink? What was that all about? And now she was smiling again and this time he wasn't at all convinced that she was taking the piss.

The journey to Harris and Son Pharmacists took under ten minutes and Eddie made a couple of passes by the entrance to the alley that ran behind the small cluster of shops, all of which were now closed up and battened down. He kept up a running commentary which Frank took in carefully. It was the fourth down and the back door was painted a light green sort of colour. The gate to the back yard was never locked and there was only one window so they couldn't go wrong. He and Lucy would park up fifty yards or so down the road and wait. He didn't bother to say the part about what would happen if the cops arrived. If that happened, it would be foot down and bye bye Frank and Mickey.

After the second pass he parked up on a non-descript section of road that ran alongside a closed down print works. It was when the engine was switched off and Frank opened his door that the reality of what was about to happen hit Mickey full on. He was about to have another frantic moan but stopped short. He hadn't enjoyed being called a coward by Lucy and he wasn't about to let it happen again. He had spent years secretly hoping that she might notice him one day and now at last the day had come. Fair enough, he had never considered that such a great event would happen under such nightmare circumstances, but that couldn't be helped. If the price he was going to have to pay to get a smile and a wink out of Lucy Tate was climbing through a chemist shop window to lift a tub of Vallies, then so be it. Life was never meant to be simple. He consoled himself with the thought that Tommy Smith would no doubt do the same in a similar tight spot. Except that he would just kick the door in. He took a last blushing glance at Lucy and stepped out of the car assuming an air of studied nonchalance about the whole thing.

As they strolled back towards the alleyway he was itching to sneak a glance back to see if she was watching. But it wasn't the thing to do. So he didn't. Instead he focused on what his brother was telling him. Frank's voice was low and urgent.

"I'm sorry about this Mickey. Honest. But it needs doing, so we'll just get it out of the way and that's that. When we get into the alley we don't piss about. We just walk down like we do it every day. No need to sneak about and look dodgy. When we get to the gate we open it and go in. Just that. Like we belong there, OK? People notice it when you look all shifty. Look like you do it every day and you're just part of the furniture. We go in. I open the window. Quick leg up and in. Alright?"

Mickey nodded. With every step his heart was speeding up. Suddenly his elation at the Lucy wink seemed a long way away. A hundred yards back up the street Lucy watched the tall figure and the short figure disappear into the alleyway and out of sight.

"You're a right bastard for this Eddie. Mickey's not like you and all the rest of them. You should have got someone else."

"Didn't have time did I? Anyway. You watch your mouth. You sound a right slag with that language."

"You know all about that don't you our Eddie, what with all the slags who you drive around in your fancy car."

"Just shut up will you Lucy. Rest your bloody great gob for once."

Lucy was about to give him another broadside but thought better of it. She knew she held a unique position in that she could talk to her brother in a way that nobody else would dare. But there were limits and she could see that he was pretty tensed up. Maybe he was right. Maybe it was a good moment to give her bloody great gob a rest. In the front Eddie lit up a cigarette whilst never allowing his eyes to leave the rear view mirror.

What happened next was yet another key module in Eddie's learning curve. He learnt two lessons that balmy evening in May. Lesson number one was that intelligence could easily slip by its sell-by-date at which point it becomes worse than useless. The reason for this lesson was that Mr Harris had only the week before invested in a new sensor alarm which was hooked directly into the local police station using the very best of modern technology. Eddie's conversation with Mary Rogerson was two weeks old which put the intell a good week beyond its sell by date. Once the McGuires reached the yard, Frank reached up and tried the window. Sure enough it opened with the barest of pressure. He pulled up a dustbin underneath and climbed on top to get a look inside. There wasn't much light in the room and it took a moment or two for his eyes to adjust to the gloom. It then took another couple of minutes to locate the spot on the second shelf where the tub of Valium was waiting for them. What he didn't know was that the very minute he had opened the window a telephone had rung in the nearest police station which was three miles away. By the time he stuck his head through, the duty sergeant was already sending the alert out over the radio network.

Now came lesson number two. A simple lesson. The lesson that sod's law always came into play. At that time of night there was only one panda car on patrol in an area that covered ten square miles. Had they been lucky, the car would have been at the far end of the zone and at least ten minutes of flashing light time away from the chemist shop. But they weren't lucky. The car was in fact just two streets away and less than a minute from the crime scene. Eddie watched with horror as the car shot towards them before skidding to a halt level with the alley. Both doors opened and two coppers jumped out and sprinted out of sight down the alley.

"Shit." He started to fire up the engine and was about to drive off when out of the corner of his eye he saw that Lucy was out of the car and on the pavement. He wound down his window so violently that he almost wrenched the handle off the door.

"Get in Lucy. Now!"

"Piss off. I'm not going anywhere. What if they get away? We can't just leave them Eddie."

"I said now Lucy. You get in or I swear I'll . . ."

"If you get out I'll scream as loud as I can . . ."

Seconds were ticking by and Eddie frantically tried to weigh up the situation. Even if he started to open the door she would probably run and she could be quick as a cat once she got going. It would be just typical to get nicked trying chase his little bloody sister around the place. What if he left her? Nothing. She wasn't involved. They wouldn't even think about it. Just a kid walking down the street. What the hell. She could just bloody well walk home and then there would be hell to pay. He slammed the gears and drove away without another word leaving Lucy feeling suddenly rather lost.

Back in the alley Mickey was halfway through the window when they heard the sound of heavy footsteps coming on fast.

"Christ all bloody mighty." Frank yanked him back out of the window and he landed hard on the dustbin lid. There was no time to cry out as he was almost immediately airborne again. Frank picked him up like a doll and tossed him over the wall and into the adjacent yard. Just before he flew he caught his brother's instructions in a low intense voice.

"I'll keep them busy. You run like hell. Just get out Mickey. Don't bother about me."

Luckily there was a pile of old cardboard boxes on the far side of the wall which cushioned Mickey's fall. For a moment he was winded and he could hear voices next door.

"OK sunshine. Take it easy. Just stand still lad. No need for any dramatics. Hands out for the cuffs. There's a good lad . . ."

"What. Just the two of you are there. Two's not enough boys. Not even close . . ."

All Mickey heard was a dull thudding sound and a groan. Had he been able to see the action he would have seen the impressive sight of Frank turning himself into a human missile and throwing himself forward so that the top of his head smashed into the lead copper's stomach.

"Little bastard . . ."

Then the sounds were all scuffle. Time to go. He nervously opened the gate to find the alleyway empty. He gritted his teeth and ran, trying to be as quiet as he could. Not that he needed to worry overmuch. Neither policeman was worried about giving chase. They were far too tied up with the considerable task of pacifying the cock of the fifth year who had clean flipped his lid and was fighting like a complete maniac.

As soon as he was out of the alley Mickey scanned the street for the Capri. Nothing. Thanks Eddie bloody Tate. Scarpered. The swine. But then he saw a small figure about fifty yards away waving to him. Could it be? Yes. Lucy. On her own.

He ran up to her and was about to speak when she shushed him.

"Stop running will you. It looks well dodgy. Here . . ."

She grabbed his arm and manoeuvred it around her waist whilst doing the same with her own. He was flabbergasted. His life had gone completely mad. First he was a few inches away from Lucy Tate. Now they were walking the pavement with arms wrapped round each other whilst two coppers were giving his brother the kicking of his life and tough guy Eddie Tate had legged it like a complete nonce and left his little sister to pick up the pieces.

"What are you doing?"

"What does it look like stupid. This is blending in. The Bizzies are looking for a lone thief running for it. What they aren't looking for is a courting couple taking a stroll. God Mickey, I thought you were supposed to be bright."

"So you're saying that you're my bird like?"

"I'm saying that we're pretending."

"Oh. OK."

She had rather hoped for something a bit more than Oh OK. For a few yards they walked in silence whilst he went through a serious split personality moment. One person was luxuriating in the mind-boggling feeling of his hand resting on Lucy's soft waist. The other person was ripped up at the thought of what was happening to his brother.

"Where are we going now Lucy?"

She gave him a grin. "Typical isn't it. All you lads are the hardest thing ever in the playground but as soon as you find yourself in a bit of shite you need a lass to sort you out? Can you hear yourself? Where are we going now Lucy?"

She regretted the words as soon as they left her mouth.

"Look. I'm sorry. Just being a cow. Don't take any notice. This is how we play it. We get a bus into the city. We go to the pictures and we keep the ticket. Then we get some chips. And then we get the bus home and keep the ticket. It's called building an alibi. OK with you Mickey McGuire?"

"Yeah. Great. How come you know all this stuff Lucy?"

"I read detective stories."

"Oh."

Another fifty yards of silence then he stopped.

"Look. I never said thanks back there. I mean you didn't have to . . . I mean I wouldn't have expected you to . . . But I'm glad you did . . . Well you know . . . Just thanks and that."

"It just shows the lengths a girl's got to go to get a lad to talk to her. Do you realise that we've shared a classroom for all these years and you've never said a word to me. That's not nice."

He swallowed on nothing and scrambled for words which were elusive. He grabbed back onto her and started walking again.

"It wasn't that I didn't want to talk to you like, it was just . . . Just . . . "

"Just that mummy and daddy told you not to have anything to do with the terrible Tate family."

"No they didn't"

"Don't lie."

"Well OK they might have, but it wasn't that."

"So what was it?"

He gritted his teeth and spat out a word. "Shy."

"So you actually wanted to talk to me then?"

He nodded and stared hard down the street ahead.

"Well Mickey McGuire, things are beginning to look up a bit. It's a good job I stayed on. Turn down here. We'll get a bus at the bottom."

By the time they rode the bus into the city centre the ice was well and truly broken. Mickey still found it hard not to feel guilty at the surging elation that he felt. It wasn't right to feel this good when his brother was in such bother. But it couldn't be helped and Lucy was right about him needing some sort of alibi. He didn't know if the police had seen him or not, but it wouldn't take an Einstein to guess where the first place would be for them to look for chemist burglar number two.

Other things were also fighting through the soaring glory of sharing the back seat of the top deck with Lucy. A passing church clock told him that it was already nearly seven and in less than an hour Liverpool would march out into the warmth of a Roman evening to kick off the greatest night of their history. As things stood it looked as if he was going to be watching a film with Lucy rather than being glued to the TV. It seemed almost inconceivable but it was true. His life had been turned on its head and dropped to the concrete. And then there was his mum and dad. What a night they were in for. First up would be the news that their eldest had been lifted for attempted burglary and assaulting policemen. Then they would get to wondering where the hell their youngest was. If he wasn't home watching the game they would know that something deadly serious must have happened. An uneasy feeling sank into him as he pictured his dad driving around looking for him. That *would* mean his dad would miss the match as well whilst his mum waited for the phone top ring at home. When the time came to put them out of their misery all he would be able to tell them was that he had taken a ride into the city with Lucy Tate to watch a film. Without telling them. Christ. What a complete and utter disaster.

A sense of foreboding took hold and he couldn't see anything but crisis wherever he looked. No doubt to cap it all Alan Simonson would bag a hat trick for Borussia and the lads would go and crash five nil. If anyone had said a few hours earlier that the time would come when he would be sitting with his arm draped around Lucy Tate's shoulder and yet still feel miserable he would have said they were mad. But it was true. Here he was sliding through the warmth of the night as the bus trundled through empty streets towards the empty city centre and his arm was indeed very much draped around Lucy Tate and more to the point it didn't seem as though Lucy Tate wasn't remotely unhappy about it. And yet he felt even more miserable than he had a few days earlier when a freak deflection off Jimmy Greenhof's shoulder had taken Manchester United to victory over Liverpool in the FA Cup Final.

"You all right Mickey?"

"Not really."

"Wish you weren't here?"

"There's nowhere I'd rather be. I just wish things were different?"

"Like?"

"Like our Frank not being banged up. Like my mum and dad not worrying about where I am. Like me getting to take you to the pictures on any other night when the European Cup Final isn't on at the same time."

She gave him a reassuring squeeze. "Well I best make sure I'm worth it then hadn't I."

There was barely a soul in sight when they got off the bus. The city had moved indoors to watch the match. Pubs were all standing room only. Families gathered in living rooms. Those who had to work hung onto every word on the radio. This was a category that included the guy in the ticket office at the cinema. Before they had gone in Lucy had passed a tenner for Mickey to pay them in. She reckoned it wouldn't seem right for her to do the honours. At first the ticket guy couldn't seem to believe that he had customers to attend to. Who in their right minds would want to watch Close Encounters of the Third Kind instead of the final. The lad certainly looked as if he was anything but happy about the situation. Christ he looked as if he'd just eaten a bucket of worms. Mind you, he had to admit that he wouldn't mind a close encounter of any kind with the bird who was with him.

In the background Peter Jones's voice wandered out of the portable radio and filled the silence of the deserted lobby.

' . . . and as the two teams take the field here in Rome it is a truly marvelous sight. Anfield has come to the Eternal City. Everywhere I

*look I see red and white. Wonderful. There must be twenty thousand .
. . Thirty thousand . . .'*

"Two please."

"Not watching the match then?"

"No."

"Bluenose are you?"

Mickey bridled. "Am I hell."

The ticket collected smirked.

"Could have fooled me."

Mickey was about to answer back when Lucy's voice stopped them
both dead in their tracks.

"Just wait a minute will you. Look Mickey, I'm not sure about this.
I'm not going to sit through two-and-a-half hours of this shite if all
you're going to do is sit and eat pop corn and sulk about missing the
game."

Mickey turned unsure what she was on about.

"What do you mean?"

"I mean you either give us a kiss or I'm off home, that's what I
mean."

"What. Like now?"

"Like right now."

He was the rabbit in the headlights for a couple of seconds and he
probably wouldn't have moved at all but for the urgent low voice
behind him.

"Bloody hell lad. Don't piss about. Get in there."

He took a deep breath and stepped into the greatest forty-five
seconds of his thirteen years on the planet. It hadn't seemed possible
for anyone or anything to come close to matching the moment when
super sub David Fairclough had won the tumultuous quarter final
second leg against St. Etienne with just six minutes left, but his first
snog with Lucy Tate was pretty damn close.

When at last it was all finished he felt as if he could barely stand as
he turned to collect his change.

"OK mate. I suppose I can let you off for missing the match like.
Bloody hell. Here you are. That's six-fifty change."

"Cheers."

'. . . of all the familiar faces in this magnificent Liverpool team it is the craggy hard one that draws the eye. What a moment for Tommy Smith. Here he is playing possibly his last game for the team that he has served since he was a boy. What an end to a great career . . ."

The words of the commentary faded into silence as they climbed the stairs to the upper circle.

"What was that all about?" He was beginning to wonder if he was actually awake.

"Two things. Firstly you need more than a bit of paper for a proper alibi. Someone else might have bought the ticket. What you need is for the person who sold the ticket to remember you. Reckon he'll remember us Mickey?"

"I think there's a good chance he might."

"Number two, I wanted to and I got the feeling that if I waited on you I'd be waiting all night and I've seen Close Encounters of the Third Kind already and it IS shite."

"Right."

Two-and-a-half hours later Mickey felt totally unqualified to pass any sort of judgement as to whether Close Encounters of the Third kind was shite or not. He was however over the rainbow and back again convinced that snogging Lucy Tate was the complete and utter opposite of shite and all things similar. As they made they're way back down the stairs to the lobby he was about to ask the lad about the score but he didn't have to. The lad was outside of the front door watching the mass of red-clad humanity that had spilled out of the pubs and bars to celebrate the greatest victory ever. The carnival had started from the moment that Emlyn Hughes had lifted the cup over his head and it was to last until the breaking dawn. As Mickey strolled out through the glass doors of the Odeon he felt as if he was floating. It was like something out of Hollywood. Everywhere they looked were smiling faces. Car horns blared. Songs echoed up and down the streets.

Later would mean getting home and the worst trouble of his life. But later was later and now was now. For now the world was as good as it was ever going to get. His team were Champions of Europe and it seemed like Lucy Tate was his girlfriend. They wandered through the crowds for an hour and ended up sitting a while on the riverside under the moonlit shadow of the Liver Building. By the time they tried to catch it the last bus was long gone so they walked.

It was well past three by the time he made it back having dropped Lucy off at the end of her road and still the streets were full. Later in life he became so familiar with seeing the three Liverpool goals on video that it seemed as if he had actually watched the match. His brain managed to fuse the memory of his time with Lucy with the memory of Rome. Similarly his memory wiped clean most of the wretched hours that passed once he got back home. Instead it dwelt on the warm May air and the time when a botched burglary took him to town with Lucy Tate on the top deck of an empty bus. It had felt as if nothing could ever be quite as good again.

And it wasn't.

On the night of 25th May 1977 Mickey McGuire missed his first European Cup Final. It wasn't to be his last.

Chapter 2
Wembley – May 1978

By the time Liverpool reached their second European Cup final in May 1978 the world had become a very different place for Mickey. In fact it had become a different place the moment he had opened his eyes on the morning after the night before. He had been under no illusions that his arrival home was ever going to be anything approaching good. But he had no idea just how bad it was going to be. Everything was bad. As bad as bad could be.

Frank hadn't just roughed the two policemen around. He had really hurt them. His human missile act had resulted in two cracked ribs and a flailing punch had broken the second officer's nose. Had he been a known and established face it would have been bad. The fact that he was a fifteen-year-old lad who was still at school just made it worse because the police were embarrassed. The book was thrown hard and Frank was sent away to a Young Offenders Institute for three years.

His father couldn't believe that his constant warnings about hanging around the Tate family had gone so spectacularly unheeded. In a single desperate evening one son had been sent down as a result of hanging around with Eddie Tate whilst the other son had disappeared off into the city centre with Lucy Tate. The police had given Mickey the third degree at the station whilst his dad had sat white-faced with anger. The questions left him in no doubt that they thought Mickey had been a part of it and his son's edgy stuttering answers did nothing to persuade him that it wasn't the case. Nothing came of it, mostly because of Lucy Tate's impeccable testimony in an interview room down the corridor. A ticket collector at the Odeon in the city was able to confirm the fact that he remembered the young couple well enough. They had been the only customers who had chosen 'Close Encounters of the Third Kind' over Liverpool 3 Borussia Munchengladbach 1. The police removed Mickey's name from their enquiry and settled for the firm prosecution of Frank. They left neither Mickey nor his mum and dad in any doubt about the fact that they would be keeping a very close eye on him from now on. They also gave some friendly advice that it would be a pretty good idea if he were to stay clear of the Tate family in future. All of the Tate family.

It all hit Mickey's dad hard. He had never been in trouble and it crucified him to have both of his sons suddenly on the wrong side of the tracks. He worked as the assistant manager at the local Co-op and suddenly everybody seemed to look at him differently. No longer was he just another respectable member of the community. Now he was the father of the son who had fallen in with Eddie Tate and got sent down on a three for battering two coppers. After two months he couldn't stand it any more and applied for a transfer to the Southport branch where the assistant had retired to Spain.

So it was that the family packed its bags and headed north to a place where their reputation could be rebuilt. Mickey had been locked down on a grounding to end all groundings from the morning after the glory of Rome. The only time he got to see Lucy was at play time and their relationship was never about to withstand the tight leash that he was kept on. Every day his mother waited at the school gates to march him home to yet another solitary night in his room. By the time they said goodbye to the house where he had grown up he hardly cared any more. What should have been the start of a golden era had become the end of everything.

The new school was OK and he fitted in quickly enough but nothing really seemed as good as it should have been any more. Nothing was the same. His childhood was far behind him and the world seemed a hard and confusing sort of place. Even Liverpool were changing. Old idols moved on and the new ones didn't seem the same somehow. Kevin Keegan upped sticks and flew away to Hamburg. Tommy Smith and Ray Kennedy went south to Swansea. Kenny Dalglish and Graham Souness came in. The team struggled miserably through the season eventually finishing fifth and losing the League Cup final. The only beacon of light was that they went all the way again in the European

Cup. This time the final was to be played at Wembley which meant a much shorter journey for the travelling reds. But to Mickey Wembley didn't seem right somehow. It seemed like everything else in his life. Wembley was OK for FA and League Cup finals. More than all right. Brilliant. But it didn't seem right at all for the European Cup. All wrong. It wasn't exotic enough. Just London. Worst of all it would always carry the ghost of Man United's win in 1968. He found it hard to get all that exited about it. The only good thing was that at least he would get the chance to watch this time.

His Wednesdays had become a set routine. As soon as the bell rang for the end of the school day he jumped on a bus into Liverpool and then took a train over to Wigan. Then it was another bus out to the Young Offenders Institute where Frank was serving out his time. Mickey hated the cold strip lighted misery of the place but he never missed. When he had gone for the first time the place had made him shudder. The guards were the hardest faced men he had ever seen and all the prisoners seemed pale and jumpy in their jeans and blue sweatshirts. He had been relieved when Frank had been led into the visiting room to join him at the plastic table. His brother had grown and looked fit. He was also quite at home in his new surroundings. It was a brutal regime but the other cons had soon got the message that messing with the tall Scouser was a pretty bad idea. On that first visit Frank had told him that it wasn't any great problem. He was just keeping his head down and getting on with it. He mentioned that Eddie had been in a time or two and that there would be a job waiting when he got out. He had asked if their mum and dad would be coming and Mickey had passed on the message that there was no chance. And he had seen a light die in his brother's eyes when he heard the news.

When Mickey had taken the train back to Liverpool he had cried in the toilets. His brother wouldn't be coming home. Not ever. He was gone. Lost. Instead he would go to Eddie Tate.

As Mickey made the familiar journey he found it hard to shift the nagging feeling of gloom that had sat on him all day. He couldn't get a hold of it somehow. All the lads at school had been getting all fired up for the match against Bruges but he hadn't managed to get into it at all. All it did was make him nostalgic. The game in Rome seemed like something from another lifetime rather than an event from just a year earlier. As he stared out of the window of the train, that whole part of his life seemed bathed in the light of a golden era. He remembered the feeling of pure exhilaration as he had woken up that morning filled with anticipation. The excitement of the playground, the big challenge match that he never played in, the magical hours with Lucy and the fantastic dreamscape of the late-night city filled with thousands of revellers. An unbelievable time, and now it was all gone. Brother, mates, school, Keegan and Tommy Smith, and Lucy. Lucy more than all the rest put together.

When he got to Wigan he had travel options. He could wait twenty minutes for a bus or he could walk. The sun was out and it was warm enough so he decided to stretch his legs. He hung his red Liverpool Adidas bag over his shoulder and set out. Forty minutes later he arrived and started going through the search routine. At first he had bridled when most of the other visitors were waved straight through whilst he received the third degree. It wasn't hard to guess the reason why it was so. The accent. He was only fourteen and he hadn't travelled a great deal away from Merseyside but he knew well enough that the way he talked governed the way the world looked at him. As soon as he opened his mouth the stereotypes kicked in. Thief. Trouble. Might get violent. As far as the officers at the security zone were concerned he was a nailed on certainty to be hiding drugs or a knife or both so they put their hands all over him without worrying too much about remembering their manners.

The first time he had complained about it to Frank but his brother had just laughed.

"Just count your lucky stars they didn't go up your arse. They've been up mine that many times it feels like the Wallasey Tunnel. Maybe I should charge a toll."

The trips to Wigan took Mickey's passion for Liverpool to a different level. He had moved past the posters on the wall stage and the hours of waiting for an autograph at Melwood. He began to understand the bigger things that lay behind the Kop singing Walk through a Storm every other Saturday. Liverpool the city was falling apart. The prosperity that had once flowed through the community from the docks was all but gone. A decade of strikes and industrial turmoil had persuaded most employers to pack up and move elsewhere. Unemployment was soaring and the evidence was everywhere. With little prospect of getting a job, more and more

Liverpudlians left school with straight choices. Stay at home and sit in the dole queue. Get on a bus and leave town to find a job somewhere else. Or stay at home and make a living from crime. Eddie Tate was merely one of many who offered career opportunities to the likes of his big brother. By 1978 it seemed that every nicked car or stereo system in Britain found its way into Merseyside to be traded on.

The city had always understood how to trade. A hundred years earlier it had been cotton and sugar. Now it was car radios and drugs. And as soon as he left his home patch and opened his mouth he was immediately judged. Little Scouse thief.

It all meant that the hour-and-a-half at Anfield every other Saturday became more important. It wasn't just about football. It was about pride. Being the Champions of Europe was a way of sticking two fingers up to the rest of the world who told the Scouser jokes and gave the job to anyone with a different accent. By the late seventies the city had fallen into a mood of isolation. It seemed like the rest of the country laughed whenever the evening news announced more job losses on Merseyside. And the laughter was always loudest in London and Manchester. He had heard from some of the lads who travelled to away games that when they went to London the home fans would wave twenty pound notes at them and take the piss. It put an edge into things. Liverpool FC became the last representatives of a once great city that had become something to laugh at. The men in red had taken on the mantle of the Beatles.

This was something that was very close to Mickey's heart. His O-levels were just a couple of years away and what he was going to try and do with his life was becoming a bigger issue with every passing week, especially as his mum and dad never shut up about it. Their message was clear and consistent. Don't turn out like Frank. He dossed about at school and look where he is now. Learn Mickey. Get the picture. This campaign only intensified after parents' evenings which were always along the lines of 'has potential and should do better'. They said that he had a brain in his head if he chose to use it. They said he needed to knuckle down and get his head out of the clouds. His parents had ideas that he could find himself a career where he would wear a suit every day and end up in a nice bungalow with a postcode from a respectable area. A place far away from the Tate family and all like them.

THE LONG AND WINDING
ROAD TO ISTANBUL

Mickey nodded his way through all these lectures but the idea didn't inspire him greatly. He could find nothing in him that wanted to be some kind of clerk turning in at nine every morning for eight hours straight of boredom. But not wanting it was one thing. Finding a way of avoiding it was quite another. He was hardly overdone with options. The visits to Frank had been more than enough to put him off any interest in taking a walk to the wrong side of the tracks. The preferred option would always have been to pull on a red shirt and make a position on the right side of Liverpool's midfield his own. But he had figured out the fact that such an idea was a pipe dream before he had reached his seventh birthday. All of which left him with just a single string to his bow. Music.

It had become apparent from the moment he was given a recorder to play in primary school that Mickey McGuire had a rich vein of musical talent running through him. Music had enjoyed star billing on every school report he had ever brought home. His dad took little notice and preferred 'the should do better' elements of Maths and Science, whilst his mum was secretly pleased. The subject which maintained the kind of distant second to music, as Manchester United did to Liverpool, was English. The female teachers of both subjects had always commented warmly that Mickey was a creative child and good to work with whilst the males who dominated the Maths class rooms and the Science labs hinted that he was a cheeky little sod who disrupted lessons.

His dad was fond of a particular speech that ran along the lines that music and poetry were all very bloody nice but they never put a meal on a table or petrol in a tank. But Mickey knew otherwise because he had grown up with a parallel set of Scouse role models who didn't pull on red shirts and conquer all corners of footballing Europe. The musicians. Scaffold and Gerry and the Pacemakers and, like giants who towered over all the rest, the Beatles. There was a well beaten track to musical fame and fortune to follow for the aspiring young Merseyside musician; a track where singer poets stood as tall as any. John Lennon and Roger McGough were his kind of guys. They were the vital link. The umbilical cord that connected the poems of Wilfred Owen to Top of the Pops. They were the ones who kept him up late at night scribbling lyrics into a notebook that he never showed to anyone. They were the ones who passed the hours in his room as he worked chords on his acoustic guitar and practised singing when his mum and dad were out and couldn't hear.

His music gave a focus to the gloom that had crept into most corners of his life. The black book was the place to get it out and down. It made him seem even dizzier than ever. Most adults were of the opinion that he had his head up in the bloody clouds. Some were of the opinion that it was better than being a violent little sod going about with a bike chain. Others said it would come to no good and he would most probably end up on drugs. Mickey was happy enough to let it all wash over him. He was focused. He was going to sing the songs of the time. He would bring the next Penny Lane into the world. He would become every bit as much an icon of his city as Tommy Smith had been every time he chopped down some Fancy Dan winger from London.

The book was in his jacket pocket as he walked through the shabby streets to the prison. Every boarded shop or gable end covered in disillusioned graffiti was inspiration. Every alley filled choked up with litter. Every thin-faced teenage mother pushing an unwanted pram. Every worried pensioner waiting for an unreliable bus. Every shop window filled with gaudy signs advertising cheap baked beans. His songs were all around him. And every step he took was like he was in some sort of film. Registering. Seeing poetry in the day to day obvious. Putting misery to music. Putting images and thoughts into a bank that he would draw on when the time was right. It meant that he didn't notice sometimes when people spoke to him. It meant that he was often miles away. Sometimes it was if he was a bit slow. Mickey Dreamer they called him. Well it didn't bother him greatly. It was true enough and he was developing a thing for the truth.

It was Mickey Dreamer who suddenly found that he had walked fifty yards past the prison entrance without noticing. Typical. For once the search was fairly quick and he was in place at the familiar plastic table ten minutes after going through the main door. His brother arrived a few minutes later in good spirits.

"All right Mickey. Didn't expect you today."

"How come?"

"Don't be daft. Bloody match of course. You don't want to hang about here too long or you'll miss the kick off."

"I'll be fine. My usual train gets in just after half past six. Loads of time. Will you get to watch it?"

THE LONG AND WINDING
ROAD TO ISTANBUL

Frank rolled a skinny cigarette and lit up. "Yeah. Mind you it looked a bit iffy for a while. The screws were worried that it all might kick off between us and the Mancs. They can't stand it. At the moment it is one European Cup each. That all changes if the boys do it tonight. They can stick their Best and Charlton and Denis Law up their arses. It will be two-one and won't they know it."

"You seem in good fettle."

"Yeah. I'm sound. All downhill now so long as I keep my nose clean. Six months and I'm out of here."

"Eddie still coming?"

"Yeah. Been like clockwork hasn't he. I know you don't like him but at least he's good to his word."

"Suppose."

Mickey passed over the carrier bag he had brought. Frank took it with a rueful smile.

"Look Mickey, for the millionth time, you don't need to bring all this stuff."

He took out a special souvenir edition of Liverpool's march to the cup final, a packet of Mars bars and a cassette of the new Clash album. "Cheers. I hope you're not spending all your pocket money on this lot."

Mickey grinned. "Got a paper round now haven't I."

"Good lad. What about school?"

"You know. Same as ever."

"Parents' Evening been yet?"

Mickey nodded.

"Well?"

"It wasn't bad. Dad wasn't happy but he never is."

"He's right Mickey. Come on, look at where I am. You don't want all this shite. Don't make a bollocks of it like I have."

"I won't."

Frank flicked through the magazine whilst he took the last scrap of smoke out of his roll up.

"We going to win then?"

"Should do. We've beaten Bruges before. It'll be like playing at home."

They fell into disecting the match for a while. It was comfortable ground. Frank always dreading his brother trying to persuade him not to go with Eddie Tate when he got out. He had tried to explain a

36

thousand times that he had no choice. No exams. No qualifications. Just another Scouser with prison time on his CV. Who would take him on? Nobody. Just the men who organised gangs of labourers to work on the black and he wasn't having any of that. Likewise Mickey hated it when Frank started to sound like his dad and give him a lecture about working hard at school and getting a proper career and some prospects. Both brothers knew exactly how the other felt and so they had learned to avoid the subjects that they found uneasy. Football was safe ground. Familiar ground.

After half an hour Frank finished a second roll up and glanced up at the clock on the wall.

"You best be off Mickey. It was my fault you missed the final last year. I don't want it to be my fault if you miss your train and miss another. Come on. Bugger off. I'll see you next week."

Mickey had lost track of time. Mickey Dreamer. He had let ten crucial minutes slide by and the train wasn't any kind of certainty.

"You're right. I need to leg it."

Outside he started to jog. There was no need to panic too much. There was a short cut he had found which saved a good ten minutes on the journey and ten minutes would be plenty enough to get him onto Platform 2 in time. The downside was that the route of the short cut ran through the kind of estate where the police would only ever enter in groups greater than ten in vans with wire mesh over the windows. The only time he had taken the short cut before it had been in February and the whole place had seemed terrifying in the thick dark of a cold rainy night. It had been miserable orange light spilling down into gurgling gutters blocked by old chip papers and used condoms. The snap shot images from his walk had provided the material for three of his better poems. He had actually considered sending one of them to Paul Weller of the Jam after he had clocked the lyrics of 'Down in a Tube Station at Midnight' which seemed to be about all the same kinds of stuff. But he hadn't. He couldn't begin to believe that anyone as totally cool as Paul Weller would take a blind bit of notice of the scribblings of a schoolboy in the fourth year. After that night he had decided that the one walk through the estate was enough in terms of material-gathering and that in future he would play it safe and take the main road route.

But now his options were closing down. The ten extra minutes were suddenly putting him into the danger zone of being on Wigan station as Liverpool kicked off their second attempt at the big prize. It meant that the short cut option would have to be taken. Missing Rome had been bad. Missing Rome and Wembley was unthinkable.

As he took the turn he decided that he had been worrying for nothing. The evening was warm and the sun was still high in the blue sky. The place was filled with kids all wrapped up in their make believe worlds whilst their mums hung out the washing or headed back to the kitchen to cook the tea. It seemed a different place altogether and the brooding cold threat of the February night seemed a long way away. It was down hill now and he quickened his stride. Piece of cake. Train, bus, match. Finally the excitement was beginning to kick in. So what that it was Wembley. It was still the European Cup. The second in two years which of course took Liverpool into territory occupied only by the true greats; Real Madrid, AC Milan, Ajax, Bayern Munich. Territory unknown to any other British team. Territory unique to Liverpool.

Trouble ghosted out from a small alley. Trouble times five. All male, all about eighteen, all looking like the worst kind of trouble there could ever be. They had pale sharp faces and three had acne that spoke of chips with everything. The leader stepped forward and pushed Mickey hard in his chest. He tried to spin round so that he could run but his balance wasn't up to it and he fell. The leader reached down and yanked at his bag, pulling the strap tight around his neck as he turned it side-on for inspection.

"Told you didn't I? A nasty little Scouser."

This caused dutiful tittering from the four followers. The leader turned his attention back to Mickey.

"We don't like Scousers here. In fact we don't allow Scousers here. Know what we do to Scousers here do you?"

Mickey knew he was in a world of trouble now. A whole great sprawling endless ocean of trouble. The words that hit him were formed from the flat vowels of Manchester. He could see the shirt under the light jacket. Red. Old Trafford red. Salford red. United red. Mancs. They were Mancs and he was dead.

"We kick the shit out of them. That's what we do to Scousers round here."

And without another word he started. The first kick caught Mickey on the forehead and threw him backwards. His brain started to work in fits and starts. He felt a kind of relief that the foot that delivered the blow was shod in a trainer and not a work boot. A thought raced in and out that he could kiss goodbye to any hopes of seeing the game. Another thought wondered if the same thing was about to go down between the Scousers and the Mancs in the prison. Another more scientific thought that his dad would have commanded his body to go into hedgehog mode and make like a ball. He had just about completed this exercise when a kick slammed his head into a wall and put all the lights out.

Later he would remember strange dreams from the time of darkness that followed. They were dreams of swimming in treacle or sinking into green quicksand or trying to slither up pink luminescent ramps liberally coated in grease. He figured out that the dreams were the manifestation of his bashed brain trying to struggle back to the surface. Apparently he did a fair amount of writhing and twitching on his bed at times and the graph at the end of the wires that were plugged into him would dance and skip. When he at last rejoined the world there was music in his head. Not actual music. Music created from the nerve ends of his brain. It was Paul Weller and the Jam and it was both logical and appropriate. Lines from 'Down in the Tube Station at Midnight' no less.

> *I first felt a fist, and then a kick*
> *I could now smell their breath*
> *They smelt of pubs and Wormwood Scrubs*
> *And too many right wing meetings*
> *My life swam around me . . .*

So Paul had suffered a proper kicking too. Nice research. Now he could have a go at doing the getting your head kicked in song. But where the hell was he? And what was going on with his eyes? He was lying in a place of blurred white. The world lay behind the bathroom window of his eyes and inside the pain rattled round his skull like a runaway train. Not just his head. Chest. Arm. Everywhere. And slowly the world was beginning to come into focus. White walls. Machines of some sort. Hospital. Well obviously. Where else? But where and when and how? He started to sit up only to find a hand gently easing him back horizontal.

THE LONG AND WINDING
ROAD TO ISTANBUL

"All right love. Just lie back like a good lad. Nice of you to join us I must say. I was beginning to think you were quite the most anti-social bugger I had ever met."

The face was big, smiling and middle aged. The voice was soft and Irish. The uniform said nurse. He tried to speak but it just came out as a rather miserable croak and she held a glass of water to his lips which tasted better than just about anything he had ever sipped in his life. The next effort at speech was more successful.

"When? When is it?"

"It's Saturday love. You've had a pretty fair nap."

Saturday! Crazy. Four days. Bloody hell.

"Who won?"

"Who won what love?"

"The match. The European Cup. Was it Liverpool?"

"Oh that match. Aye. It was Liverpool. One nil I think."

"Who . . . Who scored?"

"Oh I'm buggered if I know love. Football's not my game. Hang on though. Saw it on the news so I did. I think it was that Scotsman. The handsome one with the legs."

"Kenny Da . . ."

But the curtains were closing again. Big thick black velvet curtains that sent him back into the darkness.

"Mickey!! Bloody hell Mickey . . ."

His dad. His dad with tears running down his cheeks. No. Couldn't be. His dad never cried. Must be someone who looked like him. Someone who looked tired. All out knackered.

" . . . you OK son? Can you hear me . . . ?"

Son. Maybe it was his dad. But then again lots of men called him son. There's your change son. Mind how you go son. Steady on now son.

"Water."

A pitiful whisper. An image of a whipped Hunchback of Notre Dame. Faux pas.

"Hiya dad."

"Christ you've given me and yer Mam a scare Mickey. How do you feel?"

"Terrible."

"Well you're mending so the quack says. Passed the worst now. You'll be home in a bit."

"How long?"

His dad looked a little troubled at this. "Well you know. When you're good and ready. Not point in rushing things. It'll soon pass. Just wait and see. Your Mam has just nipped off for a brew. She'll be back in a bit. Christ she'll be glad to see you awake."

"We won dad. Dalglish."

"Too right. Wait till you see it. Souness picks it up just on the edge of the box and chips it like . . ."

Click. Return to black.

Click. Return to light. Now he is used to the five-minute bathroom window when he wakes up. Very quiet. Always quiet. An empty room with sun streaming in from outside. Nobody but him. How long? Then a sound. The turning of a page. The chair by the bedside. He turned to look and even though his eyes were still glazed there was no doubting it.

Holy Christ.

Lucy.

"Alright Mickey."

"Lucy."

Same cracked up whisper. She held out a glass and he sipped. She laid a cool palm on his forehead and he felt like floating up out of the bed and break-dancing on the ceiling.

"How?"

"Frank told Eddie when he went to visit. I had to wait until the weekend to sneak off. But here I am."

"You came."

His eyes were almost clear now and he saw that she was crying.

"Hey. Give over. I'm fine. Just a few bashes. Nowt to bother about."

"I'm not crying about your injuries Mickey. I've grown up with injuries."

"Oh. What then?"

She held up his black book which she had found by the bedside as she waited for him to show signs of life. "This."

His stomach lurched at the sight. Nightmare. Nightmare times ten. He didn't let anyone read that book not ever. And if there was anyone on the whole planet who he would least want to read his black book it was Lucy Tate. And here was Lucy Tate sitting at his bedside reading the black book and the cat was a mile out of the bag and chasing mice along the skirting boards.

"Shit." He closed his eyes and tried to pretend it wasn't happening. He felt her hand close around his.

"I read the Lucy poems Mickey. All of them."

He ground his eyes tighter shut. "Oh."

"I must have read them all ten times each."

Ten times each. Maybe that was a promising sign. Probably not. Absolutely not.

"I never meant for anyone to read them."

"I should think not. Anyone but me that is."

He risked opening an eye a millimetre or so.

"Bet you hated them."

"Don't be stupid. How could anyone hate them? They're beautiful."

"Just like you . . ."

No. No. NoOOOO! The curtain. Not the curtain. Click.

She came one more time. By this time he was well on the way to mending. There was plenty to mend. Three cracked ribs. Multiple break of the arm. Fractured skull and a whole host of cuts and bruises. The story of the Koppite who missed the match had made the Granada News and an appeal was put out by the police. They might as well have appealed for snow in Sri Lanka. The estate where Mickey got filled in didn't do information to help the police with their enquiries. Especially to help their own get sent down for doing the right and proper thing and sorting out a Scouser who was only in town in the first place to visit his thug brother in prison.

When Lucy came again he was sitting up and all his wits were back in place.

"I didn't know if it was a dream or not. You know. When you came before."

"No dream Mickey."

"And you reading my book and that wasn't a dream either?"

"No. All true."

He gave the clock on the wall a nervous glance which she noticed. "It's all right. I have everything covered. I checked. Your mum and dad are due, yeah?"

He stared down, embarrassed that he had been so obvious.

"It's all right Mickey. I had a word with the nurses on the desk. I gave them a real Romeo and Juliet thing. You know, family feuds and all that. They're all signed up so there's no need to panic. If your mum and dad turn up whilst I'm here we get a warning and they'll smuggle me out through the nurses bit."

"You're amazing."

"Absolutely. Glad you noticed. Here. I brought you some books. They're all miserable and depressing so they'll be right up your street I reckon."

He worked his way down the pile.

"You read all these?"

She grinned. "Guess who's top in English Lit?"

"They must all love that. A Tate at the top of the class."

"Let's just say they're confused."

Time flew by and after what seemed little more than seconds the nurse gave an urgent rap at the door.

"They're here. I've told them we're sorting something out. They've gone for a brew. You should be OK for five minutes then you best go."

"Thank you."

"All part of the service pet."

When it was time Lucy leaned over and kissed him. "I know it's hard for you to see me Mickey. It's the same with everybody. Eddie is getting worse and worse. But I just tell myself it won't last forever. In a few years I can go to college somewhere and just be Lucy instead of being Lucy Tate. And then maybe we might stand a chance. Anyway I'm off because I told myself I wasn't going to cry and I'm not going to."

"Lucy . . ."

But she was true to her word. One minute she was there. The next minute she was gone leaving nothing but memories. It seemed to be a trend. When the reds made it to European Cup Finals he missed the game and got the girl and lost her again.

The English dominance of Europe's most prestigious competition lasted another three years. But it was Nottingham Forest and Aston Villa who lifted the trophy. And Mickey watched all three games from the first minute to the last. But he never saw Lucy.

Chapter 3
Paris – May 1981

Lucy took a sip of coke and checked the clock. It was already past eleven and her essay on King Lear, tragedy and betrayal was barely a page long. It would be past two before she was finished and able to at last allow her leaden eyes to rest for a while. It had been the same for weeks as her A-levels drew nearer and nearer. She had been offered a conditional place to study English at Bristol and having spent a day wandering the city it was an offer she was desperate to take up. It was all she had expected of university and, best of all, it was a million years from Liverpool and her brother's growing reputation. The elation of opening the offer letter had soon been replaced with the realisation that an A and two B's were going to take some getting. There was no way she was getting an A in either History or General Studies. It would have to be English.

On her desk a small portable radio was switched low. Just background. Something to distract her from sleep. John Peel of course. It had been John Peel after ten o'clock for as long as she could remember. There was something about his voice that seemed to speak to the lonely millions who did whatever they did in the empty hours of weekday nights. The unknown bands he spotlighted howled away at the injustices of Thatcher's Tories.

Lucy was as lonely as any who sat in their small rooms with Peel's voice filling the quiet. As Eddie had gone from strength to strength she had become more and more isolated. It was her choice of course. Had she decided to join his world then she would have been the princess in the castle. That was what Eddie wanted. He hated it that his favourite sibling shunned everything that he did. He wanted her to be proud of him. He wanted to shower her with gifts. He yearned for her approval. What made her isolation complete was that the rest of the family all stood shoulder to shoulder with the family high flier. All three of her older brothers had left school to join the family business. Both her sisters were going out with guys of his. Her mum was proud as punch that her family stuck together and were doing so well. Only Lucy stood apart from it all. Only Lucy disapproved.

Eddie never tired of asking her what was wrong. Why she pushed him away all the time. Why she cut herself off from her family. He told her it wasn't right, wasn't healthy. Couldn't she see how much better things were now for all of them. The house was quite unrecognisable from the place where she had grown up. The back garden had been swallowed up by a sprawling extension that housed a lounge big enough for all of them to sit in front of the TV in deep leather. A games room housed a full size snooker table. They now had three bathrooms and no waiting in the mornings. Not that Lucy would have been troubled anyway as she was always the only one who was up as she got ready for school. There wasn't a gadget they didn't own and the fridge was full of steak and strawberries and champagne. Outside the pavement was home to a line of brand new cars that were constantly upgraded. The neighbours must have hated it just like they must have hated it when the extension swallowed up all the light from their back gardens. But they didn't say anything and they never would. Nobody but nobody ever said anything against the Tates. To do so was madness and would attract guaranteed retribution. A brick through the window. A strung up pet. A torched car. A sliced up cheek. And of course the word was that half of the coppers in the local nick enjoyed holidays in the sun care of brown envelopes from Eddie Tate.

Lucy wondered why she was the only one who seemed to see how wrong it all was. It wasn't that the rest of her family were terrible people or anything. On the contrary she loved every single one of them. They simply chose the option of tunnel vision. They saw a fabulous lifestyle way beyond anything they could ever have expected. They had moved to a world beyond the dreams of all their neighbours. It was a world where anything could be bought without a second thought. Where paying the electric was nothing. Where there wasn't a car showroom in the city where the salesmen didn't give a big welcome.

PARIS – MAY 1981

Lucy felt like she was the only one who saw where it all came from. She was the only one who didn't have a car. She hadn't even taken lessons. It drove Eddie crazy but there wasn't a thing he could do about it. Her creed was simple. She lived in the house and ate there. Until she achieved financial independence she had no choice in this. All the girls at school had weekend jobs which paid for clothes and records. She had tried for a while but it had soon became clear that nobody was about to take on a Tate. It left her living her teenage years between a rock and a hard place. She refused to take a penny from her family and nobody would allow her to earn anything.

Not having a car meant that she walked and took buses. Maybe that was why she saw what the others chose to ignore. The neighbourhood was falling apart. It was squeezed between the two T's. Thatcher and Tate. Thatcher presided over a regime that was destroying the city brick by brick. No more hand-outs. No more subsidies. No more nothing for the loudest of the Labour heartland. Unemployment was on the rise all over Britain. On Merseyside it was sky-rocketing. The growing despair of long-term unemployment provided perfect soil for Eddie to plant his seeds. Every day she saw the results as she walked to school and back. Heroin had swept through every street like a bitter wind. The addicts were all around with their sunken cheeks and hungry eyes. Every day they migrated to the city centre to steal whatever they could lay their hands on. Then they would return to cash in their loot with Eddie Tate's men. Trade goods for heroin. The trade goods were moved along a network that spread all the way over the north of England. Every town had men in certain pubs who would take orders for stereos or designer shirts or just about anything which Eddie's addicts would go out and nick to order. Wherever she looked she saw families she had known all her life ripped apart by Eddie's heroin. Mums and Dads were old before their time. Grandparents were broken by the sight of their beloved grandchildren turning into the walking dead. She couldn't ignore it. The obvious stared her in the face every lousy day. And the eyes that followed her along the pavement were filled with a loathing that seemed to know no depths. Not that she ever felt threatened. No chance. It was as if she had a force-field around her. Nobody could come nearer than ten feet. But they could stare. And they did.

THE LONG AND WINDING
ROAD TO ISTANBUL

School wasn't much of a sanctuary. She wanted nothing to do with the wannabe bad boys and girls who saw her as the ticket to a place on the Tate payroll. The ones who wanted to pass their exams and make a career shunned her. Not a single lousy one of them was willing to admit that she could be any different. She carried her surname like a cross. And she was achingly, endlessly lonely. No family and no friends. All she had was a piece of paper which promised a better life a hundred-and-fifty miles to the south where being a Tate would mean nothing to anyone. A place where she could just be Lucy and people might even like her.

She tried to drag her attention back to the nearly full page in front of her. One day her own family would probably go the same way as King Lear's. She wondered how they would stick together when the going got tough and the fancy cars and furniture were all taken away. And would she play the part of Cordelia and be the one to stand beside her oldest brother when the police at last caught up with him. Probably. She hated everything Eddie did and all the misery his monumental ambition caused. But she still loved him every bit as much as he loved her. Blood. It was easy to shun him when he was so high. But she wouldn't be able to leave him alone when he crashed.

Distractions. Concentrate. Get it done, go to bed, get the A grade. It was all that mattered. John Peel's voice was back after a blinding torrent of sound from a group from Cardiff.

'Now of course my lords and masters expect me to be impartial at all times and I hope I am. But there are times when I don't quite manage it and tonight is one of those times. I received this demo a few days ago and just about everything made me struggle with my impartiality. Why you may ask? I'll tell you. One. A Liverpool postmark. Two. The band is called Spion which I expect refers to the Spion Kop at Anfield which for any of you out there who have lived on Mars for most of your lives is a footballing Mecca in Liverpool 4. I'll tell you more after this track which is rather good and called "No More Sugar and Spice" . . .'

It was just a matter of seconds before she knew it was Mickey. Spion were a simple affair of two guitars and a drummer and a solid melody sat behind the words of the lead singer who was unmistakably Mickey McGuire. Although she had never heard him sing before and his voice had fully broken she had no trouble in recognition. More than the voice was what he sang. The words were the same as those she had read by his hospital bed. The black book. The song was a series of simple images that were as familiar to her as to any native Liverpudlian. Pictures of the empty warehouses all along the Dock Road to Seaforth. Giants in red brick with row after row of broken windows. Crumbling quaysides by sickly oily water that no ships used any more. No more sugar and spice. Or cotton. Or any of the materials of Empire that had found a gateway into Britain and its Industrial Revolution under the great white edifice of the Liver Building. The words reached down to the place inside her that would be forever Liverpool. And as she listened she knew that it would be the same for many, many others. Mickey was striking a chord that would be heard in all the places where once there had been jobs and shops that were open and a sense of belonging and pride. Coal towns. Ship-building towns. Steel towns. It could be Scotland or Tyneside or the valleys of Wales or the rustbelt of Michigan. He sang of how it once was. Of how it had all gone to hell. Of Thatcher's wrecking ball. She was spellbound. It was fantastic.

' . . . now I got a letter with my demo tape. Spion is Mickey, Midge and Tonto and they are at school in Southport. Apparently if you look hard enough you'll find them in various Merseyside pubs and I certainly can think of worse ways of spending an evening. OK. Reason number three. I've always been a sucker for an unashamedly obscure title and the next track is very much in that category. It's called 'Lovers Under Creamy Yellow' and it really is very good indeed . . .'

The electric guitars were cashed in for acoustic and Mickey's voice was like a lament. 'Lovers under creamy yellow' was a Mersey ballad of walking in the rain with Birkenhead almost out of sight the other side of the river. Seagulls and tug boats and fish and chips under a bus shelter. The ferry bouncing over choppy waters. The lights of the city in the night sky. A sharp wind and salt in the air. As tears wandered down her cheeks Lucy wrote the title down on a spare sheet of paper. Then she underlined the first four letters. LUCY. Not so very obscure Mr Peel. Not if you had taken a walk in the rain along the Mersey with the lead singer. Hand in hand and soaked to the skin and realising that seeing each other would be all but impossible for a long time. It had been two years earlier. They had managed to meet up a few times after he had at last been discharged from the hospital but it was always difficult. His parents had become doubly protective since his beating and she never seemed to have money for fares.

They had decided to do the grown up thing and wait until they both found their respective freedom. Since then there had been letters but nothing for a few months. She had begun to think he had given up on her. Well of course he had. He was a handsome lad even though he didn't seem to realise it. All he saw in the mirror was a boy who couldn't cut it on the football pitch. Of course he would never see himself through female eyes. He wanted to be like the 'Anfield Iron', Tommy Smith. He wanted to be like his big brother who had walked free from prison at six-foot-one and fourteen stone solid muscle. He didn't realise that his delicate features and kind eyes were going to become a magnet, especially once his female classmates got to hear his poems put to the music. When the letters had dried up she formed lots of images of fantastic looking girls from the big houses of middle class Southport. Summer barbeques and fathers who were lawyers or newspaper editors. Trips to watch plays at the Empire and going on summer holidays with the family to islands in Greece. They would have sunbed tans and big hair and white teeth and she couldn't stand to think about it. Whoever it was probably took him for nice meals in country pubs, hair blowing in the wind in a soft top MG. Vodka tonic and avocado prawns. And no doubt he had long forgotten Lucy who came from the wrong end of town whose brother was in the fast lane to the criminal top table.

Every day she made a solemn vow to herself that she wouldn't think about him any more. Maybe she would take up one of the offers for a Friday night date and the hell with it. The problem was that the only offers she ever got were from testosterone drenched clowns whose dreams were limited to sex and violence. The boys she secretly fancied stayed clear of her as if she had leprosy.

So every night she tended to read through one of the Lucy poems that she had secretly copied whilst Mickey lay unconscious on his Wigan hospital bed. And most nights she cried herself to sleep. And most mornings she woke with a hollow feeling and little will to get out of bed to face another day of cold stares and whispered conversations.

The hour and minute hands on her clock moved vertical. Midnight. John Peel was chatting away about a new band from Walsall who were worth a watch at the weekend. A rather drunk couple were making their way home outside. Traffic rumbled along the main road and the sky was all tinted orange. Lovers Under Creamy Yellow. He hadn't forgotten her and maybe there weren't any middle class Vogue girls from leafy streets with perfect lawns after all. Maybe, just maybe he was just as lonely as her. Maybe that was why he sang of walking by the river in the rain and eating chips from soggy paper. Maybe.

She pushed King Lear to one side and set out a blank piece of paper. Why not. Why the hell not.

Dear Mickey,

I suppose this has to be considered as fan mail. I expect you will have drooling females from all over Britain writing and begging for a signed photo or a lock of your hair. You're quite the rising star according to Mr Peel. I don't care if I sound like an old aunt but I'm going to say it anyway. I am so, so, so proud of you. There. Said it. It will be blue rinse next. Lovers Under Creamy Yellow? Not all that obscure actually. Not for the girl who got soaked to the skin. Or maybe there is another Lucy. If there is she should be aware that I will tear her hair out by the roots. OK. Time for practicalities. Although I still don't claim to be any great footballing expert it hasn't escaped my notice that Liverpool are in Paris next week. Real Madrid this time isn't it? Aren't they supposed to be quite good. Yeah, yeah. Nothing compared to the Mighty Reds. I can hear you saying it. Anyway. It occurs to me that we have a bit of tradition here. Lucy, Mickey and the European Cup. What about that for a song title? That would get Mr Peel going. So. Is the tradition to be continued. This girl would like it very much and if that sounds brazen so be it. How about meeting at Pier Head at five o'clock next Wednesday. A walk in the rain and a bag of cold chips and we could find a pub to watch the game in. If you aren't too big a superstar for such a mundane plan then write to me and I'll be there.

All my love.

Same old Lucy.

P.S. Please could you send me a signed photo for my bedroom wall?

THE LONG AND WINDING
ROAD TO ISTANBUL

She posted the letter the next morning on her way to school. For a moment she paused in front of the post box, the letter half in half out. And she wondered whether sending it was really such a good idea. Letting it loose from her grip so that it could disappear was easy. Waiting miserably for the postman wouldn't be. Writing the letter had put the gnawing loneliness of her life into a sharp focus. A reply might mean a break from it for an hour or two. But no reply would make everything so very much worse. She stood for so long that she began to feel foolish. What if someone was watching. That would give them all a good laugh. Something to talk about in the pub later. You should have seen that Lucy Tate. Standing by the postbox like she'd swallowed a glass of sour milk.

She opened her fingers and let it drop. What the hell. In for a penny and all that. As it turned out there was barely any agony at all. She did the maths and worked out that the earliest a letter could possibly arrive would be in two days time. And sure enough the postman came up trumps. The rest of the house was asleep and she had the kitchen to herself to open the letter.

Dear Lucy,

I absolutely cannot believe that you heard us on John Peel. I have been going on all week to everyone that we might be on and they all said it was all bullshit. To be honest I never thought for a minute that he would actually play it. It was the weirdest feeling I can tell you. Of course I have had an avalanche of fan mail and numerous offers of yacht trips around the Caribbean but we artists have to watch out for our street cred. Bearing this in mind I have turned down all offers that might blunt the ferocious edge that is driving Spion into the limelight. Soggy chips by Pier Head however is entirely in keeping with all that we stand for and so we have a firm date. You are quite right that tradition dictates that the European Cup should bring our ships together in the midst of Thatcher's endless grey ocean. However you failed to mention the second European Cup Final tradition. Namely, Liverpool win and Mickey McGuire's life heads off down the toilet. I have decided to convince myself that this has been a seventies thing and that all will be solved by the dawning of a new and fresh decade. The truth is that I would still have said yes even if a full brigade of

PARIS – MAY 1981

Waffen SS were waiting for me with guns trained. I guess that makes me some kind of idiot and there is a school of thought that says letting on about such things to a girl is about as cool as a boiled egg. I'm glad you got the 'Lovers Under Creamy Yellow' thing. It's a good job because there is nobody else on the whole planet who would have stood a chance.

See you on Wednesday.

Same old Mickey

It was as if they had written the weather. For a while in the morning the sun had shown some vague enthusiasm but by lunchtime a hard wind was kicking in off the sea and by mid-afternoon all was grey. Mickey pulled up his collar and sheltered as best he could. He kept telling himself that it had been Lucy who had sent the letter in the first place so there was no reason why he should worry about getting stood up. But he did worry. Every thirty seconds he looked up at the clock on the Liver Building and it never seemed to move. And the cogs of his brain started to clank around. Grey sky. Miserable grey. Bedraggled Liver Bird statues. Soaked seagulls and traffic inching office workers back to another suburban night. And the boy waits for the girl. A lone damp figure hunched in the face of the rain. The thing was that he could hardly play the tragic figure because he had turned up half an hour early which made looking at the clock every fifteen seconds all the more stupid. He decided there and then that he might as well give up all aspirations of ever being cool. If he was going to do the Paul Weller thing it would have to be lyrics only. The cool bit was way beyond him.

Turning up half an hour early was just another incidence of total lack of cool. What had it achieved? One, he was soaked to the skin. Two, he was a nervous wreck.

A cracked Scottish voice snapped him back into the world.

"Got ten pence for a cuppa tea pal?"

"Yeah. Sure. Hang on will you." His hand was so wet that it didn't want to go into his jeans pocket. In the end he had to sort of wrestle with himself to get the thing out.

"There you go mate."

THE LONG AND WINDING
ROAD TO ISTANBUL

The Scot who looked as if his last shave pre-dated the Thatcher revolution looked at the offering dubiously.

"That it?"

Mickey couldn't see what the problem was. "It's what you asked for."

"Aye, but that was a metaphor. Most people would'nae take the statement literally. Ken what a metaphor is pal?"

"Yeah. Simile's kid brother."

This brought on a phlegmy laugh which more or less instantly turned into a hacking cough. It took a while before the power of speech returned.

"That's no bad pal. I'll remember that one. Simile's wee brother. Why d'yu ken metaphors then?"

"I'm a writer."

"What kind?"

"Poems and songs."

"What d'yu write poems about then?"

Mickey's attention was away. His eyes had left the ex English teacher from Kilmarnock and had fallen on the vision that was approaching him. Familiar and not familiar at all. Same old Lucy and yet a whole new Lucy. She wasn't a girl any more.

"Her."

The bag man followed his gaze.

"Christ. No wonder. She you're bird?"

"She is when I close my eyes and go to sleep. Then I wake up and the world's a bag of shit again. Here. A quid. That unmetaphorical enough for you."

"Aye. Quid. Noun. Slang. Enough for a wee half."

"What about the tea?"

"Bollocks to it. 'Nother metaphor. I'll see you around pal."

"Yeah. Take care mate."

As one figure shuffled away the other glided in. She wore a knee-length raincoat and her hair was short. And she had make up on. He couldn't get his head around it being Lucy.

"You look like something out of a movie."

"And you look like something out of a launderette. What movie?"

"Third Man. You know. The end. That long walk with all the leaves falling and she passes the guy without a glance."

"I'll go for that. Always up for the role of femme fatale. Who was your mate."

"I didn't get his name. He was very big on metaphors though."

"Did he shake you down?"

He made the mistake of attempting a cool urban kind of shrug which made her laugh.

"How much? No lying. It's not allowed."

"A quid."

"No wonder you're struggling to find a place in Maggie's shiny new Britain. Do you insist on chips outside or could we maybe go inside somewhere? You've already done that song anyway and it was far too sad and I'm not in the mood for being sad today."

"OK. But only this once like. Happy songs don't sell you know. It's suicidal misery that gets the likes of me into the top ten. You only get away with happy, happy if you look like David Cassidy or something."

"You best stick to misery then, but not tonight."

She hooked her arm through his and they headed toward the city centre and he couldn't work out why he had been so nervous. It was like she had written. Same old Lucy. So what that she had grown up and looked fifteen shades of great. They still shared the same wavelength. The same ledge hovering thousands of feet above all the crap below.

As they headed away from the grey waters of the river they felt as if they were all alone in their own quiet world but they were wrong. Their every move was being carefully studied through a pair of binoculars which peered from the window of a Ford Granada parked up in the service bay of the Atlantic Hotel.

Behind the binoculars was DI Walter Nelson who had been seconded to the Greater Merseyside police on a six month attachment. The higher ups had been getting increasingly fed up with being told of the rise and rise of Eddie Tate. They were particularly fed up with being given the news that nobody had anything on him. Nothing. Not a whisper, not a sausage. The whole city seemed to know that Eddie Tate was well along the road to becoming a Scouse version of Al Capone but the long arm of the law held not a shred of evidence to prove it. To make things worse there was lots of whispered talk about how many officers Eddie Tate had in his pocket. Nobody dared put a figure on it but the higher ups feared the worst. So it was that the

THE LONG AND WINDING
ROAD TO ISTANBUL

Chief Constable of Greater Merseyside had a quiet word with the Chief Constable of Lancashire over a few late night whiskies after a conference. He asked if he could have a man for a while. Someone straight. Someone very hard. Someone to tear up all the files and start again. Someone to find a toehold, a foot in Eddie Tate's door. The Chief Constable of Lancashire came good. He asked about and went through his files and came up with the right sort of guy. Walter Nelson was something of a high flier having made Detective Inspector before turning thirty and had a reputation for in the face hard-nosed coppering whilst still being one of the sharpest tools in the box. Lancashire loaned him out to Merseyside for six months.

He spent a month reading up the files and taking a look at the ground. It was long enough for him to learn that the walls that Eddie Tate had built around his empire weren't about to come crashing down just because Walter Nelson had taken a ride down the East Lancs road. Once he had covered the background he made his first report. Taking down Tate was a long-term project and there was no point in pretending otherwise. In his opinion the first task was to attack the mood of resignation that seemed to prevail. He felt that Tate had built up an air of untouchablity and before any real progress could be made something had to be done about that. He was given the nod to see if he could snipe around the edges and start to get under the cracks a bit. After a month of looking for the cracks Walter had found just one.

Lucy Tate.

Lucy Tate. Seventeen-and-a-half years old. Great looker. Conditional offer to study English at Bristol which was pretty damned unusual for the little sister of a face-slashing hoodlum. Stayed in almost every night and didn't appear to have a boyfriend which certainly wasn't because of not being extremely easy on the eye.

Lucy Tate was an enigma and Walter liked that. As he poked about her life he began to come to the conclusion that against all reasonable odds Lucy Tate was straight as a die. And yet as he watched the family together in the long lens that took him through the back window into the large lounge he saw clear affection between the brother and sister. What was it all about? There was something about their expressions when they spoke with each other. Something about their body language. Most coppers would have thrown such subtlety to one side, but not Walter. He worried at it until he felt that he understood. Lucy

56

was Eddie Tate's favourite. He wanted her to be proud of him. To look up to him. To approve. And Lucy would only give him love. Never respect. And his body language told Walter all about how that must have hurt.

Slowly his theory started to take form. Lucy was bucking the trend. She was the exception to the rule in a family knee-deep in crime. She was planning her escape to a new life far from the reputation of her family. And she was Eddie Tate's little princess who must have thought he was some kind of god when she was five but now she had grown out of it. She was an Achilles Heel. A crack.

Once he had drawn his conclusions it was time to use them. Somehow he needed to use Lucy Tate as a way to send out a clear message to Eddie. Don't even begin to think that you're untouchable. The theory was fine, but putting it into practice was another thing. Lucy's life was simple to the point of being spartan. She went to school and then she went home. Sometimes she went for a walk. Every now and then she went into the city to watch a film or a play. But she was always alone. Always a quiet figure blending into the background. After giving two weeks of his life to watching her every move Walter had begun to feel sorry for her. He was losing enthusiasm for the whole idea. The concept was good but he couldn't see how he could make anything of it. He told the two young detectives in his charge that they would give it until the end of the week and if nothing happened they would move on to something else.

And now it seemed as if something might have happened. A meeting with a stranger. Arms linked in the rain. And she was smiling. It was the first time in a fortnight that he had seen that. So who was the someone? The face wasn't one he recognised from any of the files. Young. Probably the same age as Lucy. And very wet. The daft bugger must have been waiting out in the rain.

Nelson patiently laid out the facts. The meeting was well away from home turf which suggested that somebody at home wouldn't have approved. The lad had stood about in the rain which suggested that he cared. And Lucy Tate was smiling for the first time in a fortnight. It was basically next to nothing but it would probably be the best chance he would get to make anything out of his fortnight's work.

"OK lads. Let's lift them."

"What for sir?"

"For breathing. We don't need what for any more do we. Have you been asleep for the last year? S.U.S laws? Ring any bells? Maggie's little gift to all hard working coppers."

The constable blushed. "I thought it was Stop under Suspicion. Why are we suspicious sir?"

"Jesus, you're greener than last month's bread. Wake up and smell the bloody coffee. We're suspicious that he is a member of the KG bloody B. It doesn't matter. That's the whole point. It's why all the pinkos are out marching every weekend. Come on. Out you get. Time we got off our arses."

The three policemen closed the gap to Lucy and Mickey.

"Excuse me sir. Madam. A few questions."

Two sets of eyes jumped with shock. Nelson had his badge out at eye level. Lucy was the first to react.

"You HAVE to be joking."

"Just a few questions madam."

"About what?"

"Where are you going?"

"And what the hell has that got to do with you?" Desperate panic was erupting up the back of Lucy's throat. This couldn't be happening. They had only been with each other for a matter of minutes after two endless empty years and now this. But already the words in Mickey's letter were beginning to haunt her. The tradition of the European Cup final. Liverpool win and Mickey McGuire's life goes down the toilet.

"Madam, you and you friend are both acting in a suspicious manner and we would like to establish that nothing untoward is happening here. I'll ask again. Where are you going?"

She had more or less decided to keep her temper but the man was getting under her skin too much for that. Little did she know that was what Walter Nelson did best.

"Oh go to hell. What do you think this is? Russia? You can't do this."

"Actually we can Madam. And I am afraid that your behaviour is merely confirming my original suspicion. I must caution you that we have a statutory right to search your person. I would like you to accompany me to the police station so that we can undertake a proper search."

"No BLOODY WAY . . . !"

The three policemen moved quickly and before either Lucy or Mickey properly realised what was happening they had been cuffed and they were being guided toward the car. Once they were inside Lucy kept up a stream of anger which the policemen ignored with small, knowing smiles. And then she glanced across to Mickey and saw that his face was chalk white. And a horrible realisation hit her. Mickey had something to hide. Something for them to find. And it was far too late to do a thing about it. Liverpool win and Mickey McGuire's life goes down the toilet. Oh please no. And again it would be all down to her. Her surname which she carried through life like a cancer.

They were split up when they reached the station. They searched her from top to toe. A policewoman in surgical gloves humiliated her like she had never been humiliated before. Then they sat her in an interview room and made her wait for what seemed like forever before questioning her about nothing for two hours. Then they told her that she was free to go and they apologised for any inconvenience they may have caused. And she saw the look of triumph in the eyes of the Detective Inspector's eyes.

"Where's Mickey?"

"I'm afraid your friend was found in possession of a quantity of an illegal substance. He will be staying here for the night and until he appears in front of the Magistrate tomorrow morning."

"You can't keep him you bastard."

"I can. I will. And both of my parents are named on my birth certificate. Same name."

"I'm going nowhere until you let him go."

"Then that of course is your choice madam. There is a seating area against the wall there for the use of the public. The hot drinks machine vends at 30p."

She slumped down and bit back the tears that had been so close for what seemed like hours and hours. What on earth did she expect to achieve by waiting? They wouldn't let him out. Not a chance. This was all about Eddie of course. They wanted to get to Eddie through her and that meant they had to get to her. And that meant Mickey would have a night in the cells. She had been staring down at the tired lino on the floor didn't notice Nelson come over to her.

"What an interesting situation we have here Miss Tate."

She didn't bother to look up. "Really."

"Oh yes. Really. I wonder if Eddie knows you are having secret romantic meets with Frank's brother."

Her head fell and inch or so. Nelson dripped sarcasm like scalding fat.

"I think I'd better tell him. Better let him know. It's the kind of thing a big brother needs to know. No big brother likes the idea of his little sister knocking about with lads that use drugs."

"Go away."

Nelson leaned in close so that his face was very close to the top of her bowed head. "I don't go away Lucy. Not me. I'm like a nasty rash. I get all over you. All the way under your skin."

The illegal substance was £3 worth of Lebanese Red that Mickey had bought from Tonto, 'Spion's bass guitarist. He had been smoking dope for a few months and he was pretty taken with it. He liked the idea of sharing a couple of spiffs with Lucy but he hadn't been at all sure how she would feel about it. It was something he had been planning to play by ear. And now the small lump was bagged and tagged and he was alone in a cell. After a while he realised they weren't about to question him. He was unimportant. This was all about Lucy. At least that was what they had started with. Get to Eddie through Lucy. But of course they were going to get two for the price of one because now they could find a way to get at Frank through Mickey.

When he strained his ears he could just about hear the sound of Peter Jones from a portable radio at the end of the corridor. He stood and pressed his ear to the cold metal of the cell door.

" . . . as Liverpool make their way out on to the shiny green of the pitch here at the Parc des Princes stadium in Paris it is as if Anfield has moved from the Mersey to the Seine. I look to my right and I look to my left and I look straight ahead and all I see is the red of Liverpool . . ."

He managed to hear five minutes and then the duty sergeant left and took his radio with him leaving only silence. It would be the next morning that a grumpy voice the other side of the door told him Liverpool had won one nil.

Lucy lost all track of time. What did it matter. She had made her mind up to sit all night. It was the least that she could do. Not that it would achieve much. But it would be better than taking an empty bus back to her cold room and her books. Her head seemed too heavy to lift so she just stared down at the same bit of floor. The door kept opening and closing each time bringing a rush of damp air from outside. She didn't bother looking to see who it was that came in and out so she didn't see when Mickey's father came in and stood as still as stone when he saw her. She didn't see the cold rage on his face as he crossed over to where she sat.

"You."

She looked up into eyes filled with the very purest of loathing.

"You bitch. You lousy little bitch. What is it with your family? Isn't one of my sons enough for you? Do you have to take both? Just leave him alone, you hear. Keep your little whore hands off him. He has a chance, our Mickey. Just stay away."

She wanted to say something but there was no point. She was born a Tate which meant that what she said wouldn't matter. As far as he was concerned she was filth and always would be. There was no Lucy. There was only Lucy Tate. She met his eyes and found only ice. Then he marched to the desk to ask about his son.

It was time for her to go. She got up and went out into empty streets and driving rain. The eyes of Merseyside were fixed on Paris. Nobody was there to see the girl in the raincoat who leant over a rail and turned her face into the salty wind and cried and cried.

In the weeks that followed Mickey sent her letter after letter. He said he knew it wasn't her fault. He said that there was nothing she could have done to help it. He said they could put it all behind them. But after three months when she didn't reply the letters at last dried up. She got her A in English and surprised herself by matching it with a similar grade in General Studies. She duly made her escape to Bristol in October and penned a letter with an enclosed postcard of Brunel's suspension bridge in Clifton. By the time the letter arrived in Southport Mickey wasn't there any more. The three members of Spion had all got places at Newcastle Polytechnic and headed off to Geordieland. His father saw the Bristol postmark and shredded the letter into the smallest pieces he could manage.

Chapter 4
Rome – May 1984

Lucy spotted Frank McGuire as soon as he walked into the bar of the Students' Union. It wasn't hard. He stuck out like a sore thumb. It wasn't just because he stood a couple of inches taller than just about everyone around him. It was everything about the way he carried himself. The room was filled with students in their old jeans, sweaters with holes and crusading T-shirts. Most of their faces were flushed with drink and the hopeful energy of young people from nice streets in nice towns all ready to go out and change the world. Frank carried a stillness about him as he carefully scanned the room. His hair was short and expensively cut. He wore a casual black leather jacket that must have cost more than her grant for the whole term. And when his eyes met hers there was no naiveté. Quiet eyes. Hard eyes. He wasn't about to march to free Mandela. He gave her an unsmiling nod of recognition and eased his way through the crowd at the bar.

The sight of his approach fired up a small knot of anger in her. Eddie's messenger. Eddie who would never stay clear of her life. Eddie who sent his number one enforcer down to her like a ghost from another world.

"Alright Lucy."

She gave him a cold look.

"He just doesn't get the message does he? Just go home Frank. Tell him the answer is no. It doesn't matter what the question is."

"Can I get you a drink?"

"I've got a drink."

Frank gave the nearly empty glass in front of her a glance.

"Not much left."

"Look, she said she's got a drink." The voice beside her was from Keith who was from somewhere in Worcestershire. He was studying politics and he was in the same play as she was and he was a boyfriend of one week standing. His upbringing in a cosy Midlands town had obviously not taught him about what signs to look for. Threat for Keith came in the shape of the local skinheads when they overdid the cider and pissed against walls. They wouldn't have the likes of Frank McGuire where Keith came from. The quiet ones with the measuring eyes. The hard ones.

Frank moved his eyes onto the voice. "I don't think you're a part of this conversation mate. Better it stays that way."

Keith wasn't about to register the danger in the soft Scouse voice that he could barely hear over the loud music that drenched the bar in sound. Had he had three snakebites less, then he might have been less impulsive. He started to stand up to ready himself for action. Frank leaned over and took one of his ears between thumb and forefinger and twisted.

"You don't want to do this. Believe me. Just sit down and shut your face and everything will be fine. There's a good lad."

Keith would never have believed that such an unbelievable amount of pain could result from a tweak of the ear. It sobered him up in a few seconds and made him aware of the danger in the half-smile. Lucy reached up and swatted at Frank's outstretched arm.

"Look Frank. I told you. I've nothing I want to say. Just go home will you? I'm sorry that you've wasted your time but he shouldn't have sent you."

"He didn't send me. He doesn't know I'm here."

This was unexpected. Enough to stop her in her tracks.

"So what are you doing here?"

He took another look around the crowded space.

"Can we go somewhere else Lucy? Somewhere quieter?"

Next to her Keith suddenly exploded to his feet and started to barge his way towards the Gents. The shot of pain had disrupted his system to such an extent that the five snakebites in his stomach suddenly wanted out. He made it to within five yards of the door to the toilets when two hours worth of drinks exploded out of his mouth and all over a second year geography student's blouse. There were screams and raised voices and the geography student's boyfriend flailed out a punch which by luck more than judgement landed square on Keith's nose and felled him like a skittle.

Lucy sighed. Unbelievable. Frank hadn't even been in the room five minutes and already the night had turned to vomit and violence. She got up and grabbed her jacket.

"Let's go."

Outside it was the third warm night of a ten-day hot spell. Frank was uneasy.

"Look. I'm sorry about that Lucy. I just wanted to calm him down."

She laughed. "Well it didn't work very well did it?"

"No. I suppose it didn't"

Everything about his body language spoke of regret that was genuine. Maybe she should cut him some slack.

"Forget it. You've probably done me a favour. He was a mistake."

"He your boyfriend?"

"Of sorts. Not any more I think. I don't know what I was thinking of to be honest."

"Right."

They walked in silence for a few minutes. A pub appeared with a couple of spare tables out on the pavement.

"This will do. I'll have a coke please."

He disappeared inside and she took a seat and wondered what it was all about. It had been over two years since she had been back home. Her escape to Bristol had been complete. She felt like an animal released from a miserable small cage in a zoo into a million acres of the Serengeti. Her life on Merseyside was far behind her. Now she had friends. She had a life. A real life that belonged to Lucy. Her surname meant nothing in her new life and there was nothing that would persuade her to change the way things were. Of course they could be better in some ways. Money was always a complete nightmare. Her grant was barely enough to cover half a term and she made up the shortfall stacking shelves at a local supermarket. All her friends had parents who sent them cheques when times got hard. Of course she could have had a bigger cheque than the lot of them put together if she had made a single call to her brother, but it was never going to happen. If she had to work all night every night, then it would still be a small price to pay for freedom. She was serious. She was gone. And there was no way she would be going back.

And for two years the silence had been complete. The Tate family was split. And Lucy had thrived on building a life that belonged to her and nobody else. Her studies had been a great success. Her tutor wore a corduroy jacket with leather patches on the elbows and a CND badge on the lapel. He was a Labour man of thirty years standing and was delighted that his brightest protégé hailed from Liverpool. He was well on the way to steering her to a big result and he had set up the prospect of a scholarship to the University of Minnesota. Boyfriends came and went, but mainly went. There had been one who had lasted over a term but since then her relationships had been short and inadequate. Keith was the last in the line. In her quieter moments she reflected that she might never quite fit in to her new environment. She had escaped the streets of her childhood in body but they still retained a hold on her soul. The evening news often carried pictures of the grinding decline of her home city. In the last summer before her escape, Toxteth had burst into flames as the worst riots in decades had shocked a watching nation. Thatcher had dispatched Hesseltine to take a look and he had found a city on the brink of collapse. Soaring unemployment was tearing the heart from Liverpool and Yosser Hughes took the burning despair of the city into the living rooms of the whole country. It made it hard at times to settle with the growing comfort of her fellow students whose parents were cashing in on the great Thatcherite boom that was sweeping the shires of the south whilst the old industrial heartland of the north was left to fester and rot.

The more everyone tried to welcome her in, the more she felt apart. Not that she showed it. She went to all the parties and allowed her accent to drift. She made a name for herself as an actress and was always pursued by plenty of suiters. But she would never really be a part of it. And she had realised that she would never want to be. She was floating between two lives. It wasn't uncomfortable. Anything but. But it wasn't permanent. Not nearly.

Frank came out with the drinks. She was mildly surprised to see that he had chosen an expresso.

"Here you are."

She took a sip of coke and shook her head at the proffered packet of Benson and Hedges. He added a teaspoon of sugar and stirred whilst taking in the leafy neighbourhood where the price of a single house would buy up a street at home.

"Bit different from the Pool, hey Lucy."

"Just a little."

"You happy here?"

"Yes."

He nodded at this. "Good. You deserve it. Things must have been pretty shite for you at home."

"Thank you."

She had never really known Frank. He was just another one of her brother's hard guys. His quietness surprised her.

"So come on then. If my brother didn't send you, what's going on?"

He took a mouthful of smoke and let it out through his nose into the warm night air.

"Do you know what's been going on with our Mickey?"

As is if she didn't. For two years it had been a routine that ran like clockwork. Every Thursday she would be in the newsagents round the corner for a copy of the New Musical Express. For the first year there had only been snippets about Spion. Small adverts showing them supporting other unknown bands in and around Liverpool. Five-line reviews that always spoke of promise and heart and soul. The breakthrough came in the spring of 1982 as the British fleet headed south from Southampton to retake the Falklands. "No Hope Street" became an anthem for the left and made it up to number 19 in the charts. It painted the picture of dole Britain. Closed shops and boiled cabbage. Second-hand toys for Christmas. Giros blown in the pub and her at home on the Valium. It won awards for its haunting acoustic melody and it came to represent the cry of pain from all the places that paid the price for Harrods sales figures going up by 10% a quarter. And suddenly 'Spion' were in the vanguard along with The Style Council and Billy Bragg and UB40, putting anger and misery to music.

Two days after their first appearance in the top twenty, the three members of Spion walked tentatively onto the main stage at Glastonbury for the 11 a.m. slot. Traditionally it was one of the festival's short-straws as the majority of the 90,000 revellers would inevitably still be sleeping off the effects of the night before. However the effect of 'No Hope Street' meant the newly arrived Liverpudians were watched by over 20,000 and a week later their single climbed to number nine.

The next year they supported the Specials on a thirty-date tour around Britain and their first album, 'Bedsit Revolutionaries', became a cult favourite. The band attracted attention from the musical press. They were seen as something of a throw back. There was plenty of hard drinking and rumours of hotel room excesses, but they also carried a hard left-wing political edge. This became all the more relevant once the Conservative Government had secured another term of office in 1983 and the traditional opposition was left in ruins.

For a while it seemed as if the only real alternative voice to Thatcher's rampant new captitalism was to be found in the small collection of groups who sang out for the victims of the cult of selfishness that had taken such a hold of the nation.

Early in 1984 the last of the Mohicans called his men out for the final battle. Arthur Scargill did what the whole country had been waiting for him to do and he marched the miners out for their long anticipated showdown with the government. Spion heeded the clarion call and their second album, 'Barricade', was launched at a succession of fundraisers for the striking miners up and down the country. Soon these events became as volatile as the picket lines in Nottinghamshire where pitched battles raged every day between the police and the flying pickets. Spion gigs sucked in enemies from all sides and violence became commonplace as the supporters of Militant Tendency fought it out with the police and skinhead gangs who weren't all that bothered about the rights and wrongs of the strike but couldn't resist the chance of a good old rumble.

After a particularly wild night in Huddersfield, Mickey enjoyed a couple of weeks of minor fame as a Daily Mail bad boy. The indignant newspaper wondered if the band actively encouraged the excesses of the audience and demanded that the police look into the matter. At a time when the top end of the charts was dominated by highly groomed New Romantics with expensive swept back hair and jackets with rolled up sleeves, the jeans and donkey jacket look favoured by Spion became something the right-wing tabloids used to mark them down as trouble.

Every now and then Lucy would hear Mickey interviewed on the radio. The communist bogeyman sounded pretty much like the same old Mickey to her. He had certainly become a lot more political than when he had been at school, but that was nothing unexpected. He was as articulate as ever and it made her smile every time he managed to work a reference to his beloved Liverpool FC into his answers. But behind the jauntiness she sensed a tiredness in his voice. Maybe he was burning the candle at every end he could light it. Probably. She had seen lots of the lads at university go clean off the rails in their first year away from home. With a few quid in their pockets and a party every night they would gorge themselves on teenage freedom and end just about every night with their heads plunged down the toilet. Her instincts told her that Mickey and the band would be doing much the same only more. Well of course they would be. They were still students up in Newcastle and at the same time they were flying up and down the country on a rock and roll bandwagon.

There had been a couple of times when she had seen television pictures of live gigs and on both occasions her stomach had had a little twist of anger at the sight of all the girls with their faces a sheen of sweat and excitement. No doubt there would be a queue of them at the stage door every night and she found it hard not to feel a pang of jealousy.

There had been a few opportunities for her to go and see them, but she had only been once, when she had gone along to Glastonbury with a couple of friends. She hadn't mentioned that she knew the lead singer of the band that was due on stage at eleven. Both her mates had been fast asleep when she had left them and joined the surprising crowd. It had been fantastic. Unbelievable. She had eased her way up to near the front and couldn't quite get her head around the fact that the lead singer who was drawing all the cheers was Mickey. Her Mickey. Or the Mickey who might have been hers but for the way things were. And when he sang 'Lovers under a creamy yellow' there seemed to be hundreds of people all around her who knew all the words and sang along. And the tears poured down her cheeks as his voice took the rain of a Merseyside night into a warm summer's morning on a Somerset dairy farm. And she had wondered if he was thinking about her as he sang. A woman in her thirties tapped her gently on her shoulder and asked if she was all right and Lucy wiped away her tears and said she was fine. She had nearly told the woman that the song was about her but she realised that it would make her sound like some kind of nut job.

Once the encore was wrapped up she had made her way to the side of the stage with a vague notion of trying to find him, but the place was blocked off by great big security men with biceps popping the sleeves of their T-shirts. How very strange. She was still Lucy and he was still Mickey, but it would count for nothing. She could tell the bouncers she knew him for as long as she liked but it wouldn't make a jot of difference. Mickey had moved along into another world and a backstage pass was needed to join him in it.

When she got back to the flat she sat for a whole night staring at an empty sheet of paper and tried to find a way to get something down on paper. After umpteen cups of coffee she had screwed the paper up and tossed it into the bin. What was there to say? She was in Bristol and he was in Newcastle. She was by the Severn and he was up on the Tyne. Their worlds were moving apart like continental plates. She never wrote, but every Thursday morning she went in to see Mr Habib to collect her copy of the NME. And now, like a stranger from a far away land, Frank McGuire had arrived from her past.

"I've read about him in the papers. He seems to be on the up and up. You must all be very proud."

Frank eased the ash off his cigarette on the ledge of the ash tray. "Yeah, course I am."

"What about your mam and dad?"

He shrugged. "Don't know. They don't talk to me. Not since I was banged up. I'm still a disgrace."

"I'm sorry."

"No need. It was all my choice. You reap what you sow."

"What Eddie sows you mean."

He looked up warily. "Look. I know there's stuff between you and Eddie but it's none of my business. It's not why I'm here."

"So why are you here Frank?"

"It's about Mickey."

Something in his voice. Something not good at all. Something that made her heart sink.

"Go on then."

"How much do you know about Spion and that?"

She shook her head. "Only what I read in the papers. I haven't spoken with Mickey for ages. In fact it will be two years the day after tomorrow."

Frank raised an eyebrow. "That's pretty specific."

She laughed. "Mickey's timetable. Our friendship seems destined to be governed by European Cup Finals. Two years ago we had a date which lasted all of five minutes before the police lifted us and locked us up. And here we are again. Back to Rome. Remember the last time Frank?"

He grimaced. "Course I do. Eighteen months worth of remember it."

"Oh I'm sorry. That was horrid of me."

"You're all right. It's life. Like I said before, nobody forced me did they? I felt bloody awful for our Mickey though. It always seemed as if it was my fault that he kept missing the finals. First the Chemist thing then he got battered by those Mancs when he came to visit. What's so funny?"

"Nothing. Sorry. It's just I always had a feeling that it was down to me. I think I have to take the rap for the last one. Know what he told me before we met up? He said he was a bit superstitious about it. The tradition of the European Cup. Lucy and Mickey meet up. Liverpool win and Mickey McGuire's life goes down the toilet. We had a right laugh about it and then look what happened."

He grimaced at the memory of that night. "Anyway. I was saying about the band. You won't know the others? Midge and Tonto?"

"Not a thing. Colourful names."

"Not in real life. Steve Midgeley and Sean Higgins. Christ knows where Tonto came from."

"Who are they?"

"Just lads from the school in Southport. Not bad lads really, it's just . . ."

He seemed on the verge of getting tongue-tied.

"It's just . . ." She prompted.

"Well Tonto's fine. He's quite quiet really and he can't half play the guitar. But Midge . . . I mean he's all right as well . . . He's just a bit of a nutter that's all."

"I bit of a nutter. Nutter as in head butts and Stanley knives?"

"Christ no. None of them are like that. No. He's just daft. Seriously daft. It was him who got our Mickey into smoking dope."

She could see the furrow of concern on his forehead and he wasn't at all keen on meeting her eyes.

"The thing is Lucy, well things have gone on a bit from there. You know how it is in that kind of life. Birds and booze and everyone wants a piece of you."

"All I know is what they put in the papers."

"Well there's lots of drugs kicking around as well. Most of the time it's nowt much But then it can get serious. To start with they were just being stupid. Dope and speed and acid. But then Midge got into coke. And Mickey wanted to have a go as well and . . . Well you know how it is . . ."

"I haven't a clue how it is Frank. You forget I'm only a Tate by name. I left that world behind."

"Well they both started getting into it more and more, especially when the band got signed up by a record label and some money started coming in. The problem is that all the chart hits and that is all hype. The lads don't see much. Just a few quid really. Certainly not enough to feed a coke habit. That's when I got to hear what was happening."

"How?"

"Midge was buying off Trevor Birch over in Bootle. He'd run up a big tab and he couldn't cover it. It was getting to the broken bones stage when one of Trev's boys rang me for a quiet word. He said it wasn't just Midge who was doing all the lines. It was Mickey as well. Trev had let them have plenty of credit because he thought they must have been coining it from the records and that. Then when he found out they were on toss all he went psycho and told the boys to go and sort them out. Both of them. He said that if Mickey was happy enough to put it up his nose then he would have to be happy enough when he got his legs broke."

"Oh Jesus. The bloody idiots."

Frank lit up another B&H. "I went to see Trev and I settled the bill. Then I caught up with our Mickey and I give him loads. I felt like smacking the little prick. Three grand it cost me. I was going to buy a new motor. They said that was it and they would leave off it and I thought at first that they would."

"But they didn't."

Frank shook his head irritably. "It's got worse. They don't get any credit any more. I made sure of that. I got the word out so now it's cash and carry or nothing. But they seem to get hold of cash out of thin air. Midge is worse than Mickey. He's up and down like a yo-yo. I don't think he knows what day it is most of the time. He's got to using smack as well. Mickey hasn't. Not yet. I've gone on and on at him but I can't get through. He can't seem to see where it's all going to end up. But I can. I see it every day don't I?"

"One of the many joys of working for my brother."

This put his head down another notch. She didn't actually say the bit about it being OK if he helped Eddie sell his filth to other lads from other families. She didn't have to. Her unsaid words sounded like a scream in Frank's ears.

"I can't see why any of this has brought you to Bristol Frank."

He finally looked up and there was no mistaking the pain in his eyes. "He won't listen to me Lucy. It's like he's on some sort of a death wish. Maybe it would be different if you had a go. I mean you've always been . . ." He reached out for the right words and didn't find them. " . . . you know."

"Do I?"

"Special."

"Special?"

"To Mickey. More than anyone. Come on Lucy, you know that."

"All I know Frank is that I haven't heard from Mickey in two years now and I naturally assumed that he decided to sample the delights of all the nubile young things who attend his concerts."

"Course there's birds. Lots of them. He's a right lucky little sod that way. But they're all nowt really. You want to see the look on his face if anyone ever mentions your name."

"Who on earth mentions my name?"

"Well they don't exactly mention your name. Not as such. It's the song. You know. 'Lovers Under Creamy Yellow'."

She was open mouthed. "You're not saying that people know that is about me. Us."

He smiled at the look of horror on her face. "No. Do they hell. In fact I think it's only me. He told me after the Paris game. He knew he probably wouldn't get to see you again. What a mess he was. Cried his bloody heart out. I didn't know what to say. I'm not good at that stuff."

"No. I don't suppose you are. What do you want me to do Frank?"

"Have a word. I reckon he'd listen to you. If he doesn't, then he won't listen to anyone and then he's going to be stuffed. Already he's not well. Have you seen any pictures?"

"No."

"He's even skinnier now. Just a bag of bones. His head is starting to look like a skull. He's pale as a sheet and he is twitchy as a dog with fleas. Paranoid as well. He's convinced that MI5 are out to top him. Crackers I know, but try telling him that. And the more shit he snorts the worse he gets. Midge keeps telling him he needs a bit of smack to slow him back down and . . ."

His voice trailed off. The look on Lucy's face told him that she understood well enough. No need to say more.

"Have you anything in mind Frank?"

He nodded. "They're doing a gig in Wales tomorrow night. For the miners. I could get a hotel for the night and drive you up tomorrow. That's if it's OK for you to miss lectures and that . . ."

"OK. No need for a hotel room. You can have a couch."

"Thanks. I didn't know what you'd say."

"Well it was always going to be yes. I suppose it will always be yes where your Mickey's concerned."

This brought a smile onto his hard features.

"You two really love each other don't you?"

She blushed. "I haven't a clue. We barely know each other. Every time we meet the sky seems to fall in."

"You two always remind me of a Scouser version of Romeo and Juliet."

"Bloody hell. Shakespeare from a gangster. I'm impressed."

"Third year school trip. We went to see it at the Empire. I got caught smoking in the bogs and banned from all trips for a year. But I had a snog with Sheila Maxwell on the way back on the coach."

"I didn't think anyone ever snogged Sheila."

"Just goes to show doesn't it. You learn something new every day. Want another or shall we get a bite to eat? I'm starved."

Lucy got up and went to lectures as usual the next morning but she might as well not have bothered. She had barely managed a wink of sleep as her mind raced away all through the balmy night until the sky lightened to blue. It was all much too fast. It had taken her a long time to come to terms with the idea that her relationship with Mickey was about reading the music papers on a Thursday morning. Things were just never going to happen and that was all there was to it. She had vowed to be sensible, to shine in her exams and to move on to a life that was a million miles away from Merseyside. And if that meant that she and Mickey were never to be, then it would be the price she would have to pay. The memory of all the miserable lonely nights in her room and the looks on the faces of the neighbours as she walked to school were almost overpowering. She couldn't go back. Not ever.

So she had restricted herself to watching Mickey from afar. Like a fan. But now the past had reached out and taken her by the collar and as night turned to dawn she tried to get her head around the fact that she was about to see him again. And she wondered what he would be like. A cocaine addict. Mickey. It made no kind of sense. But there was no way Frank had been exaggerating. She knew that it must have taken a lot for him to take the trip south. He had only come because things were bad. She was frightened that Mickey would be a stranger who didn't want to know her any more. After all she hadn't replied to any of his letters. He probably thought that she had decided to dump him once she had escaped Liverpool.

As the hours trudged by her mood sank steadily. Of course he would be different. How would she have felt if the boot had been on the other foot and it had been she who kept sending letters away into a vacuum? And what was it that Frank had said. 'Course there's birds. Lots of them.' The horrible little cows. How many was lots? And did he sleep with every one of them? Did he sleep with two at a time? Wasn't that what rock stars did, especially when they were hoovering up fat lines of cocaine. Then she tossed herself over to her other side and reminded herself how many Keiths there had been. Four. Boring dreary sods the lot of them. And yes she had slept with them. And just like Frank had said, it was nowt. And every time as she stood in front of the mirror the next morning to clean her teeth she had thought about Mickey. So there was no point in getting all wound up about Mickey and his roadies. And Frank had said that he still talked about the song. And Lucy had heard him sing it herself at Glastonbury. So try and sleep Lucy. Clear the head. Think about how many railway sleepers you would need to build a railway to Mars. Think about swimming ducks eating bits of bread.

The lectures wafted over her head and she didn't manage to take a single note. She couldn't find an ounce of interest in whether or not Tom Sawyer was central to America's perception of itself. They could take Tom Sawyer and shove him some place where the sun didn't shine as far as she was concerned. She was in a world of her own as she left the last lecture, so much so that she actually bumped into Keith who was waiting for her with the look of a man who had just swallowed a raw haddock.

"Lucy . . ."

"Oh piss off will you Keith. I don't go for the throwing up type."

"But Lucy . . ."

"Two letters. N and O. Spells no. Means negative. Nada. Non. Niet. Nein. Get the picture? Bye bye."

She had allowed her accent to thicken and a few heads turned to watch. Sod the lot of them. She kept her head up and headed out of the lecture hall and back to the flat. Once they crossed the Severn Bridge they seemed to enter a world that felt entirely different from the prosperity of Bristol. By the time they were past Cardiff they were into a landscape dominated by coal mining and steelworks. The weather turned windy and grey and there seemed to be police vans at every road end. The gig was to be held in the town hall of one of the many half village, half towns that sat on top of the coal that lay under the ground of the valley floors. They parked up two hours before the show was due to kick off and went into a terrace-end pub for a couple of drinks.

Outside, the high street was filling up with different groups who eyed each other with hostility. On one side of the street a cluster of policemen were receiving instructions from a beefy sergeant whilst the front entrance to the town hall was controlled by NUM stewards. A group of skinheads had taken up position on a patch of grass under a grimy war memorial where they were surrounded by a growing collection of spent beer cans. The Militant Tendency group was gathering around an old Transit van where a young woman with cropped green hair and a pierced nose was passing out placards pledging undying loyalty to equality, freedom and downing the runaway battleship that was Thatcher. And there was car after car bringing in those affiliated to nothing more than the band Spion and the songs that seemed to put the way they felt about life to music.

Frank and Lucy had a corner seat from where they could watch the scene unfolding through a window which hadn't been washed for a while.

"It's going to kick off big time." There was no enthusiasm for the idea in Frank's voice. "Look at them all. They think they're different, but they're all the same. Coppers, miners, skins, they all want a ruck. They just wear different uniforms."

"You know Frank, I never realised what an interesting character you are."

"Didn't notice more like. Nobody looks very hard at lads like me. People cross the street and try and look the other way."

Lucy took a sip at her coke. "So why?"

"What? Why Eddie?"

She nodded.

"Nothing else was there. I pratted around at school and didn't get any exams. Once upon a time I'd have gone and got a job down the docks or something." He shrugged. "You know how is in the Pool for lads like me. It's what I always told our Mickey. For a while I thought he'd taken a bit of notice."

"Do you feel bad about what you do?"

"Meaning?"

"You know what I mean. Selling drugs. Breaking up families. Hurting people."

He lit up and looked outside. "It's easy to have a go at the likes of me. Sure we're bad lads. But if you want to look at social damage, then who is worse? The likes of me and Eddie or the ones who close down all the factories?"

"That's crap Frank and you know it. It's a pale excuse. Just because a factory closes it's no excuse for peddling smack. You're avoiding the question."

He turned back to her with a faint smile. "Course I'm avoiding the question Lucy. I didn't want the dole so I chose to be a villain. I don't dwell on it. I don't dissect it. I just do it."

"No dreams Frank?"

"Course I've got dreams."

She raised an eyebrow but he just shook his head and resumed his vigil on the fight waiting to happen outside.

"What do you want to do then? Shall we try to get backstage now or do you want to wait till after the gig?" He asked.

"I'd like to see the gig. I've only ever seen them once you know. At Glastonbury. Two years ago. I thought they were great."

"Fair enough. Make sure you stay close by when we get in."

"My own knight in shining armour. What a lucky girl I am."

THE LONG AND WINDING
ROAD TO ISTANBUL

By nine the small space in front of the stage was far too full. The manual of safety regulations had been the least of the problems faced by the concert organisers. Frank's prediction had come to fruition a little after eight when the skinheads had charged the Militant lines in a sudden pre-emptive strike. It was a fight that was about as even as Germany versus Poland in 1939. Within a few seconds seven followers of world revolution were laid out on the tarmac ready for hospitalisation. Then the fight was evened up as thirty miners flew into the fray with arms hardened from years of digging coal. Within another minute, five of the skinheads were laid out ready to share a ward with their left wing adversaries. Then came the police with batons crashing and the beefy sergeant to the fore with his face brick red and his eyes gleaming. The whole thing was done and dusted in five minutes and the cameraman from the local news was chuffed to bits. It had been just like Nottinghamshire and he was confident that he had nailed it to the wall.

Once the sergeant had finished breaking heads and snapping on cuffs, he entered into negotiations with the senior shop steward in charge of the doors. They agreed that the best thing would be to keep the skinheads out which would keep some kind of a lid on things inside the hall. But as all attention was on keeping out young men in Doc Martin lace-ups with number one haircuts and swastika tattoos on their forearms, nobody got round to counting the numbers which soon far exceeded the venue's safety limit.

By the time that Spion took to the stage the place was pumped up on a mixture of violence and canned beer. The band were met with loud and prolong cheering. Lucy and Frank had found a position on the edge of the crowd but quite near the front. The sight of Mickey sent a shudder through her. He was thin to the point of being almost emaciated. He strode to the front of the stage with one arm held up high with a clenched fist. His T-shirt and jeans hung off him and his hair was dead and lifeless. His face was a sheen of sweat and his eyes seemed to have been pushed back into the sockets.

He was smiling, but it wasn't the old Mickey smile. It was a wild high-octane sort of smile. Almost a leer. He was plugged into the energy all around him, high on the edge of violence that pervaded the room. And then he held his arms out wide and patted downwards to encourage silence which eventually settled into the sweat-filled smoky air. He grabbed a microphone and spoke in a strange jerky voice that Lucy hadn't heard before. And yet there was something utterly compelling about him. Especially his eyes which were almost alight.

"There's a lot of talk about red at the moment. Talk from RED top papers. Talk of the RED menace. The RED peril. REDS under the bed like Arthur Scargill . . ."

The mention of King Arthur was a cue for prolonged cheering.

" . . . we are warned about what will happen if be don't defeat these evil REDS. We'll have the RED army waiting to come and get us when they get their orders to march from RED Square. We have the RED brigade waiting to plant bombs on us. We have a RED alert all over the land and Maggie says we must man the barricades to beat these terrible REDS . . ."

The mention of Thatcher was cue for an instant chorus of "MAGGIE, MAGGIE, MAGGIE . . . OUT! OUT! OUT!"

"Well Maggie, we've got news for you tonight you horrible old bitch. The REDS aren't all that easy to beat. Remember Lenin and Trotsky Maggie. Remember The Bay of Pigs. And after tomorrow night it will be remember Rome . . . Come on then . . . Let's be hearing you . . . OH WHEN THE REDS . . . GO MARCHING IN . . . OH WHEN THE REDS GO MARCHING IN . . . I WANT TO BE IN THAT NUMBER . . . "

And without really being aware of it Lucy was hammering out the song with the rest of them, her arm raised high in a fist. For the next hour-and-a-half everything seemed possible as Mickey kept his audience roaring out defiance and support for the coal miners. After three songs he was drenched in sweat and pouring can after can of Harp down his neck. Red was the theme that ran through the set and he had his audience singing Liverpool songs and forgetting their footballing allegiance in favour of a strange cocktail of world revolution, defeating the Tories and beating FC Roma in their own Olympic Stadium and conquering Europe. For a full forty-five minutes the frenzy built until he unplugged the wires and went acoustic. He silenced the room with the ballad 'Lovers Under Creamy Yellow' which never failed to send the tears streaming down Lucy's cheeks and tonight was no exception.

By the time it was all over, Spion had rubber-stamped the allegiance of over four hundred supporters of the miners. In the lobby the plastic collection buckets were filled to overflowing. Frank and Lucy waited until the lights went on and the hall emptied out leaving a sea of cans and fag ends. A short steward came over.

"Time to be off folks. All done here isn't it."

"Actually, we want a word with the band."

The sing song Welsh voice took on a regretful air.

"Can't do that I'm afraid. Nobody allowed back there."

"I'm the lead singer's brother. Go and have a word. Tell Mickey that Frank and Lucy are here."

The genuine Scouse cadences seemed to persuade him. He scuttled off and returned a few minutes later.

"This way."

The dressing room was a scene of mayhem. Mickey was looking decidedly sheepish. There were several very drunk young ladies, two of whom were wearing surprisingly few clothes for what was after all a rather chilly night. Lucy took a quick scan of the floor to discover there were pairs of jeans and sweatshirts strewn on the rather tired carpet. The air was filled with a thick fog of Cannabis and the drummer was leaning over a fat line of cocaine with a rolled up note protruding from his nose. As they walked through the door, their miner guide's eyes nearly pooped out as one of the girls dragged a T-shirt over her head to reveal a braless torso. There was a smudge of white powder on her nostrils and she had been taken by a sudden and irresistible urge to jump up and down on a chair waving her T-shirt over her head.

It wasn't so much the surprising sight of a bouncing pair of teenage breasts that came as such a shock to the union man. It wasn't even the clear evidence that the sudden urge to bounce her breasts in public was evidently cocaine driven. It was the fact that the young girl in question was the daughter of Evans the butcher and the steward was accustomed to seeing her in a blue and white apron and measuring out portions of pork chops.

"Bloody hell fire."

At that instant she recognised a Saturday morning customer and all at the same time she screamed, covered her chest with the T-shirt and clamped her eyes shut hoping it would all go away. Midge took an almighty snort that left the mirror clean of powder and then stood up, beat at his chest and gave a better than average Tarzan impression which sent one of the girls into fits of hysterics which soon turned into uncontrolled coughing as her lungs were filled to capacity with smoke.

In the middle of it all Mickey stood with the expression of a man who wished he could be anywhere on the planet but the place where he was. He tried a smile which didn't work out very well. His eyes flitted about the chaos all around him and it was obvious that his brain was running on full revs.

"All right Frank. Lucy. This is a surprise like."

Lucy folded her arms and was in no mood to put him out of his misery. Again he looked about as if trying to find something that would make things look better. This time he tried a light laugh which was even less successful than the smile and sounded like a sort of strangled bark.

"We were . . . Well you know . . . After a gig we like to . . . Shite. Bollocks."

"I think the term is sex and drugs and rock and roll isn't it?"

Lucy's voice was like the water from an Alpine stream running down his back and into his underpants. In winter.

"I know it looks kind of bad but . . ."

Midge had joined him now and draped an arm around his shoulder. The guitarist's eyes looked as if they were plugged straight into a sub station.

"Hey it's Franko. General Franco. Franco Generalissimo. And who might this senorita be? A senorita with a generalissimo. Well bonjourno pretty lady . . ."

He grabbed Lucy's hand and was making an attempt to kiss it with flourish when she dragged it away angrily.

"I'm from Liverpool dickhead."

His face darkened in a flash. "No need for that you slag . . ."

Frank stepped forward and eased him back all the way across the room until he was against the wall.

"The lady is a friend of mine and Mickey's and you're going to behave yourself aren't you Midge?"

The cocaine was driving around Midge's overcooked brain like a rally car and it made him feel as if he could take on Mohammed Ali and Joe Frasier at the same time. Luckily there was a voice somewhere far in the distance that managed to get through and remind him that this was Frank McGuire and that messing with Frank

McGuire was a pretty poor idea. Very slowly the rush receded and he raised his hands in a gesture of supplication.

"There's a good lad. There's a couple of lasses here who seem like they want to get to know you. Why not have a chat with them and leave us be."

He gave Midge a friendly pat on the cheek that was just hard enough to hurt a little and then followed it up with a quick sharp pinch.

"No bother Frank. Sorry about that."

"It's OK Midge. We all make mistakes. Learning by them is always the key to life."

Frank pulled a piece of tissue from the box on the make up table and wiped away the cocaine from Midge's nose.

"You should be careful Midge. Loads of Bizzies out there who wouldn't like it if they knew that a bunch of Scallies had brought snow to this quiet corner of Wales."

Frank let him be and Midge was aware that his heart was banging at his chest at about sixty times the normal rate. For a moment he felt a surge of panic and his breath seemed shallow. But then a junior assistant from the local Mace store called Brenda felt so euphorically empowered by her first taste of cocaine that she leapt to her feet and thrust her tongue halfway down to his stomach.

Lucy ignored the scene and stared hard at Mickey who clearly wanted to look anywhere else but back into her face. His hand was like a trapped sparrow as it ran up and down his neck and chest scratching and scratching. He was talking fast without managing to say very much.

"Great to see you Lucy. Honest like. How long's it been? Bloody hell, bloody ages isn't it. Must be two years. Bristol yeah. What's it like? Bit different to Newcastle I bet. University not Poly. Bit Ivy League. Not many Scousers I bet. Not many in Newcastle either. Not many anywhere mind. All heading down to Rome. Like St. Paul. No he was going to Damascus wasn't he. It was Peter on the road to Rome. That's it. Quo Vadis wasn't it. Sunday afternoon special. Three hours and then a bit. Mind you . . ."

"Mickey."

"Yeah. What. Shit. Was I gabbling? Bollocks. Sorry but . . ."

"Shut up Mickey." She reached down and found an anorak which was hanging over metal chair. "Let's take a walk shall we? You look like you need a bit of fresh air."

Putting on the jacket was a task that he was not up to and Lucy had to pull one of the arms back the right way out before he could complete it. Once outside he took an almighty pull at the night air and rubbed his face to try and clear his brain of the collection of competing chemicals which were running in all directions. He clenched his eyes closed for a moment and then opened them again and shook his head like a wet dog.

"OK. That's a bit better."

"Come on."

She put an arm through his and marched him along the now deserted street at a much quicker pace than he really wanted. They were silent for a few hundred yards of tightly packed terraced cottages. Eventually they came to a bus shelter with Perspex windows covered in multi-coloured graffiti.

"Let's sit."

By this time his mind was at last slowing down and a huge sense of regret was creeping up on him. He had hoped for this moment so many times over the last two years. Planned it when he was alone in his flat with an empty page on the table and a pen in his hand. There should have been a plaque to commemorate all the late night hours he had spent leaning over the iron rail of the Tyne Bridge staring down into the inky black waters below and thinking about what he would do when he met her again. What he would wear? What he would say? Where they would go? He had thought about it more and more ever since Liverpool had booked their place in their fourth European Cup Final. Would it bring them together again? It always had before. And he had started over ten letters only to screw them up and throw them because he had already written far too many letters and never once got a reply. And he had considered taking the train to Bristol and finding the place where she lived and turning up on the doorstep with a bunch of flowers and a hopeful smile. But visions of rugby playing boyfriends in tweed jackets from Hertfordshire had jumped into his mind and he had looked at himself in the mirror and seen the grey around his eyes and yellow of his teeth. So instead of doing anything he had waited in the vain hope that she might get in touch like she had before. And every morning he went down two flights of stairs only to find the mat empty of anything from the postman.

THE LONG AND WINDING
ROAD TO ISTANBUL

When they had left Newcastle that morning he had believed that the chance had come and gone. Once they were on the road there would be no address for a letter to find and no phone to ring. He had looked for compensation in lager and dope and cocaine. Much too much cocaine. Idiotic amounts. But it hadn't seemed like it mattered because Liverpool were about to play Roma in the lions' den and Lucy hadn't remembered that they always found each other when the reds reached the summit of European football. By the time he had got up on stage he had been more wired that he had ever been before. He buried all the hurt and gave the performance of his life and the next night the lads would do the same and barring nuclear war he would be sitting in front of a TV with a few cans to watch every kick. And if Lucy wasn't there, then Lucy wasn't there. But Dalglish would be there. And Hansen and Rush and Souness and Lawrenson.

But now Lucy was here.

Against all the odds and everything that made any kind of sense the dressing room door had opened and there she was. With Frank. And a face that was a mask of sad concern. Eyes that wondered what on earth had happened to Mickey McGuire. And at the very moment when he wanted to try and say all the millions and millions of things he had been planning on saying for two years he wasn't capable of spelling his own name right. Because when Liverpool won the European Cup Mickey McGuire's life always went all the way down the toilet. For weeks he had been avoiding walking under ladders and making sure he didn't spill any salt. But none of it had done the slightest jot of good because she had come just like he had hoped she would and she had found him at the bottom of the worst.

"How come you're here Lucy? Was it the Cup Final?"

She smiled. "Actually, no it wasn't. I was going to get in touch. I nearly did twice. But I lost my nerve. It is because of Frank."

"I don't understand."

"He's worried about you Mickey. He says you won't listen."

He blew out his cheeks. "Oh right. So you're here as the worried favourite auntie then."

"Don't be so sarcastic."

"I'll be what I like. Why didn't you reply to any of my letters?"

"Because there wasn't any point. You were in one place and I was in a different place. I thought it was the sensible thing."

"Yeah right. Miss bloody sensible. How's about going with the heart for once Lucy?"

"Because life isn't like that Mickey. Maybe you don't see that because your brain is so completely frazzled that you can't even manage to put a coat on yourself."

"Just give it rest will you."

"Oh right. Fine. You want me to be like one of your little bimbos do you? Keep my mouth shut, take my drugs like a good girl and get my tits out on cue. That what you want Mickey? That what it's all about is it? Get out and preach the revolution and then have a good old grope with some sixteen year old little tart who should know better."

"Look I'm not having this. Maybe you should piss off back to your nice little middle class Disneyland and go and marry a bastard lawyer and have his nasty toffee nosed brats."

"Mickey . . ."

"Mickey nothing. You think you can come waltzing in and start preaching at me like I'm something you scrape off your shoe. Well get stuffed Lucy. I don't need this."

He was up and walking before she could say another word. At first she started to get to her feet to follow but then she thought better of it. She watched his angry strides take him back down the empty road. It would be best to let him cool off a bit. She had read that cocaine brought on paranoia and it certainly seemed like Mickey had the full dose. As she sat and stared over the valley to where the ill-defined shape of one of the slag heaps was silhouetted against the dreary orange of the night sky, she knew that she could have handled things a lot better. In a way he had been right. What right did she have to land back in his life without warning and start lecturing him like she was one of his teachers at school? She would apologise and try again. She would suggest the next morning when his head might be bit clearer. And she would stay calm and be a whole lot nicer.

But what on earth had happened to him? There was so much that was different. His appearance was part of it of course, but that was easily explained. Drink and drugs and late nights and a lousy diet. It was the anger that was new. Where had that come from? Maybe it was all the politics. She had watched it on the news with friends and they had talked about it over coffee and bottles of wine. Their objection to Thatcher was nice and cosy and theoretical. But Mickey had been out there on the ramparts where the police vans gathered by the hundred and the bricks were being thrown. He wasn't just talking it. He was doing it. And at the same time he was doing all the drugs. She nodded to herself. The morning would be better. A time to understand and listen. A time to find the easy place they had always shared. She got to her feet and started to make her way back.

Her head was down when she turned the last corner and so she didn't notice the police cars outside the town hall. She only looked up when the shock of a hand on her shoulder brought her out of her thoughts with a jerk. She was about to shout out when Frank put his face close to hers and shushed her.

"There's trouble."

She looked down the road with a feeling of familiar panic. Later it would turn out that what happened had only partly been down to the daughter of Evans the butcher. The real root of the problem had been the man who had taken a train from Paddington that morning with instructions to see if he could do anything about the Liverpool band who were making such a nuisance of themselves. The local police were expecting him having received a call in advance. He had told them there was nothing that was official. His job was to see if there might some way of picking the members of Spion up and giving them a few hours in the cells. And if that could be turned into a few weeks in the cells, then all the better. They were causing trouble and tensions were already running too high for comfort. They were skirting on the edge of sedition and there were people in high places who were getting rather fed up with it all.

The locals hadn't been much impressed with the man from London. They were becoming sick of his kind who kept turning up in the pit villages like a bad smell. But at least this time they weren't wanting them to arrest lads who played in the same rugby team on a Saturday morning. This time it was a bunch of Scousers and that wasn't so bad. The man from London had been itching to pin all the fighting in the street on the members of the band, but they hadn't even shown their faces during the trouble. Once the gig had started he had waited patiently for evidence of incitement only to hear the lead singer encourage his audience to join in with football chants. He had been about to accept a lift back to his hotel when things had kicked off again.

There was a chain of events. The shop steward who had manned the door had been enormously troubled by the sight of the teenage daughter of Evans the butcher dancing on a chair half-naked. He had a daughter himself and she was the same age as the topless wonder in the dressing room. And the shared age was fifteen. He had almost got home when he couldn't stand the incessant nagging of his conscience any more and turned around to go and knock up Evans the butcher.

Evans was known as being a man with the kind of short fuse that the Welsh are famous for. Once he had the bones of the story, he pulled on his shoes and marched up to the town hall with murder in his heart. The man from London was about to get into his car when he saw a burly figure in pyjama bottoms and a vest walk up to the side door of the town hall. Mickey had arrived back a minute or so before and had gone in. When Evans arrived one of the stewards tried to tell him he couldn't go in without a pass. Evans had taken a handful of the man's shirt and dragged him out of the doorway before dropping him to his knees with a vigorous kick to the nether regions.

Evans dramatic entrance into the dressing room coincided precisely with the moment that his daughter stepped out of her knickers and waved them above her head to the exultant cheers of her audience. The short fuse lit the dynamite and Evans attacked everything within reach in a blind rage of kicks and fists. The police arrived seconds later to find an extraordinary scene of three terrified singers, one psychotic butcher, two fully naked girls and one half naked girl. When the dust settled and the handcuffs were in place, they also found quantities of Class A, B and C narcotics. All three girls turned out to be sixteen and under. The idea that pop singers from Liverpool had come to the valleys to ply fifteen-year-old local girls with drugs with a view to God knows what, was quite enough for the Magistrate to hand down the stiffest sentences at his disposal a few weeks later. Midge held his hands up to ownership of the drugs and was given three years. Mickey and Tonto were sentenced to eighteen months each.

Spion were finished in a blaze of hysterical tabloid headlines which lasted for a week and then petered out. Midge died of an overdose in 1987 in a squat in Knotty Ash. Mickey and Tonto played occasional pub gigs, but Spion never recorded another song.

But all of this lay in the future as Frank and Lucy watched the three members of the band marched unceremoniously to a police van. They were more or less thrown into the back and the van made its way down the street and into the drizzle of the night.

Lucy spoke quietly and to herself.

"Liverpool win and Mickey McGuire's life goes down the toilet."

Frank placed a gentle hand on her shoulder. "Come on. I'll get you home."

The next night Mickey once again strained to hear a distant radio through the door of a cell. His body was drained of all life and he felt cold to the bones and sick. It took all his energy to get up from the bed and crawl across the floor to sit by the door. The radio was nearer than it had been in the police station in Liverpool and the sound was clearer.

" . . . I cannot begin to tell you what a hostile arena this is for the Liverpool players who are making their way out to the middle. Two thousand years ago this is the city where Christians were put out in the Arena to fight with lions. That is how the red men of Liverpool must feel like now. This really is the lion's den. All around we have flags and flares and noise . . . unbelievable noise . . . there is a small knot of Liverpool fans away to our left but I cannot hear them at all . . . Liverpool have been to many tough places in their long and proud European history . . . But never anywhere like this . . ."

This time the radio stayed on for the whole match and Mickey heard the drama of Liverpool claiming the trophy for a fourth time on a penalty shoot out. When the radio was switched over to a music station he lay down on the cool concrete floor and stared up at the ceiling. At least this time he had heard it all. Maybe one day he might even get to watch. Maybe one day he might even get to go. It seemed like a dream that was so distant as to be from another planet. Another universe. His life had done more than go down the toilet this time. This time it had been flushed and now he was in the sewer and up to his neck. He was going to prison. He was going to break his parents' hearts. And he had shouted at Lucy and stormed away when she had come to him.

If he had stayed he wouldn't have been there when the police had come and they might have talked, might have . . .

If.

Always if. If and if only.

A year later part of his dream almost came true. The TV in the prison recreation room didn't break down and nothing went wrong which meant that he could at last sit and watch Liverpool take the field for their fifth European Cup Final. But at quarter to eight they didn't take to the field because the field was littered with the dead and the wounded. A surge from the Liverpool end of the ground had created panic amongst the Juventus fans and twenty-nine were crushed to death against a wall. By the time the game started Mickey had returned to his cell. So he didn't get to watch after all because he couldn't bear to. When Platini scored a penalty to win a hollow victory, Mickey had his headphones on so that he could blank everything out. A complete and utter sense of despair had taken hold of him. A small hope had built up that on the day of the game he might get the news that there was a visitor waiting for him. And the visitor would be Lucy. But there had been nothing. A few days later he received a postcard from her. She said that she was in Minneapolis. She had won a scholarship to study in America. She said that if she had been in England she would have come to see him. But she wasn't in England. And she didn't come and see him. And as the corpses were put into body bags and taken to the makeshift morgue the tradition was broken. Or maybe a new one was born. When Liverpool lost the European Cup Final, Lucy and Mickey didn't find each other. And Mickey McGuire's life didn't go down the toilet for the simple reason that it was already there.

The tradition would not be put to the test for another twenty years.

Chapter 5
Bayer Leverkusen
February – 2005

The arrivals board announced that the London flight had hit the deck on time. Frank finished up his coffee and folded his copy of the Daily Post. At first he was going to tuck it under his arm but then he reconsidered and binned it. He bought the paper for local interest. The court column told him who had been sent down and for how long and the back pages charted the crazy season that Liverpool were embroiled in. Today nobody had been locked up and there was an air of general gloom about Liverpool's prospects in the last sixteen of the Champions League.

The fact that they were there at all was a minor miracle. A few weeks earlier the trap door had been well and truly open as the team had trudged off the Anfield turf at half time in their make or break game with Olympiakos. A Rivaldo free kick had meant that the only way forward to the knock out stages was for the reds to score three in the second half. The side was ripped up with injuries and they were missing all their first choice strikers which made the task seem all but impossible. But the years had been rolled back and the impossible had been achieved as the Kop had rediscovered a voice that had last been heard in the glory days of the seventies and eighties. The culmination of what had become one of the great European nights had arrived when Steve Gerrard had jubilantly hammered home a shot from outside the box to send his team onwards into the latter stages of the competition.

But that had been months before and much had happened to dampen the euphoria of the night. A string of miserable half hearted performances had culminated in a cup defeat at Burnley that many considered to be the most abject suffered by a Liverpool side in living memory. Nobody much fancied the team's chances against the efficiency of the Germans and, with Everton ahead of them in the league, the knives were being sharpened for the manager and board.

Frank had never shared his younger brother's blind passion for Liverpool but as the years had gone by he had found his enthusiasm had steadily grown. This was mainly because he now attended all the home matches. In 1992 when the new Centenary stand had been completed Eddie had invested in a hospitality box. This was typical of the new respectable veneer that coated most of his boss's activities. Three restaurants, a night club, a property company and a scrap yard on the docks gave Eddie Tate all the trimmings of legitimacy. He kept his books and paid his taxes. He had even started giving heavily to local charities. He paid extortionate fees to London accountants with public school voices who made sure all the laundered cash was clean as a whistle before being presented to the men of the Inland Revenue. The fact that every new business that Eddie opened was inevitably just another washing machine in his growing launderette was an open secret. The police knew it. The customs and excise knew it. The whole of the city knew it. But proving it was something altogether different. Eddie had always known how to keep his darker dealings at arm's length and now he was never found within ten miles of a transaction.

He directed operations from his large detached house in the leafy streets of Crosby. The respectable veneer was thickly and evenly coated. He was a regular sight strolling the fairways of West Lancs Golf Club where he played to a handicap of three. His two sons attended Merchant Taylors public school and he was inevitably the first on the guest list for anyone who was arranging a charity fundraiser. When the auction kicked off the whole room would know who would make the biggest bid of the night. There would be quiet whispered conversations on the tables around as people informed guests from out of town that Eddie Tate was the biggest gangster on Merseyside. But nobody ever said anything that was loud enough to be overheard because bad things still happened to those who crossed him.

And Frank was always there. The quiet one of the party. The one who drank coke and did the driving. The one whose eyes never stopped scanning the space around them. It was rare that Frank wasn't dressed in a suit. An expensive suit with a cut to emphasise his lean frame which he worked hard in the gym every day of his life. His shoes would have impressed both Sergeant Major and fashion guru alike. His hair was always short but not cropped. He wore a Rolex watch and favoured tie pins. Every inch was manicured and expensively clad right down to the year round tan. But his eyes had never lost the hard edge. There were a million stories about the cold violent deeds of Frank McGuire, Eddie Tate's designer clad enforcer. It was said that he was the only one that Eddie trusted. It was said that they both went all the way back. It was said that it was always Frank who was at the sharp end.

Like all rumour, some of it was true and some wasn't. Frank hadn't had to do anything particularly violent in well over ten years. Once his reputation was established there had been no need. He didn't enjoy hurting people. In fact he pretty well hated it. Now there was no need. There were so many stories that nobody was about to risk getting on the wrong side of him. In fact there had been less and less need for the rougher side of their work for some years. Eddie Tate was a phenomenally successful criminal for the simple reason that he had an innate gift for business. The fact that he had made crime his business of choice had been entirely down to the family and postcode he was born into. Once his empire started to sprout more and more legitimate elements Eddie found that he could make almost as much profit within the law as he had managed with his illegal activities.

At times Frank wondered why Eddie bothered with the illegal stuff at all. He already had more money that he would ever know what to do with. But he never thought about that for very long. Making money legally didn't carry much of a kick. All it meant was lots of hard work to grow a pile of cash that was already large enough. Crime had become a sport to Eddie. Playing the game against the authorities gave an edge to his life. Had he gone straight, he would have ended up putting obscenely stupid bets on the roulette wheel to get the juices flowing and that would never be his style. Eddie liked to control events. He liked to plan and execute. He liked to pit his wits against the best minds the establishment could put against him. And he liked to win. It was the ultimate game of chess and it was only such fun because the stakes were ten years in Walton if he found himself in checkmate.

Frank would have much preferred his boss to go straight. He found no pleasure in the crime game. It was mostly tawdry and miserable.

Frank spent more time than Eddie at the sharper edges where the addicts paid the desperate daily price for Eddie's amusement. For many years the criminal side of operations had revolved entirely around drugs. Of the drugs they were involved in, heroin was by far and away the most important. It was the cash cow. The year in, year out money machine. Increasingly their dealings had become mostly wholesale. They did a small amount of business with one or two long-standing customers who serviced the streets of Liverpool, but mainly they sold in heavy quantities to other high-level buyers around the country. They had found a level where they sold mostly in bulk quantities and they maximised profit by achieving economies of scale.

Frank oversaw the transactions. He made the deliveries and collected the cash. Others would use disposable mules to ferry the drugs around, but not Eddie. Eddie had always used Frank because he was reliable. He wouldn't sample the goods and wind up in a lay-by on the edge of overdose. He wouldn't take on board too much drink to settle his nerves. He wouldn't drive like a nutter. Frank was the ultimate steady hand with years of experience behind him.

In return Frank was an extremely well paid individual. He lived in a two-bedroomed flat on the Albert Dock which had been a gift from his employer. He drove around in a large Mercedes which was replaced every two years. He had the choice of three of Eddie's villas for his holidays. As he had reached the gateway to middle-age Frank had started to live ever more quietly. His home was his sanctuary. Inside it was gleaming and perfect and kept so by a cleaner who was paid for three hours a day and always struggled to fill the time. Visitors got an instant impression of spare expensive furnishings and books everywhere. He had started with the Open University in his mid-twenties and it had become central to his life ever since. First he had completed an English degree. Eddie had suggested economics or business studies should be next so his protégé could play a greater role at the top of the business. Instead Frank had baffled him by choosing philosophy.

He had never found any kind of long-term relationship. There had always been girls. Lots and lots of them, drawn like flies to jam by the Rolex watch and the quiet nature. Then the girls had become women, but there was always a twenty-foot high electric fence that was his reputation. For several years he had hardly bothered with girlfriends at all. Every now and then he would bring one home to gasp in amazement at the forty-two inch widescreen TV and to ask who Hegel was. Nothing ever came to anything. They were nothing more than frantic carnal interludes with the intervals in between getting longer all the time.

In many ways Frank was quite happy with life. It was certainly very comfortable. Money was plentiful and he had enough savings not to worry about the future. His work was seldom boring and he was good at what he did. His relationship with Eddie was cast-iron solid and they were easy in each other's company. But as the years rolled by Frank slowly lost his sense of contentment. Now they had so much, what possible reason did they really have for carrying on the never ending pursuit of more. They peddled human misery for their growing fortune and Frank found it a harder and harder thing to push to the back of his mind. The time was fast approaching when he would drop his bombshell and tell Eddie that he was walking. He had bought himself a property in Tuscany under a whole new identity and the time was drawing near to make his exit. Language classes had given him enough Italian to blend away out of sight in the warm air and the olive groves.

Eddie was planning his greatest move yet and when it was all played out Frank would depart the scene. He had given great consideration to the idea of walking before the new project got under way, but in the end he had decided that he owed his boss one more slug of loyalty.

Eddie's new vision was to cut out the middleman and control his supply line to as near to the source as possible. The goal was to source and purchase his heroin from sellers a long way outside the UK and therefore beyond the reach of the authorities. He wanted to be able to make a purchase and then move the goods into Liverpool with maximum control. The big new venture had been under development for eighteen months and now at last it had reached its final stages. The next twenty-four hours would hopefully see signatures on dotted lines.

The man Frank was collecting from the airport was a Russian called Dimitri Zarkhov. In a past life which seemed as far back as the Stone Age, Dimitri had been a high flier who had been fast tracked to the upper echelons of the KGB. But by the time he made Major and was allocated a fifth floor office in the Lubyanka, it was already clear that the writing was written large on the wall for those who had inherited Lenin and Trotsky's revolution. All around the great fortress of the Bolshevik Party was crumbling and collapsing. Some of his colleagues backed Gorbachev and his efforts to drag the Party kicking and screaming into a form that the world would consider to be acceptable. Others plotted and staged the coup which failed spectacularly when Boris Yeltsin hopped on board a tank in front of the world's media. Dimitri stayed clear of both camps and started to make plans.

His role had been in internal security and it gave him access to files running to millions of pages. The majority of files charted the movements of those who had tried and failed for seventy years to fight the Soviet system. Thousand upon thousand of dreamers and Jews whose journey from college to labour camp to unmarked grave was carefully noted down for posterity by armies of civil servants. Dimitri had no interest in these files. He was drawn to a much smaller body of work. The organised crime files.

Various Mafiosi had flourished quietly under Soviet rule and Dimitri's instincts told him they would flourish ten times more successfully once the Bolsheviks were removed from their perch. For two years he made discreet contacts with one of Moscow's longest established Mafia leaders and started doing favours for cash. When the KGB was disbanded Dimitri had a new job offer on the table and he moved from one office to another. The only difference between his work for the KGB and his work for organised crime was that the criminals had better technology and they were more efficient at what they did. The levels of violence used by both were much the same. Soon he was the chief executive officer for his new boss. He moved the cash and arranged the bribes. He oversaw the paperwork on purchases of night clubs and fleets of trucks. And when a killer squad dispatched by the Chechens dispatched his boss to another place care of sixty-three bullets, Dimitri was perfectly positioned to take over the top slot in the corporation.

It was a role that he had filled for ten years and he had guided the organisation to a fortune that ran into hundreds of millions. He had salesmen all over the world seeking out customers for a growing range of goods which tended to change with the times. The sale of young women from small villages all over newly democratic Eastern

Europe was his biggest growth area. But the heartbeat of his empire was always drugs and arms. Both were spectacularly lucrative and he could never have chosen which was the best. The plus point in terms of his arms trade was that all the products he traded in were easily procured in his own back yard. By the late nineties, the Russian government had reached such a state of mayhem that it was unable to pay its army. This provided perfect conditions for the likes of Dimitri to buy any kind of weaponry for a few dollars of hard currency. He had invested in fleets of trucks and several merchant ships to move the goods to delivery points all over the world. The downside was that weapons were bulky and calling in unpaid debts was often all but impossible as his customers tended to be wildly violent individuals from the more lawless corners of the world.

Drugs had many advantages. They were anything but bulky and the profit margins were astronomical. Debts were much more manageable as customers were easily found and could be dealt with in the wide open cities of the west. The distasteful part was that procuring the drugs often meant dealing with a variety of Muslims from the southern edges of the old Soviet Union and Afghanistan. Dimitri was and always would be Russian to his toenails, and he detested the Muslims with a murderous passion. He gave huge donations to the hospitals who patched up the wounds of wrecked young soldiers returning from the killing fields of the Chechen war. He punched the air when the evening news showed pictures of air strikes on Grozny. He knew that a large fraction of every dollar he paid out of heroin would find its way into the pockets of the extremists who would one day use the money to attack his homeland. He hated it, but there was no option.

This was the main reason why he had reacted very positively to the tentative approach from Eddie Tate. His representatives had first brought the name of Eddie Tate to his attention in 1999 and since then the two men had done a growing amount of business with each other. They had met twice, once in Frankfurt and once in Vienna. On both occasions Dimitri had felt that he had met a kindred spirit. They were both family men. They were both born to business and the fact that they worked on the wrong side of the law was merely a result of their backgrounds. Eddie had made several purchases from Dimitri and every time he cleared his bill on time, in full and without fuss or argument. He learnt that Eddie was primarily a wholesaler and a large percentage of the UK's heroin flowed through his networks. On the night of their second meeting they had sat up late into the night in the hotel bar working their way through glass after glass of vodka which Dimitri had brought with him and paid the barman $200 to turn a blind eye to. They sat by a window that looked out from the twelfth floor onto the deserted streets of the Austrian capital and shared a glimpse at each other's inner selves whilst their minders sat to one side and sipped coffee.

Eddie told of his younger sister who had left Liverpool to become a famous face in the media. He owned up to the fact that she left a shadow across his life. For years he had tried to persuade her to accept his olive branch and for years she had never picked up the phone. He remembered the days when he had been her hero, when she was a little girl and he would buy her dolls. Now her contempt hurt him and it was the one thing in his life that gave him pain. Dimitri told Eddie how his wife had become a shopping machine who put her fingers down her throat after every meal. He told how his two sons were miserable lazy scum who made him feel ashamed every time he laid eyes on them. And he went off into a rambling diatribe of loathing towards those who had come to Moscow from their Chechen pig sty and held hundreds of his people hostage in a cinema. His eyes burned with the very purest of hate, not only for his Chechan enemies, but for Muslims all over the planet.

What had really impressed him was that Eddie Tate had remembered every word despite being so drunk he could hardly lift a glass to his lips. He had not only remembered Dimitri's dripping hate, but he had managed to build a proposal from it. And Dimitri liked that. He liked it a lot. Certainly enough to take a flight to Ringway Airport in Manchester to dot the Is and cross the Ts. The icing on the cake was that Eddie had an executive box at Anfield and he would be treating Dimitri to the best seats in the house for Liverpool's game against Bayer Leverkusen. The Russian had grown up in the era when Liverpool had dominated European football and the trip to Anfield was something of a pilgrimage.

Frank easily spotted the Russian entourage as they emerged into the Arrivals lounge. They were hardly a discreet party. Out front was a beaming Dimitri striding out in his Crombie coat and black polo neck. He was in good nick for a man approaching his fifties and as ever a big grin was all over his tanned face. Behind him were three young women who looked as if they had come straight off a Milanese catwalk. They were all wearing designer clothes, classy jewelry and they barely weighed twenty stone between them. They knew that every male eye in the place was all over them because it was the same in every room they ever entered. They were different girls from the ones who had come to Vienna. And the ones in Vienna were different to the ones in Frankfurt. Dimitri liked his girls and he liked to change them as others liked to change cars. Behind the flouncing girls came the minders pushing trolleys laden with extortionately expensive suitcases. Frank gave them a small nod of recognition. Unlike the girls, the two minders were same guys he had met before. They had passed several hours together and he had learnt that they had both joined Dimitri from the Spetsnatz, the elite special services of the Russian Army. He knew that if he was ever required to tackle either of them he would need a lot of guys at his side and they would all need to be armed to the teeth.

"Frank! You look good. You always look good. I hate you for looking so good."

Dimitri wrapped him in a big hug and planted a kiss on either cheek which was something Frank had still to get used to.

"Hello Dimitri. Welcome to England."

"Sure. Welcome to England. When I was young we all dreamed of coming to England. And now I am here. Meet my friends Frank. This is Natasha. This is Tania. And this is Ivana. Natasha and Tania held dangled manicured hands for him to lightly shake. Ivana was too involved in taking in her first view of English soil to pay him much attention. She gave him a throw away 'Hi'

"And of course you know Vladimir and Anton . . ."

More nods. But no eye contact. Their eyes were quartering the room for threat. They were men whose eyes were trained never to stop. If they were awake they were looking.

"So. What have you planned for us Frank? What is the itinerary?"

"OK. We've got you a hotel in Cheshire. It's about a forty minute drive from here. You can settle yourselves in and then we'll meet up with Eddie for lunch in Liverpool. Then he'll show you his new acquisition. OK with you?"

"Is all good my friend. And then we go to see the match, yes."

"Of course."

"And Liverpool kick the bastard German arses, OK?"

Frank smiled. "Let's hope so."

"So why is it you smile Frank?"

"It's just the way you said that about the Germans. You sounded like my dad, that's all."

"It is how every man should feel about the Germans. My father was a tank commander. Have you heard of the battle of Kursk, Frank?"

They were walking to the exit now.

"A little. 1943. Wasn't it the biggest tank battle in history or something?"

This made the Russian very happy. "So. You know history. I like men who knows history. In Russia we never forget history. We breathe history. And OK you are quite right. The greatest tank fight of them all. The Nazi bastards threw in everything and we killed them. Thousands and thousands of them. And my father's tank killed three Nazi tanks. Three! He became a hero of the Soviet Union. And he taught me to hate the bastard Nazi Germans. Hate them always. So tonight it is like Kursk for Liverpool, OK? Tonight the reds win again, OK?"

"Sounds good to me. Here. This is us."

A people carrier was waiting outside the doors with one of Eddie's men by the open boot.

"Very efficient Frank. I like a man who is efficient. It makes me think how has he done this thing? Maybe you have paid all these people so they let you wait here, no?"

Frank merely gave a small smile and held the door open. The reality was much more mundane, just like it almost always was. He had written a simple text message to the driver and sent it from his jacket pocket as the Russians had emerged from Customs. Simple things almost always looked good.

Once everyone was loaded on board they headed for Cheshire.

"Today I need favour Frank. You can give me favour yes?"

"That's my job Dimitri."

Dimitri lit a cigarette and sucked it half way to the butt.

"Is these girl Frank. Natasha and Tania they are not any trouble. They go to hotel. They swim. They spend my money in beauty parlour. The paint their faces. So Ok. They typical girl yes?"

Frank nodded. No doubt in Dimitri's world this was very much the kind of agenda for a typical girl who had slept and scratched her way to being a gangsters' moll.

"This Ivana she no typical girl OK. She always making trouble for me. I say Ivana it will be very beautiful hotel for sure. My friend Eddie will only find the most beautiful hotel. I say there will be a pool and sauna and satellite TV and everything OK. But this Ivana she never so simple, yes? She wants to see this Liverpool. She wants to see where Beatles make their songs. She wants go to this Penny Lane OK?"

"OK. Why not? But I best warn you it's not all it's cracked up to be."

"Not in your ears and in your heart then?"

The voice from the back poured into his ears like warm honey. She sounded like a Bond girl.

"Not really love. It's just another road. But I'll take you if you like."

"Yes. I like."

Dimitri gave him a trademark bash on the shoulder. "Then is good OK. You take this Ivana for me. Then bring her to the match. She like the football. All of us we like the football."

Frank ordered coffee once they arrived at the hotel and settled down with a book. No doubt the girl would take forever to get herself ready. But he had only read a page when the voice was back with him.

"Are we ready?"

He looked up and was surprised to see her in jeans and a leather jacket that had never been near a designer shop in its long life. Her hair was pushed under a hat and her face was devoid of make up. She noted the surprised look on his face.

"I read books before we came here. They say Liverpool is a poor city. I come from a poor city. It is not good to wear expensive clothes in a poor city. It makes the people hate you. So we go?"

"Yeah. Sure. We go."

Frank had rung through for Eddie's authorisation of Dimitri's favour and he had been happy enough with it. One of the lads had driven a car out and given Frank the keys. They were soon on the M56 and headed towards the tunnel.

"Are you hungry?"

"Sure. The food on the plane was not good."

"What sort of food do you want?"

THE LONG AND WINDING
ROAD TO ISTANBUL

She turned to him and smiled. "You are a very polite man. It is true that you are a gangster Frank?"

This knocked him back somewhat. "I suppose so. Yes."

"In Russia most of our gangsters are not polite. They drink too much. It makes them cry and fight. It is the same here?"

"We don't tend to cry much."

"Does it surprise you that Russian gangsters cry Frank?"

What a strange woman. It was if she was looking all the way inside him with her Siberian eyes.

"No. I don't suppose it does."

"Why? What do you know about Russians?"

"Bits and pieces. I guess most of my impressions are out of date."

"Out of date. Interesting answer Frank. Interesting gangster. Maybe this can be an interesting afternoon. How out of date?"

"You ask lots of questions?"

"Does that trouble you?"

"No."

"Then how? Tell me."

He shrugged and lit a cigarette. She took one too.

"Books. I like Russian books. Dostoevsky, Pasternak, Tolstoy."

This stopped her in her tracks a little. She took a thoughtful draw on her cigarette and watched the road for a while.

"Did you read these books before you became a gangster?"

"Now that is a good question. I'm impressed. The answer betrays the man."

This won a smile and he continued. "The answer could be damning. Did I decide the road of crime after 'War and Peace' and 'Crime and punishment'?"

"And did you?"

"No. I was a gangster long before I ever picked up a Russian classic."

"A good answer. A very good answer. You took the road from crime and violence to Tolstoy. It makes you of interest."

"Lucky me. Anyway. We were talking about food."

"Yes. We were talking about food and I have a request."

"Fire away."

"Sorry?"

"I mean just ask."

She finished her cigarette and tossed it through the window. "My father loved the Beatles, Frank. When I was a little girl it was all I ever heard. All night it was Beatles. We lived in a small place with a gold mine. A cold place. High flats where sometimes the heating would fail and old people would die in the night from too much cold. The only light I grew up with was what came from our record player. That is why I want to see Penny Lane Frank. You take my picture and one day I put the picture on my father's grave in Siberia."

He nodded. What would he put on his father's grave? They hadn't spoken for nearly thirty years. Mickey had told him that his dad hadn't got long left. He was on the terminal ward and the cancer was chewing the life out of him. And yet he still refused to see his eldest son in the time he had left. Ivana continued the long lead in to a choice of food.

"When I grew up I won a place at college in Moscow. I escaped from Siberia. I dreamed I could bring my mother one day but she died. But I brought the Beatles with me. And in Moscow I found more music from this city of yours. Maybe it is like obsession for me. Maybe it is all I have left of my father. Maybe I am just a stupid girl."

"Maybe not. Who do you like at the moment?"

"You know this Amsterdam?"

This surprised him. "You're joking. You get their stuff in Russia?"

"If you look hard. You like this 'Does this train stop on Merseyside?' Yes?"

He stared ahead for a few hundred yards. Like wasn't really the right word. The song was all about the darker history of his home town. The slaves and the plundered goods of Empire. 'See the slave ships sailing into port, the blood of Africa is on every wall.' The back story to the money that built the mighty buildings of Pier Head. And he couldn't help but realise that what he and Eddie were doing was just an extension of the same history. Liverpool from slaves to heroin. Misery for big money. And he was a part of it. He had spent his whole life a part of it.

"Yeah. It's a great song."

"You know Spion, Frank? They not big band. They were from the 1980's I think. I don't think they play any more."

"They don't." Now he felt as if he was frozen. It was almost spooky. This weird beauty from the depths of Siberia was telling him about his brother's band.

"They have one song that I always love. It is very strange name. 'Lovers Under Creamy Yellow.' I never understand this title. It is like 'Sergeant Pepper's Lonely Heart Club Band.' Sometime my English is not strong enough."

"Not just yours. Nobody knew what the title was all about. It was a code."

"Code?"

"Yeah. The lead singer of the band was in love with a girl called Lucy. L.U.C.Y. Lovers . . . under . . . creamy . . . yellow . . . . Lucy. It was a love letter."

All the cool disappeared and when she smiled she was like a young girl.

"So it was a secret love song, yes?"

"It was."

"And did everyone know the secret? Did Lucy know?"

"She knew."

"And what happened?"

"It didn't work out. It was a modern day Romeo and Juliet."

She clapped her hands in delight. "So it was a sad story. I love sad stories."

"I thought you might."

"You ask me about food yes?"

"It's OK. I've already guessed."

This brought a frown. She obviously didn't much like being transparent.

"Guessed what?"

"Fish and chips and Pier Head. Look, it even looks like it might start to rain in a bit."

She pushed her hair back over her head and gave him a long look.

"You a very strange gangster Frank."

He could have said that she was a very strange gangster's moll but he knew better. Almost all the girls who hung out in nightclubs all over Eastern Europe were students paying their way through college with their looks. It was all part and parcel of a girl making her way in the countries of the emerging Europe. They were the lucky ones. The unlucky ones got sold to the highest bidder. It was like she read his thoughts.

"Do you disapprove of me Frank?"

He shook his head. "Maybe I even understand you. Maybe we both do what we do because we didn't have many other choices."

"I am studying and when I get my degree I will have a real life. You know this?"

Uncanny. "Sounds like much what I am doing."

"Will I like fish and chips Frank?"

"I doubt it but it'll make your father happy. Wherever he is."

Frank McGuire had hung onto his heart for forty-four years, most of which he had spent as one of Liverpool's more feared enforcers. He lost it in a single wet afternoon over a bag of fish and chips in the rain with his brother's voice singing away in his head.

Eddie was at his most effusive. He liked Dimitri Zarkhov and he wanted to impress him. It wasn't just about business. It was more. Eddie was a man of many acquaintances and no friends. He was welcomed in wherever he went but he would never feel at home. There were always whispered conversations just out of earshot. Know who that is? That's Eddie Tate. You know. The gangster. The Scouse Capone except his tax returns never have a blemish. People wanted to know him because he had more money than just about anyone they ever met. But they wanted things off him. Cash. Favours. Never Eddie. Never the man. His wife had said yes on the promise of a house in Crosby. His lads tried to pretend that all the stuff they overheard in the playground was all lies. Everyone went out of their way to be that extra little bit nice when he was with them. They made sure they never got the wrong side of him. Well of course they did because it was an open secret what happened to those who got the wrong side of Eddie Tate. Blinding pain at best and lights out completely at worst. He spent his life surrounded by people and yet most of the time he felt like the loneliest man in the world. Sometimes he would try to talk to Frank but his longest standing partner had gone all weird on him. Frank had moved off to some kind of different zone and Eddie didn't get him at all. It was like he was never really there any more. Sometimes Eddie wondered if he had started using the smack but he never saw any sign of it. Everything Frank did was perfect down to the last detail and yet he never seemed a part of things any more.

The worst of it was that he was reminded just about every night of who he really wanted to talk to. Lucy wasn't Lucy Tate any more. She was Lucy Mathews now. Lucy Mathews who always seemed to appear with a microphone and a flak jacket in the hell holes of the planet. 'This is Lucy Mathews from BBC News 24. Darfur . . . This is Lucy Mathews from BBC News 24. Gaza City . . . This is Lucy Mathews from BBC News 24. Freetown.' Just about every night he watched her in front of a back drop of distant explosions or children with big eyes drained of just about every spark of life. Her own eyes had come to match the hardness of those she reported on. The last time he had seen her had been the day she had left the house with all her possessions crammed into a holdall to take the train to Bristol. He had pleaded for her to let him give her a lift but she had refused point blank. She had turned to him from the path and simply said goodbye. It had seemed inconceivable that she really meant it but they had never spoken since.

He had watched her from afar. Her five years in America had seen a marriage to which none of the Tate's were invited. He had spent a small fortune on a firm of New York investigators who had reported that her husband came from a wealthy New England family who had been involved in banking for three generations. The newly wed couple moved into an apartment in Greenwich Village and friends of friends got Lucy a start with a local TV station. Within two years she had graduated to a national broadcaster who cottoned onto the fact that the soft Beatle traces in her accent were deemed to be downright cute by the viewing audience. She did film and entertainment and built a reputation for straight questions asked with unblinking eyes.

In 1990 the reports from the New York private eyes turned darker. The investigators reported following Lucy into a support agency for battered women. Eddie was getting ready to take a plane across the pond to kill the Yank scumbag when a second report landed on the mat. Divorce papers had been issued and then Lucy had reported her husband Lloyd to the NYPD. He had assumed she would at last come home and maybe seek the support of her family. Instead she talked her way onto a plane to Kuwait to join the team reporting on Operation Desert Storm.

When she had at last come home it had not been to Liverpool. It had been London and the BBC. Then it had been all corners of the globe and he had watched the softness of her face eaten away into hard lines. There were plenty who said that Lucy's face was perfect for television. Clean lines framed by a short crop of black hair. But Eddie only ever noticed the melancholy eyes which were so different from the little girl he had once bought dolls for. And he knew she would understand his own sadness if he was only given a chance to tell it to her. But it was clear that it was not to be. Probably never. Maybe she would come to his funeral.

All this meant that his relationship with the Russian had become important. Which meant that the day of Dimitri's visit to Liverpool was a red-letter day for Eddie and he was determined that everything was going to go to plan. They took a long lunch and caught up with each other's news and talked a lot of football. Then they stepped out into the rain and rode along the dock road along with all the grain wagons. It was only a ten minutes ride from the city centre to a gate by the waterside. Over the gate a rusting sign announced to the world that the site within was owned by:

'McIvor & Son. Coal Merchants. Est. 1963'

Except that it wasn't McIvor & Son any more. McIvor junior had tired of the long hours and graft many years earlier and had disappeared off to London where he worked as a plasterer. McIvor Snr had kept the place going until forty years of inhaled coal dust got the better of him and he put the business up for sale to pay for private medical treatment. When he sold his business his solicitors told him that the buyer was a shell company representing a German firm which was a main player in moving Silesian coal from Poland. Nobody had any clue that behind the piles of paperwork lay Eddie Tate.

His Mercedes paused by the gates whilst the driver jumped out and opened up. Inside there wasn't a great deal to see. There were no buildings alongside the wharf. Instead the old pitted cobbles were buried under a pile of eight hundred tonnes of Colombian coal that had been included as part of the purchase price. Other than the coal the only noticeable assets were a rather weary looking crane, two equally faded JCBs and a Portacabin office. There was no sign of any human activity until the door to the Portacabin opened and a small man in a grimy cap stepped out with a roll-up clamped between his lips.

"Alright Bob."

"Boss."

THE LONG AND WINDING
ROAD TO ISTANBUL

Bob had been with Eddie for twenty years and he had been the obvious choice to run the yard having previously worked up the road at the grain terminal. He had told Eddie that working the machinery would be like riding a bike, especially as it was old enough to be the same stuff he had operated all those years before. When a boat came in he had plenty of mates he could call in on a casual basis. The business was run from an office in a development park on the outskirts of Warrington where a manager and secretary organised shipping papers and sales and all the other administrative bits and pieces. It had amused Eddie when his manager had told him how much he had made on the eight hundred pile without lifting a finger. Energy prices were shooting up on the back of the oil price. It had made Eddie feel like he had the Midas touch.

The visiting party escaped the thickening rain and went into the Portacabin. Inside all was dockside usual: overflowing ashtrays and fading pin ups. Bob offered a brew from a greasy kettle but Eddie produced a bottle of vodka and glasses.

"OK Dimitri. Have you got the package?"

The Russian nodded to one of his Spetsnatz shadows who dug into a brief case and pulled out a metal pod the size of a bag of sugar.

"This is it."

Eddie took the pod in his hands and turned it around. Then he tossed it to Bob who made a rather hurried catch.

"Go out and bury this in the coal Bob. Deep. Come back when your done."

A couple of minutes later the they heard the choking sound of the old diesel engine coughing into life. Eddie laid out two glasses and poured.

"So. A chance conversation in a Vienna hotel and here we are. Here's to Russian technology."

Dimitri raised his glass. "For sure. And beating the bastard Germans, yes?"

"Yeah. That does for me."

Bob returned five minutes later.

"Done boss."

"Sound. Let's go take a look then shall we?"

Outside the rain was getting sharper and the waves out in the middle of the river were choppy on the wind. Birkenhead was becoming little more than a grey smudge on the far bank as the afternoon darkened and closed in.

Dimitri fired off a snatch of Russian to Anton who took out a small piece of equipment that looked like an oversized TV remote. A small bleeping sound grew louder as he approached the coal pile. Soon he located the general area where the bleeping was at its loudest and nodded to Bob to start digging. The JCB took a shovel full of coal and dumped it on an open area of cobble but the bleeping was still strongest by the main pile. It was only after five shovels that the bleep became stronger by the removed coal. Now Anton nodded Bob to use the JCB to thin the pile down. A minute or so later he bent down and picked up the shiny pod.

Dimitri clapped his hands in delight. "Like I say Eddie. It is perfect. The KGB scientists made this so spies could hide papers and we could locate them. Now we can hide drugs in thousands of tonnes of coal or wheat. The old world and the new world my friend."

Eddie wasn't surprised that the trial had gone so well. There was no way that Dimitri would have come all this way unless he was a hundred percent confident in his gadget. Still he was impressed. The pod moved the goalposts a long way in his favour. Dimitri had told him that the signaling technology was unique to the KGB. Even if the police got wind of the fact that there were drugs stashed in a load of coal the only way they would find anything would be to go through the pile lump by lump and even then Dimitri had shown him how they could give the metal pods a plastic coating that made them look and feel like coal. It offered Eddie the kind of direct control over his shipping that he had craved for years. Once the pipeline started to flow it would be under the control of very few men, all of whom had been with him for a very long time. The transponder which was the key to locating the pods would always stay with him. Nothing was ever foolproof, but this was as close as it was possible to get.

He turned to Dimitri and held out a hand.

"Looks to me like we have a deal here mate."

They were two well dressed men in their late forties, both a stone or so overweight, both hiding bald heads under expensive hats. They stood in the rain with matching smiles and shook on a deal that could supply ten percent of Britain's heroin needs for many years to come.

THE LONG AND WINDING
ROAD TO ISTANBUL

Anders Veervott watched the screen that showed him that Eddie Tate was on the move again. It was the daily routine. He and his partner Wilhelm Jankers would be in place half a mile from Tate's home in Crosby a little after five o'clock every morning. They would spend their day following the flashing light that told them where their mark was going. Eddie Tate had six cars and his watchers had each and every one of them tagged. Every day they followed and noted. The third member of their team, Horst Van Dyke downloaded and edited the material from the various bugs that were in place all over the Tate Empire.

The three men were the founder members of a discreet South African Company called Technical Solutions. The firm had been set up in Pretoria five months after Nelson Mandela took his legendary walk to freedom. As the world celebrated, the three men had foreseen imminent redundancy. All three had left Cape Town University in the early eighties with excellent scientific degrees. Their studies had been sponsored fully by the state which ensured that they took their technical expertise straight to the security services once they graduated. For ten years they plied their trade of high tech watching and listening and logging in the dusty shanty towns where the ANC planned their attacks on the Apartheid State. Much of their work was modelled on the stunning successes achieved by the British Army's 14th Intelligence Unit which at the same time was slowly but surely watching and tracking the IRA into submission. The technique was simple enough to be hugely successful. They watched and listened and collated and edited until pictures and routines began to emerge. As soon as a particular picture was complete, the information was passed on to the special forces who would do their stuff. It was all about getting slowly under the skin of the enemy. They inserted their electronic tape worms and sucked their targets dry of their secrets. Sometimes it happened quickly. Sometimes it took time. But in the end they would finish their pictures.

The three men realised there would be no place for them in the new Rainbow Nation and so they privatised their skills and offered their services to the highest bidders on a global basis. Their first real breakthrough came in 1996 when a maverick police Chief in St. Louis engaged their services to break into the affairs of the local drug lord. It took them a year to get enough for the police to swoop. The target was sentenced to twenty years and the Police Chief was re-elected by a landslide. With this on their company CV, they were fully booked in other American cities for the next eight years.

It was at a conference in Boston in 2004 that the Chief Constable of Greater Merseyside fell into a late night conversation at the bar with the maverick St. Louis chief who by now had been re-elected for a third time. After several whiskys the American pulled a Technical Solutions business card from his wallet and gave it to the Englishman.

When he returned home the Chief Constable went directly to the Home Office. He explained that it was time to try something different. He told them all about Eddie Tate and how he had stayed clear of a single arrest for thirty years. He told them of how he suspected that Tate was paying off his own officers all the way up to the top. He told them how it was all but impossible to launch any kind of operation without Tate hearing about it the minute it started. Then he told them about Technical Solutions. His proposal was simple. He wanted Technical Solutions to come to Merseyside and do their stuff on Eddie Tate. The South Africans would report only to him and their invoices would be settled directly by the Home Office. There would be no mention of the word Merseyside on the invoices. And he pitched the idea that if this approach worked in Liverpool then it could work in other cities. The Home Office were back in touch with a yes two days later and in September 2004 the South Africans arrived in Liverpool to start their long watch on Eddie Tate and all who sailed with him.

Two days after Dimitri and Eddie left the coal yard for the city centre the Chief Constable read of their visit in the weekly report. It had been the fourth such visit in three months. He took a mental note and smiled to himself. Slowly but surely the pieces of the jigsaw were coming into his possession. Now it would be all about patience. He reached down and opened his desk drawer. A picture of a beaming Eddie Tate stared up at him. Eddie had just purchased a signed football shirt for £15,000 which was going to help children in a local hospice. The evening paper had put the picture on page five. The Chief had cut it out and kept it. It gave him motivation.

The flight was dreadful; just like always. EasyJet didn't do flights to the places where Lucy visited. Scheduled airlines would get her into the country next door. Then it would be wads of cash to some desperado or another who was either drunk enough or crazy enough to fly the last leg. This time it had been British Airways to Kampala in Uganda and a reasonable ride in an air conditioned 4x4 to the east of the country where her producer had done a deal with a wild-eyed veteran of the Rhodesian Air Force who had agreed to fly the team over the mountains to Goma for a sum that would keep him drunk in the style he was accustomed to for a couple of months. Fitting in Lucy, producer and two cameramen had been a squeeze and no European airport would have allowed the over-laden little plane anywhere near a runway. The heavy load meant that they had to hug the forested slopes of the Mountains of the Moon, sometimes only just scraping over the higher ridges. Below them dwindling numbers of gorillas hid in the impenetrable forest. For a while Sigourney Weaver's film had brought a small influx of tourists to this wild part of the planet, but then the Hutu and the Tutsi had hacked each other to pieces with machetes and tourists had stayed at home to watch the gorillas on TV. After a stomach-churning hour the plane hopped the last ridge and the long gleaming waters of Lake Kivu could be seen stretching out for miles into the distance and Tanzania. For a while the scene was achingly beautiful, but as the town of Goma took shape the beauty faded fast.

Once upon a time Goma had been a pretty place where Belgian Colonists had plied their trade over the waters of the lake. Independence had brought years of decline coupled with lots of nasty little wars. Then a few miles over the border into Rwanda, the great genocide of the early nineties sent hundreds of thousands fleeing to sprawling refugee camps that stretched for miles around the town. These acres of human misery were then made even worse when a volcano erupted and coated the whole place in millions of tonnes of grey dust.

As the plane dropped towards the ground the scene that took shape through the smeared windows was one of familiar ghastliness to Lucy. Hundreds of thousands of people lived from hand to mouth under plastic and cardboard. They subsisted on United Nations' handouts and gave each other every tropical disease in the book. They dreamed of returning to homes which had been torched by bandit bands high on drugs and killing. To start with they were a multitude who hung on to the genuine belief that home was still a place that could be theirs again. But the months had turned into years and the years had become a decade and it had become clear that the dusty fields of Goma would be the only home they would ever have.

Lucy felt an enormous sense of weariness as the plane taxied to a halt. She knew exactly how the hot air would smell once the door was opened. Wood smoke and open sewers and unwashed people and rotten food. For her it had become the smell of hopelessness. The smell of the dispossessed. Sometimes a particular news story would alert the world to them for a while. And then there would be extra loads of food and a few tents. The sticking plaster would be put in place and people would feel better about things. And then the dispossessed would be forgotten again, less newsworthy than David Beckham buying a new pair of shoes or a secretary from Kettering winning fifteen minutes of fame by taking her bra off on Big Brother. On occasions Lucy had managed reports which caught the imagination of the public. And for a while the purse strings had been loosened and things would get a little better for a time. For years she had forced herself to be pragmatic about what she did. If her stories led to even a trickle of extra aid, then lots of lives would be saved. She banked the lives in a mental account and drew on it whenever she arrived at another place that the world had turned its back on.

When she had first started this kind of work she had been on the rebound from her divorce. She had been running from the day she had caught the bus away from Liverpool and still she had never found a place worth running to. America had given her the nice apartment and invitations to the right New York parties. She had made friends who liked to talk about what was happening in the theatre. And for a while it had all seemed close to perfect until her ivy league husband had started to beat her like a dog.

Instead of diving into a rebound relationship she had taken a plane to war. Covering the conquest of Kuwait had been a little like taking class A drugs. It drowned all the despair and loneliness in great bursts of adrenaline. And she found she was good at it. Really good. The network couldn't have been more pleased. The juxtaposition of a pretty girl reporting from an ugly place was tried and tested over many years. The prettier the reporter, the easier it was for the sales teams to make top dollar on selling advertising space. Lucy had that little bit extra. The voice. Her light Scouse twang hit the mark with millions of viewers all over Middle America who had grown up through the Sixties. They were the consumers that every market researcher dreamed of targeting. Having Lucy on the news won contracts for those looking to sell new lawnmowers to cut the lawns of Idaho and Nebraska. After a while Lucy grew fed up with being viewed as eye candy and applied for a job with the BBC. It involved a monster pay cut which her American employers couldn't get their heads around, but she took it any way. The BBC didn't do advertising. They did reporting.

She was able to bin the designer figure-hugging power suits and the plastered make-up that only lasted a matter of minutes in the tropical sun. Through the late nineties she became the face of the world's nightmares from Bosnia to Zimbabwe. Along the way she collected another marriage and another divorce, this time from a husband who found her increasingly distant. He had said that it was like she preferred to be off in any godforsaken corner of the planet rather than at their home in Surrey. And Lucy had quite agreed. It had been amicable.

She bought herself a cottage in Cumbria which became her hideaway between jobs and she started making vague plans to knock it all on the head and have a go at writing something and growing her own vegetables. The vegetables were still a pipedream but she had managed to produce her first book which was a collection of snapshots from the dark places. She hadn't found it hard to find a publisher and the book was due for imminent release. It would mean a few months at home doing the interviews on daytime television and signing books up and down the country. The thought made her feel weary but at least it would give her a break.

She had been getting tired for more than two years. Darfur had all but finished her off. The barriers didn't work any more and she was finding it harder and harder to stay motivated. Once she had been happy that her work had real outcomes. Problems were never solved, but at least they were eased. All the lives in her secret bank account provided the fuel for her to keep on putting herself in the midst of the world's latest nightmare. But the longer she carried on, the more she felt that her work was no different to chopping brambles. For a while things looked better but a few months later the thorns would be back and twice as big. For a while new technology kept disasters looking new and fresh. It took a few years for the people of the western world to lose their voyeuristic thrill at the news taking them live to distant corners of the planet where people starved and bled to death. But it was just a passing phase. There was nothing new any more. The producers in London were always looking for new angles that could give a fresh view of people slaughtering each other.

The Goma story was the latest in the hunt for a new slant. Lucy had flown into the eastern corner of the Democratic republic of Congo to meet with Sylvia Harding. Sylvia was a child psychiatrist who had left her job at a hospital in Wolverhampton to set up a centre to help a few of Africa's child soldiers to rediscover their humanity. The place she had chosen was Goma and trade wasn't hard to come by. Her camp was now home to two hundred boys and girls aged between nine and fifteen who had plumbed the lower depths of human cruelty. Her life savings had kept her going for a year. Next she sold her house at the top of the market which bought another three years. But now the money was all but gone and as a last resort she had e mailed press releases around the world and Lucy's producer had bitten. The BBC wanted a close up view of young children who were multiple killers. Sylvia wanted her project put in front of the eyes of the world with a telephone number for credit card donations.

The psychiatrist was waiting at the end of the runway in an open-topped Suzuki. She wore combat trousers and an old check shirt. Beside her a young boy of ten stared ahead as if he were in a trance. As the BBC party emerged from the door she walked to them with one hand holding a straw hat in place.

"Hello Lucy. Sylvia Harding. Thanks for coming."

"Hi. Shall we load our gear into the jeep."

"Yes. Great. Sam will help."

She fired off a burst of an unrecognisable native tongue which brought the boy trotting over to collect bags. His thin limbs showed life. His eyes showed none.

"I've watched lots of your stuff Lucy. You're good."

"Thank you."

"I really need you to be good for me. We all do."

Lucy tried a weary smile. Already the overwhelming stink of sewage was getting into her nostrils.

"I'll try."

THE LONG AND WINDING
ROAD TO ISTANBUL

Ragged children chased the jeep along pot holed roads beaming and screaming the chant of French Africa which greeted occasional white travellers. "Bonbon!! Bonbon!". Lucy never travelled without a bag of boiled sweets close to hand, and as they drove she tossed out handfuls which led to numerous scrums of small bodies in the dusty road behind them.

Sylvia's camp was just a part of the whole sprawling mass cardboard, corrugated iron and plastic that spread out as far as the eye could see. They were given a tent to share and Sylvia gave them a few minutes to settle in. Lucy drank a warm can of Coke whilst the cameramen fussed with their gear and the producer checked in with London. One by one, small faces appeared to stare at them. No smiles. Not even much curiosity. Just lots of dead eyes killing dead hours. At last a small girl who wasn't much older than seven walked up to Lucy stiffly and sat down on her knee. Lucy had been in Africa enough times to know the drill. She started to pick the lice out from the girl's tightly cropped hair and hummed quietly to herself. Once upon a time the girl's mother must have done the same thing before the sky fell in. The mother would have hummed an African melody. Lucy hummed 'Lovers Under Creamy Yellow' and wondered idly what Mickey was doing. The Congo was two hours ahead of Liverpool. That made it just by one at home. Probably raining. Probably cold. Was he at work? She had no idea what he was up to. Spion had folded and Mickey had disappeared from her radar. On occasions she had considered getting in touch with Frank and asking after him. Twice she had actually had the telephone in her hand but she hadn't dialed. He would probably be married by now. Children. Cheeky-faced little toddlers dressed from head to toe in miniature Liverpool kits. They would probably have been taught to recite the names of the '77 Cup winners before the age of three. Sometimes the thought made her smile. Other times it put her in danger of tears. Like everything else in her life Mickey was gone. Like millions of African women over thousands of years she allowed her thoughts to wander like wood smoke as she pinched lice from the child's hair. Maybe when she went home she might find him. Look him up. Stick a toe in the icy waters of the past. Then again, maybe she wouldn't.

Sylvia came and they started their tour. Same old huts and tents and faces bothered by flies. Same shining stick arms and legs. Same big

116

eyes overflowing with memories that brought nightmares. They took their shots and images. Lucy talked with Sylvia as they walked while the cameras sucked in close ups. The star of the show was Michael. Michael was an angelic looking eleven year old who had a stump for a left arm care of a grenade which had gone off too soon. There was nothing unusual in that. It was the manner of how it happened which made it unusual and gave the story the new slant.

Michael had been kidnapped and drafted into a small band of guerrillas who fought out of the mountains. One day they had swept into a village and killed most of the inhabitants. They had stripped the chief and his wife and staked them out face down. The leader of the group had given Michael his instructions. His job was to take a grenade, pull the pin, thrust it up the wife's backside and then beat a fast retreat.

He managed it, and the group had erupted with delighted laughter as the woman's body had exploded like a pomegranate. He was then told to repeat the process on the chief himself. The man knew what was coming and took a last revenge on the boy who had executed his wife. He clamped the muscles of his anus for long enough for the grenade that killed him to also remove the boy's hand.

The group decided Michael was of no further use and left him to bleed to death. Somehow he had managed to blunder his way down a path which led to a small mission centre where they were able to patch him up and eventually turn him over to Sylvia's care. He told his story as the African night thickened and closed around them. Sylvia translated his soft spoken words whilst Lucy held his dead little hand. When he finished he allowed himself to be hugged and they left him sitting in his own corner of the hut.

Lucy did the wrap up as a big fat sun sank down into the waters of the lake turning them to blood red. *"Lucy Mathews. BBC News 24. Goma."*

It was time to go home. Maybe it was time to stay home.

She looked so tired. Mickey never went a day without watching a full bulletin of BBC News 24. Some days his heart would take its customary skip when the anchor man would tell the audience that they were headed out God knew where for a report from Lucy Mathews. Then there would be days and weeks on end when there would be no sign of her. Was she some place where there wasn't a story after all? Or maybe she was back home on a break. And then his mind always wanted to know what was she doing and it winced at the images of Lucy in the kind of London restaurants that would cost him a week's wages with blokes from Hugo Boss adverts with square chins and pearly teeth. Google told him the bones of Lucy's story. Degree from Bristol. Masters in America. Marriage and divorce. A career in network news. BBC. Marriage and divorce. Thousands of hits on the name Lucy Mathews. They read like a list of everything bad that had happened in the world for a decade and a half. For fifteen years he had watched the bones stretch her skin that little bit tighter and the light fade from her eyes like a long summer's evening. Tonight she seemed all washed-out. Who wouldn't be? The nearest he had ever got to Africa was South Wales, but after watching so many of Lucy's pieces it had become familiar to him. Dust and death and smirking killers in their rag bag uniforms and mirror sunglasses. He had written poems about it. About how the ones who lived rode Toyota 4x4's and the ones who died watched from the dust.

The news moved along to the economic downturn on the High Street and Mickey checked the clock on the corner of the screen. 6.30. Where the hell was Tonto? He had been due to knock off work at 5.30. He had probably drifted off into dreamland on the top deck of the bus and missed the stop. Mickey pulled out his mobile and hit send.

Tonto's familiar drawl answered on the third ring.

"Where the hell are you?"

"Just through Old Swan."

"Bloody hell Tonto, what have you been doing?"

"I met a couple of Germans. Outside the flat like. Took them for a pint. Seemed like the thing to do."

"Look. I'll meet you off the bus. I need to be out of here before Ellie gets in."

"Fair enough."

6.33. Christ it was getting iffy. Ellie was on a ten 'til six shift and she would be walking through the door any second and that would be a complete catastrophe. He and Ellie had been an item for close on two years and the cracks had been widening for all but three months of their time together. He had met her in the canteen a few weeks after he had started as a porter up at the hospital. He had been reading the back page just like always and wondering if he had time to take the long walk through the corridors to get a quick fag before returning to duty. Suddenly he was joined by two nurses in their mid-thirties who were giggling like twelve year olds.

"Are you Mickey McGuire?"

"That's me."

It was how every one of his six long-term relationships had kicked off. Like his other partners, Ellie had been into Spion when she was a teenager. She had once adorned her bedroom with pictures of Mickey who all her friends agreed was well cool. And of course the theme tune that had played behind her moments of teenage heartbreak had been 'Lovers Under Creamy Yellow'. She had spotted him from across the room and she had wondered. The man closing in on forty wasn't all that different from the man who had once enjoyed prime space on her bedroom wall. His face was rather lined now and he had the greyish look of a solid smoker. But his hair was still a thick mess and he carried no spare poundage. She had blushed right down to her chest when she'd admitted to once having him on her wall, and when he'd asked her out she had said yes. Three months later he moved in with her and things had started to go downhill almost straight away. Most of the trouble stemmed from his untidiness. Regulation clothes on the floor, pots in the sink and hairs in the bath stuff. Then it started to be about money. The flat was in Yuppyville and the rent was a serious item. Ellie had moved out a fellow nurse to accommodate Mickey and she not unnaturally expected him to pick up half the tab for living in such a prime location. Mickey tried, but his porter's salary wasn't up to much. Had he budgeted properly as she had recommended, then there would have been no need for problems. But Ellie's idea of a proper budget was not in line with Mickey's. She had two very major issues which got bigger and bigger every time he couldn't find his share of the rent.

Number one was the £10 a day that went into newsagents tills for two packs of Benson and Hedges. She couldn't get her head around how someone who worked in a hospital could be so stupid. £70 a week. £300 a month and he couldn't find the cash for the rent and the power and the cleaning stuff and she told him that it really, really pissed her off. At times he pointed out that just about everyone who worked at the hospital smoked like Chinamen, but that was much like tossing a jug of unleaded onto a bonfire. Never a day went by without her slipping in a reference to him giving up and freeing up £300 a month which might just mean them going on holiday for once.

Then there was the equally divisive issue of football. The football rows worked around the fixture list. The mother of them all had erupted when he had taken a new credit card on and loaded £400 straight on board to renew his season ticket for the season. That had been a Vesuvius class explosion. How could he? How could he tell her there was no chance of taking an EasyJet flight for a nice weekend somewhere in Europe one day and then go out and spend £400 on a bloody season ticket the next? Once she was on a roll her anger blossomed and grew like a mushroom cloud. Eleven overpaid yobs in red shirts. Childish. Idiotic. And then there had been a silence that lasted a whole week. After the season ticket battle there were skirmishes of two varieties. One was the brief exchange of small arms fire which accompanied most home matches. These fights were not usually about money because the money on the season ticket was already spent. They were about it being very nice for him going swanning to Anfield for a few pints with that cretin Tonto whilst she stayed in because she had paid almost all the rent again that month.

The skirmishes which escalated to rocket-propelled grenades and occasional air strikes broke out around Cup games which were not included on the season ticket. The first such battle the previous August had not been too bad. The club had guessed that the preliminary Champions League round tie against AZ Graz would struggle to half-fill the stadium and so they had sold the tickets cheap. £10 hadn't been too big a hurdle to get over. It was when the group stages started and the first game against Monaco had set him back £30 that things had really started to turn bad. By the time he used the card to draw the money for the Olympiakos decider things were becoming serious. That night had been the worst because the stunning second-half comeback and Gerrard's story book winner in the dying seconds deemed it imperative that he and Tonto celebrated properly with a few pints. The few pints took him past the last bus and meant a taxi home, and that made the whole evening fifty quid which was not so much a red rag to a bull as an electric prod up the bull's backside.

Mickey hadn't thought it possible that the situation could get any worse, but it did. Ellie got to hear that he had been booked in for the night shift and that he had done a bunk to go to the game which resulted in a verbal warning. A second verbal warning because he had done the same to go and watch a Carling Cup match. And what would happen if he got the bloody sack for skiving off she had wondered. What would they do about the rent then and how would he pay off his credit card and did he think she was about to keep him on the dole because if he did he had another bloody think coming. And the night after her mother had come to call and it had been two against one and he knew the sands of time were running out on their relationship.

The Bayer Leverkusen game was always going to be a disaster waiting to happen. There was no avoiding phase one of the disaster. Another £30 spent in a month where he had yet again fallen well short of meeting his share of the rent. The second phase of the disaster had all hinged on whether or not he would draw an evening shift. He had. This time it would be a written warning and the next time it would be curtains. When the rota for the week had been posted the week before, he had known what it would show with a sinking dread. And there it was. McGuire M. 4 p.m. to Midnight. Trouble.

Of course there was always the option of giving the game a miss and keeping the extra £30 on the credit card to himself. For a while he had considered it. Maybe it would actually turn out to be smart play in more than one regard. Ellie would be impressed by the fact that for once in his life he had put her and work in front of football. And then there was the wretched state of Liverpool's season. A mixture of injuries and downright pathetic crap had put the season on the edge of crisis. His heart was trying to tell him that the reds would sweep by Leverkusan like the reds of old would have done. But this lot were but a pale shadow of the reds of old and Gerrard was suspended and his head told him that the Germans would probably win 2-0 and it would be just another night of feeling miserable about everything. Maybe he would be best to cut his losses, win a Brownie point or two with Ellie, hang on to his job and spare himself an hour-and-a-half of Teutonic humiliation.

But what kind of a fan would that make him?

And how would he feel when he sneaked off to the storeroom to grab a listen to the radio to hear every man and his dog singing 'Walk through a storm' whilst he was wheeling Evertonians to and from X-Ray and listening to how they were the dogs bollocks and that

Liverpool were crap. No way. Not a chance. Not when it was the last sixteen of the Champions League. If the reds were going to crash and burn then he was going to be there to crash and burn with them and stuff it.

He grabbed his lucky scarf off the hook and clicked off the lights. Lucky scarf. That was a joke. If it had once been lucky it had lost its powers years before, but he wore it all the same. Before stepping out onto the pavement he took a careful look up the street to check that the coast was clear. It wasn't. Ellie had just turned the corner and was coming on fast with sharp click clack steps. Christ. He ducked out of the door and jammed himself between the wheelie bins and the low hedge that always looked like it grew empty beer cans as some kind of exotic urban fruit.

The sharp footsteps drew nearer and louder and then she was there. He looked up at her as she unlocked the door in the dull glow of a street lamp. It seemed unbelievable to him the hard angry face above him was the same one that had blushed scarlet in the canteen a couple of years earlier. He held his breath as she opened and closed the door and then he darted away to meet Tonto off the bus. 6.45 p.m. Christ the bloody thing best hurry up.

It rumbled into view five minutes later and the rather plump figure of Tonto stepped off. As ever he was crammed into his favourite denim jacket that sparkled with over a hundred small Liverpool badges that he had collected over the years. Mickey could remember the jacket from his first day at the school in Southport. Then it had been not a bad fit, but the onset of middle-age spread meant that it was now a good three sizes too small and doing it up had become out of the question many years earlier. The sight of his friend climbing down from the bus gave Mickey a sudden shot of sadness. Tonto wasn't young any more. Just like he wasn't. They had both crossed the big forty line and it was showing. Where the hell had all the years gone? It only seemed a matter of weeks ago that they had been chasing up and down the country and playing to packed halls. But it wasn't a few weeks. It was twenty years and in between was prison and Midge's funeral and an empty feeling that would probably never go away.

"You alright Mickey?"

"Not bad. We'd best step on it. We want to get in well before kick off."

This thought brought a big smile to Tonto's big open face. "One of those European nights Mickey."

"It is."

"Think it will be like the old days?"

"It'll never be like the old days. But maybe it'll be like Olympiakos."

"Olympiakos was brilliant."

They walked in silence for a few minutes and Mickey heard his friend's breath grow a little short. They had always enjoyed a strange sort of relationship. But any sort of relationship that anyone would have with Tonto was always going to be strange. Because Tonto was strange. He always had been. Mickey could remember him from the first weeks at their school in Southport. He had hardly ever spoken but it hadn't seemed to bother him any. He had been one of those lads who had just been there. He hadn't been much use in class and the teachers tried to be nice to him. It was only when he and Midge formed the band that Mickey had actually spoken to Tonto. At that point the band had numbered two and things didn't look all that promising as Midge was a drummer and Mickey's guitar skills were basic to say the least. They had been bashing away in the Assembly Hall one lunchtime when the door opened and Tonto had come in with his normal semi-vacant smile. He had taken a seat at the front and listened for a while. The two players had ignored him at first, but then he had spoken up as they took a pause between songs.

"S'cuse lads."

"Yeah."

"You reckon I could have a go like. When you next play."

"You play do you?" Midge's voice had been all suspicion. The idea of a lad like Tonto in his band didn't fit what he had in mind at all.

"Yeah. Guitar."

"Electric or acoustic?" The tone made it clear that Midge suspected an acoustic guitar and a medley of badly played Rolf Harris numbers.

"Electric."

"Any good?"

"I'm all right."

It was clear that Midge was preparing a no way mate answer and Mickey didn't think it seemed fair somehow.

"Come along tomorrow. Bring the guitar. You never know."

THE LONG AND WINDING
ROAD TO ISTANBUL

The next day Tonto had shuffled in and plugged himself in and proceeded to knock their socks off. It turned out that he had spent three years of his life sitting in his bedroom playing along to his beloved Pink Floyd. He couldn't just play. He could play like God and all of a sudden Spion became something. Midge talked them into the gigs. Mickey wrote the lyrics and developed a voice. And Tonto gave them the musical class. As he had got to know Tonto better, Mickey realised that there were more than a few pieces missing. The tranquillity was of the sandwich short of a picnic variety. His life was very straightforward. Two things mattered and nothing else. Guitar playing and Liverpool Football Club. Everything else was superfluous. He left school without a solitary exam and no great regrets. It meant he could play his guitar for ten hours a day instead of four and he became the rock that everything Spion achieved was built on. It was during his first year out of school that Tonto discovered his third great passion. Cannabis. He took to cannabis like the proverbial duck to one of the Stanley Park ponds. Every day was a series of joints that took him from getting up to going to bed. They also took him off to another world where nobody else seemed to be around. His eyes developed a vacant look and the smile became a fixture on his face. There had never been too many threads attaching Tonto to real life and the cannabis snipped away most of them.

Mickey had been worried for him when they had been sent to prison but Tonto had sailed through like a barge wandering down the Mississippi. When they had got out, his probation officer had found him a job as a night watchman down on the docks and he had kept it for twenty years. It suited him down to the ground because it meant he could sit all night in a Portacabin and play his guitar and smoke joints. His wages were plenty for a season ticket, a one bedroom flat, beans on toast most nights and half an ounce a week. Most of the time Mickey envied him his straight forward life.

"I might need a favour Tonto."

"Yeah?"

"Yeah. I was supposed to be working tonight but I've bunked off."

Tonto gave a frown. "Wouldn't they give you the night off?"

"Not a prayer."

"What's up with them Mickey? Don't they know it's the Champions League?"

"Oh they know it well enough. They just don't give a shite. I reckon they put me on the four 'til midnight deliberately."

"Evertonians are they?"

Mickey laughed. As far as Tonto was concerned most bad things in the world were down to Evertonians.

"Worse. My boss hates football and she hates everyone who watches it and me most of all."

"Why's that Mickey?"

"Christ knows. Why are zebras born with black and white stripes."

"I think it's for camouflage isn't it?"

Mickey rolled his eyes. "Anyway. This favour. I'm going to get a written warning when I go in tomorrow and Ellie's going lose the plot."

"What does that mean Mickey?"

"It means she's probably going to chuck me out and I might need to sleep on your sofa Tonto."

Now Tonto's frown deepened a couple of extra notches.

"But I haven't got a sofa Mickey. You know I haven't got a sofa. I've only got two chairs."

"Well a sleeping bag on the floor them"

"I haven't got a sleeping bag Mickey."

"I've got a sleeping bag and you've got a floor."

"That's right. I've got a floor."

"And if Ellie chucks me out will I be able to sleep on it?"

"Yeah. Course you can Mickey. Long as you like. But you won't have to most of the time. You can have the bed when I'm working nights."

"You're a pal Tonto. It won't be for long. I'll sort something out"

Tonto gave the thought a grave nod. "It's not easy with all these Evertonians. Especially if they finish fourth. It'll be really bad if they finish fourth."

Mickey figured that all the Evertonians certainly had a lot to answer for. His job,. Liverpool's prospects for next years Champions League, the chances of long term peace in the Middle East and Global warming to name but a few. But all the Evertonians couldn't stop him taking up residence in a sleeping bag on Tonto's floor which at least meant he had some kind of fall-back position.

By the time they turned a last corner and got a view of the towering roof of the Kop they were part of a throng. There was a buzz about the

THE LONG AND WINDING
ROAD TO ISTANBUL

conversations. It didn't matter how bleak things got in the league, there was always something special about European matches under the floodlights. The players pulled on the history along with their shirts and they always seemed to play like a different team. They could hear the crowd in the ground and all around them those approaching the stadium picked up the pace. It was the moment when unpaid gas bills and bad school reports and bullying bosses all got forgotten. It was the moment when the wall to wall greyness of life could be tossed for a couple of hours. It was the Champions League and it was the last sixteen and all of a sudden nothing else mattered.

And then he spotted his Frank a few yards ahead. His Frank with some bird. Interesting.

"Hey! Frank. Hang on a sec . . ."

He jogged up and tapped his brother on the shoulder. It had been months since they had last spoken and Frank's face showed pleasant surprise.

"Bloody hell Mickey. Long time no see. How are you?"

"Ah you know. Up to me neck and sinking fast."

"Still with Ellie are you?"

Mickey gave resigned sort of a shrug as Tonto caught up. "I doubt it after tonight."

"He's coming to my place. He's got a sleeping bag and I've got a floor like."

"Sounds like a match made in heaven lads. Anyway we best be getting along . . ."

Mickey's eyes had been drawn to the vision at his brother's side. Who the hell? And how the hell?

"Hang on a sec. Are you not going to do any introductions?"

It was pretty clear that Frank didn't want to, but now he was on the spot.

"Oh yeah. Right. This is Ivana. She's from Siberia. Well Moscow now like. But she grew up in Siberia. A mining town like. Ivana, this is me kid brother Mickey and this is his mate Tonto."

Mickey took the proffered hand and couldn't quite get his head around Frank bringing a bird like this to the match. She must have been something to do with Eddie Tate of course, but even so. He noticed a widening of the oriental eyes as she was introduced to Tonto. Then there was the Bond girl voice.

"Frank. Are you not telling me something here?"

"Yeah. Well. Maybe not everything I suppose."

She was smiling now and every passer by noticed.

"I do not believe there can be too many Tonto's, even in Liverpool."

Tonto shook his head gravely. "I've not heard of any. Except me of course. And I'm forty-one."

Mickey gave his brother a quizzical look. What was this all about? Ivana noticed his confusion. "And of course I see now. Frank McGuire. A little brother called Mickey. So Mickey McGuire yes?"

"Sure. That's me."

"And once you are both in a band called Spion, no?"

"Yeah. Bloody years ago, but yeah."

"With how you say Midge, yes."

Mickey was really intrigued now. "That's right. With how we say Midge."

"He doesn't come to the football?"

"Not any more. He's dead."

"I'm so sorry. I am insensitive."

Frank was flapping a little and looking to get a word in and failing.

"Oh you're all right love it was years ago. Christ getting on twenty years now. Overdose. Anyway. What do you know about Spion then?"

At last Frank grabbed a toehold in the conversation. "Ivana has a collection of Liverpool music. It comes from her dad. He was a big Beatles man in the sixties and seventies."

"In Siberia?" Beatles and Siberia were not two things that Mickey normally associated with each other.

"For sure. In Siberia. But now I live in Moscow. I order my music from Amazon. It is how I buy Spion CD. It is how I find 'Lovers Under Creamy Yellow.'"

"You like it?"

"It is beautiful. I always think that the man who writes this could be a Russian. You understand what it is to be sad. To be sad can be something that is beautiful. In Russia we know this. I think you know this also."

Bloody hell. Who was this woman? And what was he supposed to say to that? He was still looking for any kind of response when Tonto beat him to the punch.

"It was the first song I did with my new guitar."

Frank made a show of checking his watch. "Look guys. We need to be getting in."

Mickey's half smile faded out. "Don't keep Eddie waiting whatever you do. That wouldn't do at all."

"Just leave it out Mickey."

"Yeah. OK. We'll go on the Kop now. You hop along to your nice executive box. Sip a bit of champers like. And stuff the poor bastards who pay for it."

"Mickey . . ."

"Yeah, yeah. I know. Don't go on in front of the nice lady from Siberia. I'm sorry Ivana. Family stuff. It's the little brother who wishes the older brother would stop selling smack conversation."

"Mickey, I'm serious here . . ." The hard edge. The oh so familiar hard edge. The thirty second warning of a kicking voice.

"OK. OK. I'll see you around Frank."

"Mickey."

He turned to see a smile on the girl's face.

"You find Lucy?"

What the hell? How?

"Frank told me. So. You find her?"

Christ. He felt like he had been smacked by a cold gust of wind off the Mersey.

"I see her almost every day but I'm hardly ever within a thousand miles of where she stands. A riddle. Maybe Russians like riddles."

"You must find her Mickey."

"And why is that might I ask?" She was getting under his skin a bit.

"Because of the song Mickey. If a boy wrote that song for me I would expect him to find me. To find me wherever I went. They are words you cannot run away from. So you find her OK?"

"OK."

Frank took her arm and walked her towards the main entrance of the Centenary stand whilst Mickey stood with his mouth slightly open.

"She a mate of Lucy's then is she Mickey?"

"Seems like it."

"We should go in Mickey. They'll be singing Never Walk Alone in a minute."

"Yeah. That's right. They will."

Two hours later a Hamman free kick made it three nil and despite a goalkeeping howler in stoppage time the win was enough to send Liverpool through to the last eight. And Mickey became acquainted with Tonto's floor.

Chapter 6
Juventus – April 2005

Strangely enough the demise of Mickey's short and uninspired career as a hospital porter did not come as a result of football-related absenteeism. A few days later and it would have been the case because the week after his dismissal Liverpool were due to take on the mighty Juventus in the Stadio Di Alpi to defend a 2-1 first leg lead achieved at yet another tumultuous night at Anfield. He didn't usually bunk off to watch away matches on the tele. That was pushing it a bit. He had worked during the second leg of the Leverkusen game and had spent the evening ducking in and out of the laundry room where he had hidden a radio.

But the Juventus game was different.

Any kind of draw would send the reds into the semi-finals where they would probably play Chelsea. That meant they would be just two games off the final in Istanbul of all places. 180 minutes against a team they had comprehensively outplayed at Christmas and been within a quarter of an hour of beating in the Carling Cup Final. It meant that it was possible. Not likely, but possible. After twenty slow years which had seen his life drift and collapse into middle age, the reds were once more poised to claim the greatest prize of them all. The city was collectively trying to do as Rafa Benitez instructed and take each game as it came. No point in thinking of springtime trips to Turkey when the might of Juventus was still blocking the way.

Hanging on to a slender one-goal lead in Turin was always going to be a big ask. What made it even bigger was the fact that injuries had stripped the squad down to the bare bones. The captain was suspended and it would be a near scratch team that would take the field for the club's biggest game in years. Every logical analysis said Liverpool had no chance if they were lucky and probably even less than that. But the red half of the city was in no mood for cold analytical logic. Instead there were thousands like Mickey and Tonto who took refuge in a dogged belief in history and superstition.

History was a comfortable bedfellow and one they had relied on for years. The crowing of Manchester United fans would always be met with an enquiry as to how many times they had won the European Cup. What? Only twice? Piss off and come back when you've got something to talk about. Liverpool fans were dab hands at playing the 'form is temporary, class is permanent' card. Although this was a card that had been played for years against the enemy from Manchester, it was now played against Juventus and Chelsea. Juve like United had only claimed the trophy twice. And Chelsea? For all their Russian millions they had never even got close. Maybe things could be looked at differently when the final came along and AC Milan, because they were senior members of the élite club. They had won the thing six times, which meant they deserved proper respect unlike the likes of Chelsea and Man United.

Then there was the superstition card, which was being played with growing enthusiasm. All sorts of things that had happened in 1978 when Liverpool had beaten Bruges at Wembley were repeating themselves in 2005. Statisticians had dug out the fact that back in '78 Liverpool had finished fifth, lost the League Cup Final and gone on to become champions of Europe. There had also been a dead Pope and a Royal Wedding. As the 2005 season drew to a close it was looking eerily familiar. The reds were coming to terms with the fact that they were more than likely to finish fifth in the Premiership behind Everton. They had lost the league Cup Final to Chelsea. The Pope was dead and Charles and Camilla had tied the knot. Which of course gave lots of straws to clutch at when it came to the Champions League campaign. So the fact that it was a semi-reserve team that was due to take on the Italians in their own back yard suddenly didn't seem so bad after all. And the fact that Juventus were odds on to win the Italian League was neither here nor there. What chance had eleven seasoned internationals against the tide of history and fate.

Mickey had considered the whole situation long and hard whilst trying to find sleep on the threadbare carpet that did nothing to ease the hardness of Tonto's floor. He had decided that hospital portering wasn't for him anyway. He'd done it for a while and it was time to move on. It had become even worse in the weeks after Ellie had thrown him out. He seemed to bump into her at least three times a day and the look of withering contempt on her face was not good for morale. It was a straight choice. He could miss the game and keep a job that wasn't all that well paid and that he didn't enjoy much. Or he could watch the match and be a free agent in a world pregnant with opportunity. No contest.

And then once his mind was made up he saw a small item in the paper that made the whole process redundant anyway. Waterstones Bookshop was proud to announce that Lucy Mathews would be giving a talk on Thursday night about her new book 'Stories from Bad Places.' Tickets were available at £4 each and anyone who wanted to come along was urged to get their tickets early because a sell out audience was anticipated. As he read it he could hear the words from the mysterious Siberian beauty who had been with Frank on the night of the Leverkusen match. "Because of the song Mickey. If a boy wrote that song for me I would expect him to find me. To find me wherever I went. They are words you cannot run away from. So you find her, OK?"

That was all well and good to say when you're an exotic Russian jetting about the world in the world of blue chip crime. It was a bit different for a hospital porter with a bursting credit card and a girlfriend threatening to garrote him with piano wire if he didn't come up with his share of the rent. All very easy to say. Sure. Find her Mickey. And where is she? Oh, no problem. Only the back end of darkest bloody Africa. That's fine then. Get a 32 bus from Pier Head and tell the conductor to stop when they reached Kilimanjaro. But the bloody woman had sunk a hook into him. He had fallen into a comfort zone on the Lucy front. Lucy was someone he watched on the TV. He kept a distance of a million miles. She was someone he had known once and so of course he watched her. He wanted to know how she was getting on. Nothing wrong with that. It was only natural. And watching was one thing and finding was quite another. There was nothing to find. He had stomped away from Lucy years earlier in a blighted little Welsh coal town. She had given him his chance and he had blown it into a million pieces and taken the road to prison and oblivion. Lucy on the other hand had taken a different road to where she was now. A celebrity. A face known by the watching millions who tuned in to early evening nightmares from the place where Thomsons didn't do self-catering with optional excursions.

Fair enough it hadn't all been strawberries and cream. Google had told of two divorces and no kids, but even so he had no doubt that Lucy's life would be full enough. Certainly far too full for her ever to have the slightest interest in a twenty years out of date minor pop star who couldn't even nail down a job as a hospital porter.

Find her. Yeah right. Just like that. Ivana's words had bugged him all the way into the first half until Luis Garcia had scrubbed them away with his opening goal. But all of a sudden it was different now. It wasn't a case of a non-discount long haul flight where food was still served. It was a bus into the city to Waterstones. It was ten minutes instead of ten hours. It was 80p instead of £800. It was possible.

He collected a ticket the next day and saved everyone some time and effort by going to see his supervisor to resign. The woman looked like all her Christmases had come early. She had been confident enough that she had followed all the required procedures that had to be in place before she could actually fire Mr Michael McGuire. But you could never quite tell. Many colleagues had been similarly convinced that they had done everything by the book only to find themselves up in front of a commission- only lawyer at an industrial tribunal a few months later. And now all the trouble was saved with a short two-line hand-written letter of resignation. She had put on her glasses to make sure it really was true. And it was.

"Well. I wish you the very best of luck Michael."

"It's Mickey."

"Yes. Of course. Mickey."

He left her with the thought that Mickey was a better name for a mouse than a middle-aged man with a chronic football addiction.

When he arrived at the bookshop the staff were digging about for extra chairs to accommodate the larger than usual crowd. He took a chair from a young assistant who gave him a smile that flashed with the silver of a brace. Like always his mind jumped about like a rabbit on speed. Brace. Silver. Jaws in James Bond. Which one? Moonraker. As if a fifty-odd-year-old Roger Moore wouldn't have got a complete and absolute kicking if he had picked a fight with Jaws. Bond as in

Bond girl. As in the kind of voice you hired at hundreds of pounds per minute to convince punters to pay £50 a bottle for perfume. As in sensational beauty from the frozen wastes of Siberia. As in 'So you find her, OK?' Well Miss mystery Ivana, I've found her in a bookshop in Liverpool city centre.

Almost all the chairs had been filled and the manager was checking his watch and wondering whether to kick things off. Mickey had taken a place right at the back, a good thirty feet from the table where she would sit. He had also decided to wear a baseball cap and a pair of sunglasses because he wanted the decision whether or not he actually spoke to her to be his decision. Not her decision. So he would stay in disguise and play it by ear. Because in the end it might not feel like the right thing to do at all.

The last chair was filled by a figure he only just recognized. In fact, but for seeing pictures in the paper he wouldn't have recognized Eddie Tate at all. The last time he had seen Eddie had been sat in the back of Eddie's car en route to robbing a chemist. He had been thirteen and Eddie had been twenty. Which made Eddie forty-eight now. There was nothing much of the young thug to be seen in the man who took a seat at the back. Eddie had filled out and lost hair. A pair of glasses made him nondescript. He wore the clothes of a man who had come straight from working in a bank. Nobody seemed to recognise him. He seemed smaller than he did in the pictures. But Eddie had never been particularly big in stature. It was his reputation that was massive. And here he was in the midst of the literary middle class who would discuss the spring programme at the Empire over wine and nibbles once Lucy had done her turn. Little did they know that a man who ordered the slashing of faces and the snapping of legs was sitting in their midst in his Harris tweed jacket and sober tie. Was he in contact with Lucy? Maybe she had relented. Maybe a close up of the biblical horror of Africa had brought her to the conclusion that her big brother wasn't so bad after all. Or maybe Eddie was on the same mission as he was. Maybe he was clutching at the same straw. And if he was, Lucy would be in for an eventful night.

The lights were switched off and the manager took the floor.

"Well thanks for coming everyone. We certainly have quite a crowd. And why not! We all know Lucy Mathews of course. We have watched her on the news for many years. We know she is a committed

THE LONG AND WINDING
ROAD TO ISTANBUL

journalist who with professionalism and sensitivity takes us to places
we would never dare to go on our own. Her new book 'Stories from
Bad Places' is an important book. A moving book. Heartbreaking at
times. Uplifting at times. I look forward to hearing about what led
Lucy to write it. And before I introduce Lucy, I would like to remind
those of you who may not know it, that Lucy is one of ours. Lucy
grew up right here in Liverpool and I for one am delighted to claim
her. Ladies and gentlemen. Lucy Mathews."

And there she was. She was so much thinner than she looked on the
tele. In the flesh she looked almost ill. The years under the tropical sun
had done her no favours. Her skin looked stretched and tired. She
smiled and said 'good evening' and she looked nervous. Maybe an
audience from her home town was more daunting than the familiar
unthreatening lens of a camera. She spoke quietly but the room was
quiet so it was easy to hear her. Her talk was much more political than
he had expected. She talked of arms sales and crippling levels of debt
and wholesale corruption. Her voice carried an undercurrent of anger
and she left her audience in no doubt as to where the blame lay for
most of the horror she had witnessed. She spat bitterness at the
corporations who trampled whole countries for the God of the bottom
line. She spoke with neither notes nor frills and when she answered
questions she told it straight. After an hour and a quarter the manager
once again stood up and let the audience know there was cheese and
wine and that there were plenty of books ready and waiting to be
bought and signed.

Part of the audience headed for the refreshment tables whilst others
joined the queue for a signature. Mickey sat for a while and wondered
what to do. He could just go. He had come in secret. He could go in
secret. He could save himself the humiliation that he knew would
come when he saw the look in her eyes. But then he would have to
walk home and try and find some sleep on Tonto's floor with his brain
running at a thousand miles an hour. If he chickened out he would
regret it and there would never be another chance. If he joined the
queue he would probably regret it even more. It was a no winner and
he put off making up his mind Finally he gritted his teeth and joined
the back of the queue and he was leafing through his copy of the book
when a commotion broke out up at the front.

"Come on Lucy. It's been years . . ."

"I don't care how long it's been Eddie. I don't want to talk to you and I would like you to go please."

"Bloody hell. Can't you even spare a few seconds for . . ."

"Not a minute, not a second. We're finished Eddie. Now please go."

Eddie's voice was rising. "I'm going bloody nowhere . . ."

The manager was there now looking like a man with chronic piles.

"Please sir. I think it would be for the best if you leave now."

"Shut it you jumped-up little prick. Now you listen here Lucy . . ."

"Sir, I really must insist . . ." The manager had put a hand on Eddie's shoulder. Eddie suddenly seemed to freeze. Then he turned slowly to face the man who had entered what he considered to be his space.

"You take your hand off me pal or I'll make your face look like a takeaway pizza. OK?"

The manager lifted his hands clear and went as white as all the millions of sheets of paper that filled the shelves around him.

"Look. I'll have to call the police unless . . ."

"Eddie, for God's sake stop it."

Eddie turned back to her and registered one of the assistants scuttling through a door to a back office. No prizes for guessing what number they would be calling. Unbelievable. No way was he going to give the Bizzies the pleasure of lifting him on a breach of the peace in a bookshop. It was time to go.

"You shouldn't forget family Lucy. You should never forget family."

She looked him straight in the eye.

"I have no family Eddie."

They held the stare for a few seconds than he turned and barged his way past the astonished onlookers and crashed out through the door. Mickey along with everyone else in the room stood like a statue whilst the manager and Lucy held a quick conversation. She then packed up her things and left through the door at the back whilst he made a rather strained speech thanking everyone for coming and apologising for the unfortunate end to the evening and hoping he would see them all again soon.

The flashing blue lights of a police car streaked by Mickey as he was half way to the bus stop. No doubt Lucy was already on her way back to whichever hotel she was staying at. And then tomorrow she would leave the city and probably not come back again. Ivana had said to find her. Well he'd done that. And he had even dug out the courage to speak to her. And now he had lost her. And right on cue it started to rain. There was a drunk guy across the road shouting that God would soon be coming to burn all the sinners. Mickey couldn't care less if he did.

Two days later it was his turn to step out into the literary spotlight. Years earlier he had emerged from prison with three exercise books full of poetry. A small local publisher had given it a go and Mickey had become a bit-part player in the City's art scene. At first his readings had been reasonably well attended. His audiences were drawn from the residue of the Spion fan base as well as rubber-neckers who were interested to see what a man who had been crucified in the tabloids looked like in the flesh. He got a few decent reviews and every now and then a modest royalty cheque landed on the mat. Two more books had followed and he became a fixture on the arts circuit. He got occasional bookings to go and do some work in school and every couple of months or so he would do a reading.

As the years had passed the audiences had thinned out and now he was lucky to see twenty on a good night. Commercially it would have never stood a chance, but the Arts Association always had a few quid to pay for a drop or two of culture for the oppressed masses. His reading in a community centre in Bootle would give him a £50 lifeline which he promised himself that he would put in an envelope at the back of a drawer to make sure he could run to a ticket for the semi-final. If they made it. Which of course they would. Because it was all just like it had been in 1978. And of course when Liverpool won the European Cup Mickey McGuire's life always went down the toilet and right now he was swimming in the pan waiting for the gods to flush again.

The reading was billed to start at 7.30. When the appointed hour arrived the audience consisted of two. One was a rather large woman wearing a thick brown coat buttoned right up to the neck and a light blue woolen hat that could double up as a tea cosy. As soon as she had sat down she had pulled an open packet of Tesco Value digestives from a carpet bag and proceeded to eat them with focused concentration. Audience member number two had started off the day with a bottle of White Lightening cider five minutes after leaving one of the city's hostels and had topped it up through the day with eight cans of Dutch lager which were on special 'buy one get one free' offer in Haddows.

He had clocked the poster advertising the reading in the middle of the afternoon. It had been the mention of 'refreshments provided' that had attracted his particular interest. Past experience had taught him that the promised refreshments were always kept back until the reading was finished so within five minutes of taking his seat he had lowered his unshaven chin onto his chest and was snoring softly.

The young woman was the secretary of a local writers group. She had filled in the application to fund three nights of poetry and now she was trying hard not to look too anxious. She gave her watch the third check in as many minutes and adopted a confident brisk sort of tone.

"People are often a little late Mr McGuire. We'll give it another ten minutes or so shall we?"

"Whatever you want love. And it's Mickey."

This seemed to put her in a fluster for some reason.

"Yes. Absolutely. Mickey. Of course. Oh bugger."

And then she was gone, away over to the table to make sure that there was milk in the fridge even though she had only checked a couple of minutes earlier. Like her mum said, how would she ever get a fella if she went into a complete tizzy every time she opened her stupid mouth. Bugger, bugger, bugger.

By 7.45 things had looked up. The sound of hostel man's snoring and tea cosy ladies chewing was drowned by the conversation of the seven members of the local writers club who had met up round the corner in the pub. As far as Mickey was concerned this was exceptionally good news. If they had met up in the pub then it was a hell of a solid bet that they would be returning once the formalities of the evening were complete. And were that to be the case it would be only natural that they would invite the speaker to accompany them and it was generally the case that such groups had a budget to entertain the poet for the night and buy him a few jars.

"I'll get things under way shall I . . . urm . . . Mickey . . ."

"You do that. Let's get the show on the road. Give them hell darling."

"Well I don't know about that actually . . ."

"Course you do. I need them warming up. Let's have a bit of song and dance. A floor show. Can you sing?"

"No of course not . . ."

"Bet you can dance though . . ."

"Absolutely not. Goodness me. Really."

THE LONG AND WINDING
ROAD TO ISTANBUL

She turned away and tried to fold her arms as tight as she could across her chest.

"Urm . . . Good evening ladies and gentlemen . . . and . . . And thank you all for coming for tonight's reading . . ." She was almost hyper- ventilating as she unfolded her neatly written notes. "Yes . . . Now . . . some of you might remember tonight's guest as a pop singer from the 1980s. Mr McGui . . . Mickey's band . . . Spion . . . became well known for their songs which touched on the issues of the time. You might remember the song 'Lovers under . . .'"

But Mickey wasn't listening any more because the door at the back of the hall had swung open and a late arrival had come in. The last member of the audience took off her wet raincoat and hung it over a chair and then took a seat at the back.

Lucy.

So she hadn't gone after all. Instead she had stayed and somehow found out that he was doing his stuff in a community hall with peeling walls, failing heaters and a notice board full of redundant drawing pins. How on earth had she found him? Then it occurred to him that she had made a career for herself as a reporter. It was what she did.

" . . . urm . . . excuse me Mr McGui . . . Mickey . . . I wonder if you could . . . well you know . . . start . . . sort of . . ."

He snapped out of the shock and realised that all eyes were on him.

"Ah. Yes. Thank you . . . er . . ."

"Elizabeth."

"Yes. Totally. Right. So here we all are then . . ."

He was actually pretty good at readings. He had twenty years under his belt and he knew how to give his audience what they wanted. The small band of humanity that constituted the Mickey McGuire fan base liked his poems because they knew what they meant like. He stayed clear of long words and tried to paint pictures that would ring a bell with the people who shopped in the Spar. When he was done there was a polite smatter of applause which roused Mr Hostel from his slumber and Elizabeth pointed them all in the direction of the Tesco's own brand biscuit collection and choice of orange squash, tea or coffee which Elizabeth dispensed with yet another tremendous blush. Mickey stayed at the table and shuffled with his papers, answering a few polite questions. Lucy passed on the refreshments and stayed at the back and read. After a while the audience took their leave, the majority of them headed for the pub next door. They had indeed extended an invitation to Mickey but he had told them he needed to be somewhere. Hostel man hoovered up the last of the biscuits and shuffled over to the table. Mickey was wondering if he was about to pass judgement on the poems, which would have been tough since he had slept through the whole thing. Instead he fixed the poet with bleary eyes.

"Could you spare a man a quid for a half?"

Mickey thrashed his pockets for change only to discover that the only coins in possession were three, two pence pieces and a two pound coin. Just his luck. He passed the two pounds which was duly accepted.

"You're a gent pal."

"That's good to know."

"Aye. Well then."

"Absolutely."

Elizabeth was back in arms folded over chest mode. "I don't think you should encourage him. He was only here for the biscuits."

"And what did you consider to be the better offering my fair Elizabeth. The biscuits or the verse? The food for the stomach or the food for the soul? It is a question that cuts to the very heart of life itself."

"Well really . . . I mean it isn't as if . . . well it just isn't . . . oh bugger."

"Bugger indeed Elizabeth. Bugger indeed. Is it cash or cheque tonight?"

"Cash." She dug the notes out of her purse and started stacking chairs. Mickey helped her until he reached Lucy who had joined in without a word.

"Hello Lucy."

"Hello Mickey."

"Lucy. This is Elizabeth. She was going to start the evening off with some dancing but there just wasn't time."

"Hello Elizabeth."

Elizabeth was beyond blushing. She was beyond just about everything. She was going home and she was going to pour a whole tumbler full of her mother's sherry and if the old bitch said a single solitary word she would tip it over her head. Her troubled face creased with slight recognition as she shook Lucy's hand.

"My goodness, you're not . . ."

"She is."

"Good God. Could I . . . well I mean . . . if it isn't too much trouble
. . . perhaps?"

Lucy reached into her bag and pulled out the reporter's notebook
that had been a constant companion for so many years. She scribbled
and tore off a page. "To Elizabeth. Thank you for a wonderful evening.
Make sure you leave time for the dancing next time! Lucy Mathews."

Elizabeth read and blushed on cue.

"I wasn't really going to dance . . . I don't dance . . . it was Mr
McGui . . . Mickey . . . I think he was being funny . . . and . . . bugger."

Outside the rain was fully up to speed and the street looked as it
hadn't been used in thirty years. Elizabeth offered a lift but they said
they would be fine. Mickey flourished his fifty pounds.

"Shall we have a drink? It's on the Community Arts Initiative Fund."

"How could a girl possibly say no."

They by passed the first three pubs to avoid Mickey's white lie
being exposed by the writers group. Pub number four had been made
over with bookshelves filled with job lots of volumes from car boot
sales. Mickey got the drinks and joined Lucy at a corner table. And it
was the same as always. They had both agonized about whether or not
they dared find the other because they were frightened to talk after so
many years. But there was no need.

"I think your poetry has got better Mickey."

"How do you know? You've not seen me in twenty years."

"Amazon my dear. I tap in Mickey McGuire and it shows all. I
have every book you've ever written believe it or not."

"Bloody hell."

"And in my humble opinion you've got better. Sadder, but better."

"Thank you."

"You're welcome."

"You're pretty good yourself. I don't suppose I've missed many of
your stories. You've made me a news junkie. Tell you what. You've
got some front to call my stuff sad."

"OK. Touché. At least I made the effort to come and see you. It
obviously escaped your attention that I had a gig of my own the other
night you miserable sod."

"I was there."

"You're joking."

He shook his head and took a sip of his lager. "I went in disguise. I wasn't sure if I would have the bottle to talk to you."

"Why on earth not?"

He cast his eyes down to the scratched graffiti on the table top. "After what happened last time I suppose. You know. In Wales. I was a complete git."

"For God's sake Mickey. It was twenty years ago. Surely you didn't think I'd hold onto a grudge for that long?"

"I don't know. It's what I'm like these days. Ever since prison I suppose. I don't have a lot of confidence about anything any more."

"So you wear disguise to go and see your old girlfriend." There was a twinkle of amusement in her eyes which he had thought had been scrubbed away.

"Yeah. Well you can't be too careful."

The twinkle faded out. "I suppose you saw what happened then."

"Yeah. In full technicolour."

"I should have known better. I thought that after twenty years he would leave me be."

"I'd have thought you'd know your Eddie better than anyone. He doesn't do forgetting. Doesn't do forgiving either."

She was deflating at the memory. All the memories. "And what about Frank?"

He smiled. "Oh you know Frank. Same old same old."

"He's still with Eddie then?"

"Yeah. Mind you a few things have changed. He does a lot of studying now."

"What kind of studying?"

"Open University. He got a degree in English. He's on with philosophy now."

"Bloody brilliant. Good on him."

"Actually. Come to think of it there's something else."

He lit up and recounted his meeting with his brother and the mysterious Siberian. The story re-energised her, especially when he told her how the girl with the Bond movie voice had issued him instructions to go and find the girl from the song.

"My, my. What a story Mickey McGuire. And so like a good boy you donned your disguise and sought me out. Who said romance was dead. Who do you think she was then?"

"No idea. Something to do with Eddie I dare say. But you should have seen the look on our Frank's face. I've never seen him like that before."

"So there's still never a dull moment on the banks of the Mersey then."

He stubbed his cigarette and gave a weary sort of smile. "Dull moments is all I've had for years. Thousand after thousand of them. You're best away Lucy. Seriously. You had it right all along."

"It isn't a prison Mickey. There are trains that leave Lime Street every hour. And they named an airport after John Lennon in case you didn't notice. Why do you stay?"

"Too scared to leave I suppose. Liverpool is all I know. The big wide world seems too big. I only really left town once and look what happened."

She suddenly flared. "Oh for Christ's sake Mickey. You were just a kid. All of you were. Maybe you still are. Look. You know how I feel about you . . ."

"No I don't."

"Well you wrote the bloody song. The Russian girl was right."

"Lucy. I don't understand."

"Think about what she said. But it's not on a plate Mickey McGuire. You have choices. Choice one. Sleep on your friend's floor and get old and tired and read a few rather beautiful poems to people who can't wait for you to shut up so they can get into the pub."

She paused and looked all the way into his eyes.

"Or do as the girl said. Find me."

He was shaking his head, unable to keep up at all. "But . . ."

"No buts. Here is how it is. We toss our lot in with the gods. One last chance Mickey. One last throw of the dice. Here is how it plays. It hasn't escaped my notice that Liverpool are in Turin next week. A draw and they make the semi-final. Then it's Chelsea. Fate again I think. Chelsea with their Siberian billionaire. Then it's the final. Remember the tradition Mickey?"

"When Liverpool win the European Cup we come together."

"Very good. And I am a girl who likes her tradition. So I have been doing my homework. The final will be played on 25th May at the Ataturk Stadium, Istanbul. Here. This is my mobile phone number. I will be there from six o'clock. When you get there just call."

She flipped the card onto the table and was suddenly a flurry of movement. It was all too fast for him. "Jesus Lucy, hold up will you . . ."

But she had her hands on his cheeks and her mouth over his. Then she pulled back.

"Find me Mickey. Break out. Or stay. It's your choice . . ."

And she was leaving and he still had millions of stuff to tell her.

"But what if we don't get there. Bloody hell Lucy, we're away at Juventus and we've got injuries . . ."

She was half out of the door, turning back to him with the same smile he remembered from when he was thirteen and Tommy Smith dished it out at the back.

"All you need is to believe Mickey. See you where the east meets the west."

She blew him a kiss and the door swung shut. He felt as if he had been flattened by a thirty-eight tonne truck and it was all he could do to light up a smoke. He hadn't noticed the guy come over from the bar.

"S'cuse mate."

Mickey looked up. "Yeah?"

"Her that just went out. Is she the bird off the tele. You know. The news and that?"

"That's her. Lucy Mathews."

The man shouted to the landlord in triumph. "Told you it was her. That'll be ten quid my friend."

He turned back to Mickey. "She your bird is she?"

"If we get a draw against Juventus, beat Chelsea and I beg, borrow and steal my way to Istanbul, then yes, she might be."

"No chance then is there. Juve's going to kill you. Liverpool are shite."

Like Tonto always said. You had to watch out for those Evertonians.

"You're bloody quiet today Frank."

Frank was staring down at the snow-capped peaks of the Alps a few thousand feet below their southbound plane.

"I'm always quiet."

"Well today you're quieter than usual, that's all." Eddie had been finding it hard to get his spirits up ever since his miserable experience in Waterstones. It had been many, many years since he had needed to duck into an alley to avoid the police and he hadn't enjoyed the experience.

"Put it down to Friedrich Nietzsche."

"How the hell is that?"

"A German philosopher. He was the guy that Hitler got his ideas from. He's my latest module."

"Jesus Frank. I don't know where all this stuff comes from."

"Horses for courses Eddie."

"Yeah, well give me Aintree any time."

Frank smiled and resumed his study of the mountains below. Although the Friedrich Nietzsche stuff was true enough it had nothing to do with the reason for being quiet. His life had been topsy-turvy for over a month now. The steady rhythm of his life had been disturbed. Not just disturbed. Wrecked. Fire bombed. Torn open like a Christmas present in the hands of a four-year-old. The ominous thoughts of Nietzsche had washed over him without registering because every corner of his brain was taken up with thinking about Ivana. She had got in through his pores. She had possessed him and there seemed nothing he could do about it. And now as the captain informed them that the plane was starting the descent to Turin, it was getting worse.

They were once again combining business with pleasure. The pleasure was the best seats in the house at the Stadio Di Alpi to see if Liverpool could hang on to their slender 2-1 league and progress to the Champions League semi-final. The business part was to dot the 'I's and cross the 'T's on the deal that would cement Eddie's position as one of the UK's top purveyors of heroin.

All the elements of the deal were now in place. Dimitri's demonstration had been the final piece of the jigsaw. The heroin was to be purchased from Goran Jankovic who would be paid by bank transfer once the goods were delivered to Dimitri's agents in Constanta, Romania's largest port on the Black Sea. The consignment would then be packed into the pods Dimitri had demonstrated at the coal yard and hidden in a boatload of coal to be delivered to McIvor & Son in Liverpool. Goran was the seller. Dimitri was the haulier and Eddie was the buyer. Tonight they were to all meet up and shake each others hands. If all went to plan the first shipment would arrive in a couple of months time.

Frank had been given the job of making initial contact with Goran six months earlier. Eddie had being buying consignments of heroin which originated from his network, for a while. By the time they reached Liverpool they had always passed through more pairs of hands than Eddie was comfortable with, and so he had arranged for Goran to meet with Frank with a view to their trading directly.

It had been a trip that Frank had no wish to ever repeat. Goran's Empire was centred on a cluster of crumbling high rise flats that looked down on the city of Sarajevo. A few years earlier the flats had provided a home for Serbian snipers to pick off anything that moved in the streets below whilst the watching world gasped in horror at the carnage. Before the Bosnian war had broken out, Goran Jankovic had been nothing more than a low grade thug who drifted in and out of police custody on numerous petty offences. The war was the making of him. He joined up with one of the paramilitary bands that defended the flats from attacks from the neighbouring Muslims and he found his niche. As the conflict descended into depths of barbarism, Goran went down into the pits like a natural. He excelled in atrocity and soon became a leader of one of the more beastly bands in an utterly beastly conflict.

When a kind of peace at last arrived in Sarajevo, Goran kept his group intact and retained control of the flats where he had grown up. He had come a long way in a few short years. The end of the war saw him and his followers armed to the teeth and steeped in violence. Crime offered an obvious road for him to follow as the city fell under the control of various militia groups. Within a few years he was one of the top dogs. He controlled a large chunk of the black market. He ran prostitutes and sold drugs. Soon he was selling both of these commodities overseas. The prostitutes were trafficked out through Albania to all corners of Europe. But it was heroin which became his greatest earner. The complete lawlessness of Sarajevo provided a perfect base to run a drugs empire. Every official in the city was up for sale and nobody in their right mind would consider any kind of attack on Goran's high rise stronghold. The city was geographically well placed more or less half way between the poppy fields of Afghanistan and the rich markets of Western Europe. By the end of the century Goran was worth millions, most of which were stashed away in a variety of bank accounts all over the world.

THE LONG AND WINDING
ROAD TO ISTANBUL

The approach from Eddie Tate suited him well enough. He had heard a little of the man from Liverpool and had been impressed. If Eddie wanted to buy direct that was Ok as far as Goran was concerned. It meant less small consignments, which made life easier. His men had collected Frank from the airport and taken him through the shelled out streets in a convoy of three black Mercedes. Frank had known plenty of hard men in his time. It had been his career. His life. But these guys were in a whole different league. He had read up on the war before taking the plane and had blanched at the atrocities that both sides had committed. The men in the car with him made his skin crawl. There wasn't anything he could really put a finger on. It was as if the very air in the car was polluted by something evil. It was a feeling that never left him during his two day visit. Every face in every room had the dead eyes of a multiple killer, none more than Goran himself who made Frank's blood run to ice. Never in his life had he been happier to feel a plane take off than he had when he left the brooding tower blocks of Sarajevo far below him.

But the deal had been done. Prices were agreed as well as methods of payment. Goran had confirmed that moving the consignment to Constanta would present no problem. He said he knew plenty of people in Romania. It was where most of his girls came from. And then he had given an order, and two of his men had brought three girls into the room. Not one of them was over sixteen years old and their eyes were blank and dull with heroin. Goran said they were from Romania. He said he would make $5000 each for them. He said he made the best money when they were young. He said that Frank could have his pick if he liked. Not to keep. Just for the night. And they all found that funny. And when Frank had told him thanks but no thanks they had sneered at him.

The flight back to Liverpool had been when Frank had made up his mind that it was time to get out. He had been in the company of some pretty unpleasant individuals for as far back as he could remember. In fact there was no point in pretending that he wasn't a pretty unpleasant individual himself. All he owned had come as a result of his enforcing Eddie's empire. There was no way he could sugar the fact, not even to himself. But the men he had spent time with in Sarajevo were from a whole different world. These were men who had drunk at the filthiest trough of them all. Doing business with men who might get a tenner in Walton for armed robbery was one thing. Dealing with characters on the wanted list for war crimes was quite another. Eddie wouldn't care of course. Just so long as his smack was cheap, pure, delivered on time and kept at arm's length, then Eddie Tate was a happy man. As his plane had swooped down towards John Lennon airport, Frank made his mind up once and for all. Once this one was done, he was out. Right out.

And now he would be meeting up with Goran again. The Serbian had been delighted with the idea of signing things off in Turin and then going along to watch the match. He had said that all his guys were big football men. It would be a summit meeting of three of Europe's most senior drugs industry executives. It wasn't just the thought of being in the company of the stone-cold killers from the Sarajevo flats that was making Frank quieter than usual. In fact that was hardly the reason at all. By far the biggest reason was the same reason that he had been quieter than normal for over a month. Dimitri Zharkov was going to be in Turin. And Dimitri Zharkov liked to travel with his pretty girls. And one of those pretty girls was Ivana. And Frank couldn't get his racing brain away from wondering if the girl from Siberia would be in Turin as well. And if she was, then how would she be? Would she be cold and ignore him? Or would she give him some sort of sign that their day in Liverpool had meant something to her as well? He had failed to clear his head of thinking about it for days and it was becoming annoying. It was pathetic and he couldn't believe that he had so little control over his brain. But he hadn't and now it was getting close. Really close.

The plane touched down five minutes early at 10 a.m. and an hour later they were checked into their hotel. The receptionist passed a note from Dimitri saying that they should come to his suite when they were ready. Frank showered and changed into a suit and joined Eddie. Goran was already there with two of his guys. They seemed well enough at ease in their casual jackets and polo necks. Their clothes spoke of days of golf and nights at the theatre. Their eyes were all about executing whole villages using lump hammers to save ammunition. Dimitri clapped his hands with pleasure when one of his Spetsnatz guys opened to door for Eddie and Frank.

"So. My English are here. Is good for sure. Come. Come have coffee. Have champagne. Have pepper Vodka. You must meet Goran Eddie . . ."

THE LONG AND WINDING
ROAD TO ISTANBUL

Eddie shook hands with Goran who had stood up from his armchair. Frank casually nodded to the two Serbian minders. One returned the nod. The other gave his lip a slight curl at the memory of Frank being too squeamish to accept the offer of a free Romanian girl.

The consensus was that coffee was the best idea. The champagne and pepper vodka could wait until they had concluded their business. The suite came complete with a meeting table and six chairs. It was a place where Fiat executives had once done deals on thousands of cars, the perfect corporate environment for executives from companies with open cheque expense accounts. And today the deal was all about moving consignments of heroin from A to B. Eddie was planning on fifty kilos for the first run. It was £750,000 to Goran when the goods were safely delivered to Constanta. It was £750,000 to Dimitri once the consignment was retrieved from the coal at McIvor & Son. It would put heroin guaranteed at 60% pure into Liverpool at £30 a gramme. Eddie would double the weight and wholesale at £40 a gramme. Five million. Three-and-a-half million profit. It would be his greatest ever transaction and Frank could see that his eyes were bright with excitement. And why not? It was a long way from robbing a chemist for a tub of blues.

Frank was about to join the other minders when Dimitri took him to one side.

"My friend, once again I need to ask for you help."

Frank felt a shiver of hope.

"This Ivana. I say you go for sauna, OK. I say take swim and do hair. I say look in shops and spend money. Is this so bad? Yes! Is so bad! Shops are boring. Swimming is boring. Hair is boring. All is too much boring Frank. Everything boring."

"That's a pity."

"For sure. A pity. And she drive me crazy with all these boring. And this some girl from small place in Siberia. You should see these place Frank. They not even have shops."

"You want me to take her out again?"

"This is what she say. She say, Dimitri, you tell Frank to take me to Milan. She say she need to see Milan. Not Turin. Not Ivana. She needs Milan. Some castles. Some churches. So what can I do?" He spread his arms in a gesture of hopelessness.

"You could tell her no I suppose."

"Sure. I could tell her this. I could leave her at home. I could do this, for sure. But I like it to make Ivana happy. Maybe I'm crazy old man OK. So maybe you can take her to see these castle and church Frank?"

Frank shrugged. "Not up to me Dimitri. You best ask Eddie."

It was no problem as far as Eddie was concerned. He made a show of pulling four, five-hundred Euro notes from his wallet and handing them over with two match tickets. He was the big hearted Eddie. The fat wallet Eddie. The nothing could be too much bother for a mate Eddie. Already he was getting the hang of the East European back-slapping routine. No doubt he could learn a few of Dimitri's old KGB tricks as well. Like throwing traitors into an open furnace.

"Go on Frank. Get yourself a hit of culture and we'll see you at the match later. Behave yourself. Don't go singing 'Scouser Tommy' on the train."

"I'll try and remember not to Eddie. See you later."

He left the suite and felt really impressed with himself. He had wanted to do an Irish jig. He had wanted to jump up and punch the air. He had wanted to do all sorts of daft stupid things and instead he had played it cooler than cool. Frank the quiet gangster. Frank who would snap your legs and then go and read the paper. Frank who never in a million, zillion, trillion years would get himself smitten by a Siberian student who found hair boring.

Her room was a floor down and his heart was banging his ribs as he knocked. Again she was casual. No make up. None needed. He wanted to say something suitably cool but he didn't get the chance. Before he could dazzle her with any brilliant Scouse repartee she took his cheeks between cool hands and kissed him so that his knees felt like they weren't there any more.

"Christ almighty." Was the extent of his repartee when she released him.

"So. A kiss and you ask for your God."

"Yeah. Well. I suppose."

Her smile widened in pleasure at his discomfort.

"So my philosopher is dry of words. Come. We can go."

Going meant a taxi to the station and a train ride across the flat fields of the Lombardy plain.

"Dimitri told me you wanted to see castles and churches."

"Maybe I only wanted to see you. But OK. There is also one castle. Big castle. Maybe you know this one? Castello Sforzesco?"

"Sorry love. My knowledge of Milanese architecture ends at the San Siro."

"San Siro?"

"Built for the 1990 World Cup. Capacity 80,000. Home to AC Milan and Inter. Notable for the tower walkways that make it look like something that could land on the moon."

"So this one is a new castle. A football castle. My castle is old. I will teach you."

"Teach me what?"

Enigmatic smile. Visions of umpteen billion acres of frozen pine forests.

"Be patient philosopher. You shall see."

The taxi ride took only a few minutes. They got out on a huge roundabout where newsagent stalls all carried the same pictures of the riot at the San Siro the night before. The two Milanese giants had been drawn together in the quarter-finals and emotions had overflowed. The Inter fans had arrived at the stadium prepared for a pyrotechnic plan B should their heroes fail to overturn a first leg deficit. When it became clear that there was no way their team was going to progress, they had rained hundreds of flares down on the pitch, frazzing the AC goalkeeper's shoulder and causing the game to be abandoned. It took a while to cross the road to where the towering walls of the Castello towered like they had towered for six hundred years.

Once they were through a vast set of doors the courtyard was vast and peaceful. The city was left behind. Suddenly the only sound of the twenty-first century was the muffled sound of distant horns. There were small knots of tourists. Japanese were making it digital. Americans were trying to look interested in what their guides were telling them. A couple of Finns consulted the guidebook. Frank looked about and felt the power of the place. It was impressive enough now. It must have sent out quite a message in the fifteenth century.

"So. We are here now. I tell you about Francesco Sfortza OK."

"OK with me. I don't expect he played in the hole behind the front two did he?"

"The hole?"

"Never mind. Go on. Let's hear about him."

"You must know where he started. What he was. And where he finished Frank. This is what is what is important. Where he finished, OK?"

He shrugged. No doubt it would all come clear in the fullness of time. He took in the high walls built from countless thousands of tiny red bricks.

"So Francesco was born in 1401. He is not coming from rich family. Only poor. But he is strong boy. Very strong. And he becomes strong man. In those times the kings and Popes they not have armies of their own. When they need to fight they rent army. Rent, yes? Like car?"

He nodded. "Sure. A bit like Halliburton in Iraq."

"So Francesco he becomes a paid fighter. I think you say mercenary." She raised an eyebrow to confirm her English.

"We say mercenary."

"At first he is only strong. He is famous because he can make to bend iron bar with his hands. But soon he proves he has good brain. He knows how to do very good fighting. And soon he is a commander. So many wars OK. And he make these wars so good that the Duke of Milan says OK now you marry my daughter Bianca. It is spoiling war, no?"

"Spoils OF war."

"But when this Duke die he has no heirs and so Francesco he become Duke of Milan himself. And many people feel scared OK. Their Duke he is fighting man. Man for the wars. A man who bends iron bars. But they have big surprise OK."

"OK."

"You see Francesco he make only peace. And builds this place here."

She took in the Castello with an elegant sweep of her arm.

"And there is more. He pays the artists in the city. And he makes too much peace all over Italy. And all the people they love this Francesco. They never forget him."

"Right."

He was standing with his hands in his pockets and trying to work out where it was all going. Maybe it wasn't going anywhere in particular. Maybe he was waiting for a punch line that hadn't been written. She took his arm and they walked.

THE LONG AND WINDING
ROAD TO ISTANBUL

"You cannot see can you philosopher?"

"I don't think I can."

"You can be my Francesco. Like you tell me. You are from poor home. You are mercenary. You are mercenary leader. And this Eddie he is Duke of Milan OK. You can do like this Francesco. You can walk free of being mercenary. You can make a finish with fighting."

So there it was. She had brought him across the old landscape of the Renaissance to this place of old power to tell him what he had already decided. First it was Goran and his psycho henchmen. Now it was the clean lines of the Castello hard against the clear blue of the sky.

"Funny you should say that actually. Any chance you might consider the role of Bianca?"

"We can see. Now you buy me lunch. I want spaghetti and Parma cheese and Chianti wine."

It was past six by the time their train pulled into the station in Turin. A taxi deposited them outside the ugly grey concrete walls of the Stadio Di Alpi and Ivana was the one to ask the stewards for directions as there was a thick sense of hate in the air. It wasn't a place for a Scouse accent. The others in the party barely noticed their arrival as the afternoon had been given over mainly to vodka. Dimitri was all softened edges and he looked for all the world like everyone's favourite uncle. Eddie was bright-eyed and almost tripping on the whole experience. Goran looked like he wanted to turn a machine gun on the whole stadium. The three had shaken on their deal and sealed it with a toast and smashed their glasses in the hotel bar. The under manager had been about to say something but his line manager had laid a hand on his shoulder and stopped him with a small shake of the head. Now they were passing flasks to each other as an explosion of flares greeted the arrival of the two teams.

Frank leaned over and tapped Eddie on the shoulder.

"All right boss?"

"It's the big league Franko. Them on the pitch and us in the stands. Big league."

Them on the pitch were every bit as successful as Eddie had been in completing their business. A side ravaged by injuries turned in one of the finest performances any Liverpool side had produced in years. Jamie Carragher at the back rekindled memories of Smith and

Thompson and Hughes. The Spaniard Xavi Alonso returned from a broken ankle to shackle the prodigious talent of Pavel Nedved, Juve's flaxen haired Czech star. The famous black and white shirts hammered away at a red wall for ninety minutes as the home crowd became almost hysterical with frustration. The red wall stood firm. And as the stands emptied, a small corner of the ground was given over to the sound of the celebrations of the four thousand travelling fans.

The news drifted over the Alps that Chelsea had negotiated their trip to Munich without undue problems. It was to be the semi-final that everyone had wanted but had hardly dared to hope for. It was to be an all English affair. It was to be the nouveau riche Londoners with their Abramovich billions against the faded glory of the Mersey reds. It was to be history against the modern world. It was to be the crumbling port of the lost Empire against the high rise wealth of the capital. It was to be red against blue. Football shirts and politics. Old Labour against old Tory. Hatton against Thatcher. Rich against poor. Mersey and Thames. Terrace against Mews.

And beyond it all lay the Ataturk stadium. A great concrete vision of the Muslim Crescent perched on a bleak hill in the industrial outskirts of Istanbul.

Waiting.

Eddie was on a roll. "Lads. You're coming. All of you. And it's non-negotiable. My box, OK. My treat. "

And his new found mates were more than happy to accept. Because this was a game that was about to capture the attention of the whole football world, from the boarded-up terraces of Kirkdale to the million pound flats on the Kings Road, to the dachas in the forests around Moscow, to the bullet riddled concrete of the high rise flats that stared down onto the old killing zones of Sarajevo

Chapter 7
Chelsea – May 2005

Mickey's first and overwhelming emotion having found Lucy again after twenty years was one of complete euphoria. Cloud nine wasn't even in the same neighbourhood. The feeling stayed with him all that night as he walked the damp empty streets of the city until a watery dawn shone over the river.

It was beyond comprehension. It wasn't just that she had taken the trouble to find him on her return to the city. She had said that she was his for the asking. And she HAD said it. No matter how many times he replayed her words in his head, there was no doubting the fact that she actually had spoken them. "Find me Mickey. Break out. Or stay. It's your choice . . ."

The trouble was that along with the dawn came the doubts. The adrenalin of hope had kept him up all night and now he was both soaked and starved. 7.10 a.m. Where the hell had all the hours of the night gone? Not that it mattered. He was officially a man of leisure once again. The Job Centre had been duly informed that he no longer enjoyed secure employment at the hospital. There had been no getting away from the fact that he had left this employment of his own accord and so the woman behind the security grill had fixed him with a stare and informed him there would be no possibility of income support for a statutory period.

A job was certainly something that would have to be considered at some stage. But not in the short term. There was far too much going on for scouring the small ads sections for the kind of jobs that were on offer for middle aged men with pop star and jail time on their CVs. It would be completely pointless anyway. If he got a job it was a nailed-on certainty that time off for a jaunt to a European Cup Final at the other end of Europe would not be on the cards.

He decided to take one thing at a time. Do like Rafa says. Each game as it comes. Focus on the next task. So what was that? Find somewhere warm and grab a bite to eat. Could it be done? Course it could. He still had £40 left in his pocket from his poetry reading. So that was a good start. Problem; cold and hunger. Solution; a double sausage and egg meal in McDonalds.

He took a seat and flipped the complimentary newspaper over to the back page. And suddenly everything looked really tough. The cold light of day was positively Arctic. It was OK for Lucy to give him an enigmatic smile and tell him to trust in fate. How typical of a bloody woman. Trust to fate. Don't even consider the fact that Gerrard is suspended and Hamman is injured and Xavi Alonso would be playing straight out of a bloody wheelchair. They couldn't even get a bloody draw at Southampton or Birmingham and Lucy said trust to fate and the reserves would go out and do the business in Turin.

Yeah right.

Ridiculous. He wondered what she would do when the floodgates opened and the black and white shirts rained in the goals. He dug in his pocket and took out the card she had given him. Not just a phone number. An address. Somewhere in Cumbria. Birch Cottage. He took a bite of sausage and egg and pondered. Maybe it wasn't so bad. In fact, maybe the best thing that could happen would be for the lads to crash out three nil. They could focus all their attention on nicking the fourth place spot from Everton and he would have the excuse to call Lucy and catch a bus to the Lake District rather than trying to find a way all the way across Europe.

Much to his surprise the thought cheered him up greatly. He had discovered a treasured place for any football fan. Suddenly he had made the game on Wednesday night a no lose affair. If by some complete and utter miracle the lads came away from Italy with a result, he would be made up. Of course he would. No matter what was going on in life there was no escaping the fact that making the Champions League semi-final was hallowed ground. But if the logical thing happened and they got beaten, then he would find the road to Lucy a hell of a sight more manageable.

CHELSEA – MAY 2005

As it happened the theory didn't work all that well in practice. He and Tonto were in place in a nearby pub with widescreen at six o'clock to ensure they got a decent spot. By the time the teams took the field all thought of no-lose situations had vanished. Ninety minutes later he felt like a wrung out dishcloth. There would be no call to a mobile and a bus ride for a couple of hours or so. Well not yet anyway. Because once the coverage of the match finished it started to sink in that in two weeks time they would be playing Chelsea in the Semis.

It wasn't might be playing Chelsea. Could be playing Chelsea. It was WOULD be playing Chelsea. And as the cold night air cleared his brain of some of the lager the enormity of the task started to become apparent. In the pub amidst all the singing it had looked easy. Chelsea, who the hell were Chelsea? League wins – One. European Cup wins – none. Nothing to compare with the reds with their museum full of triumph. And everybody had been talking about all the 1978 stuff and how history was on their shoulders. With a dead Pope and a royal wedding and a League Cup final defeat on their side, what chance had the Johnny-come-lately Londoners. Nobody wanted to focus on the finishing fifth in the league part of the prophecy because that would mean conceding fourth place to Everton and nobody was about to do that. Basically it was in the bag and talk had turned to who it would be in the final. Not much doubt about that. AC Milan or PSV Eindhovan? No contest was it. It was going to be Milan.

It had all sounded great in the exultant noise of the pub. Once they were outside and walking back home it suddenly didn't seem all that easy after all. Chelsea had been pretty well indestructible all season. They'd only been beaten three times. The defeat at Man City had been a freak where they had created enough chances to score ten. They had looked a good bet to beat Barcelona in the Nou Camp until Drogba had been sent off by a dodgy ref. And they probably lost on purpose in Porto because they had already qualified from the group stages and Mourino would have wanted his old club to progress to the knock out stages. Other that that they had swept all before them. Maybe if it had been a one off game there might have been a chance. Anything could happen over ninety minutes. But it was two legs. So there was no chance. Not if he was going to honest about it. It didn't make him a bad supporter or anything. He would be there in the Kop yelling his head off with all the rest of them. But Chelsea were like a relentless blue machine built at a cost of 200 million pounds. Dead Popes wouldn't come into it. And neither would Lucy's fate. Maybe if Cisse was fit and Morientes wasn't cup tied . . . but there were no maybes. It would be a call to the mobile and a bus to Cumbria. End of story.

Two weeks later it didn't seem so certain any more. They had taken up the same spot in the same pub and watched the blue shirted machine look almost completely ineffective. The weekend had seen Liverpool succumb one nil to Crystal Palace in a performance that went a long way beyond pathetic. It had made it all but certain that Everton would indeed achieve the unthinkable and claim the last Champions League spot. The chances of anything other than complete, utter, and miserable humiliation at Chelsea seemed slim to say the least. But against all sensible odds, a completely different Liverpool took the field and made the Champions elect look every bit as pathetic as they had looked themselves a few days earlier. It had finished 0-0 and there was no escaping the fact that it could have been even better as the Reds had started to pick them off on the break towards the end of the match.

Which meant that all they needed to do was to win at Anfield and they would be in the final. Which made it a one off. And anything could happen when it was a one off. And the dead Pope factor suddenly seemed to carry a bit of weight again. And maybe Lucy's talk of fate also needed to be taken seriously.

It was April 27th. The Final was set for May 25th. Twenty-eight days. Four weeks. If Liverpool did indeed roll back the years and come good in the home leg, it would be three weeks. And suddenly the reality hit him hard.

He had four weeks. And getting to Istanbul wasn't something that was going to just happen. It was something that was going to need a load of cash. And he had no job, no available funds on the credit card and the last of the Arts Council money had been spent on the ticket for the home leg against Chelsea. For the first time he really saw what Lucy was doing. She had said it. She wasn't going to make it easy. Of course she wasn't. She wasn't going to make it easy because she had absolutely no interest in the loser Mickey, who had wandered his way through twenty years of easy come, easy go jobs and easy come, easy go girls.

From the first night they had met when Emlyn Hughes had lifted the European Cup into the warm night air of Rome, Lucy had always seen something in him that he always missed. She'd been dropping hints for almost thirty years. She wanted him to stick his neck out. To make the jump into the cold water for once. To leave the comfort zone. To stop playing it safe. She must have guessed that he didn't have tuppence to rub together. That was the whole point. The road to Istanbul was nothing more than a metaphor. In the end it was simile's kid brother. He was going to have a choice. He could either tell himself that it was out of the question and impossible and that Lucy was a rotten, cruel bitch for expecting him to try, and he could embark on a self-pitying sulk for the rest of his life. Or he could take the road. By hook or by crook.

Lucy had been the clever one. Just like always. She had found a way to resolve a thirty-year question. Lucy wanted Mickey. Lucy loved Mickey. And Mickey loved Lucy. But she didn't want the loser Mickey. She didn't want the walking shell who had walked out of the prison gates all those years earlier. She wanted the Mickey from the third year. Mickey dreamer. Mickey who believed he had the world at his feet. Mickey who had believed that Scargill would bring down Thatcher. Mickey who believed his songs would make a difference. And the Mickey she wanted would find a way to make it to the Ataturk stadium no matter what it took.

Tonto was humming happily to himself.

"Tonto, I've been thinking."

"Yeah?"

"We might beat Chelsea you know."

"Course we'll beat Chelsea. They've never won nothing."

Things were always simple for Tonto. It wouldn't have mattered if Liverpool had been playing a Solar System Best Eleven, Tonto would have taken victory as guaranteed. Whenever the reds lost Tonto would find the whole thing highly confusing for a while but it never for a moment dimmed his complete conviction that they would win the next match, no matter who they were playing.

"They beat us in the Carling Cup."

"Only cos they got a lucky own goal."

"They're going to win the league."

"That's different to Europe. You need a track record in Europe. Like we've got."

"The thing is . . . Well if we win, we're in the final aren't we."

"Course we are. This is the semi-final."

"We've got to go Tonto."

This caused a look of mild concern. "You mean not watch it in the pub?"

"That's right."

"But the final's not at Anfield Mickey."

"No. It's in Istanbul."

"I don't know where that is Mickey."

"Turkey."

The frown got a shade deeper.

"I don't know where that is either."

"It's bloody miles away, that's where. And if we're going we're going to have to get some cash together in a big hurry."

"Like how much?"

"Christ, I don't know, a grand each?"

Tonto shook his head at the figure. "I haven't got that much money but I suppose I could start saving. What if I try and put twenty quid a week to one side?"

Mickey paused to light up then shook his head. "That's no use. We need to think of something. We've got four weeks Tonto. Four weeks and we need to come up with a big lump of cash."

"Why can't we just watch it in the pub Mickey?"

"Because we're going. It's been twenty years Tonto. The last time we were in a European Cup final we were both still in prison. This could be a once in a lifetime chance. So the pub is out. Right out. OK?"

"OK Mickey."

They walked another two hundred yards down the road as Tonto's brain wrestled with the stunning problem of raising a thousand pounds in under four weeks. Then his brow smoothed a little as a thought jumped into his head.

"Why don't we borrow it from Frank Mickey? Frank's loaded."

And of course it was exactly the same thought that had leapt into Mickey's head as he had embarked on his all night city walk following the poetry reading. But it didn't work. If he made it to the Ataturk stadium to call Lucy's mobile, honesty would be paramount. The journey was everything. The journey was the thing that would prove that a new Mickey had emerged from the ashes of his life. Lucy wanted to see if the new Mickey was willing to dig into his past and find the energy and life to make it all the way across Europe to get the girl. And that wasn't about borrowing the cash off big brother because every last penny of big brother's cash came from the Eddie Tate Empire. Lucy's big brother. And of course that wouldn't be acceptable. So borrowing off Frank was out of the question. Which meant that the question was still huge.

"No we can't do that."

At this point most lads would have asked why this was the case, but Tonto wasn't like most lads. He took things at face value. It made life easier to understand. He was a lad who would always pay the first asking price of a Moroccan souvenir vendor.

Once again he furrowed his brow and concentrated. The next thought made the lines deeper.

"We're not going to have to sell stuff are we Mickey? All I've got to sell is my tele and my guitar. I don't want to sell my tele and my guitar Mickey."

And Mickey stopped as the answer jumped into his head like an Israeli paratrooper.

"Tonto, you're a genius."

Tonto was somewhat taken aback by the unexpected compliment. "Yeah?"

"Too bloody right yeah. You said the magic word. Guitar. As in music. As in Spion. As in a comeback gig to raise the cash."

"What? Me and you?"

"Well Midge isn't going to join us I'm afraid."

"No. I don't suppose he is. Midge is dead."

The ghost of their former drummer hovered between them for a moment. The street was quiet now. A rather ill tempered cat was the only other living thing in sight. For a moment Mickey saw the near impossible range of the long-shot he was suggesting. They were two middle-aged guys, one rather fat and one rather thin. They hadn't played a note in public for a decade and their drummer was six feet under in a cemetery in Southport. And they had never been all that famous in the first place. His own meagre fame had withered to such an extent that his last reading had attracted an audience of ten. But one of those ten had been Lucy and that had been like a miracle. A miracle that had led to a lifeline. And the way that Liverpool had just made the multi-million pound talents of Chelsea look like a collection of blue-shirted donkeys was something of a miracle. It was a time of miracles. Like Lucy had said, it was fate.

"Think about it Tonto. Let's say we could get three hundred at a fiver each. That's £1500. Then we'll get Baz to burn off a few of the old CDs. Let's say we sell a hundred at a fiver each. And I might sell a few poem books. Christ, we can do it."

In his heart he knew these were big, big numbers, but if it was a time for miracles and fate, then maybe they might not be quite so big after all.

"Sounds about right then Mickey."

Tonto wasn't troubling himself over much with the numbers. He was happy to take Mickey at face value. When all was said and done, three hundred times five was a sum that was a little bit beyond him.

"Look Lucy, I'm really not sure at all about this."

Christ she hated him. She hated every artificial inch of him. Roger Templeton had been her boss for eighteen months and she would have liked nothing better than to pass on his details to an Al Quaida killer squad. His family ran a factory in North London that specialized in air conditioning and throughout the Thatcher boom they had prospered. It had meant a move from a small house in Enfield to a big house in leafy Rickmansworth and a place at Eton for the son and heir. Roger had absorbed the whole Eton thing like a dry sponge and had developed the airs and graces of a man who came from a family whose thousand-acre spread had been gifted by William the Conqueror as reward for services rendered.

There wasn't a single aspect of his personality that she didn't detest, from the affected plum voice to the pathetic, street clothing. He was a born political animal and by the age of thirty three-he had smoothed and smarmed his way into control of the news department that included reporter Lucy Mathews.

Right now he sat back with a smug sort of look on his sunbed-tanned face, and made a show of playing with a set of worry beads. Those bloody beads. She had heard him spout off more than once about how he had brought them back from the West Bank as a reminder of how things looked at the sharp end of the news. He would then go on to explain that a leader could only lead if he knew the sights and sounds of the front line. The smell of cordite. The surge of adrenalin in the veins. It was a story that he wheeled out for silly girls in wine bar happy hours with studs in their bellies and God knew where else. Who saved their pennies for two weeks in Ibiza and a bigger pair of tits. One of the camera team had told her that his close up view of the West Bank had been taken through a pair of binoculars from the balcony of his room in the King David Hotel whilst he sipped his gin and tonic. Arsehole was far too good a word for him. As he fiddled with the beads she fantasized about lacing his pretentious expresso cup with Rohypnol and dumping him on the streets of Kirkby wearing nothing but his designer boxer shorts.

"And why may I ask are you not sure about this Roger?"

He eased back a designer frayed cuff to reveal his Rolex in all its splendour. Wanker.

"Good God. It's almost six. Why don't we adjourn somewhere where they serve alcohol and talk it over?"

"Why don't we just sort it out now Roger."

He had finalised a divorce six months earlier and told everyone in the office who was under fifty and wore a skirt that he had moved into an absolute blinder of a pad on the South Bank. This was the point when he had decided to embark on a campaign to lure Lucy back to his shrine to Ikea chrome and to add her to his treasured list of conquests. When he was really pissed at the Christmas party he had staggered over to her and confessed that he watched her on the screen and had fantasies. He had told her that she was his ice queen. She had smiled sweetly and slipped a handful of ice down the back of his designer faded jeans and taken her leave. She would have preferred to have taken a more vigorous approach and kicked him as hard as she could in the balls, but it wouldn't have been the smartest of career moves. Unfortunately he had taken her slipping ice into his smalls as a sign of intimacy and if anything he had become even more insufferable. Maybe it would be better to lamp him one in the bollocks and take him to the cleaners in a sexual harassment hearing. As he leered across the desk the idea was certainly tempting.

"It's just not our thing Lucy. We do news. You know that. Hard news from the hard places. 'Stories from Bad Places'."

He grinned and it seemed like he expected her to leap over the desk and seduce him because he had remembered the title of her book. "This really isn't our thing at all Lucy. It's for Sport or one of the documentaries."

She took a long breath and folded her arms tightly across her chest. Maybe one day he would catch some of the body language.

"Bugger off Roger. Look at the world. The news world. We have 150 thousand American soldiers in Iraq. And eight thousand Brits. And they are in Afghanistan and Uzbekistan and Kuwait and most of the near East. We have suicide bombers doing their stuff every day. We have religious nuts on one side driving jumbo jets into high buildings and religious nuts on the other side opening up a multi-million dollar Museum of Creation in Kentucky where Adam and Eve flounce about with dinosaurs."

He looked a little confused and a little angry at yet another rebuff. "So?"

"So it's all about east meets west Roger. Islam meets Christianity. Rich meets poor. Teenagers with stones and petrol bombs meet tanks and helicopter gunships. This is the Crusades revisited for Christ's sake."

"I don't see what on earth you're driving at Doll."

"Roger, if you call me doll one more time I might just re-arrange your face so it looks like tomato puree."

He liked that. "OOOHH. Doesn't the lady get fierce. Christ you don't half turn me on when you talk violent."

She got to her feet and paced. One day. One day she really would kill the preening bastard.

"OK Lucy. It's like the Crusades. And East is meeting West and the sparks are flying. So what does that have anything to do with this programme idea of yours?"

"Where does the East meet the West Roger?"

A shrug. "A geography lesson now is it."

"Istanbul Roger. As in the place that started out as Byzantium and became Constantinople and became Istanbul. A city that sits either half of the Bosporus. A city that spans two continents. And into this very city at the intersection of all that is going on in the world we are about to see forty-something-thousand Scousers introduced into the mix and you sit there and tell me that isn't a story."

"That is of course assuming that Liverpool beat Chelsea which I think is pretty bloody unlikely."

"Oh. I forgot. You're a Chelsea fan of course. I just bet you never missed a match when they were in the second division getting ten thousand if they were lucky."

This flustered him a little. "Well of course I did. I was at school."

She gave a derisive sort of snort. "Having lots of fun and games in the showers no doubt."

She regretted the words the minute they left her mouth and saw red take over from sunbed-brown.

"Maybe you might remember that I am your boss Lucy." She thought the red hue was down to anger. In fact it was blind undiluted panic that somehow she had got to hear about that one and only time with Lionel Evans-Smythe.

"OK. Sorry. Let's just assume for a moment that it IS Liverpool, then even you have to admit that the prospect of forty-odd-thousand Scousers begging, borrowing and stealing their way across Europe to Istanbul is pretty bloody newsworthy. It'll be the biggest invasion since Gallipoli."

"It won't be that many Lucy. I checked. There are only twenty thousand tickets for each of the finalists."

This drew a laugh. "That might make a difference for the prawn sandwich brigade that follow your lot but it won't up on Merseyside. Believe me."

His composure was all up the spout. She had gone through him like a dose of salts. And he was trying to work out if the look in her eyes was anger or triumph. Did she really know about Evans-Smythe? It was inconceivable. Hardly anybody knew about it. But then again she had so specifically mentioned showers. Jesus. It had been nearly twenty years ago and it had only been bloody once. But then again. Maybe it would be best to play safe.

"OK. If in the unlikely event Liverpool DO make the final I'll allow you to take a news team down to cover the story. But before you get all excited I suggest a look at the Premiership table might be a good idea. The last time I looked there is something of a gap between Chelsea and Liverpool. All we need is a one all draw and you can kiss your little programme goodbye. League tables don't lie, Lucy."

She placed her hands on the edge of the desk and leaned in to him. "Roger. There is something you should know. Form is temporary. Class is permanent." She spoke in broad undiluted Scouse and he looked as shocked as if Evans- Smythe himself had walked into the room. Dripping wet.

There aren't many who set their stall out on a career path at the age of twelve and make it all the way to the finish line. Jennifer Wilson was one of the rare ones who did exactly that. Only one job ever held any appeal to Jennifer; she was always going to be a reporter. She started writing for the school magazine at twelve and by the time she reached the lower sixth she was the Editor. It was a similar story at college, and her enthusiasm and CV were more than enough to win her a place as a cub reporter on the Echo.

Twenty years later she was an assistant editor with a nice three-bedroomed house in Maghull, a husband called Stan and two teenage daughters who went about like a pair of underdressed tarts but could have been worse. All in all, Jennifer's life was almost an unqualified success. She had set out her stall at an early age and had got there before turning forty.

Sometimes in quiet moments when she had the house to herself and was able to light a few scented candles in the bathroom she would review her life to date and all in all there were very few things that she had missed out on. Hardly any in fact. Just one if the truth were to be known.

When she had sat down for the first class of her third year her eyes had been drawn to the new boy who had moved from the city. As far as she was concerned it had been love at first sight. Mickey McGuire was without doubt the most devastatingly fantastic boy ever to walk the planet. It was a state of utter smittenness that stayed with her for years. It lasted through school and well into college when his poster was ever present on her wall. It lasted all the way to the day when she had shed bitter tears when she read of his eighteen-month sentence.

The problem was that her love had always remained unrequited. Mickey had always been friendly with her. She was a mate. During the early days of Spion she had been a willing volunteer who would go out on Saturday afternoons and to plaster the walls of Southport with home made posters which she helped to make. She had her first direct contacts with the media as she penned press releases for the local free papers and the music rags.

CHELSEA – MAY 2005

And through it all Mickey treated her like a pal. Nothing more. Every now and then he would have brief flings and she would cry herself to sleep. But never once did he ever think to ask her out and make her life perfect.

Then one day after work a lad called Stan joined her at a table in a city centre pub and she had agreed to let him buy her a drink and the rest was history. Thoughts of Mickey McGuire faded but not all the way to black. On three occasions she had turned out for his poetry readings and seen how the years were taking a heavy toll. His talent was still prodigious, but he obviously was going to be one of those people who would never find the key to turning ability into anything worthwhile. The last time he had noticed her and they had gone for a couple of drinks and it had been like it always was. They were pals. And she had written quite a long piece about the great Scouse hope of the early eighties who had matured into a poet of substance.

And then it had been occasional drifting memories in her B&Q bath with the flicker and scent of the candles and the distant hum of the traffic outside.

She was working on a story about the continuing difficulties at the Ford factory when the front desk receptionist buzzed her with the news that a Mr Michael McGuire was hoping to see her. And all of a sudden she was fourteen again and frantically working on her face and hair in a mirror as he took the elevator.

"All right Jenn."

"Mickey. Hi. Brilliant to see you. Please. Have a seat. Tea? Coffee?"

He sat and the fact that he was clearly middle-aged hit her rather hard. Because if he was middle-aged, then she was middle-aged too and her own girls were now older than she had been when she had worshipped the very ground he walked on. He really didn't look all that well. His clothes were at the stage where the best place was a jumble sale table and his face was tired and pale. But there was still a trace of the old energy and his eyes still sparkled as they took in her office.

"Coffee would be magic. Bloody hell Jenn, you've done great haven't you?"

She fussed about with the kettle and cups.

"Oh you know. Not bad. What about you?"

This brought a rather surprising laugh. "Terrible. Like always. Single and unemployed and not a bean to my name."

"But still writing poems?"

"Yeah. Still writing poems. The hungry poet part is something I've got nailed down. Hey, guess where my place of residence is now."

"Go on."

"A sleeping bag on Tonto's floor."

This lit her face up. "Oh my God. Tonto! You're still with him. How is he?"

"Tonto is Tonto and always will be. He takes every day as it comes and continues to occupy a completely different planet to the rest of us."

"I can't believe the two of you are still together."

"Is that a good thing or a bad thing?"

She placed a coffee in front of him. "Not for me to say. I report. I don't judge. Anyway Mickey, is this social?"

A voice in her head was screaming silently. Please don't ask me for money Mickey. Please don't have slipped that far. If you ask I will give, but it will break my memories like china plates.

"Well not really. I'm looking for one of those for old times sake favours Jenn."

No. Please no. Not a tenner till Friday. Not that.

"I'm all ears."

"You'll remember that I'm a massive red?"

This drew a smile. "It wouldn't be easy to forget."

"No. I suppose I was always pretty up front. Well here it is. We've won the European Cup four times and I've never seen a single one of the finals. Not live. Not on the tele. Not at all. Every time we made it through, some big disaster would blow up and I'd miss the game. Twice I was banged up and once I was out for the count in a Wigan hospital."

"And the fourth?"

"Always the reporter hey Jenn? The fourth time, which was actually the first time, I was watching 'Close Encounters of the Third Kind'."

"Instead of the match?"

"Instead of the match."

She was beginning to feel pretty confident that he wasn't about to ask her for a tenner. And this was interesting. Really, really interesting. She could think of absolutely no logical reason why Mickey would have gone watch Spielberg's most dreary film instead of watching Liverpool win the European Cup for the first time. She fell into familiar newshound mode.

"May, 1977 yes?"

A nod.

"Three one against Borussia Monchengladbach?"

Nod.

"The biggest night in the history of Liverpool Football Club and you were in a cinema?"

Another nod.

"I think you're going to have to give me some details here Mickey."

He pulled out a crumpled packet of cigarettes and looked hopeful. She got to her feet and opened a window and slid her metal bin to his feet.

"It will have to be edited highlights. I spent the evening with a girl who will have to remain nameless. And from that night forth she became the love of my life. But it has never happened. She went one way. I went another way. But we always seemed to come together when the lads made it to the final. And things always went all to hell. And then I never saw her for twenty years until last week."

He took an anxious draw and seemed unsure where to go next.

"A straight question Mickey."

"Go on."

"Is this the girl from 'Lovers Under Creamy Yellow'?"

Nod.

"Fish and chips in the rain by Pier Head? All true?"

Nod.

"You know I used to lie awake at night thinking of ways to tear her eyes out with my fingernails. Even though I never knew who she was. The problem was that I never could grow a decent set of nails. Look. Still can't."

This led to a drag from the cigarette that was more akin to a gasp for air.

"Bloody hell Jenn, you mean . . .?"

"Oh yes. Hook, line and sinker. I don't suppose I was the only lovesick teenager you left emotionally shattered with that bloody song of yours."

He looked rather startled. He never ceased to be amazed at the continuing legacy of 'Lovers Under Creamy Yellow'. First the mysterious Siberienne and now Jenn. His mate Jenn who had obviously felt very differently about him to the way he had felt about her.

"I gather the name of the lady in question is a state secret?"

Nod.

"Well pray continue."

Another frantic drag. "OK. Like I said. Twenty years goes by and she reappears. And she says this is the last chance. The only chance. But there's strings like. Big time strings."

"Like?"

"Like she gave me her mobile number and said I have to make it to the Ataturk Stadium on May 25th and she will be waiting. She knows I'm flat broke you see. She knows I'll have to break free of all the shite and find a way to make it."

"A quest?"

"Yeah. A quest."

She sat back in her chair and made a steeple with her fingers.

"This really is the most outrageously romantic story Mickey. It's borderline Mills and Boon. Even though I hate your mystery woman with a passion I have to admit that she has a bit of class."

"She's got more class than Kenny Dalglish."

"Ever the poet. You still haven't got to the part where you want me to take the stage in your costume drama."

"No. Right. OK." He lit another cigarette from the dying butt of the first. "We've come up with a plan Jenn."

"We?"

"Me and Tonto. We're going to do a gig. A fundraiser. We reckon if we could get three or four hundred at a fiver a head and sell a few CDs we might just scrape up enough to get to Istanbul."

"And what if Liverpool don't make it? I believe a certain team called Chelsea may still play a part in things."

"No chance. This is all about history and fate Jenn. Think about 1978 . . ."

"Ah. The dead Pope and royal wedding card. How very New Age Mickey."

"Some things are meant to happen Jenn."

She smiled. He might be residing in a rather tired body but he was still a big kid at heart. He always would be. The Mickeys of the world didn't do growing up.

"You want a story I expect."

"Well. You were always the one who told the world Jenn. You can stick a few posters up as well if you like."

"I think I'll stick to the story. Where and when?"

"I went to see Eric Thompson. You remember? The Berlin Club?"

"So Eric is still on the scene. Is he charging you much?"

"He says if we can knock out more than two hundred tickets he'll do it for what he makes on the bar. It's two weeks Friday. The twentieth. Eight o'clock. Fiver on the door."

"Cheaper than Coldplay then."

"Well we were always value for money."

She picked up a pen and started making a few notes. "I gather that the part about the girl is strictly off limits."

"I'd rather it was."

"Pity. But I rather like the angle of the penniless voice of the early eighties making a last bid to raise the cash for Istanbul. It plays for me. I think we will be able to come up with quite a spread. I also have two or three good friends in local radio. I think I can get plenty of airtime for some of the old tracks. So the answer Mickey is yes. And you now have a mere 197 tickets to reach Eric's target. I shall bring my two daughters to see the authentic voice of a world that isn't with us any more."

For a moment he felt like crying. At last life was looking as if it might turn.

"Thanks Jenn."

"My pleasure Mickey. Really. Go find a happy ending."

Frank found it hard to comprehend just how much his life had changed in the few short weeks that had passed since he had last waited on a plane at Ringway Airport. The last gasp of winter had become the first warmth of spring. His cruise control life had become a rollercoaster in a typhoon. The last time he had waited by the Arrivals gate he had felt a dull boredom at the prospect of entertaining the Russians. It would be a day of hanging around whilst Eddie and Dimitri did the vodka and the handshakes and back slaps and declarations of undying loyalty. Then it would be a game against Leverkusen and no doubt another few nails in the coffin of Liverpool's season.

THE LONG AND WINDING
ROAD TO ISTANBUL

How completely wrong he had been. Instead of the anticipated hours of dreariness, Ivana had walked into his life and lifted him ten thousand feet away from the mundane. And against all odds the reds had cruised past the Germans and made it look easy.

Now he waited with a stomach that was full of tension. The same questions as Turin. Would she be there? Would she go with him? What would they do? Was it a beginning or an end?

And as the passengers started to emerge he saw that she was there. And soon it was agreed that once again Dimitri wanted her to go with Frank because she wanted more Liverpool to take home to her room at the university. And the moment they had got into the car they had fallen into each other's arms and kissed. And he knew once and for all that he was completely, utterly and conclusively stuffed. Only one thing mattered in his life anymore. Ivana and nothing else.

"So. That was very nice my gangster. I think about this for so many days. You know this my gangster?"

"I'm no different. What's the plan for today then?"

"Today I think you can take me to where you live."

He gripped the steering wheel and stared ahead at a family who were trying hard to fit luggage into a car boot, without the success that those in the adverts always seemed to have.

"You're sure?"

"Of course. And you?"

"It means we cross the line Ivana. You know this."

"OK. I know this. I cross line. I have made decision. I can be this Bianca. So I need you to be Francesco. So we cross this line. You can cross line for me Frank?"

He smiled and gave a rueful shake of his head. "I expect I'd jump into a molten volcano if you asked me. Let's go."

Crossing the line with Ivana was the kind of thing that was promised to suicide bombers by fast talking Imams. Except no seventy-two virgins of paradise could ever have come close. Frank made coffee in his chrome kitchen and for the umpteenth time had to convince himself that he really was awake. As the kettle started to hiss he took a look through the louvre doors to where she was sitting. She was at the table by the window in his dressing gown. Behind her a cluster of seagulls flapped about in the blue sky. Siberian beauty. River Mersey. His flat. And he was awake. Nothing made any kind of sense and he couldn't care less.

He poured two cups and put them on a tray. She pushed her hair back and cleared some space. In front of her were all the photographs he had taken when he had bought his small house in Tuscany.

"Maybe you have Spion CD Frank?"

"Maybe."

"Maybe you can play this one OK?"

His brother's voice filled the room and made everything feel even weirder still as she sang along, word perfect as she moved from photo to photo.

"So this is where I am Bianca?"

"The very place."

"Is smaller than the Castello."

"A little, but the view is better."

"You can make wine here, yes?"

"So they tell me."

A smile.

"I think it looks like good place Frank. I think we can go here."

"When?"

"I will give you one email address. You can give me one email address. So we can talk. And I come when the time is good."

"Do you have money?"

"I have some money. Maybe more money can make it more easy for me. I need passport. Plane tickets. Not too much. Only some."

He reached for his wallet and pulled out a credit card.

"Take this. The code is 1977. Take what you need."

She turned the card over and over in her fingers and looked at a view of low hills under a baking sky.

"And we can be happy Frank?"

"Yeah. We can be happy."

By the time they reached Anfield it was more than clear that it was about to be a night of nights. Of course the media build up had been hysterical and then some, but even after all the endless hype there was still something extra special in the Mersey air. Many column inches had been given over to talking up the influence of Liverpool's star player. Their twelfth man.

The Anfield crowd.

THE LONG AND WINDING
ROAD TO ISTANBUL

After twenty years the old stadium had once again become a place to be feared by visiting teams. It hadn't escaped anyone's notice that the sheer barrage of sound that hit the experienced Juventus players in the first half an hour of the quarter-final had knocked them backwards. By the time they regained their composure they were two down and on their way out.

Chelsea had been making confident noises about looking forward to the challenge but nobody really believed them. The world was waiting to witness the kind of arena where Gladiators had once fought to their deaths. It had become more than a mere football match in many different ways. Jose Mourinho, Chelsea's flamboyant Portuguese manager, carried an arrogance about him that had infused the whole club. They had more money than every club on the planet put together and they worked on the certainty that in the end the big bucks would always come through. Mourinho liked to be known as the 'special one' and he more than anyone was going to have a twenty-first century lion's den experience having shushed the Liverpool fans in the Carling Cup Final in Cardiff.

Chelsea and Mourinho were all about London. They were £1000 for a season ticket and £250,000 for a nothing special house. They were about ostentatious wealth and they looked down their noses at the rest of the world. Already the FA and UEFA had fined them for various acts of misconduct and they had made it more than plain that they couldn't care less how much they were fined. Because what did money matter when all was said and done? As the price of oil continued to climb like a thermometer in the Sahara, their Russian owner couldn't spend money faster than he was making it.

They had the players and they had the money and they knew it. So what that Liverpool represented the greatest of the old guard? Those days were long gone. What mattered now was the size of the cheque book. Tradition and history counted for nothing. To start with, a 0-0 draw in the first leg had seemed like a great result for the Merseysiders. But by the time the day of the Anfield game arrived most of the media experts had concluded that it was in fact a great result for Chelsea after all. They had conceded no away goals. A one all draw would be enough. They had the best defence in the land. And they were simply bound to score. And of course they were twenty plus points ahead of Liverpool in the Premiership. And the league table didn't lie. Well it just didn't.

So the morning papers told the world that it was an open and shut case. Liverpool had exceeded all sensible expectations, but enough was enough. It was the day when they would finally be found out. Chelsea was just too downright wonderful and rich for anyone to seriously consider it possible for them to be beaten. The view was unanimous. Chelsea. Chelsea, and probably at a canter. But the one niggling doubt in the back of everyone's mind was the player who hadn't cost a penny and had no international caps at all. That twelfth man. The crowd.

As the streets around the stadium filled up, it became very obvious that the twelfth man was taking the job seriously. By the time the teams took to the pitch the noise was so loud that it seemed like it was almost alive. Later, some scientists were to announce that the forty thousand who made up the twelfth man had broken the world record for the loudest sound ever generated by human beings. And before five minutes had elapsed the barrage of sound had cut right through two hundred million pounds worth of blue shirted arrogance. The great defence was suddenly at sixes and sevens. The keeper sythed down his Czech Republic colleague Milan Baros and just as everyone was preparing to scream for a penalty the diminutive figure of Luis Garcia was skipping away from the goalmouth like a hyperactive elf.

A whistle. A finger pointing to the centre circle. Goal. Unmitigated utter deafening bedlam. One nil. And Mourinho was thrashing up and down the touchline giving a great impression of Achilles with an arrow sticking out from the back of his ankle.

Many were to say that the six minutes of added time at the death of the game were the longest six minutes in history. They were to say how time itself seemed to stop as a ball broke to Chelsea's Icelandic international Eider Gudjohnsen with just a handful of seconds left in the game. And when his shot flashed by the post to safety Mickey couldn't believe how calm he felt about it all. Normally he would have died a thousand times in those frozen nanoseconds. Instead he stood like a man with a strange light about him. The feeling of fate and history was strong upon him. From the moment the goal went in he had felt utterly serene. Because some things were just meant to happen and that was all there was to it. Fate and history. And a dead Pope. And a royal wedding. And a defeat in the League Cup Final. And when Liverpool win the European Cup, Mickey and Lucy find each other. And those honeyed words from the woman from the other side of the Ural Mountains. Find her Mickey. And Lucy turning to leave the pub with a glint in her eyes. Because there was only ever going to be one winner that night. And the winner was the team with the history and the passion of a city behind them. It wasn't a night where money counted for a thing.

And so the blues were sent back south to lick their wounds and to complain about the referee. Not that anyone listened much. The football world gave them about as much sympathy as Hitler got when he lost the battle of Stalingrad. Mourinho sounded like a petulant child as he bleated away about how it was that the best team had lost. And no doubt some marketing guys at American Express must have wondered why they had spent such a fortune to have him advertise their credit card. Mourinho or De Niro? Be serious. But none of the moaning mattered because Liverpool were to play AC Milan in the European Cup Final in Istanbul on 25 May 2005. It was written down. It was real.

Up in the executive box, the champagne flowed as fast as the stewards could keep up with it and even Goran was all smiles. Eddie was on the roll of his life and insisted they should all reconvene for the final in Istanbul and it would be his treat. He told them that they were like a talisman. He raised his glass high and proposed a toast to the last leg of the journey. In the midst of the celebrations the look exchanged between Frank and Ivana was barely noticeable. But it was noticed by Anton who had been discreetly noticing everything that had happened all day because Dimitri had asked him to notice.

Outside the crowd had cascaded out of the stadium and onto the terraced streets that had seen so many glorious nights down the years. The eleven men who had hung on for eighty-five minutes of normal time and six minutes of added time had done their work and retired to the dressing room. The twelfth man wasn't nearly finished and the night bounced with songs of triumph. Songs of victory. Old songs that had been taken from where they had waited at the back of a cupboard for twenty years. And there were new songs that had never been sung before. Songs of Istanbul. The great Merseyside Crusade to the gates of Asia commenced the very minute the referee at last put the suffering thousands out of their misery and blew his whistle. Within minutes keyboards were being attacked and by the next day every flight was full and every internet available room taken.

Unlike Tonto, Mickey had no voice left to join in. He just floated along with it all with a smile of the very purest of joy on his face and after a while he was in a pub without really noticing that he had got there. All around complete strangers were shaking each other's hands and waking up to the fact that the previous two hours had really happened. Lucy had been right. Fate and history had been the thirteenth and fourteenth men out there. Fourteen against eleven. No wonder the arrogant Cockneys had been dispatched back down the M6. The lads had pulled on the shirt and remembered what it meant. They had done their part and left all the experts and journalists spitting their tea out. The team that was lying fifth was in the final. The team that was twenty odd points behind was in the final. The team who had been written off every step of the way was in the final. The airwaves were alight with people wondering aloud just how the hell it had happened. But Mickey knew exactly how it had happened. It was fate and history which were forces way more powerful than two hundred lousy million quid's worth of dodgy Russian money.

The lads had come through and the twelfth man had roared them over the line. Over the course of a couple of hours Istanbul had moved from being a mirage to a reality. Now it was down to him. All that was left was a couple of thousand miles and a few hundred quid and his life would at last find the tracks again. Twenty years had been far too long. He had paid the price of allowing his paranoia to take control on that terrible night in South Wales. A terrible price of months of prison and years of nagging self-loathing. And now, thanks to eleven men in red and the twelfth man in the stands, he had been handed the chance to put it all right.

Two thousand miles and a few hundred quid. Compared to beating Chelsea it was nothing. He took a great long swig of his pint and felt the cold chill all the way down his neck. The road to the East was wide open.

Lucy had considered watching the game in the hotel room that the BBC provided for her when she was in London during the intervals between postings. But as she had left Television Centre she had changed her mind. A taxi had dropped her on the Kings Road and she had chosen a big, brash pub with a giant screen. By half past seven the place was packed to bursting with red faced Chelsea fans, most of them fresh from the offices where they worked. As the game kicked off they were loud and proud and confident and chanting at the screen. A few minutes later they were screaming abuse at the referee as the sound of the Kop seemed to threaten to lift the screen off its wall mountings. By the time the game was over they were all but silenced and she sat with a small smug smile as they left before the experts had time to explain just how they had got it so very wrong. Outside she took out her mobile and picked Roger Templeton's number out of the memory.

"Roger. It's Lucy."

In the background she could hear the sound of subdued wine bar. It was a night of thousands of disappointed yuppies.

"Thought you might ring."

"I can take it the programme is on can I?"

"Suppose so."

"Great. Have a wonderful evening Roger."

"Yeah right."

It was much later that Dimitri arrived back at his hotel. His head was flying and he decided on a last drink before hitting the sack. The bar was deserted and the young barman was clearly fighting sleep.

"Is OK my friend. Only one drink and we go for sleep. We have whisky. Two whisky. Big whisky. Best whisky you sell OK?"

Dimitri took a table whilst Anton collected the two big whisky at £22.95 each.

Once the ex special forces man sat down they spoke in Russian

"So. You followed them?"

"I did. They went straight from the airport to a block of flats. I presume it is where he lives. They stayed until just after six. Then they went straight to the stadium."

Dimitri swilled the honey-coloured malt around the glass thoughtfully.

"We will wait a little time and then we deal with this. Two weeks. You can come back with Vladimir and let him know that nobody touches what belongs to Dimitri Zarkhov. It will be discreet OK. I don't want Eddie to know. It isn't any of his doing. I like Eddie."

Anton took an appreciative sip of his drink which was the first of the day.

"And the girl? You want me to deal with her when we get home?"

Dimitri shook his head. "No. For some reason I like this girl. She is different. For sure she is headstrong, but this is good. She will not see this Frank again. So she will forget all about him. We will do nothing with Ivana. We carry on as normal OK."

"Fine. Your call boss."

"For sure. My call. We have one more whisky. And in two weeks you let this Frank know that nobody touches what belongs to Dimitri Zarkhov."

Twelve days later Mickey paid his fifth visit of the afternoon to the newsagent shop around the corner from Tonto's flat. The Bengali owner gave a him big grin.

"Papers they are arrive now sir."

"Magic. Here you go." Mickey passed a pound coin and was already flicking the pages by the time the newsagent had come up with the change. The article was on page seven. Not only was it on page seven, it was page seven. All of page seven.

"Bloody hell Jenn, you're an absolute dancer."

"Please sir?"

"Here. Look at this. Talk about fan-bloody-tastic."

He held the full page spread up for inspection and the man behind the counter reached for his glasses. The headline read "Singing all the way to Istanbul" and underneath was an archive shot of a 1984 Mickey leaning out into a sea of young faces with a microphone close in to his face.

"This is you I think sir."

"You bet. Me, twenty years ago. Me, before everything went down the drain."

"You were singer?"

"I was singer."

"And now you make sing again?"

"Too right I am. Friday night down the Berlin. I've got some tickets on me if you fancy it. Fiver each."

The thought of a concert made the old retailer look a little anxious. "I think I have too much work sir. We not close early here. Always ten o'clock I am."

"You don't worry about it mate. It's the thought that counts. I'll see you."

Mickey was about to leave to read the body of the article.

THE LONG AND WINDING
ROAD TO ISTANBUL

"Sir. Please. You are not taking your change."

"Oh right. Course."

"And maybe I can be taking two of these tickets please. My two sons they are very much liking music. I think maybe they can come to this music of yours."

"That's really good of you mate. Here you go. Two tickets. Tell them to enjoy themselves."

Outside it was warm and sunny and absolutely everything was going right. Already the Berlin had sold over a hundred and twenty tickets and that was before Jenn's article. A whole page! Unbelievable. Maybe they would get more than three hundred. It would probably be a pretty middle-aged gathering. Lots of fellow campaigners from the eighties who had taken the fight to Maggie and got a proper kicking. It was like time had gone into reverse and the world had lost twenty years. Liverpool were once again in a final. Spion had dusted off the guitars and were practising for five hours a day. The old armies of the left were once again gathering to have a go at the leaders of the G8 who were due to meet up at the Gleneagles Hotel in July. And Lucy was back in his life. No wonder the sun was shining.

He found a bench and lit up. Jenn had done him more than proud. The text told of one of the lost Liverpool groups who had shone out briefly for a couple of years and then had disappeared. She recalled what the late John Peel had said about them. She recalled the time when they had made it all the way to number nine in the charts. And she told of a boy she had known at school who lived and breathed Liverpool football club and had spent a whole lifetime dreaming of making it to a European Cup Final. Now the boy had grown into a man and he was hitting the come back trail to raise the cash to make the trip to Istanbul. The end of the article brought a smile to his face.

'There must be many women out there who are just like me. We are in our forties now. We look in the mirror and we see cellulite. Our teenage children drive us to despair. We buy clothes that are four sizes larger than the ones we used to buy. And sometimes when the house is quiet we might choose a record from our past and remember the days when we were younger and more beautiful. The record that I tend to choose is in my opinion one of the most beautiful songs ever to be written in this musical city of ours. 'Lovers Under Creamy Yellow'

deserves to be spoken of in the same breath as 'Yesterday' and 'Eleanor Rigby' and 'Ferry across the Mersey'. It's all about being young and full of hope and head over heels in love and eating fish and chips in the rain at Pier Head. I know for an absolute fact that I am by no means alone here. There must be thousands of us who sat up late in our bedrooms and cried over that lovely song. Mickey McGuire and Tonto provided a soundtrack to our teenage years. Now is a time for us to forget the wrinkles and ignore the hip-measurement and roll back the years. Let's shell out a fiver and buy a ticket back to our youth and put Mickey and Tonto on the road to Istanbul.'

When they arrived at the Berlin Club later on in the afternoon Eric Thompson told them that the phone had been ringing off the wall. He had knocked out another two hundred tickets and the punters were coming in thick and fast. They were already well over three hundred and there was still a day to go. It might even get past five hundred at this rate. And the road to the East was more open than ever.

The story ran in full on the Echo's website and Google picked it out of the ether for Lucy who had been entering the keywords Mickey and McGuire and Spion into the search engine for two weeks. There it was again. The song. So many women all over the world seemed to have been affected by Mickey and Lucy eating their chips in the rain. Now it looked as if many of these women would send Mickey on his way to Istanbul at a fiver a time. It was beginning to look as if her faith hadn't been misplaced after all. She had nearly gone back to find him on two or three occasions after the poetry night. Maybe she was being unreasonable. In her world insisting on a man making a journey to Istanbul to get the girl wasn't much of an ask. In her world men had credit cards and secretaries to make the booking. The problem was that Mickey had never been close to that world. Maybe he might have a credit card but he didn't look to her like a man who would have much action in the available funds section of the statement. He had no job and no prospect much of finding one. But then she had remembered him telling her all about the first final in Rome and how almost thirty thousand Liverpool fans managed to make it down there. He had told her that they could play a final on the far side of Saturn and the lads would make it there one way or another. And so she had decided it was only right and proper that he should get to walk the walk.

THE LONG AND WINDING
ROAD TO ISTANBUL

Her background research for the programme had tended to back-up his get-there-through-hell-and-high-water theory. The story of the Scouse trek to the east was a story that was growing every day. The planes that flew direct from anywhere in the UK to Istanbul had been sold out within hours of the semi-final. A few days later most flights from other easily accessible European capitals had been the same. Stories of all kinds of weird and wonderful routes were emerging every day. There was Romania, Hungary, Bulgaria and even Albania although she shuddered at the fate of those who thought a bit of sweet talk would cut much ice on the Kosovo border. She had been on the Kosovo border with Albania. It wasn't a place for sweet-talking. It wasn't a place for sweet anything.

When she had finished the article she felt pretty confident that he and Tonto would have the required funds to make the trip. Surely they would get over three hundred. Maybe they would get five hundred. Enough. Next he would have to pick a route. Vague memories from school recalled that geography had never been one of Mickey's stronger subjects. Her mind painted a picture of him down in the local library turning the pages of an atlas to the South Eastern Europe pages and scratching his head. M62. Turn right on the M6 and keep heading south Mickey. Her mobile phone was lying at the edge of the table. The days were ticking down. It was beginning to look as if it would ring after all. Then? Then was then.

Frank parked his car around the corner from the Berlin and locked it with a beep of the remote control. Jenn's article had made him feel melancholy on several fronts. The stuff about the song rattled a couple of chords. He had always felt saddened by the fact that his little brother and Lucy had never found a way of being with each other. He had never really known Lucy until he had taken his trip to Bristol. The girl he had found had impressed him greatly. It was amazing that the same blood ran through her veins as her older brother. And yet when he had considered things, it wasn't all that strange after all. They had both grown up to be successful individuals on the back of ability, hard work and determination. They differed only in the fact that Lucy carried a fierce belief in right and wrong and Eddie didn't. For years 'Lovers Under Creamy Yellow' had played at the edges of his life. Sometimes in the background in restaurants. Sometimes on late night radio when he was driving. Sometimes he even played it himself in the flat.

But now it had become so much more. Now it had become a theme tune for his own life. Because it wasn't only the song of Mickey and Lucy now. It was also the song of Frank and Ivana. And the second level of his feeling of vague sadness was that he would have so loved to have taken Ivana to see the Spion comeback night. How she would have loved it. She would have taken in every minute detail of the faded backstreet venue that for thirty years had provided a first stage for the budding bands of the city. He had emailed her the link to Jenn's story and she had emailed back saying that she would be there in spirit. And she had confirmed that Dimitri was taking her on the trip to Istanbul. And she had said that she would ask that Frank should take her on a tour like he had done in Milan and Liverpool. And she had said that he should buy two tickets for a plane to Italy. Because she had made her mind up and she wanted to go to the cottage with the view over the hills covered in olive trees. And she said that if anything was wrong she would get away somehow and wait for him between three and four on the afternoon after the match. She would wait at the Blue Mosque. And she asked Frank to tell Mickey to find his Lucy.

The final level of melancholy was that Mickey felt he had to put himself on the line with the concert at all. Frank would have paid for the trip gladly. For years he had tried to persuade his brother to allow him to help with one financial crisis after another but Mickey had always refused. Because Frank's money was Eddie's money and Mickey didn't want any of Eddie Tate's money because it was filthy. It reeked with the stench of human misery and greed. So all that Frank could do to help Mickey and Tonto down the road to Istanbul was to pay his fiver along with the rest of the audience. When he had first heard of the plan he had dreaded how it would be. He had a picture of an audience of about ten and another dream burst like a balloon on a birthday. But as he turned the corner he was greeted with the sight of a queue. How many? There had to be over a hundred in the line to the door and there was still an hour to go yet. So Jenn's article had done the trick. The audience was well over three quarters female and Frank knew that the turnout was all down to the song that had become as much his own as his brother's. Did Lucy know about the gig? Maybe he would dig out an email contact address at the BBC and send her

Jenn's article. And maybe she might think about contacting his brother. It was a hell of a long shot, but they were living in strange times where anything seemed possible.

He gave the stage door a bash and Eric Thompson opened up after a few minutes.

"Christ almighty Frank. Long time no see. You look fit mate."

"Fit enough Eric. You don't look so bad yourself for an old bastard. Mickey in is he?"

"Yeah. In the dressing room. You remember where it is?"

"Sure do. Looks like a fair turn out."

"I reckon we'll have over five hundred."

"And I trust you're not ripping him off."

Eric gave a look of horror. "As if I'd do that Frank. I'm doing this for bar takings only. Be rude not to wouldn't it. I'd hate not to help the boys get down there to the game."

"Eric, you restore my faith in human nature. You really do."

The older shook his head. "If you want to talk about human nature Frank maybe you could persuade your boss to ease off on the protection rates he charges. A man can't make a decent living like."

"You make a living Eric. So don't play the suffering old git card. It doesn't suit you."

"Ah piss off. I'm going to make sure the lasses at the front are managing."

A stab of memory hit Frank as he knocked and went into the dressing room. What a different scene it was from the last time he had been with Spion backstage. Then it had been half-naked Welsh girls and a whole host of class A drugs. How very different now. Instead of three young lads with their eyes fired up with cocaine there were two middle-aged men. Tonto was working through a few chords with a serene look on his face whilst Mickey was pacing the room looking altogether more nervous. And Midge was six feet under, like so many of the customers who had spent their money with the Eddie Tate empire over the years.

Mickey's face broke into a smile at the sight of his brother. That was something that had never changed through all the years of their divergent lives.

"Alright Mickey. All set?"

"Not bad. We've been rehearsing all week and the rust is mostly scraped off. Christ I'm nervous though. I've never been this nervous."

"I don't blame you mate. There's about a thousand middle-aged birds out there getting ready to have a good old scream for old times sake."

Mickey pulled a rueful sort of face. "You saw Jenn's piece then."

"Who didn't? I was thinking I might try and dig out an email address for Lucy and send it on."

For a moment Mickey was about to tell him. But somehow it had become a superstition thing that he should keep it to himself. Fate was doing him proud at the moment. No point in tempting it. "Oh. Right."

Frank smiled at his brother's squirming discomfort. "Ivana wishes you all the best."

This cleared the squirming look and replaced it with open interest. "Who is this Russian bird then Frank?"

"I think she's my Lucy. We did the fish and chip thing you know. Down at Pier Head. The rain and everything. It was on the afternoon of the Leverkusen game."

"What? You and her like?"

Frank nodded. "And the fish and chips."

"Bloody hell."

"What?"

"Hell. I don't know. It's just not like you I suppose Frank."

Frank wondered whether he should mention the cottage and the olive groves and the plane from Istanbul but thought better of it. Dimitri wouldn't be best pleased when Ivana took the jump and he might put two and two together and get to asking a few questions, especially when he heard from Eddie that Frank had disappeared off the radar at the same time. If it was to happen, then Mickey's best protection would be to know nothing.

"Maybe it's time for me to stop being so self-controlled. You know I would have paid for you to go don't you."

"Course I know. And you know how it is. Especially after Midge and all that."

"I know. And I'm dead proud of you for sorting all this out. Seriously. It's brilliant. I won't be able to stay all the way through I'm afraid. I've got something on later."

Mickey's face clouded over. Something on. An errand for his lord and master. Another batch of poison to be delivered. Another wad of dirty money to be brought back.

Frank avoided the familiar look on his brother's face and turned to the strumming Tonto.

"You OK Tonto?"

"Great Frank. We're going to Istanbul you know."

"Read about it in the papers mate."

Tonto gave a grave nod. "Istanbul's the capital of Turkey Frank."

There didn't seem a lot to say to that.

"That's right enough."

"It's a good job we're in the final Frank. Those Evertonians were all getting too big for their boots."

"And we can't be doing with that, can we Tonto?"

"No way Frank. But they'll shut up when we win the European Cup again. Mickey says we get to keep it this time."

"If we win."

"Course we'll win. We're the best aren't we Frank. I reckon they'll put it in the museum. What do you think?"

"Nailed on certainty I reckon. Anyway boys, I'm going to grab a pint and leave you in peace. All the best, OK?"

"Thanks Frank. I wish Midge was here."

"I know Tonto. We all do." And he gave a look to Mickey that said please don't say the obvious thing and spoil a good moment. And Mickey caught the look and read it and gave a small nod. "See you around Frank."

"Yeah. We'll catch up before you head off to the final."

"Are you going with Eddie?"

Frank nodded.

"Maybe we'll bump into each other then."

"Maybe. That would be a thing wouldn't it."

It was a very different sort of Spion gig from those that had gone before. Not having a drummer any more obviously caused a major cramping of style. Mickey had decided that the best way to get around this deficiency was to play to the audience. The Berlin was never going to be filled with a sweating throng of angry teenagers all fired up and ready to change the world. The ones who heard Jenn's call were always going to be the generation who had been that way twenty years earlier. Now they would be an audience with mortgages and gardens with barbeques. This meant that Spion reined in the loud and angry and went sad and acoustic. They added to their own repertoire. They threw in a couple of the sad Beatles songs and John Lennon's 'Imagine'. They did covers of the some of the left wing laments from the eighties including a number of Paul Weller songs and 'Shipbuilding'. The tears started to flow in earnest when Mickey chose Neil Young as a memory of the fallen Midge. "And every junkie's like a setting sun . . ." And by the time they did 'Lovers Under Creamy Yellow', there was barely a dry eye in the house.

A couple of hacks from the music press went to describe a night of near unbridled middle-aged emotion that hit an unlikely crescendo as the members of the band hit the stage for an encore that was all red. First the audience joined in with the 'The fields of Athenrye', an old Irish Republican song adapted into a song for Celtic FC adapted to a Kop anthem. And then the night ended in 'You'll never walk alone' as five hundred voices put Mickey and Tonto squarely on the road to Istanbul.

When it was all over CD sales were of the hot cakes variety and by the time Eric clicked the lock on the front door the money count had risen to well over £3000.

They had their ticket to ride.

Frank had to leave after an hour. It was a complete downer but it couldn't be avoided. Tonight was the monthly Glasgow run and he was due up in Pollock in the early hours. He got into his car and set out on the short run back to the flat to get ready to leave. His head was still full of music and he felt surprisingly uplifted by the whole evening. He no longer felt sad that Mickey hadn't asked him for the money. It was so much better this way. It would count for more.

Behind him Vladimir tapped the send button on his phone.

"He's leaving."

"Is he coming to the flat?"

"Can't say yet. I'll keep you posted."

As Frank's Mercedes worked through the lights on the waterfront it began to look more and more likely. When the indicator pointed to the flats it was confirmed.

"OK. Three minutes."

"Fine."

Frank swiped a card and gained admission to the underground car park that was part of the package. Nearly ten. That was fine. Plenty of time. He swung the car into his space and climbed out. It was as he turned to lock that he felt metal on the side of his forehead. Then he heard a soft Russian voice that he remembered from a late night hotel bar in Vienna.

"Hello Frank."

"Hi Vladimir."

"You stay still, OK?"

"OK."

His mind hit overdrive. There was only one conceivable reason why Vladimir was in the car park at ten o'clock on a Friday night with a gun to his head. Dimitri knew about him and Ivana. And Dimitri was pissed off. Pissed off enough to send his man back to Liverpool to collect the bill. He saw movement in the entrance to the car park. A jogging figure, jogging in the way that a man jogs who could jog for thirty miles with a twenty kilo pack on his back. Anton. Shit. Two on one. Not that it needed to be two. One would have been plenty. Frank was handy enough but he was Southport to Liverpool compared to these guys.

"We go up to flat now. No stupid OK Frank?"

"OK."

Out of the car park. Into the lift. Not a soul in sight of course. It was Friday night. The residents were out in theatres or wine bars or newly opened Vietnamese restaurants. And if not, they were in their slippers watching DVD's with bottles of wine recommended by the Observer colour supplement. Corridor. Door. Inside. Light on.

Did Eddie know? Probably not. In fact almost certainly not. Eddie was a hell of a customer who paid cash and lots of it. Dimitri was pissed off, but there was no need to get the wrong side of one of his best customers. So this was an unofficial visit. And whatever was about to happen to him would be blamed on somebody else. Eddie had no shortage of enemies in the city who might have a go at his main man. The last thing anyone would consider was that the cheerful Russian with the big smile had sent his ex-special-forces-guys all the way to the banks of the Mersey to sort out business. So what was about to happen? Were they about to execute him? It seemed pretty likely. The Russian view of killing was much more relaxed than in the UK. Murder was a thing that happened out there every hour on the hour. Putting much of a value on a human life was never going to happen in a country where over fifty million had perished in every kind of nightmare over the course of less than a hundred years. Anton seemed to read his thoughts.

"We're not going to kill you Frank OK. You can relax a little. For sure, we hurt you. We hurt you a lot. But you live this time."

Frank closed his eyes and allowed the breath to leave his lungs. So he wasn't about to die. And as soon as he realised that these were not to be the last minutes of his life his mind switched channels. Ivana. Holy Christ. Ivana.

"What about the girl Anton? What has happened to her?"

Anton shrugged. "Nothing. Dimitri like this girl. Sure, she a little crazy but that is why he like this one. So he say nothing. He say she will forget you. She even come to Istanbul. I think it is good that you do not go Frank. You tell Eddie you need to stay here. Make up story. Because maybe if you come to Istanbul you not leave OK."

"OK." Relief. Massive relief. So there would be some pain. No doubt a huge amount of pain. But pain was something that could be handled and put in the past. If they had killed her that was something that he knew he would never be able to handle and put in the past. But they hadn't killed her. At least not yet. And Dimitri was so confident that he was even going to take her to Istanbul. And that meant that there was still hope. It meant that she may still be at the Blue Mosque at the appointed hour.

Anton had opened the small rucksack and removed a hand towel.

"OK Frank. So now you open your mouth. We don't need any noise right now."

Frank duly stuffed his mouth and Anton fixed things with some silver duct tape.

"OK. Here is the next. You put your hands on something that belonged to Dimitri. You know this Frank. We all know this. It is no good. So now we need to make punishment. There are two ways here. You take punishment and we go. Or you make struggle and we hurt you some. Then you still take punishment. Then we go. I think you maybe a man who can take punishment, yes?"

Frank had a mouthful of towel so he just nodded.

The Russian reached back into his bag and removed a large square piece of wood. "So. We are going to punish your hand Frank. Because you put this hand where it is not allowed. Sure, we understand. This

Ivana is pretty girl OK. Maybe Anton and Dimitri like to put hand on this girl. But this girl is Dimitri's girl. So we put hands on other girls OK. You have girls here in Liverpool Frank. Plenty girl. Pretty girl. These are the girl to put hand on. Not Dimitri's girl. So we punish you hand Frank. OK."

Frank didn't have to wonder very long about the nature of the punishment. Next out of the bag came a claw hammer and a thick six inch nail. Oh Christ.

"Yes I know Frank. Is not good. But it could be worse OK. We could kill you but we don't kill you. We could punish you in right hand. Right hand is best hand, no?"

Frank nodded, his eyes glued to the big hammer.

"So we punish left hand. It make very big pain. But in three or four months it is not too bad."

He talked in conversational tones as he took a small bottle and opened the cap. Vladimir had brought a desert bowl from the kitchen and placed it on the table. Anton poured bluish liquid all over the nail and talked in conversational tones.

"Iodine OK. This nail he is sterile. No infection. Like I say. Three four months you can be fine. So. Is time now. You can sit here."

Frank sat at the table where he drank his morning coffee.

"So. You hold out this left arm. You put back of hand on this wood here. Is good. And you spread fingers OK. Good. Vladimir will hold this hand here. I make with nail now. You are ready OK?"

Like hell he was. What man in the history of the universe had ever been ready to have his hand nailed onto a cube of wood. But there was no choice. If he tried to fight they would simply beat the living daylights out of him and do it anyway.

"First I place camera OK. Dimitri he need to see this. When he see this he can say OK this is all finish now."

He placed a portable DVD camera on a work surface and fussed for while as he checked that all of the action would be properly recorded in clear focus.

"Is good. Nice pictures. Dimitri can be happy. OK. So Frank I am going to do this now. You make ready now. One . . . two . . ."

Frank screwed his eyes shut and waited on a world of wall to wall pain.

It is sometimes said that all publicity is good publicity. In fact it is said quite often. The benefits of publicity had been conclusively proved as well over five hundred people had turned out to fill the coffers of the Istanbul travel fund on the back of Jenn's homage to the past. By eleven-thirty the money was all counted and stowed away in Mickey's backpack. Next stop was the pub and several celebratory pints. And the next day was to be all about travel agencies and plans. Eric leaned back in his chair with his hands behind his head and a cigarette dangling from his lips.

"Plenty enough then lads?"

"More than. How was the bar?"

"The bar was spot on lads. Loads of shorts and mixers, which are the ones that add up. A good night was had by all. You know, you were pretty good out there. This a one off or can we expect the big comeback?"

Mickey grinned. "We're just taking each game as it comes. So there's no point thinking about Top of the Pops and videos with glamorous birds in bikinis. We're just doing like the gaffer says and focusing on Milan on Wednesday night."

Outside the air was warm and the sky all full of stars. Life wasn't just looking up. Life was taking off.

"We never made a video before Mickey."

"No. That's right enough."

"Never got on Top of the Pops neither."

"Never say never though, hey Tonto."

"Which song would we do for birds in bikinis Mickey?"

"I think I'll have to write one, mind you . . ."

Fast steps. Trainers on paving stones. Running. An empty street. Bang.

And one theory was proved and one theory was disproved.

The theory that was disproved was the theory that all publicity was good publicity. Jenn's efforts had filled both the Berlin Club and the cash bag. They had also attracted the attention of Keith Taylor who lived around the corner from Tonto and went by the nickname 'Skull'. The nickname wasn't greatly imaginative and referred to Keith's choice of hairstyle, which was basically the shaved to the bone look. Keith was the leader of a gang of four who were tightly bound by a shared view of the world. They co-habited in a squat and enjoyed speed and cans of strong lager. They had swastika tattoos on various parts of their bodies and they were signed on to the view that Hitler's Holocaust was: (a) greatly exaggerated and mostly made up by the Jewish Media and (b) even if it did actually happen then it was no bad thing and it served the hook-nosed Yids right.

Mickey and Tonto had been involved in a couple of altercations with Skull and the gang in the local pub. These could easily have been about contrasting political opinions, but the cause had in fact been football. Because each of the shaven-headed followers of the Fuhrer also had tattoos of the Everton badge to go with the Swastikas.

So it was that a theory was proved right. Tonto's theory that you had to look out for the Evertonians. Always. Skull was a woeful specimen of humanity in all respects, but he wasn't remotely thick. Quite the opposite. And he worked out a plan to suit the needs of the night. He knew where the gig was on. He had a good idea when it would end. He knew Mickey and Tonto would be emerging at some stage with the cash from the night. And all this knowledge made planning how to relieve them of the cash a relatively simple affair.

The plan involved waiting for them to come out of the Berlin. Then kick their heads in. Then take the money. And that was exactly how the plan went. They waited. They kicked in heads. And they took the money. And it was all over in under a minute.

Mickey was flat on his back staring up into the stars which only minutes earlier had seamed like a million beacons of hope. He didn't really want to move. His brain tried to identify where things hurt the most. His nose was pretty bad and the sticky feeling around his mouth told him it was bleeding. There had been a couple of booted kicks to the stomach and he had fallen badly. But it was soon clear that this wasn't Wigan revisited. This time it wasn't going to mean a few weeks in hospital. Not that it mattered much because all the consequences were slamming home one by one. No cash. No road. No match. No Lucy. Liverpool win the European Cup and Mickey McGuire's life goes down the toilet. Again.

He took his eyes away from the stars and turned his head to see how Tonto was faring. He seemed to be doing OK. He was sitting and rubbing his head and looking rather bemused with life. But there was nothing all that unusual about that.

"Told you, didn't I Mickey? Told you about the Evertonians."

"Yeah. You did Tonto. Told me for years."

"I think they've busted my guitar as well . . ."

Tonto's flow was broken by the sound of Mickey's phone, which had been left unstolen in his pocket.

"For Christ's sake . . ." He dug it out and hit receive.

"Yeah."

"That you Mickey?" Frank. Frank sounding like he'd never heard him before. Not ever.

"Frank?"

"Mickey. Come round to the flat will you. Quick like. I mean real quick."

"But Frank, me and Tonto, we've just . . ."

"Please Mickey. Just come. I need you to come."

What in the name of hell was going on?

"OK. Give us ten minutes."

He hauled himself to his feet and gave Tonto a hand up. What could it be? Frank had sounded terrible. Something really bad must have happened. But what? He was at the flat. What the hell could have happened at the flat? He wiped at his face with his sleeve and covered it in sticky red. Bollocks. No point in thinking about it.

"That was Frank. He needs us to go to his flat."

"OK." No explanations needed for Tonto. He bent down and collected his ruined guitar with a troubled frown. "Let's go then."

Ten minutes would have been right on a normal night, but they were a pair of walking wounded and it took them over quarter of an hour to reach the front door to the block. Mickey buzzed.

"That you Mickey?"

"Yeah."

"Come on up. And look. You best brace yourselves like. It's not pretty up here . . ."

"How . . ."

"Don't ask. Just come up."

The door was open when they got there. The first thing Mickey noticed was all the blood on the floor. Then there was Frank sitting at the table guzzling whisky straight from the bottle. He had his hand on some sort of piece of wood.

It was only when he got right up close did Mickey see that the hand was nailed onto the wood by six inches worth of steel.

"Oh Christ Frank . . ."

His brother spoke through clenched teeth. Already his words were slurring on the back of a good half bottle of Bells.

"Get a grip Mickey. You need to hold it together. Here. Have a swig of this and calm down."

Tonto was looking on with more confusion than normal.

"They've nailed your hand onto that piece of wood Frank."

"That's right Tonto."

"Was it the Evertonians Frank?"

"No. Not the Evertonians. Not them."

"The Evertonians took our money Frank. And they busted my guitar."

Frank took the bottle back and gulped down some more.

"Right. Go to the kitchen. Cupboard under the sink. Pliers. I need you to pull this bastard out Mickey."

"We can't pull that out Frank. No way. You need a hospital. Look. I'm calling an ambulance . . ."

"No!!" Frank's voice snapped across the room like a rifle shot on a frosty morning. Again he closed his eyes and tried to calm himself. "Mickey. You can't do that. It isn't an option. I really need you help me. I need you to pull this out. I really need you to do this."

Mickey stood for a moment and looked hard into his brother's eyes and for the very first time in his life he saw real desperation.

"Right. Whatever."

He found the pliers and then Frank stuffed the towel back in his mouth and nodded. Tonto held Frank's arm whilst Mickey pulled and after a tortuous five minutes the nail was clear and lying in the blood pool on the floor. Frank kept the towel in his mouth and his eyes rolled up into the top of his head as he poured the remainder of the whisky over both sides of the wound. He then got Mickey to bring a First Aid kit and talked him through dressing the wound. Eventually the hand was bandaged and Frank half-staggered over to the sofa where he collapsed.

"I'm in trouble Mickey. Real trouble."

Mickey sat down next to him whilst Tonto pushed blood around the wooden floor with some kitchen roll.

"I kind of noticed. Was this Eddie?"

Frank shook his head. "No. Eddie knows nothing about it."

"So who?"

"A Russian called Dimitri Zarkhov. Well not himself. His lads. Two of them."

"Why?" Mickey's voice was flat. He stared ahead and waited for some talk about a drug deal gone bad or money unpaid. The answer surprised him.

"Ivana."

"What. The girl from Siberia?"

"Yeah. Dimitri's a Mafia type. Sells smack to Eddie. That's why he came over. He brought Ivana and a couple of other birds. She wanted to see the city. Wanted a tour. Wanted to do the fish and chips at Pier head thing . . ."

His voice trailed away and Mickey saw tears on his cheeks. The last time he had seen Frank cry he had been three and Frank had been six.

"Is she all right Frank?"

"They said so . . . said as long as I stayed away from Istanbul . . . said I shouldn't have put my hands on her . . . that's why . . . said Dimitri liked her . . . liked her best of all of them . . . ."

He took a handful of painkillers from Tonto who had retrieved them from the cupboard in the bathroom.

"Shit. I'm slipping Mickey. Going . . ."

He forced himself to sit up and rubbed at his face with his good hand.

"Look. There's more. I can't stand to ask you this Mickey . . . I have to . . . if it wasn't for Ivana, I wouldn't . . . you know I wouldn't . . . ."

His eyes slid closed and his head sank to his chest. Mickey tapped his cheeks and brought him back.

"Tell me Frank. You're all right."

Frank sat forward and forced himself to hang on to consciousness for a while longer.

"There's a drop. Glasgow. Tonight. If I don't do it Eddie will find out. If Eddie finds out, I'm stuffed Mickey. OK. Fair enough. Serves me right, I know. But Ivana's going to be waiting. Two o'clock. Day after the match. The Blue Mosque. So I need to keep it together. I need you to take me Mickey. To drive me."

"What. To Glasgow? Piss off Frank. You're not fit for Birkenhead."

This seemed to wake Frank up some.

THE LONG AND WINDING
ROAD TO ISTANBUL

"But can't you see Mickey. I've got to go. If I don't go I won't make it to the Blue Mosque. I can't just leave her there Mickey. Just standing there . . ."

Mickey lit a cigarette and felt the whole thing start over. History and fate. History. A chemist's shop with a tiny back window. Fate. A car with Lucy in the back. Mickey and Lucy and Frank and Eddie. So many years gone by and here they were all back at the start line.

"Just tell me where I need to go and what to do Frank. I'll take Eddie's smack." Frank was so drunk by now that his words were all but unintelligible.

"I don't know how to thank you Mickey . . . honest . . . ."

"Frank. Shut up with the sentimental shite. I'm not in the mood. Just give me the details."

Frank ran him through how it worked and Mickey wrote it down carefully.

"The thing you need to remember is that all of this is just routine. I make the run every month. The only way anything is going to go wrong is if you do something stupid that makes you stand out. The skill is to make it boring. Ordinary. Just another night."

One of the reasons that Eddie had purchased the flat was the small doorway in the back of the block, which led out to a yard where all the bins were kept. A service road ran up to the gate of the yard for the bin wagon to use once a week. When Frank made a delivery run, he left the lights on in the flat until timers knocked them off one by one at just after one o'clock. Any watcher killing the boring hours outside would see plenty of evidence that Frank McGuire was retiring to another night on his own after a quiet night in. There was a gap in the fence half way along the service road that opened onto a building site where yet more up-market flats were under construction. Beyond the building site it was a short walk to a twenty-four hour garage where a car was waiting with the load on board.

Frank completed his directions on how to find the rendezvous point in Glasgow. It was all straightforward enough. Motorway all the way to a junction, that was a mile from an industrial estate. Mickey was to call a number when he was five minutes away and the door would be open and ready. The gear was in the boot. Ten Kilos. They would have the cash on a table. £400,000. It would be in £5000 bundles. He was to count one and then count the bundles. Then put the whole lot in the holdall in the boot. Then come back.

"You'll be in and out in twenty minutes tops. There's no need to worry about it. They're not nutters or anything. They want to buy a product and they buy it all the time. It's just normal. They'll be expecting me of course, but it won't be any big deal. Once you're done, just drive back and put the car back in the garage. That's it." He glanced up at a clock on the wall. "Midnight. Three hours there. Half an hour tops to do the business. Three hours back. Make a couple of stops and grab some breakfast or something. That will put you back in town just as the traffic is building. You got everything?"

"Yeah. I've got it Frank. I'll see you tomorrow." Mickey's voice was flat and resentful. The thought of what he was doing disgusted him. The ten kilos of heroin would turn into a million pounds of misery on the streets of Scotland. A million pounds. Most would be stolen from mums and dads and grandparents and wives and brothers and sisters. Some would come from shoplifting. Some from prostitution. And once the batch was all used up, some would be sweating and vomiting in the cells. And some would have caught Hepatitis C. And no doubt one or two would have overdone it and gone the same way as Midge. A million pounds worth of damage and he was about to deliver it because when it came down to it he wasn't about to let his brother take a fall.

He took the keys and was ready to leave.

"I'm getting out Mickey. I'd made my mind out already. Before all this."

Mickey shook his head. "Lads like you don't get out Frank. The likes of Eddie don't allow it. You're on a lifer."

"Trust me. I'm getting out. Just get me through tonight Mickey. Give me time."

Mickey shrugged. "I'll give you time Frank. Come on Tonto. Let's hit it mate."

The back door and the path were easily found. The black BMW was waiting just like Frank said it would be. Instead of heading straight out of the city, Mickey took a detour to the flat.

"I'll only be a few minutes Tonto. I'll grab a few tunes. We might as well enjoy the sound system."

Five minutes later he was back and an old Clash CD took them out through Bootle and onto the M58. It was routine. Just like Frank had said it would be. Once they were on the M6, Mickey worked out how to use the cruise control and set it to seventy. The Clash became the Style Council as they passed Wigan, and at Kendal the baton was passed to the Housemartins. By the time they cleared Carlisle the wind was up and the wipers swept thick layers of rain from the windscreen. As the blue signs announced that Motherwell was on the right, Mickey slotted in Travis and gave his friend a smile.

"Big Celtic fans this lot. Seems appropriate."

"Kenny Dalglish came from Celtic, Mickey."

"That he did Tonto. That he did."

The telephone conversation was just a few words long. Three in fact.

"Five minutes."

"Right."

The warehouse was easily located and the roller shutter door was up and ready. It was three thirty in the morning and the rain was cascading from the Glasgow sky. The industrial estate was deserted. The whole world was deserted.

Mickey drew the car into a space between piles of cardboard boxes and three men waited by a table.

"All right lads."

"So where's Frank?"

"Couldn't make it."

"So who was it then?"

The code. A bit of Glaswegian mischief. Who scored the winner for Celtic at Anfield to knock Liverpool out of the UEFA Cup.

"John Hartson."

"That'll do us. Package?"

Mickey popped the boot and passed a travel bag.

"OK. You count, I'll test."

Mickey did it like Frank had suggested. One batch. Two-hundred-and-fifty, twenty pound notes. Eighty batches. By the time he had finished the count the heroin had been tested and approved.

"We done then?"

Mickey nodded, amazed at how calm he felt about the whole thing.

"We're done."

"Send my regards to Frank then."

"I will."

He reversed out carefully and by the time he had turned the car around in the yard outside, the roller shutter door was already down.

"We going back now Mickey?"

"Yeah."

It took Lucy a long time to find sleep that night. Her cottage was on the side of a hill that faced out across a valley. Beyond the valley were high mountains, then the Irish Sea, then Ireland, and then thousands of miles of grey Atlantic. The weather was pounding in from the boiling waves of the ocean and the rain was loud on her bedroom window. Ever since she was a little girl she had loved the feeling of being warm in her bed whilst a storm raged outside. It had been one of the reasons that she had chosen the cottage.

A branch from a hawthorn bush tapped erratically at the glass and kept her brain ticking over. The next morning she would drive to Penrith station and take the train to London. And on Sunday morning she would take a plane to Istanbul to start filming the red invasion. It looked like Mickey was going to be a part of the invasion. She couldn't believe that the Spion gig wouldn't have drawn a crowd after the article in the paper. How many? Three hundred would have been plenty. A smile played on her lips as she thought of Mickey and Tonto making their preparations. When would they leave? Maybe tomorrow. Maybe they would be heading out of Liverpool as she took the train south. All roads lead to Istanbul. As she drifted into sleep she had an image of thousands and thousands of Liverpudlians on the journey across Europe. She would be one. And Mickey would be another. And maybe at last things could go right for once.

She woke as the window framed the battleship grey of a wet dawn. A car? Maybe. Odd. Traffic was all but non existent, especially at this time. She strained her ears over the sound of the wind and she thought she could hear the sound of an engine heading back down the valley. And then sleep reached out and took her.

Harry Walton was on his tenth cup of coffee of the night and he had just returned from his sixth piss. His radio was on low and the newspaper was read. Half of a sandwich was left for later on and a packet of rich tea biscuits was half eaten. Just after five. Three more hours and he could get his head down. In front of him there was a map of Northern England on the screen of his computer and a small light was blinking it's way down the blue line that was the M6. Past Carlisle now. Penrith next. Kendal. Lancaster. Preston. Wigan. Right and down through Skelmersdale and back to the garage. Routine. Same old boring routine. But Eddie always kept an eye on things. He sat up and gave his eyes a rub as the light moved away from the blue line. This was new. What was happening? Probably needed a piss. Or a crap. It moved a few miles and then stopped. Five minutes. Back moving. Headed east again. Back to the blue line. Back heading south. It was strange. It was something that had never happened before. He would report it to Eddie in the morning. But he wouldn't wake him up about it. No way. The morning would be fine. It was certain to be nothing. All there was up there was millions of miles of bugger all.

The sound of the telephone dragged Frank out of sleep and back to a world of throbbing pain. The whiskey had worn off leaving only an overwhelming urge to throw up and his hand felt like it was in a toaster. He sat up and reached for the handset. The number display said 'Mickey Mobile'. Clock. Almost six. At least he'd slept for four hours.

"Hiya Mickey. Everything go OK?"

His brother's voice sounded strangely detached. "You best sit down Frank because you're not going to like this."

Frank sank back and braced himself. What the hell had gone wrong?

"Go on."

"On the table there's an address and a mobile number. It Lucy's. She's got a cottage in Cumbria. It's about twenty minutes from Penrith."

Frank frowned. So what if Lucy had a place in Cumbria? His brain was fighting to get clear of the thumping headache that was the residue of all the medicinal whisky. Mickey kept up his monotone. He sounded almost like a recorded message.

"You said you wanted out Frank. So get out. There is a shed at the side of the cottage. Inside you'll find a cardboard box full of tools and stuff. Look at the bottom. We've left half the money. It should be enough for you to get out . . ."

"Mickey! What in the name of Christ are you telling me . . . ."

"Me and Tonto got done over last night after the gig. We lost it all Frank, every penny. I've got one chance Frank. After twenty sodding years and I've got one chance. So I'm going."

"What do you mean going? Bloody hell, Mickey slow down will you, I'm all over the shop here. Going where?"

"We're going to Istanbul Frank. Me and Tonto. It's where Lucy is. You can leave a message with her. I'm not talking about it . . ."

"Mickey!!!!!!"

"Bye Frank."

"Mickey, there's a . . ."

But already the line was dead.

For a moment he stared at the handset in complete incomprehension. It wasn't true. It couldn't be true. Even his stupid, dozy pratt of a brother wouldn't rip Eddie off. He couldn't. Surely he couldn't. But there had been something so utterly weird about the voice on the other end of the phone. And with a horrible certainty it dawned on Frank McGuire that his little brother had taken £400,000 of Eddie's money so that he could go to the Champions League Final in Istanbul.

"Christ all bloody mighty."

He lit a cigarette and forced his thoughts into some kind of order. Number one. Money. Money and immediate consequences. Lucy.

He stood up too fast and only just made the toilet to throw up a large amount of the scotch. Cold water brought some kind of focus and he shovelled a handful of pain killers into his mouth and swallowed them down. The address and number were where Mickey had said they would be. He lit another cigarette and dialled. This wasn't about to be an easy call.

"Hello?"

"Lucy?"

"Yes. Who's this?"

"It's Frank Lucy. Frank McGuire."

A long pause. It had been a long time.

"Hello Frank." Careful. Suspicious.

"Where are you Lucy?"

"Frank, I'm not sure that is anything to do with you."

His turn to pause. Nightmare.

"Will you give me a few minutes Lucy. Just listen OK. Don't interrupt. You're going to be really pissed off."

An edge now. "Look Frank, I'm sorry, but I have a train to catch. We'll have to do this another . . ."

"Lucy. You need to listen. Believe me."

"Oh for God's sake. OK then. Three minutes and that's it. I'm not missing my train."

"Thanks. OK. Last night I was badly injured. I couldn't make the Glasgow run. I couldn't tell Eddie. So I needed someone who could do it in a hurry. I asked Mickey."

"You WHAT . . . ?"

"Look. Lucy. Please just listen. I can explain better later. When there's more time. Now you just need the facts."

"Go on." Now her voice was all ice.

"He's just rung me. He's . . . Jesus Lucy . . . he's not coming back. With the money."

"What do you mean not coming back?"

"To Liverpool. He's legged it."

Another pause. He could feel her trying to work things out.

"And this is my brother's money, yes?"

"Yes."

"How much Frank?"

"£400,000."

"Oh please God no."

"There's more Lucy. I told him that I was getting out. Before he left. He called me to say that he has left half the cash in a shed by your place. It's in a box. Under some tools."

"In MY shed!!"

"So Mickey says."

"Well if you're calling for me to bring it to you then there's no way in hell . . ."

"I'm not. Look I tried to tell him Lucy. But he cut the line. Says he won't talk to me again."

"Tell him what Frank? Please try and be clear."

"About the car. The BMW. It's got GPS fitted. Eddie gets one of the lads to watch the car all the way there and all the way back when there's a drop on."

"So?"

"So they'll have seen the car turn off the M6 and come to your place. Maybe they thought nothing of it at the time, but they sure as hell will once the car carries on past Liverpool. I don't give a damn what you do with the cash. Chuck it in a river for all I care. I just wanted to warn you that's all. You need to get away from there. All hell's about to break loose."

Now the pause was much longer. At last she spoke and her voice was much smaller. Afraid. Confused.

"Why has he done this Frank?"

He sighed. "Do you know anything about this gig of his? Well him and Tonto."

"I read about it, yes. On the internet. There was a piece about it in the Echo."

"It was last night. I went for an hour. They had over five hundred tickets sold. More than enough. But they got mugged outside. I never knew Lucy. He never said a word when he came round. He's only just told me now. If he'd have said I wouldn't have . . . That's why you see. To go to Istanbul. For a stupid football match. He's signed his bloody death warrant for a game of football. Jesus Lucy."

A new voice this time. As flat has Mickey's had been.

"It wasn't for a football match Frank."

"What do you mean?"

"It was for me. I gave him an ultimatum you see. I said that it was his last chance. If he wanted us to be together he had to make it to Istanbul. To the stadium. And call me on the mobile. I wanted to make him break free Frank. I wanted to . . . Oh God what have I done . . ."

He couldn't think of a thing to say. He was still working on it when she spoke again. "This is down to you and me Frank. Agreed?"

"Well. Yes. I suppose so."

"We keep him safe Frank. No matter what it takes. Agreed?"

"Yes. Of course. Safe."

"Knutsford Services. Café on the southbound. Two hours. You'll be there?"

He felt the throbbing pain shooting up his left arm and thanked his lucky stars his car was an automatic. "I'll be there."

Harry Walton's eyes were only just hanging on. The blip on the screen was past Charnock Richard now. A few miles and he would tune right onto the M58. Then it would be half an hour and he could hit the sack for a few hours. More coffee. And the other half of the sandwich before it dried out completely. He did stretches whilst the kettle boiled and added a third sugar for luck before going back to the computer with the morning paper which had hit the mat whilst he was stirring his cup. He was in the process of turning to the back page when he noticed that the blip was past the M58 and still heading south.

Strange. Maybe there had been an accident or something on the M58. He started reading but couldn't quite drag his attention from the screen. If the M58 was closed or something the next obvious choice would be the East Lancs Road through Haydock. Two more junctions. Five miles or so. But the junction came and went and Harry started to feel a prickle of anxiety. Normally he wouldn't have been all that perturbed, but this was the second strange thing that had happened on the return journey. There had been the unexplained diversion into the Cumbrian Hills at half past five.

And now this. There was a cut across to the M62 which was the next option. Nothing. Only the M62 left now. No. The blip kept straight on headed due south. And Harry knew it was time to call Eddie.

"What?"

"Something not right boss. He's missed all the turn-offs and he's still going south."

"How far south?"

"He's on Thelwall now."

"Stay on the line."

Eddie picked up his mobile and flashed up Frank's number. *'The Vodaphone you are calling may be switched off.'*

He kept hold of his temper. Maybe there was an explanation but alarm bells were going off all through his head.

"Harry. Was there anything else?"

"There was something. He turned off the motorway at five. Went into Cumbria a bit. Stopped for a couple of minutes. Then he went back to the M6."

"And you didn't think to tell me?"

Harry was suddenly very cold. "I didn't want to wake you boss."

"You didn't want to wake me. Well of course not Harry. I MEAN IT'S ONLY FOUR HUNDRED BASTARD GRAND ISN'T IT YOU COMPLETE MORON!!!"

"Sorry boss."

"Sorry? Christ if this is what I think it is, you're going to be more than sorry Harry. You're going to wish you'd never been born. Keep watching the screen. I want to know every movement. And I mean

EVERY movement. You got that?"

"Yes Boss."

Eddie stared at the walk around phone for a long minute then screamed loud enough to make his throat raw and hurled the phone through his study window. The commotion brought his wife racing in from the kitchen looking anxious in her dressing gown.

"Eddie . . . is everything all right Eddie . . ."

He turned to her with a look she had never seen before. It was a look that went all the way down to her toenails.

"Get out."

"But Eddie . . ."

"I SAID OUT!! CAN'T YOU UNDERSTAND ENGLISH YOU STUPID BITCH!!"

For a moment she just stood there frozen by the shock of the sheer violence in his voice. On his face. In his eyes. Then she turned and fled to the bedroom to throw clothes into an overnight bag. Five minutes later she had dragged her two sons from their beds and set out for her mother's house in Alderley Edge.

Eddie took no notice of the sounds of their departure. They could wait. More consequences. So the silly bitch thought that was bad. He'd see about that. And those two jumped-up sons. It was time to crack the whip. But not yet. First things first. The next call put two cars with six of his guys on the road. He told them to head south and not to worry about getting a ticket. In between calls, he got updates from Harry.

8.32. Sandbach Services.

8.43. Keele Services. Thirteen miles in twelve minutes. Frank was playing it cool then. Steady seventy and not risking getting a pull. How far was he headed? No way of telling. The boys were out of town and flying up the M62. Thirty miles behind. He just hoped Frank was going a long way. Far enough for the distance to close.

By 8.45 Anders Veervott had heard enough. More than enough. It had been four months. Long hard hours of watching and waiting and listening. Waiting for a chink of light. The coal yard and the Russian had been the first break. The Chief Constable had been very pleased with that. But after that there had been nothing.

And now the man had gone crazy. It wasn't hard for Anders to work out what was going on. The man called Harry was watching a satellite tracking device. The name 'Frank' had come up. No doubt Frank McGuire. McGuire was obviously on his way back from making a drop. It must have been from up north because Harry had mentioned a detour into Cumbria. And now instead of returning to Liverpool, Frank McGuire was heading south. With £400,000 in cash. And Eddie Tate had gone clean ballistic and his wife and boys had scuttled away in terror. Two chasing cars had been dispatched and Tate was receiving constant updates on the pursuit.

The Chief Constable was all ready to leave his house for his regular golf game at Hillside when the South African had caught him in the hallway. At first he was angry at the interruption to his day off, but the anger was very short lived indeed. As he digested the facts of Eddie Tate's bad morning a smile spread all the way across his face.

Pay dirt.

He told Veervott that he would be with him in half an hour and asked him to text over all the number plates of all known Tate vehicles . . .

"So Eddie. At last we've got a sight of your short and curlies. Time to make you dance a bit."

"Sorry dear?"

His wife had emerged with his waterproof jacket which had been left forgotten in the airing cupboard.

"Oh nothing. I won't need the jacket thanks."

"But it looks like rain. And the forecast wasn't good at all."

"No golf this morning my dear. This morning I have a much better game to play."

"Oh. How nice."

The text dropped into his phone as soon as he was through with leaving a 'no show' message for his golf partners. He pulled over and got hold of the head of traffic who duly noted the numbers and ran them. Both cars were big BMW's. Perfect. Good solid German technology that was good for 130 mph. He gave instructions for every unmarked car they had to get to the end of the M62 to look out for them. Half an hour later as he listened to the Tate house with Veervott, the news came in that both cars had been stopped. One was clocked at 112 mph. The other had hit 118 mph. There were six very pissed off tough guys all on their way to local nicks.

Through his earphones the Chief heard Eddie Tate's temper grow and spread like a mushroom cloud as he tried to get hold of the pursuit cars. A call came in from the team he had sent round to Frank's flat.

"Nothing boss. It's deserted here. Something must have gone down though."

"Tell me."

"There's blood. Loads of it. There's a sort of lump of wood. Square like. And it's covered. And the table and the floor."

"Check the phone."

"Hang on. OK. Dialled numbers. Number one. 01768 753 245. Nothing else."

"Times."

"The first call was 8.27."

"Do 1471."

"Telephone number 07770 443483 called today at 8.22 am."

"Check the phone memory. See if you can find either of the numbers. Ring me back."

Eddie forced himself to stay calm. There was no point smashing things up and losing it. He needed to think. He needed to work it out. Somebody had been in the flat at 8.22. Who? At that time the car was passing the last junction into Liverpool. So was it Frank in the car? Or was it someone else? Blood. Lots of blood. Had someone broken into the flat and taken Frank hostage? Tortured him for the password and sent someone up to Glasgow for the drop? Was 01768 753 245 something to do with it. 01768? What code was that?"

He dialled 118500 and asked. Penrith. Cumbria. As in the five in the morning detour. Cumbria. Had they dropped off the cash there? Maybe. The next call was to one of the policemen on the payroll.

"It's Eddie."

"I told you never to call me at home . . ."

"Shut up and listen. Got a pen? Good. Write. 01768 753 245. Where is it and who is it? Ten minutes and it pays a grand. I'll ring you back"

"Come on Eddie, that's well out of order, I'm on a day off here . . ."

But the policeman was talking to himself. The Tate Corporation didn't do annual leave.

Eddie was about to telephone Harry again, but decided to call round instead. It was only ten minutes. He grabbed hold of his car keys and left the house with a hefty slam of the door.

In a van two streets away Anders Veervott let his colleagues know that Tate was on the move. Next to him the Chief Constable of Greater Merseyside reached into his inside pocket and took out a cigar. Once upon a time he had been a two pack a day cigarette man. Now he was down to a cigar a week, a treat he generally saved for the golf club bar after his Saturday round. This week it was the cramped confines of the back of a van and he couldn't care less. He raised an eyebrow to Veervott who shrugged.

"You pay the bills man."

As the policeman lit up and took the smoke down into his lungs the van started to move, following a flashing icon on a map of the city.

Harry heard the doorbell and gritted his teeth. He had just spent half an hour wishing that he could wind back the clock and have his time over. Why hadn't he rung? Just one lousy phone call. But he hadn't and now Eddie Tate was at his front door and everything was going to hell.

"Boss. Look, I'm really sorry . . ."

"Shut it Harry. Where is he?"

"Going past Stafford."

"Still south then. Where's the bastard headed?"

He pulled a new mobile out and tried the pursuit team again. Nothing. What the bloody hell was going on? Unbelievable. Next he returned the call to his police contact.

"Have you got it?"

"Yes. Got a pen? OK. Birch Cottage. Overthwaite. Penrith. Cumbria. A Miss Lucy Mathews."

"Say that name again."

"Lucy Mathews."

Eddie stared at nothing in particular for a moment. It would have been less of a shock if the policeman had told him the cottage belonged to Nelson Mandela. Lucy. What on earth had Lucy got to do with all this?

"Stay by the phone. If you switch it off I'll cut your nose off and make you eat it, OK?"

"Now listen here . . ."

But the line was dead again.

CHELSEA – MAY 2005

"Got a fag Harry?"

"But I thought you'd given them up."

"Just give me a bloody fag will you. I need to think. And a pen. And some paper. Come on, move it will you."

Harry scuttled off and set his boss up at the kitchen table with a packet of Mayfair, an ashtray and an A4 pad and Bic.

"Want a brew boss?"

"Coffee. Black. Three."

He started to write it down so that he might make some sense of it. The drop must have gone OK or he would have heard. So the smack was in Glasgow and it had been paid for. The only way that could have happened was if Frank had either made the drop or told someone else what to do. There was a bunch of blood in Frank's flat. Torture? Maybe. The car had taken a dawn detour to a cottage in the Lake District. Lucy's cottage. He could hardly stand to write it down. A betrayal that involved both Frank and Lucy. He sucked in smoke and forced his mind to remain focused. Someone had been at the flat at eight in the morning because they had received a call. Mickey McGuire's mobile. Frank and Lucy and Mickey. And Eddie. The four of them. Tied in. Linked. And an eerie feeling crept up his back as he remembered the botched raid on the chemist shop all those years ago. Eddie and Lucy. Mickey and Frank. And here were all the names on his A4. And a car was cruising past Stafford with £400,000 of his cash.

Where were the links? Franks's flat. A call in from Mickey. A call out to Lucy. The drop made in Glasgow. The car which Frank had the keys for. The drugs that Frank had the code for. And blood. Why blood?

So what next Eddie? He had terrible vibes about the lads who were chasing down the car. Once again he tried their mobiles. Nothing. And that meant that something must have happened. No answer on one was conceivable. No answer on both meant trouble. Which meant that the car was away and clear. But at least he knew where it was.

At least he knew where it was. Of course. Because he was tracking it just like he always tracked it. And Frank knew that better than anyone. So surely it wasn't Frank in the car. Because Frank would know full well that he was watching it all the way. If it had been Frank, he would have had another car waiting in Glasgow. And then Eddie would never have known about the visit to the cottage. And

211

THE LONG AND WINDING
ROAD TO ISTANBUL

Eddie wouldn't have had the first idea where the money was. But he had an idea. He could see it on the screen. So who was in the car?

He dialled the policeman again. "Take theses details down." He gave the make, colour and registration of the BMW. "I can give you an exact position of the vehicle at any time. I know you lot have CCTV on the motorway bridges. I need a picture of the car as it goes past. A good one. Good enough to ID who is driving."

"You're joking."

"If you can't pick up from the tone of my voice that I'm so beyond joking here then you need a lobotomy you cretin. Get the picture and get it quick. email it."

The email came in an hour later as the blip on the screen was approaching Rugby. The picture was far from perfect but it was good enough. Mickey McGuire and Tonto. In his car. With his money. Heading south. Two dead men.

He had spent the best part of two hours trying to second guess where the mystery driver might be headed. Now he knew. He knew because everyone who had read a copy of last Thursday's Echo knew where Mickey McGuire was headed. Spion had come out of obscurity to raise the cash to make the trip to the Champions League Final. For some reason they must not have raised enough. Because they had decided to steal his cash and his car and now they were headed south down the M1. And now another strand bound them all together.

Istanbul. Mickey had sung for his ticket. Eddie had seen Lucy on the tele talking about how she would be covering the red invasion. And Frank was to travel with him. Eddie and Lucy. Mickey and Frank.

All on the road to Istanbul.

Chapter 8
The Road to Istanbul
May 2005

"Are we not going back to the flat then Mickey?"

"No. We'll go straight there."

"To Istanbul?"

"To Istanbul."

Tonto considered this for a moment or two.

"I haven't got my lucky waistcoat Mickey."

"We're not going to need any luck for this one Tonto. It's in the bag mate. Written."

"Are we using the money from that factory then?"

Mickey nodded and lit a cigarette.

"Who's money is it Mickey? Is it Frank's money?"

A shake of the head. "No. It's Eddie's money."

"It's good of Eddie to help us out isn't Mickey. I thought we'd had it when those Evertonians beat us up."

"Eddie's a red. That's why he gave us the cash. He didn't want to see the Evertonians win out."

Tonto was very comfortable with this thought. It was essential that all reds maintained a constant state of alert against the Evertonians.

"I haven't got a toothbrush Mickey."

"We'll pick all that stuff up on the road. We can afford it can't we. We're travelling in style this time. Thanks to Eddie."

Picking up stuff like that on the way hadn't been something that had occurred to Tonto. It was a good job that Mickey was with him. Mickey had always been good at stuff like that.

"Do you think they sell guitars in Istanbul Mickey?"

THE LONG AND WINDING
ROAD TO ISTANBUL

"Best in the world last time I heard."

"You reckon Eddie would mind if I got myself a new one. Out of the money like. I mean it was them Evertonians that busted it wasn't it Mickey."

"I had a word about that. He said no problem. He said you should choose the best one in the shop. Hang the cost, he said."

And Mickey switched up the volume on Bob Marley and laughed as the big German car ate up the miles.

Frank arrived at the café first and took a double expresso to the smoking area. He didn't notice Lucy at first. The student Lucy he had last laid eyes on twenty years ago was long gone. The woman Lucy was thinner. Her face was a series of hard edges that were drawn with worry.

"Hi Frank."

"Can I get you a coffee or anything?"

"I'll have the same as you. You look terrible Frank."

She watched him make his way to the counter and saw the lines of pain on his face. He had a large bandage on his left hand and he obviously couldn't use it at all as he did all the work with his right.

"Here you go."

"You've hurt yourself. Is that a part of all this?"

He shook out a cigarette and lit. On the drive out from the city he had come to the conclusion that the only way forward was the truth. There was nothing left to keep covered up.

He nodded.

"So you better tell me then."

"Eddie's putting together a big deal at the moment. His biggest ever. He wants to buy his stuff at source. Well, as near as he can get."

" 'Stuff' being drugs?"

"Yeah. Heroin." He leaned forward and dropped his voice a notch even though there was no-one sitting within twenty feet of their table. "He's dealing with two outfits. One is a Bosnian outfit who source the smack. The second is Russian Mafia. They ship it. Eddie's bought a coal yard on the docks. The Russians deliver the gear as part of boatloads of Romanian coal."

"I fail to see the relevance in any of this Frank."

"Look. Just bear with me OK. There have been several meetings to set the whole thing up. First it was Vienna. Then Dimitri came to the Pool."

"Dimitri as in Russian Mafia, yes?"

"Yeah. Dimitri Zarkhov. Well he came with these three birds on his arm. You probably know the type. They looked like they'd walked straight off the cover of Vogue."

"I know the type." And she did. She knew them from various stories she had covered from the emerging countries of the old Eastern Block. She knew them from the bars where only western currency would do and the top men from the world of organised crime liked to show off their bling. Two years earlier she had done a story about the trade in young village girls from Romania and Moldova who were sold into prostitution in the west. She had seen plenty of Dimitri Zharkovs. And plenty of the young beauties who hung on to their coat tails.

"Well I went to collect them from Ringway airport. And he asked me a favour. He said one of the birds wanted a tour of the city. Said she didn't fancy hanging around the hotel and getting her hair done and that. So I took her . . ."

His voice trailed away as his mind was once again filled with the danger facing Ivana, even though Anton had said she was not to be hurt. Lucy's voice was more gentle now.

"I heard about her. Ivana. Yes?"

"Heard about her? I don't understand."

"Mickey told me. A strange Siberian beauty in a road outside Anfield. I gather she is something of a fan of Liverpool music. Spion in particular."

"It was unbelievable. There we were driving into the city and she started talking about 'Lovers Under Creamy Yellow'. I couldn't get my head round it. She wanted to do the fish and chips on Pier Head thing."

"And did you?"

A nod.

"And was it raining?"

"Pissing down."

She sat back and pushed a hand through her hair. The song again.

"She told Mickey to find me. She said that if a man wrote a song like that for her, then she would expect him to find her."

"I know. It obviously worked then."

"It did. Although when he found me we never got to speak. I had to dig him out in the end. Anyway, that's neither here nor there. You were telling me."

"We all met up a couple of weeks later. For the Juventus game. Second leg. In Turin. Dimitri asked me to take her again. We went to Milan. To this castle. Castello. And she told me about Francesco Sfortza. And Bianca. And we had pasta and Chianti."

"I get the drift. Did Mickey know?"

" Not until last night."

"What did you tell him?"

"I told him that Ivana is my Lucy. My oxygen."

This turned her crimson. "Anyway. We're ahead of ourselves. After Turin?"

"They all came back for the Chelsea game. The semi-final. This time we went back to my flat. Me and Ivana. We agreed that we were both going to get out. I have a cottage in Tuscany you see. Nobody knows about it. Not even Mickey. I said I'd arrange tickets from Istanbul."

"And something went wrong."

"Dimitri must have suspected. He must have had us followed. Seen us go to the flat like."

"And he wasn't happy."

Frank shook his head. "He sent his lads back. They came last night. Grabbed me in the car park."

"And?"

"They hurt me. For being with Ivana. They said I shouldn't have touched her."

"So they hurt the hand that touched."

He stared past her and the memory of the claw hammer and the blinding pain was back with him. He shuddered.

"Will you tell me?"

He shook his head. "You don't want to know."

She leaned across and took his good hand between hers. "You know the places I have been Frank. You know the things I have seen."

He was quiet for a moment. "They brought this big lump of wood with them. Square. They nailed my hand to it."

"Oh God."

"I was just about to make a drop for Eddie. To Glasgow. So I was completely stuffed. I couldn't let Eddie know what had gone on or there would have been no way I would have been able to make it to Istanbul. And Ivana is going to be waiting at the Blue Mosque on the day after the match . . ."

"So you needed someone else to make the drop. Someone who had nothing to do with my brother. Someone you could trust."

A nod.

"So you rang Mickey."

"There was nobody else. Jesus Lucy, you must know that if there had been another way, I would never have rung him."

"I think I know that."

"Well he came round with Tonto. I was more or less pissed out of my head by the time they arrived. I made him pull the nail out. With pliers."

The thought drained the colour from her face. "And what did he say when you asked him to make the drop."

"At first I didn't think there was a chance he was going to do it. You know how Mickey feels. Well course you do. Same as you isn't it. It was only when I told him about Ivana that he agreed. When I said she was my Lucy."

They were silent for a while, both trying to get a grip on the guilt.

"So he went."

"Both of them. Next thing I knew I was spark out and the phone was ringing. It was Mickey. He told me that they had been done over after the gig and all their money had been nicked. So he said that he was going to Istanbul on Eddie's money. Well, half of it. He told me he'd left the other half in your shed. Said I should use it to get out like I had promised." He put his head down and avoided her eyes. "He said it was his last chance Lucy. Said you'd given him a last chance. That he had to get to the stadium and call you. That's why he did it. It wasn't the game. Even our Mickey's not that daft."

Now he looked up and into eyes that were swimming with tears. "He'd do anything for you Lucy. You do know that I hope."

"Well I do now, don't I. Why the hell didn't I just behave like a normal decent human being and buy him a ticket and take him? Why did I have to be such a nasty clever bitch and set him a test? Jesus Frank, it's all my fault isn't it?"

"Our fault Lucy. Both of us. And we'll sort it. But we've got a few problems."

This brought a brittle sort of a laugh. "Oh really. And there was I thinking we were in the bloody pink. And what problems are these Frank?"

"He cut the line before I got the chance to finish talking to him. I've kept trying to ring, but his phone's switched off. My guess is that he won't switch it on again until he gets to the ground. The car he's in has a GPS system. It's the same with all the cars we use when a drop is made. Eddie gets one of the lads to watch it all the way there and all the way back again. It's in case anyone gets any ideas."

"So my brother is probably watching right now?"

Nod.

"And Mickey doesn't know?"

Head shake.

"What will Eddie be doing about it?"

"He'll have sent the lads out to catch them up. I guess Mickey will probably have an hour's start or so. Not enough."

Now there was real panic on her face. "He's going to kill him isn't he? Oh god Frank."

Her voice was rising and a few heads were beginning to turn. He put a sharp edge into his voice.

"Calm down. He's not dead yet and he's not caught yet. Now stay cool will you?"

"But it's hopeless Frank. There's nothing we can do."

"There is and we'll do it. Whatever it takes."

"Tell me."

He lit another cigarette. "I can do a trade with the Bizzies. Eddie's been their number one target for twenty years. I can give him to them on a plate. I know where all the bodies are buried Lucy."

The icy cold tone of his voice shocked her. "But what can the police do?"

"I know all the number plates of the cars the lads will be driving. The Bizzies can pull them. That will buy some time."

She considered this and he could see that she understood the logic. "How can I help?"

"I need your contacts. Eddie owns half the coppers in the city. I need to go all the way to the top. I'm almost certain that the Chief Constable's clean. I need his mobile number Lucy. Can you get that?"

"I think so."

"Well do it then."

She was reaching into her handbag for her phone when he remembered one more thing.

"What did you do with the money Lucy?"

She shot him a suspicious look. "I thought you said that you didn't care if I threw it in the river."

"Well, did you?"

"No. It's in the boot."

"Good. I have a feeling that hard cash might be something we're going to need over the next few days."

Sir Hubert Mattinson had enjoyed many good days in his twenty-year career in the police, not least the day when he had received confirmation that he was to be Greater Merseyside's next Chief Constable. The visit to Buckingham Palace to receive his knighthood had been pretty good as well. But he could seldom remember such a feeling of elation as he had enjoyed in the back of a cramped van with a sweaty South African geek, when he should have been striding the sandy fairways with the wind in his hair. Elation barely covered it. For years he had been haunted by Eddie Tate. He felt as if the man mocked him every time he fixed his uniform in the mirror before leaving the house in morning. For years he had found it hard to nod off to sleep because the image of Eddie Tate's smug, self-satisfied face wouldn't leave him. Eddie Tate at the races. Eddie Tate at a Cancer Relief dinner. Eddie Tate at some opening night at the theatre. And through all the years he had felt as if he had a stomach full of maggots because he never really knew how many of his officers enjoyed a holiday or a new car or a brand new kitchen care of brown envelopes care of Eddie Tate.

It seemed almost unbelievable that things had suddenly started to unravel. The sheer unexpected shock of what had happened had made Tate lose his famous cool. He had yelled at his wife. He had put a phone through the window. And all of it was on tape. Not that the tapes would be worth a candle in a court of law. That didn't matter. What mattered was that Hubert suddenly had a fly on the wall view of trouble in the heart of the Tate camp. And with a bit of luck he would be able to work away at the trouble until a few more cracks opened up.

Already he had six Tate heavies locked up on a variety of charges. Two drivers were dead and buried on speeding offences. Two others had been found to have heavy-duty knives on their person. The other two were being loosely held for six hours as aiders and abettors. He had made sure that none of them had access to a phone for as long as possible which meant that Eddie Tate was climbing the walls wondering what the hell was going on. Which of course made him madder and madder. And that was just perfect because the madder he got, the more likely it would be that he would make a big mistake.

Sir Hubert had decided that it was all going so completely swimmingly that he had climbed out of the back of the van and walked round the corner to a newsagents to treat himself to a second cigar. They didn't sell singles so he bought a pack of five King Edwards and decided to have a stroll and a smoke for a few minutes before resuming his place in the back of the van. There was no escaping the fact that he wasn't really young enough for long periods in cramped spaces. He found the entrance to a park and decided it would be a good place for ten minutes or so of stretched legs and fresh air.

By the time his phone rang he had found a bench and was watching a grandfather instruct his toddling grandson in the art of duck feeding. He checked the incoming number. None. Probably Veervott

"Yes."

"Is that Sir Hubert Mattinson?"

A Liverpool voice. Unfamiliar. "It is."

"It's Frank McGuire. I don't know if you know me . . ."

Know him! He had to be kidding. Hubert had been hearing his name for two hours, and not in any kind of flattering sense either. Instinctively he checked the surrounding park for signs of danger. Nothing. Two dog-walkers. One young mother with pram. One three-a-side game of football, with an average player age of nine.

"I know you. How did you get this number?"

"Initiative."

"What do you want?"

"What do you think? A deal."

Two magic words. A deal. It was hard to keep the excitement from bursting out in his voice.

"Then talk."

"My brother has just ripped off Eddie Tate this morning. I'm talking big time ripped off. Four hundred grand and a top end Beamer."

"I expect Eddie's thrilled to bits."

"Eddie's going to kill him. If he catches him that is. My brother is driving to Istanbul and Eddie has a SatNav tracking system on the car. He's watching him right now. When he catches him Mickey's a dead man."

"A deal, you said."

"Sure. If Mickey makes it to the stadium in Istanbul in one piece, I'll give you Eddie on a plate. Full testimony in court. The lot. I'll give you all you need to take him down. You know that I'm in a position to do that don't you Sir Hubert?"

Hubert was almost exploding. He would never know how he managed to keep his voice as calm as he did. "I know this."

"Good. So we can start with a trade. I'll give you the number plates of all the cars that may be chasing my brother right now. You organise for them to get pulled."

"So that's my end. What about you Frank? How are you going to prove that this isn't some big wind up?"

"Got a pen?"

Sir Hubert reached into his jacket pocket and pulled out notebook and pencil.

"I have."

"Wye-tech Ltd. Branch Rd Industrial Estate. Haydock. There is a locked room where they keep all the cleaning materials. It's the third door on the right when you go down the corridor to the office suite. At the back, there is a hidden hatch in the floor. You'll have to move all the bottles and boxes to find it. Look inside."

"And what will I find Frank?"

"Fifteen kilos of heroin. Over half a million quid's worth. I hope that's enough for you to accept my credentials."

"Bloody hell."

"I'll take that as a yes then shall I? I expect you'll know how to get a warrant on a Saturday morning. Let's say three hours shall we. I'll call you. Think about the number plates Sir Hubert. The heroin will give you nothing but Brownie points. There's not a thing there to tie it to Eddie. The only way you get Eddie is if I give him to you. If my brother winds up dead in a ditch somewhere, that isn't about to happen. So stop the cars Sir Hubert. My guess is that Mickey is heading to Dover. When he gets on the ferry you can organise a

CCTV photo. Later I'll give you an address to email the picture. Once I have proof that he's on board you will get another appetiser. That work for you?"

"That works for me."

"Splendid. We'll talk later then."

Frank killed the call and was surprised to find that he was actually shaking. Lucy was looking much happier now that they had found a way of achieving some kind of control over the situation.

"Let's hit the road shall we?"

"Let's."

"Bye the way, that really was very good indeed. I'm actually quite impressed. It must be all those courses Mickey told me you were taking."

"I'll take that as a compliment then."

By the early evening Eddie was in danger of becoming obsessed with Harry's computer screen. His eyes felt dry and scratchy and the blood was being chased around his arteries far too quickly as a result of caffeine overload. He had no real idea why he was still fixated on a tiny flashing blip. It hadn't moved for over an hour now and he knew exactly where it was going. The car had edged round London on the orbital motorway and then gone on down to the coast. Dover. Which meant a ferry. He had done lots of calculations to work out if he could get some guys to a port either side of the British Channel but it wasn't a possibility.

Eddie Tate wasn't used to being powerless but that was how he felt now. He knew who they were, he knew exactly where they were, and he was pretty sure that they had four hundred thousand pounds of his cash with them. And yet there wasn't a thing he could do about it. As the car had at last made it all the way round London and pointed itself in the direction of the white cliffs, he had sent Harry out to buy an Atlas. At first his idea was to work out where to fly some guys to wait to make an interception, but he had soon dumped the idea. There was no glaringly obvious route across Europe and the car would almost certainly use motorways. His lads were pretty effective in Bootle but he had little confidence that they would get their act together to find the BMW somewhere in Germany or Austria. Sending them would mean a guaranteed fiasco.

Things got more interesting when he turned to the map of south-east Europe. The Balkan Peninsular was like a giant funnel which was fat at the top and then got more and more narrow until it tapered away to a bottleneck with Istanbul at the very end. Here the roads seemed smaller and he knew that these were lawless places. There would be three options. The first would take them down through Austria and then on through Slovenia, Croatia, Bosnia, Kosovo, Macedonia and Greece. The second would use Serbia as a route down to Greece. The third would involve heading out further east and then swinging down through Hungary and Bulgaria.

There would be opportunities whichever of the three routes was chosen. Goran's territory was along the western route. And he had little doubt that Dimitri would know people in the old Soviet satellites to the east. This was where the opportunity would come. And after a very, very long day Eddie finally smiled. He would have the little toe-rag right where he wanted him.

As Eddie at last tore himself away from the computer screen, Lucy and Frank were checking into a hotel in London. On the drive down they had decided that it would be best if they stayed together and Frank joined the BBC team as they headed out to Turkey. Frank made the first use of the money from the shed to pay for his ticket. All that was available was the most extortionate First Class ticket that the airline dared to put a price on. Well, Eddie could afford it. Once he was booked he found an internet café and checked one of his Hotmail accounts. Sure enough there was mail waiting for him. Pictures. Blurred, but good enough. Images of Tonto and Mickey seen through the windscreen of a BMW as they boarded the ferry. He let out a slow breath of relief. At least they were out of immediate danger. It wouldn't be for long, but it meant that he and Lucy would at least have a day or two to decide what to do. Instead of going straight back to the hotel he decided to take a walk to try and clear the cobwebs and to take his mind of the jackhammer throbs that ran up his left arm from his perforated hand.

Something wasn't quite right. It had been nagging at him all the way down the M6 and it was still there. He knew that there was a piece of the jigsaw that had fallen off the table and bounced under the couch. The whole situation was such a chaotic mess that it was hard to put things in the right order. Maybe a walk might help. The streets were filled with small clutches of celebrating Arsenal fans. Their joy meant that Man United must have lost the FA Cup Final and finished the season empty handed. That must have helped Mickey with his journey. A few years earlier and the result would have been a surprise. But the days of strutting Mancunian dominance were finally starting to ebb. What was that he had just thought to himself?

The Mancs weren't what they were? No. Not that. Something else. A few years ago it would have been a surprise. Would have been a surprise. Should have been a surprise. And now he was on his stomach rooting under the sofa with a ruler, dragging out the missing jigsaw piece.

It was the Chief Constable. He had been far too cool. "I know you. How did you get this number?" That was what the man had said. As if he had almost been expecting the call. Well, that was plainly impossible. So maybe he had been hearing the name Frank McGuire already that day. So although the call was a surprise, then the name wasn't.

He lit up and took a fierce drag, determined to keep the train of thought going. The only logical reason why his name would have been a part of Sir Hubert Mattinson's Saturday morning was if the police had some sort of inkling as to what had gone down. Yes. Of course. It was obvious. Which of course was why he showed a similar lack of surprise when Frank had demanded that he pull the pursuit cars. The giveaway had been the man's reaction when Frank had given him the location of fifteen kilos of forty percent pure. Then the copper had almost jumped down the phone line. Because that WAS a surprise.

How could they know? A tout? Not very likely. The only ones in the know were Eddie, himself and Harry who would watch the SatNav. Was it Harry? No way. Harry would have an on the spot coronary at the very thought of touting up Eddie. He discounted the thought.

They had Eddie's place bugged.

Had to be. But Eddie had the place swept every fortnight. Had the sweep failed? Frank had harboured doubts for a few months that the team Eddie hired in from Birmingham were all mouth and too much Hollywood. Maybe the Bizzies had out done them? How would Eddie have reacted when Harry called to tell him that the car had missed the turning? That wasn't hard to guess. He would have gone plot lost plus ten. And maybe someone had been listening in on the whole thing. And they had contacted the Chief Constable direct.

Now that was interesting. Not just anyone would ring the boss on a Saturday morning. Which meant that whoever had made the call was pretty close to the top man. Maybe they even worked directly for him. This thought pulled Frank up in his tracks. Maybe the Chief had by-passed the rest of the local force and set up an operation himself. If it was the case, it would all make perfect sense. It wasn't much of a secret that Eddie owned more coppers than cars. So who would it be? Bizzies from out of town? Freelancers? What mattered was that the thing was unorthodox and that meant more opportunities.

Opportunities that he could turn to an advantage.

He tossed his cigarette and jumped a cab back to the hotel. Lucy opened her door and gestured him inside. A table was covered in preparation notes.

"You manage everything OK?"

"Sure. All booked. I need to make another call. I've got an idea."

"Are you going to tell me?"

"Just listen in. You'll get the gist."

He lit and dialled.

"Sir Hubert. Frank again. Picked up that smack yet?"

The policeman was clearly annoyed at Frank's tone. "All in good time. Did you receive my email?"

"I did thanks. The wonders of modern technology, hey Hube. Whatever next?" He reached into an inside pocket and passed a folded A4 print out of Mickey and Tonto boarding the ferry.

"Frank. If you ever call me Hube again this deal is dead in the water. Understood?"

Frank gave Lucy a wink. "Absolutely. Proper title only from here on in Sir Hubert. Now, I'm sorry to tell you that you've slipped up. Not a lot. All in all you've done great. It was only a small thing, but you know how it is with the small things."

"Please just get on with it McGuire."

"You weren't surprised enough. When I rang you. It was like you were half expecting it. I wondered if it was just that you were that down and cool, but when I gave you the location for the fifteen Keys you were like a kid who'd got a new bike at Christmas."

THE LONG AND WINDING
ROAD TO ISTANBUL

"What is all this about McGuire?" Sir Hubert masked his irritation with a firm, formal Chief Constable-ish sort of tone. The wretched man had read him like a book.

"I tried to work out how. The only reason you would have been talking about me was that you must have already known what had gone down before I called. That can only come from one of two places. A tout or you've got Eddie bugged. I'm closer than anyone to this. There's no way there's a tout. The only one it could be is Harry Walton and there's no way in a million years that Harry would have the bottle. Which means that you have our Eddie bugged. Not locals either. Someone from out of town who only reports to you. Am I right or am I right Sir Hubert?"

"You don't seriously expect me to comment do you McGuire?"

"Not seriously, but it would be nice. OK. Not to worry. I'll tell you how this needs to play and you can stop me if I'm out of order."

"Go on."

"The SatNav is on Harry Walton's computer. I know that Eddie has his place swept for electronics every two weeks. In fact they were in last Monday. And they found bugger all, which of course tells me that the boys you've brought in must be pretty shit hot. If they're that good, then they must be able to tap into Harry's system and log onto the SatNav. And that means that you can see where our Mickey is just like Eddie can. And you tell me. OK?"

There was a long silence at the other end as Sir Hubert weighed it all up. Mickey McGuire was an irrelevance when all was said and done. Frank McGuire was the key. Frank McGuire in a witness box in front of the whole wide world. Frank McGuire dropping the bombshells to send Eddie Tate down all the way to Bus Pass day and beyond. So the key was to keep Frank McGuire on board.

"There are possibilities I suppose. I will need Harry Walton's name, address and phone number please."

Frank did as asked.

"Don't forget what counts here Sir Hubert. All you need to think about is our Mickey turning up at the ground in one piece. So if you guys hear anything whatsoever, you are going to tell me. All of it. Word for word. You good to do that Sir Hubert?"

"Yes. I can do that."

"Excellent. Now then. Good boys get rewarded for doing well so get your pencil out and I'll give you another five Keys as a special treat."

When he was done Lucy gave him a quizzical look. "You look more satisfied than it seems like you should. It will be nice to see how they're getting on of course. But I can't understand why it is so important."

"Have you looked at a map yet?"

"She shook her head."

"I have. I've been trying to get into Eddie's head. I don't think there would have been time for him to get any lads over to meet Mickey off the boat. In fact I'm sure of it. The first teamers are banged up on speeding charges. He would have needed to send out the reserves and they wouldn't be up to it. No chance. Eddie knows that as well as I do. Likewise, there is no way of telling which way Mickey will go for the first part of the journey. And even if there was it wouldn't do him much good. Sending a bunch of Scallies across town to nut someone in Huyton is one thing. Getting them to the right place at the right time somewhere in Southern Germany is a completely different ball game. Eddie's lads didn't tend to finish at the top of the class."

"He must be missing you."

Frank screwed up his face at the thought. "Yeah, well life's a bitch isn't it? The thing is, he won't want Mickey to make it all the way to Istanbul either. That would be a right needle in the haystack job. Think about it. Two of them in the middle of forty something thousand Scousers on the piss. No chance."

"So he'll try to get them somewhere in between. I still don't understand Frank."

"You won't like it much when you do. Our Mickey was never much of a top-notcher at geography. He will have picked up whatever map he can find at a service station. My guess is that he will go as the crow flies. I can't see him thinking any further than that."

"OK. So?"

"That will mean something like Munich and Vienna on the motorways then down through Slovenia. Maybe he'll head for Belgrade and down, but the straighter route is through Bosnia and Montenegro."

"I know what you're thinking, but Bosnia really is much better now. I was there a few months ago. Of course there are problems with organised crime, but it is nothing like as bad as it was."

He grimaced. "You just said the magic words Lucy. Organised crime. As in Goran Jankovic."

"You've lost me."

"Goran is one part of Eddie's Golden Triangle. He puts the smack into the docks in Romania for Dimitri to bring in. I had to go out there to kick the deal off last year. He's based in some high rise flats in Sarajevo. Like the end of the bastard world it was. And his guys were like nothing I'd ever come across before. I've been around plenty of hard cases, but this lot were different. Cold-eyed killers. Christ alone knows what they got up to in the war."

Now Lucy was with the programme and white as a sheet. Frank may not have thought that Christ knew what went on in Bosnia, but Lucy did. Lucy knew it only too well and she had seen it. She knew the Goran Jankovics. The psychopaths who found their own little heaven in the primordial cruelty of those years.

"You think Eddie is going to call him, don't you?"

He nodded. She rubbed at her temple and considered. Her memory was of quiet roads running through empty, bomb-smashed towns and villages. Sure it was getting better and the place was being rebuilt, but it was still a dead zone. The SatNav would take Mickey and Tonto straight into an ambush and there would be nobody about to stop it. Suddenly she felt sick as images of the Balkans flashed through her mind, until the video stopped at the very last image from her trip. A field by a deserted farm. A rusted up tractor with weeds growing through the wheels. A couple of crows sitting on the roof of a barn with a gaping hole care of a shell from a T62 tank. A ridge of glowering pine trees throwing a blanket of cold silence over the valley below. A feeling of creeping evil that seemed to get into her clothes and hair like smoke from cheap cigarettes. Nobody lived in the village any more. Nobody had lived there from the day in 1994 when the Serbian militia had come to town and killed every last man, woman and child. Now she was covering the story of a British Army unit who were following-up on intelligence and digging up the field that had once been home to thirteen goats. Very quiet squaddies with spades and a small JCB. A tall Captain watching with folded arms and barely restrained tears as the long dead corpses came out of the ground one by one. For three nights he had told her that she was the girl of his dreams. Half in jest, half in the earnest. They had shared bottles of wine and things had very nearly moved on. Now he was a million miles away from a chat up line. Now he was staring horror straight in the face. In three hours they had brought out 36 bodies. In the end it would be over a hundred. Forensic experts from Sweden were trying to find if there was any trace left of the butchers. Maybe there might be something that could lead to a trial in The Hague at some future date. A half-noticed conviction for a nondescript baker or railway clerk from some small town in Serbia who had descended into becoming a monster.

Telling Lucy about Goran made Frank realise that knowing where the car was wouldn't really do any good at all. Maybe there might be some way of getting a message to Mickey or something to warn him off, although he hadn't the first idea how to do it. The thought of his brother being the wrong side of Goran's men made his spirits sink.

"You're right. No point in getting smug about knowing where they are."

"Any plans?"

"Hell I don't know. I'll have to try and do something, but I haven't a clue what. I'll need an army to go up against those mad bastards."

To his amazement she smiled.

"Best you leave it to me then."

"Lucy. I'm not sure if you were listening just then."

"Of course I was. I'm a very good listener. Always have been. You said that this man Goran is a very, very bad man and his camp followers are even worse. Oh, and you would need an army to do anything about them. So fine. You want an army? Leave it to Lucy. Armies are us."

"What are you on about?"

"A beau my dear. A suitor. A rather dashing young man who would dearly love me to be his girlfriend."

"Oh." He wondered if he was being a bit dumb. It wouldn't be all that surprising if he was. He was rattling with pain-killers and his hangover was still a long way from exiting stage left.

"I refer to Captain Jeremy Telford of the Royal Green Jackets. We met when I was doing a story in Bosnia a few months ago. The darling man fell head over heels in love with me and proposed after three days. He is the knight in shining armour type if ever there was one. Best of all, he has fifty men and three Warrior armoured cars at his disposal. So like I said. You want an army? I can do army. All part of the service."

"And he's there now is he?"

"Indeed he is. I only got an email a few days ago of him looking lovesick and not a little handsome on his big white armoured car."

"Bloody unbelievable."

"I would have thought that you more than anyone would know that it is never a good idea to underestimate the Tate family. My dear brother Eddie has got used to having it all his own way for too long. It's time he had a run for his money."

"Eddie. You are feeling good, OK?"

"Fine Goran. In the pink."

"In what pink is this you say?"

"Never mind. Just Liverpool talk. I'm well. And you? Ready for the match?"

"For sure. Ready. AC Milan they can die, I think. I hope for this."

Eddie pulled a face and felt like it was more than just a thousand miles that separated them. Not for the first time he thanked his lucky stars that Goran Jankovic did his business in Sarajevo and not Liverpool.

"Goran. I need a favour. Not a free favour. I'll pay."

"You tell me favour first. Maybe no pay needed this time. Maybe this Final ticket is enough for pay."

"I've been ripped off Goran. Robbed. Some little bastard has had money from me. He's nicked a car as well."

"I have no understand Eddie. How you need Goran for this thing?"

"The reason he stole the money was to go to the match. He's driving. In my car. I have a SatNav system installed, so I know exactly where he is. As we speak he seems to have stopped for the night somewhere in Croatia. I reckon the road he'll take tomorrow will run right by your front door."

Now the Bosnian was with the programme. "So. OK. You can tell me where he is, this thief OK?"

"To the nearest ten feet."

"Then this thing is too easy. You call me as soon as he starts journey. We stop him no problem. You want him make die quick or slow?"

THE ROAD TO ISTANBUL MAY 2005

Eddie couldn't quite believe the question he had just been asked. You want him make die quick or slow? Bloody savages. Headbangers. Jesus Christ. "Just quick like. And there's two of them. Bang, bang. Back of the head. No need for any drama. What do I owe you?"

"Bang, bang. Back of head. This is nothing Eddie. We can do this bang, bang. One ticket is enough OK."

Eddie wondered whether the slow death option would have meant a fee. "If they have any of the cash in the car you can keep it. This isn't about money Goran. You know that."

"Sure. People who steal need to die. If this man steal from Goran he make die slow. Too much slow."

"I bet. But I don't want to hold you lads back or anything. Bang, bang will be fine. You still checking in on the Tuesday night mate?"

"Sure. I see you OK?"

"Yeah. See you then."

"And this AC Milan make die, OK?"

"Absolutely."

Eddie killed the line and wondered if the Bosnian intended the Milan team to make die quick or slow.

Mickey pulled up and sank back into the driver's seat and closed his eyes for a moment, then opened then straight away because he knew that if he left them closed for more than thirty seconds they wouldn't open again for hours. One of the papers he had read the week before had said that it was seventeen hundred and five miles from Anfield to the Ataturk Stadium. At the time that hadn't seemed too big a deal. Certainly it wouldn't seem so for the ones who climbed on a plane and climbed off about three hours later. But he felt like he had been driving forever and he was all done.

He took a look around. He really had very little idea where they were. Somewhere in Croatia and the signs said that the road was the right one for Sarajevo. He had set the milometer to zero as they passed the M58 junction and there were now well over 1200 miles on the clock. Not bad. They had seventy-two hours to kick off and five or six hundred miles to go. Well maybe eight hundred because the BMW certainly wasn't a crow. The time and distance equation was fine. They were on target.

THE LONG AND WINDING
ROAD TO ISTANBUL

The town wasn't much of a place. A one-streeter with little sign of people about apart from six youngsters kicking a football about a piece of waste ground across the road. The light was all but gone and a lit window down the pavement suggested a bar.

"Come on. Let's go and get an ale or two. Maybe they have rooms in there. If they don't, we'll kip in the car again."

Tonto stretched and got out. They had both changed on the ferry and put on their Liverpool tops, which immediately caught the attention of the kick around boys who gave up their game to run across. Neither Mickey or Tonto could make out much of what they were saying except that the word Liverpool seemed to appear in most sentences and there was a lot of enthusiastic smiling.

The red shirts had a similar galvanising effect when they entered the bar, which was both busy and smoky. The bar tender had as much English as they had Croatian but a pointed finger at a fellow customer's beer was enough. The first two glasses didn't remotely hit the sides and by the time they started on the second round they were ringed. At last an English speaker elbowed to the front.

"From Liverpool, yes?"

"That's right mate."

"Liverpool too much good I think."

"Better than that mate."

"Igor Biscan. Too much good I think."

The beer had flown up to Mickey's head and all of a sudden he was euphoric. All the nightmare events that had rolled out one after the other from the moment they had left the Berlin two nights earlier seemed to step back into the background. He felt like an iron filing being drawn towards a giant magnet. Liverpool and Eddie Tate and Tonto's threadbare carpet and poetry readings for sleeping-bag men and biscuit-munching women were all behind him. His whole miserable underachieving life was all behind him. None of it mattered any more because now everything lay ahead. A few hundred miles and as many years as he had left on the clock. He hung an arm around the shoulder of the English speaker.

"You know what we sing about Igor mate?"

This brought a big smile. "I know this sing OK. He is called Kop I think."

"Spot on mate. That's what he's called all right. And this is how we do it."

He put his beer down on the counter and raised a clenched fist to the nicotine stained ceiling.

"EEEEEEEE . . . GOOOOOOOOR!!!"

The other drinkers soon got the gist and joined in. By midnight the bar had done a pretty good job of learning 'The fields of Anfield Road' and Mickey was struck with the irony of the situation. He had three hundred pounds in his pocket and damn near £200,000 hidden with the spare wheel in the boot of the car and he couldn't get a round in no matter how hard he tried.

The next morning they woke sprawled in a heap on the English speaker's front room floor under a pile of blankets. Without a vigorous shake of the shoulder, they would have slept on past noon.

"You need to make wake up English. I am working now. My wife she has food OK? You can win these AC Milan. So. Now I go."

"Hey. Thanks mate. Hell of a night."

The English speaker's wife had no English of her own and she blushed the colour of their rumpled shirts as she served up bread and olives and salami. Half an hour later they were back on the road and heading south.

Eddie was reading the morning paper when Harry Walton called to inform him that the blip was again on the move. Straight south on the main drag to Sarajevo. He called Goran to confirm what they had both pretty well worked out the night before.

"OK. You can look at your map. There is village called Zedice. He is maybe seventy kilometres from Sarajevo. We wait two kilometres outside OK. This side. Sarajevo side. So you can watch I think."

"Nice one Goran."

Eddie sat back and looked out across his large garden where the sun had broken free of big white clouds. So many years since he had driven a sulking Mickey McGuire in his Capri. The boys had become men. And the girl had become a woman. Who could ever have predicted their lives? And now here he was with his coffee and his paper and a great echoing house with no wife and no sons. He had everything and he still had nothing. Lucy despised him. Frank had betrayed him. His wife had left him. And he had just confirmed the execution of Mickey McGuire by a band of Bosnian war criminals. He was taking his dish of revenge as a cold platter and it tasted worse than filthy in his mouth.

Anders Veervott made the call immediately to Sir Hubert.

"He has just spoken with the Bosnian again. They talked about a map. The Bosnian said Tate should find a village called Zedice. North of Sarajevo. He said he would wait there."

"Thanks Anders."

Sir Hubert had by now been hooked up to the same images that Harry Walton was watching. The blip was closing in on the Bosnian border. Overnight he had made several phone calls to various colleagues across Europe and what he had found out about Goran Jankovioc had made the hairs on the back of his neck stand up. The man was a killer who made Peter Sutcliffe look like a choirboy. And now he was waiting outside a village called Zedice with his motley band of ethnic cleansers. Would it be kinder not to make the call to Frank McGuire? There wasn't a thing that anyone could do. Not unless Mickey had switched his phone on and there seemed little chance of that. He realised that the professional thing to do was to make the call. It didn't look like Mickey would be making it to Istanbul after all. But his brother needed to know that the Chief Constable had done his best to keep his end of the bargain. Maybe he would still make the witness box to exact his revenge.

"Frank?"

"Yeah. That you Sir Hubert?"

"It is. The news is bad I'm afraid. I expect you know a man called Goran Jankovic?"

"I know him. Eddie's called him about our Mickey has he?"

"You guessed then."

"Course I guessed."

"Jankovic and his men are going to wait outside a village called Zedice a few miles north of Sarajevo. I'm sorry Frank. Mickey and his friend are already nearly at the border. Unless he answers the phone there isn't anything that can be done. I'm sorry."

Frank was impressed by the genuine regret in the voice on the other end of the line. Sir Hubert went up in his estimation.

"Don't be sorry just yet. I've got a thing or two up my sleeve. I'll call you later."

This left the policeman feeling completely bemused. The man's brother was headed into an ambush in some godforsaken part of the Balkans and Frank McGuire reckoned he had something up his sleeve. The whole thing was getting stranger and stranger. He just hoped that the card under the cuff was an ace.

"Jeremy, it's Lucy."

Jeremy Telford was chewing through a round of toast in the makeshift officers' mess.

"Hang on a sec. Mouthful of bloody food. That's it. Right oh. Got some news have you?"

Around the table the faces of his fellow officers came alive with interest. Their captain had already briefed them about the two crazy Scousers who had ripped off Merseyside's Gangster Number One and were now making a dash through the Balkans with the spoils. When he had told them that a dirty deal had been done which meant that Goran Jankovic and his guys would be lying in wait they had wondered for a moment if their gallant leader had been munching some magic mushrooms.

"Yes we have. Jankovic will be waiting about two kilometres south of a village of Zedice."

"Zedice? Oh right. Know the place. Two clicks south you say?"

"That's right."

"Yep. I know just where he has in mind. There's a cutting. Thirty-foot high rock walls either side of the road. There's a lay-by half way through. It got used for this kind of thing in the war. Where are your two chaps?"

"Ten minutes ago they were just shy of the border."

Telford looked at his watch and pulled a face.

"Bloody hell. It's going to be tight. Tootle pip my dear. We need to hitch our wagons up."

"Thank you Jeremy."

"Oh don't you worry my fair one. An invoice will be in the post and payment in full will be expected. And you should know it is never a good idea to avoid a bill from a man with three Warriors at his disposal."

He heard a chuckle. "I'll wait on the post. Let me know as soon as you can."

"Okey dokey. Ciao for now."

THE LONG AND WINDING
ROAD TO ISTANBUL

He rammed a last piece of toast into his mouth and spluttered out crumbs as he issued his orders.

"Time to saddle up gentlemen. We're gone in ten. This is going to be a little tight. I hope these Liverpool boys don't go like Schumacher or we might just find a couple of corpses."

Luckily the Liverpool boys were not even close to doing a Schumacher. Mickey's head felt like it was stuffed full of cotton wool soaked in used washing-up water. He was working his way through a big bottle of mineral water and waiting to feel half way human again. The morning was clear and fine and the countryside as easy on the eye as a postcard. The whole landscape was like a recuperating patient. Nature was glowing in the warm morning. It was a place of hills and valleys and soft meadows. It was where mankind came into the picture that the legacy of the madness of the Nineties was all around them. Wrecked buildings. Rusting and smashed military vehicles. Walls filled with bullet holes. Villages of burned-out and long-deserted homes. The sun could do little to make these places feel warm. The memory of what had happened seemed to have seeped into every crack.

The high spirits of their big Igor night faded with every mile south. A sense of dark foreboding filled Mickey whilst Tonto snored softly beside him. When he had looked at the map in a service station a few miles past Munich, this had seemed an obvious route to take. One or two of the place names rang distant bells from the news, but that had all been a long time ago. Things had improved now because Lucy had told him. He had watched her only a few months before as she had delivered a special report. She had spent a few days with a British Army unit that was involved in rebuilding schools and getting the electricity working properly again. There had been images of squaddies playing football with village kids and an electrician putting on a brave face when he opened up a burnt out circuit board. Mickey remembered the piece well because of the officer who always seemed to be by Lucy's side as they did the rounds. He was a tall blond-haired handsome git with an easy smile and voice from some school that must have cost his mum and dad £4000 a term. There had been no mistaking the expression on his face every time he looked at Lucy. Mickey had snapped off the television in jealous disgust and gone straight out to get drunk as a skunk.

What had seemed like a place of the green shoots of hope on the BBC News, seemed altogether different as he drove through it. There was a feeling of evil hanging in the air and he didn't like it one bit. Why the hell hadn't he taken the long way through Budapest and Sofia?

He braked as they came to another small, broken little village. Zedice. It was as quiet as all the other places. One or two bent old women dressed all in black, with carrier bags filled with bread. A group of four old boys at a table outside a café making their coffee last. A malnourished cat. A few bored looking crows lined up on a rooftop. And then they were back on the near-empty road south. Maybe Zedice had been on the news once. It would have been when something completely horrible had happened. Men would have come in balaclavas and mud splattered 4x4s. And the men would have killed because when they were little boys their uncles and grandfathers had taught them how to hate the other side. When he had been a boy it had been all banter between red and blue. Taking the piss. Having a laugh. Here the two sides killed each other with hammers.

They were in a cutting now and the sun was hidden behind the rough walls of rock that had been blown open for the road by high explosives many years before. There was something going on up ahead. A couple of cars were sideways on across the tarmac. An accident? The cars seemed OK. Maybe just a skid and a near miss. There were a few blokes standing by the cars and they all seemed to be OK. Mickey eased on the brakes and beside him Tonto's eyes rolled open.

"What's up Mickey?"

"Don't know. An accident maybe . . ."

But he could see guns now. Lots of guns. He forced the brake pedal to the floor and looked in the mirror. Maybe he could reverse. Maybe if he could get back into the open and back to the village.

Not a chance. Two more cars had pulled out of the lay-by and blocked the way back. His brain registered Mercedes. Black Mercedes. Four black Mercedes. And guys with guns. And nobody else in sight. And the sun hidden behind the high walls of rock. And when Liverpool win the European Cup, Lucy and Mickey come together and Mickey McGuire's life goes down the toilet. And Mickey McGuire never gets to see the match.

THE LONG AND WINDING
ROAD TO ISTANBUL

But this was a long way beyond all that had gone before. It wasn't a gang of Mancs on a Wigan council estate. It wasn't a night in the cells. This was the nightmare at the end of the rainbow. The nightmare a mile or two outside a place called Zedice where bad things had happened.

He switched off the engine and waited as the men closed the space.

"Who are these men Mickey?"

"I don't know Tonto. I don't think they're going to try and persuade us to take out a subscription for Sky TV though."

"No. They don't look like it."

A hand opened the driver's door and a gun waved for him to get out. The process was repeated on Tonto's side. Mickey stepped out and felt the cool shaded air on his face. The same air that was going in and out of his lungs much faster than normal. Faster breathing for a faster heartbeat. Were these lungfuls of Bosnian oxygen to be the last breaths he would ever take?

Nobody seemed in much of a hurry. The man who stood before him glanced to where a taller man stood with a mobile phone to his ear. It struck Mickey that the conversation was in English.

"So OK. They are here. I call you when is finish."

The man snapped the phone closed and dropped it into his pocket.

"So. You are here English."

Mickey didn't know if he was expected to answer or not. He nodded and hoped that would do. There was something weird about the man's face. What was it? It was a face that was neither handsome or ugly. A face about ten years younger than his own. An ordinary face really. Then he got it. It was an empty face. Empty face with empty eyes. A house with the lights off.

"You can die now I think. Mickey."

The sound of his own name was shocking. "You know me?"

"For sure I know you. You are thief. And now you can be dead thief. Where is this money Mickey. Eddie say you have money."

"Eddie! Like Eddie Tate?"

A shrug. "Sure Eddie. Why not? He is friend. We watch football OK?"

The strands. Same old strands. Same old strings. Same old Mickey the puppet being yanked about by the gods. When Luis Garcia had flipped the ball in at the Kop end to put the reds onto the road to Istanbul, Mickey had been stupid enough to think that fate was on his side. He had got it into his stupid, thick head that Istanbul would be all about redemption and finding Lucy when all hope seemed lost. Bollocks. Luis had merely set him on a path to this dark little cutting in a land where nightmares were as common as beans on toast. The milometer in the car read over twelve hundred miles and still he was in the shadow of Eddie Tate and the old life. The life where there were tubs of Valium through chemist windows. The life where his parents hadn't spoken to his brother for close on thirty years. The world where he and Lucy never seemed to have a chance because her surname was Tate. And now he was going to miss yet another final because some empty-eyed Slav pal of Eddie's was going to execute him for a bag of cash.

"Get the bag out Tonto."

"But what about the tickets Mickey? We won't have enough for the tickets."

"We'll sort something out. Don't worry about it."

Tonto popped the boot and took out the holdall which was passed on to Goran who poked about inside. He was about to issue more orders when his attention was caught by the sound of growling engines entering the cutting.

A few seconds later the first Warrior appeared round a shallow corner closely followed by two others. By the time they reached where the cars were parked the sound was huge. They pulled up in a line of three and a tall figure jumped down from the vehicle in the centre.

A familiar figure. A blond figure. A figure Mickey had last seen on the TV news making public school eyes at Lucy.

"Good morning, good morning, good morning." Jeremy clapped his hands together and gave the scene a look that suggested it was a jolly fine morning for duck shooting.

"Awfully sorry we're late. These old girls aren't exactly in their full flush of youth. Of course if we were American we would be in Bradleys and we would have been here in time for all the fun. Anyway. Better late than never."

Goran's face was no longer empty. It was full of freezing hatred.

"Ah. Goran Jankovic I presume. We haven't met of course. I'm Telford by the way. Captain Jeremy Telford, British Army. It isn't a pleasure to meet you because you are the scum of the earth. What would be a pleasure would be to kick you in the balls and toss you in the back of one of the cars and send you off first class to the war crimes people in The Hague. Now that would be a truly splendid way to spend a fine morning in Bosnia. But it isn't on the cards Goran. Not today. Because you have paid off lots and lots of people with lots and lots of money haven't you Goran? So today we have different business."

He was close to Goran now. Looking down with contempt from a height advantage of three inches.

"Now. We have two British nationals here and Her Majesty requires her soldiers to make sure that no harm comes to her subjects. Especially from chaps who like to kill children with lump hammers. So this is what is about to happen here. These two are going to get into the cars and we're going to go our separate ways. Now I can see that all of you have lots of nice shiny toys Goran. But that's all they are. Toys. Little toys for little thugs. You should know that the guns on my Warriors are toys for grown-ups. So if any of you tries anything I can have you all turned into very dead people very quickly. Do you understand that Goran?"

The Bosnian never moved a muscle.

"I'll take that as a yes then. OK. We'll be on our way then. I'm afraid you'll have to leave the car here chaps. I need you in one of our vehicles. Any luggage?"

"Couple of bags."

"Go grab them then."

Tonto did so and Mickey took a step forward and eased the money holdall from Goran's grasp. For a moment it seemed as if Goran wasn't about to let go, but he flicked a glance at the line of white death that stared down at him and realised it was hopeless.

"You are dead men. All of you."

Jeremy leant in even closer. "Oh really. You know where our base is Goran. Why not pay us a visit. Any time you like. Open invitation."

They held each other's eyes for a few seconds then Jeremy turned and marched up to his armoured car and climbed aboard. Mickey and Tonto were pulled in through the hatch at the back, which snapped shut. One by one the cars turned and headed back the way they had come, leaving Goran standing in the road with a head full of images from the back end of Hell.

As soon as they were out of the cutting Jeremy swapped his position in the turret with his sergeant and joined his passengers in the belly of the vehicle.

"Bloody hell lads. That was too close for comfort. You OK?"

"Yeah. What happened there? I don't understand."

Jeremy shook out cigarettes and they all lit up. "No. We must have come as something of a surprise. A good one I hope?"

"I thought the cavalry went out with Custer."

"You have a fairy godmother chaps. An email and a couple of phone calls and hey presto, help is at hand."

"Lucy?"

"Indeed. The lovely Lucy. How could a man say no?"

"I did once. I've regretted it for twenty bastard years."

Jeremy leaned his head back on the metal wall and blew out a long plume of smoke.

"So I gather. It would have served you right if I had left Jankovic to have his way."

Mickey gave him a sharp look. "What do you mean, you gather?"

"Lucy spent some time with us a few months ago to do a feature. I have to admit I was more than a little taken with her. Well. More than taken. Downright smitten to tell you the truth. We had a couple of nights with the whisky and she played me that song of yours. 'Lovers Under Creamy Yellow'. Rather wonderful actually. I must congratulate you. Made me jealous as hell, all that fish and chips in the rain stuff. She explained that she had been on the rebound for twenty years after a rather dismal night somewhere in Wales. Two marriages and a whole lot of bad endings. So she said sorry Jeremy, no more rebound. She said she was going to dig you out and take you by the scruff of the neck. Lucky bastard. Then the next thing I hear is that you are driving down the road to Sarajevo in a stolen car with a bag full of some gangster's money with Goran Jankovic and his merry men lying in wait. Funny old life isn't it?"

Mickey really couldn't think of a thing to say. More than anything his spirits had clambered out from all the ghostly nightmares that had haunted him all morning and soared up into the clear blue Balkan skies. The programme had been months ago and even then Lucy had said that she was going to find him. And maybe fate wasn't such a bastard after all. Because maybe that shot from Luis

THE LONG AND WINDING
ROAD TO ISTANBUL

Garcia hadn't been over the line after all. And maybe the Warriors might have landed ten minutes later to collect him and Tonto with bullets through their brains. And against all the odds they were still headed south.

Jeremy stubbed out his cigarette on the floor.

"The next problem is what on earth to do with the pair of you. We'll go back to the base now and I'll make a call or two. I don't expect you have any particular plans."

"No. Not really. Just get to match. That's about it."

"Well we'll put you back on the road. I have someone in mind."

As the Warriors disappeared from view, Goran reached into his pocket and redialled the mobile.

"Is Goran."

"All done?"

"No. Not done. We have problem."

A pause.

"What kind of problem?"

"I think is your problem Eddie. The car he come OK. These thief they are here. I get money. I ready to make dead. Then soldiers come. British soldier. Three armoured car. They know me, these soldier. They know Goran. And they know these thief. You have traitor Eddie. Maybe some police they listen to your house. Maybe they listen now. You call on different phone. We no speak now."

Eddie stared about his study in horror. It couldn't be? He'd only had the place checked a few days ago. But Frank had warned him that he reckoned they were cowboys. He didn't dwell on it. Twenty minutes later he was at a pay phone with £50 worth of change.

"You can talk safe now?"

"Yeah. No problem. Where are Mickey and Tonto?"

"I think they will go back to British base. I have make call. One of my men can watch this place from hills. He can tell me what happens. So I tell you."

"Thanks Goran."

"So I no come this match now Eddie. If people know I go maybe they try to find me in Istanbul. It is not safe. You must tell Dimitri OK. You make safe in your Liverpool. So we wait some time now. Then business can be still good."

Eddie took it in and nodded. The Bosnian was right. They would have to wait whilst he worked out how much the police might know. The coal yard was a goner for a start. It was a setback. Nothing more. What had been built once could be built again.

"Fair enough mate. I'll be in touch. You'll let me know if you find out anything?"

"Sure. I call."

"Hello Lucy. Mission accomplished and all that . . . Absolutely. Yes, they're both with me right now. Want a word do you . . . no . . . OK . . . I'll relay the message."

Mickey raised an eyebrow. Jeremy smiled.

"Doesn't want to talk to you I'm afraid. She says the deal is still the same. You get to the stadium and call her mobile. Tough lady."

"Comes from a tough family doesn't she? Anyway. You said you had something in mind."

"I did. I had a few days leave last month. I went to Sofia, you know in Bulgaria. It's not far from here. I didn't book anything so it was all a bit wing and prayer. Spur of the moment. I got a ride into town from the airport in a cab. Chap called Nicholai. Absolute topper. He sorted a hotel and everything. He took me about for three days and we got to know each other pretty well. He said that he liked the long distance stuff best. Greece, Hungary, Romania, wherever. He said that if I ever wanted to come back to Sofia all I needed to do was to call him and he would collect me from the base. He assured me it would be much cheaper than taking a plane."

He reached into his tunic pocket, took out his wallet and drew out a business card. "Here's the man. Nicholai. I thought it might be an idea to call him up and get him to come down for you lads. It seems that there are lots of Liverpool fans taking the Bulgaria route to the final. If Nicholai gets you to Sofia, I'm sure you'll sort things out from there."

Jeremy's confidence in the cab driver was not misplaced. Seven hours after he made the call Nicholai pulled in through the front gates of the base. As he loaded Mickey and Tonto's cases into the boot, the cab was clearly visible from the trees on the hillside that overlooked the base. The watcher duly noted down a number plate from Sofia, Bulgaria and made his report to Goran.

Who in turn forwarded the intelligence onto Eddie Tate.

Just before it was time to go Jeremy took Mickey to one side. "Just one last thing. I arranged a fee of $500 with Nicholai. That a problem?"

Mickey grinned. "No. In fact I was wanting a word on the subject of cash. You know that bag I took off Jankovic?"

"I do."

"Well it's stuffed with cash. Eddie Tate's cash. I nicked it because it was the only way I could get down here."

"I see."

"Well, I know it's bang out of order, but how would it be if I laid a few grand on you so the lads can get a few ales in on me and Tonto. For the match like. And if any of the kids round here need anything. You know football kit, balls, anything really."

Jeremy took a theatrical look about him.

"Actually, I can't seem to see any senior officer about the place. Can you see any Mickey?"

"No."

"Well hand it over then."

Mickey passed over a carrier bag which was quickly thrust deep into a coat pocket.

"Right then. You best be off. You should be in Sofia for midnight with a bit of luck. Get Nicholai to take you to the place in the city centre. You can sit outside and the kebabs are bloody spot on."

"Thanks Jeremy. We owe you."

"Just get yourself there and make her happy."

"I'll try."

Eddie took some time to work things through once he had finished with Goran. There was no doubt that things really couldn't have gone a lot worse. It was time to try and settle himself down and do some clear thinking. So far it had all been about anger and emotion and that meant that he had made some mistakes. Time to slow down. Time to write a few things down and make sense of the situation.

He took a cab into the city and ducked in and out of a few pubs, on three occasions exiting via the back door. The final exit took him into a back alley where he had ordered another cab to wait. This time he left the city altogether and took a ride to a hotel near Preston.

By the time he checked into the room and made a coffee his mind was becoming clearer. Things were not nearly as bad as they seemed.

In a way it was a pity that Goran wouldn't make the match, but in a way he was quite pleased. The man was a superb heroin supplier and his quality and price and reliability were all excellent. He was also just about the scariest individual Eddie had ever met and it would be no great hardship not to have his dubious company in Istanbul. He knew that he had to call Dimitri and it was a call that he would need to take care with. The Russian had become a friend, but Eddie was under no illusions of the extent of the friendship. How many of his problems was he going to own up to? He would have to come clean about the listening devices. Goran had already worked that part out and Goran would probably tell Dimitri at some stage, so hiding the fact would be idiotic.

Would that scupper things? Maybe. But then again Dimitri was ex-KGB and he had spent half his life planting listening devices on people. Surely he would have some sympathy with the fact that the Bizzies had jumped a step ahead on the technology front. He would ask Dimitri for a referral to a new outfit to make sure all his sites were properly swept. And once they were both happy that he had a clean bill of health, they could work on putting the deal back on the tracks.

The good news was that there was absolutely no hurry. Cash wasn't an issue. All of them had piles of cash up to their ears. None of it was about cash. It was about playing the game. And sometimes a strategic retreat was the best way ahead. Dimitri was Russian and strategic retreat was something they knew better than most. Whenever the going got tough they would torch the wheat fields and move the tank factories back to the other side of the Urals.

Then there was the Frank question. Luckily neither Goran nor Dimitri knew Frank's surname. At least he was pretty sure they didn't. That meant that neither of them would be likely to make a link between Frank and the Balkan runaways. Eddie still hadn't come up with much of an explanation for what had happened. Frank was obviously involved to some extent, but how? Nothing made any sense. Especially all the blood. And as soon as the cash had been pinched the whole thing had been amateur hour. Frank knew about the tracking device. Frank had been to Sarajevo to negotiate with Goran and he had returned pale-faced and quiet. So if he was in touch with his brother, he would have told him to take a route that by-passed Sarajevo by about a million miles. Instead Mickey had driven more or less right up to Goran's front door.

THE LONG AND WINDING
ROAD TO ISTANBUL

Conclusion? Frank wasn't in touch with Mickey. Eddie started to write down a few facts. Blood in the flat. Mickey makes the Glasgow run. Why? Because his brother asked him to. Why? Because Frank was injured and couldn't do it himself. Why Mickey? Obvious. Family. Blood. The only one he could trust.

So Mickey and Tonto turned up at the flat and picked up the keys and got their instructions. And then they made the run. No hitches, no problems, business as usual. But then things started to go weird. They take a detour to a flat in Cumbria which turns out to belong to Lucy. They make one call to Frank as they are about level with the turn off to Liverpool and keep heading south.

Of course! Frank fully expected them to return the car so that he could cover the fact that he hadn't made the drop. But it didn't work out that way. Mickey turned into a loose canon. Something must have gone wrong at the Spion fund raiser and Mickey never had the cash to make it to Istanbul so he decided to keep hold of the bag from Glasgow and make a run for it. And the call to Frank was to let him know what was happening.

Of course. Frank hadn't betrayed him after all. Mickey had stitched-up Frank and left him right up the creek without a paddle. There he was with some kind of injury and his brother telling him he had pinched close on half a million quid off his boss. Stuff of nightmares. It must have meant that Frank was all out of options. He had to get out of town quick and he had done.

So what was the Cumbria thing all about? The car was only stopped for a matter of minutes and then away again. If it was something that quick, it could have been done on the phone. Unless they had to be there in person. To deliver something or to pick something up. To deliver something. That was it. Mickey wasn't the type to keep all the cash and leave his brother in the lurch. He must have halved it and stashed it away at Lucy's. He knew exactly what he was doing. He had always hated Frank's work, especially after what had happened after the Chemist shop thing. This was his way of forcing Frank to take a bow. And he made sure his big brother had enough of a stash to get away.

He felt much better having worked most of it out. That was why Mickey and Tonto had blundered their way to near death. They didn't know what they were doing because Frank wasn't telling them.

So what was Frank doing now? Well, there wasn't a lot he could do. He had £200,000 on top of what ever he had put by over the years. It was plenty enough to get out of the country on a false ID Then he would just lie low and kill the days with his bloody philosophy books. Frank hadn't betrayed him. He had been stitched-up by his own brother and whoever had hurt him. Maybe at some stage Eddie would lay a few bob on some investigators to track him down. Then again maybe he wouldn't. Frank had been his top lad for well over twenty years and he had never put a foot wrong. It wasn't his fault that his little brother was a dickhead. Maybe he would just leave him be.

So the call to Moscow wasn't going to be so bad after all. He would tell Dimitri that a couple of clowns had ripped him off to make a run for Istanbul. Everything had been covered and he would have had them in the bag before they made Birmingham except that the cops had managed to get a bug into his house and they had pulled the lads making the chase on speeding charges. Plan B had been Goran, but that had also gone wrong because the cops had managed to deploy an army unit to pick the runners up before Goran and his boys had the chance to whack them. But that had revealed the fact of the surveillance and now Eddie would be able to resolve that issue. With Dimitri's help. He ran through it all one more time until he was happy with it. He wouldn't mention Frank at all. Dimitri would probably ask when they met up in Turkey and Eddie would just tell him he was on other business. The Siberian bird would probably be disappointed. No doubt she would want Frank to show her round some bloody Mosques or something. Well that was just tough. She'd have to make do with a tour guide.

He was about to pick up the phone, but decided to take a stroll down to the sauna instead. Now his mind was nice and clear he could take his time. A swim and a sauna and a couple of nice fat gins and then he would make the call.

As Eddie was making his way down to the lavishly refurbished leisure, area, the Chief Constable had arrived home to the smell of roast beef wafting through the house from the kitchen. It reminded him that he hadn't eaten all day and was ready to eat a horse. Before he had chance to go through to his wife, his mobile rang.

"It's Frank."

"Any news?"

"All sorted. The boys are right now in a taxi and headed for Sofia."

"What happened?"

"The British Army happened. A favour owed and all that. Don't worry. There are no bodies to count. It was all very civilised."

The Chief couldn't even begin to get his head around any of it. The reach of these people never failed to astonish him. The Army for goodness sake!

"Well, that is good news indeed. Well done. I suppose. I'm afraid I have some less good news. The Bosnian sussed us out. He alerted Tate to the fact that he must be under electronic surveillance. Tate left the house and lost us somewhere in the city. We haven't a clue where he is now. Do you have any suggestions?"

"Sorry. He could be anywhere."

"Well I can't really see what else we can do at this point."

"You best think of something. You know the deal. Mickey makes it to that stadium or you won't get me within a mile of the stand."

"I'm aware of that."

"Good."

He was about to make another attempt at going into the kitchen when the phone rang again.

"Veervott."

"Oh hello Anders. Anything?"

"Na. All gone quiet as hell. He's taped us man. You hear about those lads?"

"Yes. They're safe. Apparently they're now in a cab to Sofia."

A short silence.

"That's Bulgaria, yes?"

"It is."

Another pause. Sir Hubert could sense the South African's brain ticking.

"You might want to call your man at the Home Office."

"Might I?"

"Ya. Think about it. Bulgaria used to be Soviet Bloc, ya? They were the most loyal of the loyal remember. The KGB used to get their guys to do a lot of their wet work. I remember it man. They sent a few of their hitters down to South Africa in the eighties."

"Go on."

"Think about it. Dimitri Zarkhov is ex-KGB. The odds are that he will still have some cronies down in Bulgaria. Old boys network, ya? So if he knows the boys are headed that way he might be able to pull a string or two with some of the pals from the old days. Maybe Eddie might have worked out that one."

"So why the Home Office?"

"Eddie's gone off road on us. But if he is going to make contact with Zarkhov he's going to use the phone. I don't suppose there will be all that many calls made from the North West of England to the Moscow area on a Monday night. You get the Home Office to ask GCHQ in Cheltenham to listen in for a few hours. They can do that. No problem. Maybe we might get lucky, hey?"

Clever boy. Clever, clever boy. Sir Hubert realised how old he was getting. Out of touch with the outrageous possibilities new technology offered to good old fashioned coppering. But he was still young enough to know how to make a decision. How to pull a string or two.

"OK. I'm on with it. I'll let you know."

The beef would have to wait.

It turned out that the man from South Africa was wrong on one count. The seventies and eighties had been a time when all of Eddie's attention was taken up with local issues. He had never paid a great deal of attention to the posturing of the Americans and Russians and their Cold War. He had worked on a simple philosophy that if they dropped the bomb there wasn't anything he would be able to do about it, although he wondered what good the Ruskies would achieve by bombing Liverpool. It wasn't as if they built warships in Birkenhead any more. His knowledge of Bulgaria pretty well ended with the fact that they were dirty bastards on the football pitch who had a halfway decent striker called Stiotchkov. So it was Dimitri who made the connection.

The Russian had reacted to all the news just as Eddie had hoped he would. He had said that these things happened. It was inevitable. The key was to remember that they were mere setbacks. Of course the police would have their moments. Just like the Nazis. But in the end, that was all it would ever be. Moments. In the end they would both prevail. It was rather a stirring speech and it made Eddie feel better all the time.

"So tell me one thing my friend. You say that Goran saw these traitors leave the army camp, yes?"

"That's right. They were in a taxi. Apparently it was Bulgarian."

"How did he know this?"

"The writing on the side I think. And the number plate."

"Did he write him down, this number plate?"

"Yeah. I've got it."

"Then it is good. You can give this to me. I have some friends. Old friends. Old friends from old days. They can help me I think. Maybe they can find something with this number plate? You can find out many things in places like Sofia for a few hundred dollars. So maybe I can find these traitors for you OK. And maybe not. But we try I think. It is not good when people steal. There should be a punishment."

Eddie gave out the number plate and felt even better still. He didn't care that it wasn't professional, but he really, really wanted to see Mickey McGuire's head on a spike.

"So. Can I call you? Is safe?"

"Very safe. I lost the Bizzies in the city. I'm at a hotel now. Hang on. Here's the number. Room 417."

"So we can speak later I think. Maybe in the morning. You can enjoy your night OK?"

"OK Dimitri. Thanks pal."

Gregori Malenkov was finishing up a dreary sort of a day when his mobile phone rang. Most days were rather dreary. They had been so for sixteen years. Once upon a time Gregori had been a high flier on his way to a fifth floor office and a chauffeur-driven car and a dacha in the forested hills that looked down on Sofia. He had been fast tracked straight from University into the Secret Police and the future that lay ahead of him was bathed in uninterrupted sunshine. And when one of the big-hitters from Moscow had come to town to give some advice about a few dissidents, it had been Gregori Malenkov who had been given the job of taking him about the place. When the job was done and the dissidents safely locked up in dark places on mind altering drugs, the Russian had taken the young man with prospects to a restaurant in the hills and got him drunk on the best vodka they had.

That had been a high point. It had been 1988 and three days later his long-term girlfriend had said yes when he had asked her to become his wife. But less than a year later everything had gone all to hell. The Communist states had crashed like a row of rotten dominoes and everyone was burning every file they could lay their hands on. Some of the more senior people had managed to salt away enough cash to get out of the country.

But not Grigori. He was too far down the ladder. All he could do was to burn what files he had and hope not to be denounced. He had gone home and his new wife had become a screaming harridan. She hadn't wanted to marry a two-bit loser. She had thought he was a man with prospects. Now look at him. Unemployed and probably on his way to prison. And that had been the low point.

For weeks he had sweated it out and waited for a knock at the door that never came. They didn't care about the likes of Grigori. The small fish. Everybody was altogether more excited at the fact that all of a sudden the borders were open and there was Coca Cola on sale. When he realised that there wasn't going to be retribution, he had applied for a job as a policeman and he had been successful. And for fifteen years he had inched his way up the ladder, but his wife never forgave him for not coming good with a dacha in the hills. They lived on the twelfth floor of a tower block that was too hot in the summer and too cold in the winter and had walls that were paper thin.

It had been a dreary crap day and now the clock said it was time to catch the tram back to his dreary crap flat with his horrible dreary crap wife for a dreary crap supper of cabbage and fatty meat. Then he would sleep and get up ready to ride the seven o'clock tram into the city for another dreary crap day.

He picked up the phone with the vague hope that it might mean an hour or two of overtime. He had been quite optimistic of a good few hours of overtime over the weekend. The city was full of English football fans en route to the big final in Turkey. There had been talk in the canteen that they might run amok and every policeman in the city would be on double shifts at double time. Fat chance. The English had come to town to drink and sing and shake everyone's hand. The nearest any of them had come to running amok was to piss in every alley they could find.

"Yes. Malenkov here."

"So. The boy is now the man. And the man is still alive. Is good. It means one day we can drink vodka again I think."

"Who is this?" He asked but he already knew. At least he thought that he did.

"Maybe you don't remember me. Many years ago my friend. Many, many years ago. 1988. When they still had pictures of Lenin in that beautiful city of yours. We locked up some bad guys. Then we drink a little vodka in the hills. Now you maybe know, yes?"

Grigori smiled. Unbelievable. "Yes. I know."

"I ask and I hear maybe life isn't too good for you my friend. Maybe times are a little hard?"

"More than a little. Life is shit."

This induced a hearty laugh. "OK. So maybe we can make it better. Make a few dollars OK. Maybe $3000. You can maybe do some things for this kind of dollars, yes?"

"I think I would do most things for this kind of money."

Another big laugh. "There is a taxi driver. From your city. This morning he picked up two passengers from Bosnia. I think he brings them to Sofia. You can find where he has an arrangement with a hotel. All these taxi drivers have arrangements with hotels, yes?"

"They do."

"You find this and you wait OK? When he brings these passengers you can call me. I have a man on a plane now. He will come in Sofia for nine o'clock. When he lands he will come to this hotel to meet you. You can find out which room these people have. Find number. Make sure you know if they are inside or outside. OK? Is everything. You do this thing and my man he give you the money. Too much simple. And life not so shit any more. I send vodka as well. Good vodka. Best vodka. When you take this money you can drink some and make toast for old days OK. You can do this my friend?"

"I can do this."

"So now I give you number plate. First you tell me one thing."

"If I can."

"I speak with friend. Maybe one month ago. A friend from old days, OK. He had been in Sofia. He told me about the Red Army War Memorial. I know this one I say. Is near football stadium. Is in big park. Sure, he says. This is the one. And now it is skate park. Like in America. All graffiti and kids on skateboards. For me, I think this is not possible. This is statue for men who slaughtered the Nazi bastards at Kursk. Heroes. And now they make like some America. You tell me. Is this true?"

"It's true."

"Then this is a sad thing. A shameful thing. Everywhere is America. Nowhere is history. Maybe I get old I think."

"I'm sorry."

"Sure. But things change. Now you can get some money. Maybe less shit. So you call. You call when they arrive."

"I'll call."

He rang his wife to say he would be late and cut her off mid-scream. He took a tram out to the airport and soon matched the number plate with Nicholai Viskov. They all knew Nicholai. He was great. The life and soul. Didn't give a shit. Not Nicholai. He'd go anywhere would Nicholai. Greece, Turkey, Macedonia, Romania, Moldova . . . Anywhere! Crazy guy! Sure, he had a deal. He worked with the Hotel Varna. At least that was with the tourists who could afford it. It was no problem. Nicholai did OK.

A tram took him back into the city centre and he found a seat in a small café opposite the Hotel Varna and waited with a newspaper and an expresso. The taxi arrived at eleven and he matched the number plate with the one the Russian had given him. Nicholai was a jolly man in his early fifties who bounced out of the driver's door like someone who had just driven around the corner for a loaf of bread rather than someone who had just been to Bosnia and back. His passengers climbed out more gingerly and stretched out cramped limbs. They both wore bright red Liverpool shirts and Nicholai was speaking away in English. He idly wondered who they were and what on earth they were doing riding a cab from Bosnia to Sofia. Maybe they were on their way to the big game. He had heard the English were taking all kinds of crazy routes down to Istanbul. Crazy people. More money than sense. He took his phone from his pocket and dialled the number in Moscow.

"So they are here. Hotel Varna. Any taxi driver will know it. There is a café across from the front door. I am there. I have a blue jacket and a red shirt."

"You are very good. My man he is at the airport. He will be with you soon. So now is goodbye, OK? Maybe one day we can do more."

"I would like that."

THE LONG AND WINDING
ROAD TO ISTANBUL

"Goodbye my friend."

He strolled across the road and spun a light line to the girl on the desk who was way too bored to be suspicious and was more than happy to tell him the English were in room seven and get back to watching the TV.

Nicholai and the Englishmen emerged a few minutes later and headed off in the taxi. A bar probably. Now there was a nice idea. A bar and a plate of meat with no fat on it. Maybe that was exactly what he would do once he got paid. And the miserable bitch back in the flat could just go to hell.

The man arrived five minutes shy of midnight. He was nondescript and middle-aged and used as few words as possible.

"You have number?"

"Seven."

"So. You take this."

And he was gone. Grigori opened the envelope and took a peep inside and in the dim light of the street lamp he picked out the features of George Washington and smiled.

Sir Hubert had told his wife that they would have to use the beef for sandwiches and returned to his office in the city to call the man at the Home Office who signed off the Technical Solutions invoices. At first the man had made lots of noises about the whole thing being quite out of the question but it was only posturing. After a few minutes he agreed to do what he could and was successful enough in his efforts to ensure that the multi-million pound electronic ears of GCHQ in leafy Gloucestershire were wide open when Eddie made his call to Dimitri. A transcript of their conversation was emailed to the Chief Constable who then busied himself in getting a warrant to tap the hotel phone.

Then he called Frank but only got an answer service because Frank was sitting next to Lucy at 35,000 feet in a plane heading for Istanbul. It had been many years since Sir Hubert had used the camp bed in his office, but it looked as if this would be a night for the Hollywood approach. He tossed his tie, filled up the coffee machine and waited.

Frank called from Ataturk International Airport as soon as his switched back on phone registered a message.

"Any news?"

"Actually, there is. We listened out for any calls from the north-west of England to the Greater Moscow area."

"That was clever."

"Wasn't it. Not my idea I'm afraid. I'm much too old for all this new-fangled stuff. Anyway. Tate gave us the slip earlier after Jankovic alerted him to the fact that we had him under surveillance. Now we have him tagged again. He's holed up in a hotel outside Preston."

"What did he have to say to Dimitri?"

"Edited highlights. I think he was a little nervous that Zharkhov would take a walk from the whole thing."

"And did he?"

"No. Quite the opposite. He is taking the retreat to behind the Urals approach. And I'm afraid that once he heard that the lads were headed for Sofia he volunteered to pull a few strings. Secret police pals from the good old days."

"Damn. I was worried about that."

"He won't be doing anything just yet. He said he would look into things and call back. Maybe tonight, maybe in the morning. Then we'll know more."

"What are you doing now? Just waiting on the call?"

Sir Hubert gave his deserted office a weary smile. He hadn't a single officer on his whole team who he trusted enough to help him and yet here he was planning every move with a career criminal of thirty years standing.

"That's about it."

"Maybe you could make a start on something."

"Like?"

"Get hold of your oppo in Istanbul. Try to persuade him to find out where Eddie and Dimitri are booked in. They always book in their own names. It shouldn't be all that hard."

"I think I could manage that."

"Top man. Call me as soon as you hear anything."

"Will do. What's all that racket?"

"I've just got off the plane in Istanbul. It's like bloody Anfield here. Unbelievable."

"Possibly it would have been nice if you could have told me that you were leaving the country."

"I suppose it would. Sorry about that."

"Are you going to tell me where you will be staying?"

"I don't think so."

Time to kill off the conversation. Lucy raised an eyebrow as they queued for the immigration counter. Her two cameramen were shooting off footage of the hundreds of red-clad figures whose songs filled the gleaming chrome of the Arrivals Terminal. She reached into her bag and gave him a match ticket.

"Here. You'll need this. They are accepting sight of a ticket in place of an entry Visa. What is the news?"

"Not great but not disastrous. Eddie went off-road once Goran tipped him off about the bugging. But one of the Bizzies was a clever boy. They monitored all calls out of the north-west to Moscow. They got Eddie making a call from a hotel in Preston to Dimitri."

Lucy gave a low whistle. "Bloody hell Frank. That must have come from GCHQ. Sir Hubert is certainly going the extra mile."

"He's going to have to. Anyway Dimitri has offered to help. He said he's got old mates in Sofia who he'll call up. He'll be ringing back either tonight or in the morning."

She had allowed her spirits to rise on the flight from London. Thanks to Jeremy the threat had been lifted. All Mickey needed to do was to make the last leg of the journey and everything would be all right. But now the danger had returned. And she knew of no Jeremy in Sofia. All she would be able to do would be to call Mickey and by hook or by crook persuade him to report to a local police station. But would that be safe? No doubt Dimitri's pals probably wore uniforms. A police station would probably be the worst place to go. Frank noticed the raw fear that jumped into her eyes.

"Hey. Panic when it's time to panic. Right now we can't do a thing except wait."

She gave a small nod.

They took two taxis to make the twenty kilometre journey to their hotel in the city. It seemed like just about every taxi that edged along the road four abreast was carrying figures clad in red. They hung out of the windows and sang. And all along the pavements young Turks raised their fists high and shouted with them. Despite her gnawing fear, Lucy couldn't help but smile at the ridiculous sight. In the taxi behind, both of her cameramen were hanging out of the windows filming the whole thing. It was like a red army had come to liberate the city and the good people of Istanbul were making it more than obvious how they felt. For whatever reason the host city had chosen red almost to a man. All along the road that ran along the banks of the Bosporus there were locals wearing red. They did not have the replica shirts like the fans in the taxis. They had cheap T-shirts bought at the market for a couple of pounds. She started mental notes for the programme which one way or another still had to be made.

This was a hook she hadn't anticipated. But the more she worked the thought, the more she liked it. It was no accident that the people of the city had chosen red. As the game of football had gone more and more corporate over the years, Liverpool had been left behind. They had hung on to the old principles of the Boot Room. They had tried to believe that it was enough to try and just be a football club. After all it had served them well enough down the years. So they had never really managed to go down the road of David Beckham duvet covers and zillions of replica shirts in Japan. They had stayed in their own back yard and been left behind to such an extent that there were lots of rumours that the finances were in a proper state. The extent of this slippage had been cruelly exposed in a league season that had seen the once mighty reds finish thirty-seven points behind the brash Champions from the banks of the Thames. Worse still, they had finished behind Everton and missed out on a Champions League berth for the next season.

That meant an income drop of ten million, minimum, and things would probably get worse again. Like Leeds United before them, they would have to sell players to appease their edgy bank manager. And yet there was still just one flickering hope. Despite their dire league form, the team had defied every prediction and made it to Istanbul. And the football world had watched with an open mouth as the money men of Juventus and Chelsea were unceremoniously dumped in the cauldron of Anfield. And much of the football world had bought into the story big style. And for the first time as she looked at the remarkable scenes outside the open window of the taxi, Lucy began to properly understand the story it was her job to tell. It was the story of Gerrard's outrageous half volley in the dying seconds that had unleashed a flood of emotion from the Kop. It was the story of a Spaniard and a Frenchman who had returned from broken bones to fight through in the seething hatred of Turin. It was the story of the

THE LONG AND WINDING
ROAD TO ISTANBUL

world record breaking barrage of sound that had finally broken the seemingly invincible Chelsea. A team gently guided by a soft-spoken manager who refused to join in the fashionable hype and posturing that the tabloids all loved so much. A team driven forward by a heartbeat that was made in Liverpool. Stevie Gerrard and Jamie Carragher didn't do the Versace clothes and mobile phone adverts and pretend to be pop stars. They spoke with voices that were born and bred Merseyside. They had grown up in tough streets and they had dreamed of playing for the team down the road. They didn't go about kissing their shirts. They didn't have to.

And then there was the twelfth man. All forty-four thousand of him. The twelfth man whose huge voice had entered the Guinness book of records. The twelfth man had swept the team forward with pure unquestioning belief. And there was an unquestioned rough glamour to the twelfth man. The twelfth man came from the same city as the Beatles. A poor city that had seen better days and been kicked in the teeth and kicked again. A city that had been stripped of wealth but never pride. And so when the twelfth man roared the eleven other men home, it was about more than just kicking a football around. It was about fighting the odds. It was about refusing to bow to the rules of the all-conquering capitalist world. It was about bucking the trend. It was about the small guy winning out for once.

And that was why they now lined the streets. Young men in cheap clothes from the poor parts of town. They weren't cheering because the big corporations told them to. They were cheering because the big corporations had been kicked up the arse for once. These young men were the same as young men she had seen on street corners from the Balkans to the Middle East to the darkest places in Africa. They had no jobs and no money and the shining temples of the capitalist world were out of reach. They were the ones who had missed the boat because the boat had never come into the harbour.

And now they had found themselves a kindred spirit. That was why they stood to welcome the twelfth man into their city. And for the very first time Lucy knew what it was to be a part of Mickey's world. She had travelled her world looking in from the outside. She had run away for so many years. Watching. Reporting. Hurting. Grieving. But never part of it. Never a part of anything. But she was part of this. Just like Mickey was. Because this was all about the city where she had been born. The city she had run from and never returned to. The city that had almost died in the dark misery of the eighties when the face of Yosser Hughes came to symbolise the Thatcher losers. The city that had somehow hung on and hung on until at last finding one last chance at redemption. Just like she had hung on for Mickey McGuire. Just like Mickey McGuire had hung on for her. And now the cards were about to fall, one way or another. Mickey had three hundred miles left and the men in red had ninety minutes. By midnight the next day it would be done one way or another. And Lucy for the first time knew what Mickey was talking about when he said that there were times when a football match was about more than twenty-two overpaid blokes kicking a football about.

"So. Here is restaurant. Very good. Very nice I think."

Mickey couldn't get his head around the Bulgarian taxi driver's energy. The man was in permanent overdrive. The restaurant was on the pavement under big red awnings opposite a dome-roofed church straight out of Dr Zhivago. Four tables were taken up in red-shirted fans adding to an already impressive array of empty bottles.

"All right boys."

Heads turned. Thumbs were raised. And the singing kicked off again. Mickey and Tonto joined the nearest table and he waved a waitress over and ordered beer for everyone in sight. Only a few hours earlier they had stared death in the face. Now they were back on the road again. Part of the army now. Only three hundred miles to go. Nothing. Seven or eight hours according to Nicholai who was all lined-up to take them the next morning.

Then a sudden thought jumped into Mickey's head like a two-footed challenge.

"Oh shit."

"What's up Mickey?"

"We're a right pair of dickheads Tonto, that's what's up."

"Why Mickey?"

"Because all we'll thought about for days is getting here isn't it?"

"Well we had to get here didn't we. We wouldn't have been here if we hadn't got here."

The stunning simplicity of Tonto's logic stopped him in his tracks for a moment.

"Yeah. That's right enough. But just getting here isn't enough is it?"

"Why not Mickey?"

"Because we haven't sorted out any bloody tickets yet have we?"

"Oh."

"Mickey absent-mindedly gave a signal that meant another round to everyone who wanted one. The waitress seemed troubled by this and disappeared off inside to have a conversation with the manager. He emerged a few minutes later with an anxious smile. He leaned close to Nicholai and they had a murmured conversation. The taxi driver nodded understanding and tapped Mickey on the shoulder.

"Mr Mickey, manager he is worry now. Maybe bill is quite big now. So he think can these English make pay?"

"Oh. Sorry about that. Here. Sort it can you Nico. There's a good lad. Tell him to get the ale in for those inside as well."

He passed over a handful of twenty-pound notes, which took away the anxious smile.

"What are you going to do Mickey?"

"When we get back to the room I'll text Lucy. Maybe she will be able to sort a couple of tickets out. Otherwise we'll just have to try and buy one when we get there. Surely there'll be plenty of touts."

"OK Mickey."

At last the bar started to empty out and they rode through the empty streets back to the hotel. They agreed that Nicholai would collect them at nine for the final leg of the journey. Once they were inside the room Mickey's eyelids suddenly felt like lead. He switched on his phone and tapped out a text message and sent it. The screen told him there were lots of unread messages waiting for his attention. It also told him that he only had one bar of signal left and he had left his phone charger at home. No chance of checking messages then. One bar would be good for one phone call and he only needed to make one phone call.

He killed the power and fell asleep in seconds without bothering to get under the covers.

Mickey was the exception rather than the rule when it came to finding sleep in the early morning hours of the night before the big game. The time difference meant that it was just past one o'clock when the phone by the bedside rang in Eddie's hotel room.

"You are not sleeping, no?"

"No. Not even close. How have you got on?"

Dimitri was at his desk in Moscow. He was very proud of the desk which he had procured in the crazy days following the collapse of Communism. Once upon a time, Czar Nicholas the second had signed his papers at the very same desk. It would have fetched a small fortune at any auction house in the world. Sitting behind its perfect lines made Dimitri feel good about himself. And he liked to feel good about himself. It was how he felt now. The man with a finger on the pulse.

"So yes, my friend. I have news. Is good news I think. My friend in Sofia, he find the taxi. And when he finds the taxi he can find the hotel because these taxi men like to make a commission, you understand?"

"I do."

"So I tell him he can wait and he can see if these thief might come to this Hotel Varna. And yes, for sure, they can come. Then I am thinking after we speak what else it is that I can do, OK? Maybe I can find a man who can make some killing. OK. Is possible. Bulgaria is only poor place. There are men who do this thing. Maybe $5000. Nothing. But then I think there can be problem here. You see, I like to think Eddie. The police they knew about Goran. We know this thing. So maybe they know the name Dimtri. Sure. Why not? It isn't a problem right now. But if these thief make dead in Sofia maybe there can be questions. Maybe some people say maybe this Dimitri have some friend in Sofia. So they can go to files from old Lubyanka and they find that Dimitri has once been in Sofia. In 1988. And they can find who his friend was at that time. So maybe they arrest this friend and he can tell them that it was Dimitri who say, OK, you can find someone to make these thief dead. So I cannot make this risk Eddie. But I still like to help my friend. So I can send one man on plane OK. When these thief leave hotel room this man I sent he can go into this room. He finds mobile phone, OK. He has put tracking device in this phone, OK. So tomorrow when these thief go to Istanbul you can find out where they are. So maybe when you come tomorrow you can also bring man. A man who can make these thief dead maybe. This hotel you stay, Eddie. It has computer suite, yes?"

"I have a computer to use in the room."

"Then you can do this thing and you can call me back very soon. You can find search engine. Type Georgi Markov OK. You read how it was with this Markov. If you think this is good, then I can help your man to make same with this thief. Is not a big problem. You can look and then you call me OK?"

"Sure Dimitri. I'll be with you in a minute or two."

Eddie switched onto the computer and got onto the internet. He loaded Google and was rewarded with a screen full of hits. He selected a BBC page. 'FLASHBACK: DISSIDENT POISONING'

'The poison Ricin was famously used to murder Bulgarian dissident Georgi Markov in 1978.
Markov, a BBC World Service journalist and a strong critic of the communist regime, was killed in London when he was injected with Ricin while he waited at a bus stop.
Nobody has ever been charged with the murder, but it is widely believed that the Bulgarian secret service and the KGB were behind it.'

As he read Eddie remembered elements of the case. It had made front page news at the time. Well of course it had. The killer had injected Markov with poison from the sharpened tip of an umbrella as the dissident had waited for a bus on a busy London street. Which of course made the whole thing like a Bond movie. Which ensured that the press lapped the whole thing up like thirsty cats. He finished the article and sat back to stare at the screen. What had Dimitri said? "I can help your man to make same with this thief." It could only mean one thing. Dimitri was offering to bring a KGB killer kit with him to Istanbul and Eddie could nominate a guy to go and do a Markov on Mickey McGuire. It was all elegantly simple. The tracking device in the mobile phone would lead the assassin right up next to the target and then it would be a quick pin prick and away. As he considered it, it became clear that there would be the perfect venue and opportunity for such a kill. Outside the stadium a couple of hours before the match in the midst of 45,000 hyped up singing Scousers. Who would notice if one of them got a small prick in the crush? Who would notice if one suddenly fell ill? Then what? The St John's ambulance and a hospital in Istanbul. No doubt the KGB would have gone more sophisticated in the decade that followed the Markov execution. Whatever Dimitri had in mind would probably be untraceable at autopsy.

By the time he read the article through for a second time he was smiling for the first time in many hours. He dialled up the Russian.

"It's Eddie again."

"So you can read about this Georgi Markov, yes?"

"Yes. And the answer is yes. You're a top man Dimitri."

"And you can find a man before your plane leaves in the morning? Maybe Frank?"

"Frank can't make it. I need him to take care of some things at this end. But there's no need to worry Dimitri. I don't need a man. Sometimes when a job needs doing, it is best to do it yourself."

This brought an appreciative chuckle. "So. You can make it yourself. Is good Eddie. Is very good. This is how we can make it in Russia. I think tomorrow can be a great day. First you can punish these thief. Then Liverpool can make very nice win. Then we can drink too much vodka. Men like you and me, we don't have problems. We are men who like win I think. No problems Eddie. Only victory OK?"

"Like at Kursk?"

"For sure. Like Kursk. We can kill every Nazi bastard in our way. Like Kursk. I can see you tomorrow OK."

"You can count on it."

Eddie poured himself two of the whisky miniatures from the mini bar and drained the glass in a single gulp. It had been a bad few days. The worst he had known for many years. But the next day he would have the toothpaste back in the tube. He would have just a fleeting glimpse into Mickey McGuire's eyes. Surprise at the sudden unexpected pain. Surprise at seeing the face of Eddie Tate. And then he would wonder whether it had really been Eddie at all. And he would wonder what the hell that pricking pain had been. And then he would forget the whole thing because he would be so focused on the game.

But he would never see the game. Instead he would fall ill and die in some god forsaken Turkish hospital. And Eddie Tate revelled in the thought. He was going to get things back under control and killing Mickey McGuire would make the perfect start.

Lucy had finally nodded off when the ring of Frank's mobile woke her. She peeled her eyes open and listened.

"Sir Hubert?"

"It is."

"Working late?"

"Yes. Bad news Frank. Really bad news."

Lucy saw Frank's face slowly grow pale as he listened to the transcript of Eddie's conversation with Zharkov. At last he spoke in a voice that was suddenly very drained.

"Thanks. Really. I'm going to think about this for a while and I'll call you back. You're not going to bed or anything are you? Good. Give me half an hour or so. Bye."

He snapped the phone shut and met Lucy's enquiring expression.

"Do you remember Georgi Markov?"

"No. Why?"

"He was a dissident who was murdered by the Bulgarian Secret Police in London back in 1978. He was waiting for a bus when the killer pricked him with an umbrella. The tip was sharpened and coated in Ricin."

"Actually I think I do remember a bit about it now. There was a real stink on the news wasn't there?"

"Yes. It's all bad news I'm afraid. Zharkov's man came good. He tracked the lads to a Hotel Varna in the centre of Sofia. He's managed to get someone into their room and to put a tracking device in Mickey's phone. Tomorrow he's going to bring the same kind of kit that the KGB used to kill Markov. And a tracking device. Eddie will use the tracker to get up close to Mickey and then . . . Well you know. Same as Markov."

"What. Eddie himself?"

Frank nodded. "Said sometimes you need to do a job yourself."

"Oh God Frank. What have I done?"

"You've done nowt yet. I just need to think this through a bit." He lit up and the cigarette tasted completely foul but he smoked it anyway. "Any chance of a brew?"

"I suppose so." Her voice was flat and defeated.

"Look Lucy. It's not as bad as it could have been."

"Oh really. How do you work that one out?"

"If Zharkov had paid for some cowboy to whack the lads in their room in Sofia we probably couldn't have done a thing about it. At least we've still got some time to work things out. So cut the panic stations. We're going to be OK here. Trust."

She could see why her brother had kept Frank McGuire by his side for so long. She had always prided herself on her ability to keep her cool in the toughest situations and time had tested this ability to the full. But Frank McGuire was up in a different league. He looked like a walking corpse and her mind boggled at how much his hand must have been hurting, and yet he still kept everything together with machine-like determination.

She made them both coffee and took up a station by the window, which looked out across the moonlit river to the winking lights of Asia on the other side.

Her phone peeped out the fact that a text message had landed in the inbox. She picked it up without much enthusiasm and read. Then against all the odds, she smiled. Frank looked up and noticed.

"What's that?"

"Your bloody stupid brother. That's what. Here we are worrying ourselves sick about how to save his wretched life and guess what is troubling dear Mickey?"

"Go on?"

"He and Tonto haven't had the chance to sort out tickets with all the excitement. Can I get them some? See you tomorrow. Kiss, kiss. Mickey."

Frank joined her in a rueful grin. "Well you don't suppose that having a group of Bosnian wackos trying to top him in some godforsaken middle of nowhere was ever likely to distract him from the main event?"

"No. I don't suppose I do."

"They won't be all that easy to come by mind. You'll have to get on with it sharpish in the morning."

"No I won't. I am an organised career woman remember. I planned ahead. I bought two tickets off ebay a fortnight ago. That was when all of this seemed like good idea."

He got to his feet and took a long stretch. "OK. I've done some thinking. We have tonnes of options and no need to get all down and miserable. Want to hear them?"

"Course I do."

"Option number one. I call Sir Hubert and ask him to pull Eddie at the airport and bang him up on any old charge. No Eddie. No poisoned umbrella threat. No problem."

"Jesus Frank, why the hell didn't I think of that? It's bloody obvious."

"Bloody obvious and bloody flawed."

"Why?"

"Because Eddie will beat the charge and get out on bail. Then he'll be like a demented rhino. You know him Lucy. He'll stop at nothing to get to the bottom of what's happened, especially when he finds out there are missing bags of smack all over the Pool. So option one means we have to spend the rest of our lives looking over our shoulders and I guess he'll get us in the end. And remember my mum and dad still live in Southport."

The thought sent a chill down her spine.

"I see. Option two?"

"Risky, but not all that risky. We call Mickey in the morning and have a chat. Then we make sure he gets met by the local Bizzies when he is well out of town. Then we'll need Sir Hubert to stick his neck out further than he's ever stuck it out in his life. It's a long shot, but something tells me he might go for it."

"Tell me."

And he told her. Then he made a call. Then he called Sir Hubert who sounded tired to the bone.

"A question, Sir Hubert. Give me the truth, OK."

"I'll try."

"Do you want to take Eddie down for the glory and the headlines or do you want to take him down because he is a murderous bastard and needs sorting out?"

"I have no idea what you are talking about."

"Yes you have. If Eddie went down hard and you didn't get your picture in the papers would you be happy?"

Now the policeman got the drift. Of course public recognition was always nice but he already had his knighthood. And his hatred for Tate had certainly deepened a few notches over the last few days. McGuire obviously had something in mind and his instincts told him that it was going to be unorthodox.

"I want to see Eddie Tate no longer a cancer on the city of Liverpool. And I'm open to offers."

"Good. I hoped you'd say that. Want to hear a plan?"

"I've nothing much else to do right now."

"Well don't interrupt. Just hear the whole thing out then you can have your say. I just made a call to a guy I know. He's a Dutchman.

Willie Kuyppens. He flies chartered flights in a Gulfstream Jet. Eddie has used him a time or two when he wants to impress people. I have arranged for him to be at John Lennon Airport at seven in the morning. You catch the plane and he'll bring you to Istanbul. But there is something you need to do first. You're not going to like it, but just keep listening. I'm going to give you the location of half a kilo of smack. You go and collect it now and bring it over on the plane. You need to arrange for a senior cop to collect you from the airport when you get down here. With me so far?"

Sir Hubert's heart was thumping away like a jackhammer. "I hope you're not expecting the Merseyside police to pay for this Dutchman's services?"

"No. I arranged to meet him at this end and pay him cash. I have a bag of it remember."

"Out of interest, how much?"

"Hundred grand."

"Bloody hell. Carry on."

"When you get off the plane, you leave the smack under your seat. I'll collect it when I pay Willie. What you do then is sort a few things out with the Turkish Bizzies. Lucy will call Mickey and arrange for him to meet up with the local cops somewhere outside of the city. They go to the game with him. Lots of them, plain clothes types. They're bound to have some tasty guys for this kind of thing. Once he gets to the game he rings Lucy as agreed and everyone waits on Eddie. The locals grab him before he gets within twenty yards. That will give you possession of a KGB killer toy with intent to kill. The trouble is that all of that is still pretty James Bond. Eddie will hire in the best lawyer money can buy and he'll probably beat the rap and be back in the Pool in a couple of months. So we need some insurance. I'll plant the smack in his room and you organise the locals to get a warrant and raid it once Eddie sets off for the game. Now we're talking nailed on. A KGB toy and half a kilo is something even Eddie's not going to beat. Especially down here. It means he's going to die in a Turkish Jail and the last years of his life will be as unpleasant as he deserves them to be."

"Good God. I wouldn't want you as an enemy."

"Remember not to order any nutjobs to kill my kid brother then. There's one last thing. When the locals raid Eddie's room you need to get them to do the same on Dimitri. They won't find anything but that doesn't matter. You need to get them to arrest a young woman called Ivana Petrovich. Get them to take her back to the station and keep her until I pick her up. So. That's it."

"You're not asking for much then. What on earth makes you think that the Turkish Police will play ball?"

"I'm supremely confident in your powers of persuasion. Besides, it's going to look great for them isn't it. Catching a Liverpool Mafia Chief with a poison dart and a room full of smack. I bet you would jump at it if the boot was on the other foot."

Sir Hubert considered this and had to reluctantly concede that he probably would. Both men knew that if the plan went forward the Chief Constable of Greater Merseyside Police would be breaking every rule in every book that had been written. But they also both knew that it was a plan that would finish Eddie Tate on a very permanent basis. Once he was locked away on a thirty-year sentence in some nightmare prison, every bit of his energy would be taken up with the daily task of not getting his throat cut. He would have no time for any retribution at home. And that idea had huge appeal. It was a rare chance of justice as pure as water from a mountain stream with no five-hundred-pound-an-hour lawyers to screw the whole thing up.

"If I do this, I will expect a full report on absolutely everything you know about Eddie Tate's business."

"And I will expect a guaranteed cast iron letter of immunity from all charges for me and Mickey. So have we got a deal?"

The older man took one last moment then took the plunge.

"So where do I find this bloody heroin then?"

Chapter 9
Istanbul – May 2005

By eleven o'clock, the day was going better than Suliman Vardar would have dared to hope. As the head of Istanbul's police force he had been feeling the squeeze of political pressure for many months. The number one aspiration of his political masters in the Parliament in Ankara was for Turkey to finally be granted leave to join the European Union. The feeling was that the day when this would happen was getting nearer. It meant that everyone wanted the country to be painted in the best possible light at all times. They wanted to look modern and European and democratic and to put as much blue water as they could between themselves and the crazies on the other side of the borders with Syria and Iraq.

All this meant that the city being given the honour of staging the Champions League Final was always going to be a double-edged sword. Of course it was an opportunity for the city to show off its best face. But it was also a potential banana skin. If things went wrong, it would give ammunition to all those who wanted to keep the Turks away from the top table.

He had wrestled tirelessly with two main problems. The first was the stadium. Maybe Allah had some inkling as to what was in the minds of those who chose the site for the Ataturk Stadium, but Suliman certainly had not. The great concrete bowl was placed miles from the centre of the city in a few hundred acres of tussocky wilderness ringed by factories and crumbling high-rise estates. Istanbul was a city of many postcards and magnificent vistas, and all of them were a good twenty miles from the new stadium. There were no rail links and the roads to the vicinity left a lot to be desired. The roads to the actual stadium itself were a complete catastrophe. Just a couple of months before the final there had been just one and it was only wide enough for two cars to pass each other with great care. Those in charge had promised that on the day there would be more. He had paid the site a last visit the day before and found that this was more or less true, although in many sections the tarmac was still wet.

It was his job to try and ensure that over seventy thousand visiting fans managed to make it from the city centre to the stadium in some kind of order and no matter how many plans his people put in place, it still looked like it was going to be a complete nightmare. A few months earlier Istanbul's two premier teams, Galatasaray and Fenerbace had faced each other in the cup final. Had the game been played in the city centre, the stadium would have been sold out more than ten times over. But a mere 18,000 chose to make the trip out to the Ataturk Stadium. The locals had voted with their feet and watched the game on TV.

After all the planning, he knew that it would all come down to the city's thousands of cab drivers coming good. One way or another over 10,000 of them would have to do the donkey-work of getting the people out to the stadium and back again, and if things went really, really well it would be touch and go. If things went badly, it would be a complete disaster and umpteen million viewers all over the world would tune in to the sight of thousands of empty seats and the story that the local infrastructure had failed completely. And there was no doubt who would catch the blame.

The second pressure point had been building from the moment that two English sides made it through to meet each other in the semi-final. The prospect of massive numbers of visiting English fans had been something that had given police chiefs all over Europe goose bumps for over thirty years. There were any number of factors that had been keeping Suliman awake at night. It was to be a final played between an English team and an Italian team, just like it had been at the Heysel Stadium in Brussels twenty years earlier when twenty-nine Italian fans had ended their night in body bags. The big difference now was that the Italians had not only caught up the English in terms of football hooliganism, but they had clearly overtaken them. The pyrotechnic display of flare throwing in the all Milan quarter-final had offered ample evidence. Then there was the recent case of the two Leeds United fans who had been stabbed to death before a Champions League tie in the city. And then to cap it all the Prime Minister of Britain along with his stunted pal in Washington had spent a good four years brainwashing the western world into the fact that all Muslims were religious maniacs champing at the bit to become suicide bombers.

When he had put all the factors together, he had come to the conclusion that one way or another his career was about to come to a shuddering halt. A patsy would be needed when the city became gridlocked and mass brawls broke out among the jammed up traffic. And the patsy was in all likelihood about to be Suliman Vardar.

But it wasn't happening that way at all. In fact it had been almost the complete opposite. The English invasion had been building steadily for several days and the reports that landed on his desk were all the same. All over his city the visiting fans and the locals were getting along like they had known each other for years. The people of Istanbul had adopted Liverpool almost to a man and it had been a time of handshaking and photographs. If anything, the place had been much quieter than normal as many of the city's bad boys were clearly more interested in meeting the English than causing their usual bother.

For over twenty-four hours an armada of charter planes had been landing at both airports and disgorging thousand upon thousand high-spirited Liverpudlians and still there wasn't a hint of any trouble. It had been his plan to spend most of the morning in Taksim Square which was where the fans would gather with their banners before embarking on the cross city trek to the stadium. But then he had received another mysterious call from the Chief Constable of Greater Merseyside. The day before he had duly obliged a request to find out the hotel where an Englishman and a Russian were staying. Now Sir Hubert had told him that something big was about to happen and that he was flying over in a chartered jet. This had certainly got Suliman's mind racing. Maybe things were done differently in Liverpool, but there was more chance of the Pope getting the job as head preacher in the Blue Mosque than him ever been given the funds to fly almost two thousand miles in a chartered jet.

He had made his way to the airport in plenty of time. As he approached, a constant stream of yellow taxis were headed out in the opposite direction, almost every one of them filled with cheering red clad fans. An airport official informed him that the jet was on time and a slot had been arranged for five to eleven. Suliman had watched it glide down from the grey sky and taxi up to where he waited. A few minutes later the hatch opened and a tall, distinguished looking figure descended the steps and strode briskly over to shake his hand.

Suliman suggested that his opposite number might be hungry and maybe he would enjoy some lunch and Sir Hubert was indeed particularly keen on the idea. By one o'clock an accord had been reached. Suliman had made his calls and issued his instructions. A discreet watch was placed in the lobby of the Ritz Carlton Hotel in Taksim. It was reported that the Russian had checked in at ten-thirty with a party of four, two male who both looked like ex-military, and two females who both looked like they were straight off a magazine cover. At 12.30 his men reported that the Englishman had checked in alone. Then as the two policemen took strong coffee just after one o'clock, it was reported that both targets had left the hotel along with one of the military minders. A team was following and one of them had heard them ask the taxi to take them to one of the city's more expensive restaurants.

"Have you got Tate's room number?"

"Of course. It is 613. A suite. He is not poor, this man you come for."

"No he is not poor. Not yet. Do you mind if I make a call?"

"No. Please. I will give you privacy."

Suliman waited at the bar whilst Sir Hubert dialed. "Frank?"

"Yeah."

"Did you get the package?"

"Yeah. No problems."

"OK. It's room 613. Tate and Zharkov have just gone out. They told the taxi to take them to a restaurant. Zharkov's suite is on the floor above."

"Good. Any news on Ivana Petrovich?"

"She was checked in with Zarkhov's party. There were two men who sound like the minders you told me about. One of them has gone to the restaurant. The other has stayed at the hotel."

"And what about Eddie?"

"He came alone."

"Perfect. OK leave it with me. I'll call you when the package is in place."

Apart from his two-hour trip to the airport, Frank had spent the morning with Lucy and the team who were filming the growing crowd in Taksim Square. By lunchtime it had become an awesome sight. Every square inch of wall space was covered by hundreds of banners and by noon the place had become a sea of red humanity. He was amazed at Lucy's professionalism. They had both managed no more than three snatched hours of sleep and yet she went about her work with an easy smile and infectious energy. What made it all the more amazing was that he knew that inside she was being eaten up with a gnawing terror that was growing with every passing minute. In the early hours of the morning the plan had seemed foolproof once the Chief Constable had agreed to leave the rulebook in his desk drawer in the cause of justice. But every plan has a weak point and their plan had started to unravel over breakfast when Lucy had made the call to Mickey.

"The Vodaphone you are calling may be switched off."

The minute the words fed through into her ear, a cold fear took hold. Everything hinged on talking to Mickey and letting him know what was about to happen. If she couldn't get through he would arrive at the stadium in complete ignorance of the danger that was waiting. She had tried the number every ten minutes until she felt like smashing her phone into a million pieces. And in between her failed calls she managed to put on her reporter's face and do her job.

Frank was about to update her on the news from Sir Hubert when she gave a shake of her head, pointed at her ear-piece and mouthed the word 'Live'. Then she squared herself in front of the camera and spoke with a smooth smile.

"As you can see, the scenes here in Taksim Square are really quite amazing. We've been here since ten o clock and the whole thing has just built and built. There are plane loads of fans landing every twenty minutes or so and Taksim Square is the magnet at the heart of this great city that is drawing them together. It really is the most remarkable sight . . ."

The second cameraman stood on a portable stool which enabled him to pan his camera over the sea of heads and flags. An eager crowd of fans clutching cans of beer had by now gathered around Lucy to make leering faces at the camera.

THE LONG AND WINDING
ROAD TO ISTANBUL

*". . . Let me see if I can get a word here . . . When did you arrive sir .
. ."*

*"Bloody hell. You're the bird off the news aren't you? I've fancied
you for years!"*

"I'm delighted to hear that, so when did you guys arrive . . ."

"Hey darling, is it true that you're a Scouser or what . . ."

"Yes. I come from Liverpool. . ."

"Come clean then. You a red or a bluenose then?"

"The BBC is always impartial . . ."

This was drowned out in a torrent of booing which cracked Lucy's
face into a smile.

"Oh, go on then. Red."

One of the younger ones was less than convinced.

"Yeah. Bet you're only saying that cos we're all here like."

Lucy allowed her accent to revert to how it had once been when she
was thirteen.

*"Listen up sunshine. I was watching the lads lift the European Cup
when your Mamm was still learning you to clean your teeth on your
own."*

This brought on a big cheer and a huge blush to the face of the young
doubter.

"Come on boys. Let's have a song then."

They obliged with a version of Yellow Submarine.

*"We all dream of a team of Carraghers . . . a team of Carraghers . . .
A team of Carraghers . . ."*

*"So as you can see. Things are building up here in Istanbul. You
see what this lot are like now. Just imagine what the noise will be like
when Steven Gerrard leads out the Liverpool team in a few hours*

time. This is Lucy Mathews. BBC News 24. Taksim Square . . ."

"And number one is Carragher . . . number two is Carragher . . . Number three is Carragher . . . And number four is Carragher . . . We all dream of a team of Carraghers . . ."

She turned to Frank.

"I'll try again."

"The Vodaphone you are calling may be switche . . . ."

Again she fought back the overwhelming desire to smash the phone to pieces.

"Hey darling. Let me kiss your hand will you."

Before she had much say in the matter her hand was at the lips of her long term admirer and the moment was caught forever by the camera on his mobile.

"Cheers love. You're a doll. I knew you'd never be a bluenose."

The panic was starting to rise and she wasn't sure how much longer she was going to able to keep a lid on it.

"We need to do something Frank."

He was feeling every bit as bad, but there was no way he was going to let her see it. Ever since the first failed call over breakfast he had managed to keep up an exterior of steady confidence.

"Look Lucy. There's no need to get in a state about this. The local Bizzies are on Eddie's tail so even if we don't get chance to talk to Mickey, we still have things covered. Anyway, there's hours yet. He's probably just saving his battery or something. Knowing our Mickey, He'll have his phone switched off because he's worried you're going to call him to give him a bollocking about the tickets. You know what he's like."

Christ it was lame. But what else could he say? It was his plan and if it all went pear-shaped he would have to live with it. Not that there was a chance in hell of that. If he allowed Mickey to be killed, it wasn't something that would ever go away. Every element of the whole situation was down to him. If he had got his head down at school and not played the hard man, then none of this would have happened. He cursed himself for wasting his mental energy on the dreaded 'what if' routine. None of it could be helped. All he could do was to focus on what he could control. And to hope and pray that his toss-pot of a brother would just switch his bastard phone on.

THE LONG AND WINDING
ROAD TO ISTANBUL

"Look Lucy, I need to go and dump this package. I have to say I feel a bit dodgy kicking around with half a kilo of smack in my pocket. The hotel's just around the corner. Give me half an hour OK?"

"Fine." She was biting at her lip and the crowd that was swarming all around was making her feel claustrophobic.

"I won't be long."

She reached for the phone again but forced herself not to. Wait ten minutes. Surely he would answer in ten minutes. He had to.

Ivana had a deep sinking feeling. It had started on the plane. She hadn't seen anything of Dimitri for several days and she had been starting to worry that he had tired of her. It would have been no more than par for the course if he had. Dimitri's girls were in and out of his life on a revolving door basis. Already she had been part of his court for longer than any of the others. He said it was because she had a brain in her head. Beauty and brains. A rare thing he had said. Rare like the Siberian tiger. Rare like snowflakes in June. He hadn't called until Sunday night and she had all but given up hope of being able to make the trip to Istanbul.

When he had called there had been something different. It was nothing obvious. Nothing she could properly identify. Just something. Almost a kind of smugness. It made her feel uneasy as she packed her things and waited to be picked up. On the plane he had ordered champagne and been his normal buoyant self. But again there had been something behind the high spirits. It had taken two hours for her to summon up the courage to ask if he would allow Frank to show her the city like he had done in Milan and Liverpool. And there had been something in his eyes when he had told her that Frank wasn't able to make the trip. Something had apparently come up in Liverpool which he had needed to deal with. He said that it was a shame because he knew she was going to love Istanbul. Wonderful city. But he said that she should not worry because on the day after the match he would take her around himself. They would see all the sights. They would eat wonderful food. They would walk the bridge from Europe to Asia. And in the back of his small eyes there was a coldness that made her want to shiver.

Frank wasn't coming. Frank wouldn't be at the Blue Mosque. Did Dimitri know? Had he told Eddie Tate? And had Frank been . . .

No. She wouldn't think about it. She refused to. If Frank wasn't coming this time, there would be a next time. And he had her email address. And she could wait because she was a Russian and Russians knew how to wait. To wait and to bear.

Her unease deepened once they checked in to the hotel. The other girl was new. Yelena. A dumb bimbo from somewhere in the north. She was giggly and excited and asked if she could go down to the beauty parlour. And Dimitri had slapped her backside and said of course she could and he had given her a $100 bill that had made her giggle even more.

"Maybe I will go too."

But Dimitri had shaken his head. "No. I don't want this my Ivana. Today you can stay in room I think. You can sleep. Rest. Watch the match on the TV. Vladimir he will keep you company. And tomorrow when you have recovered from the journey, I will show you the city."

She had wanted to argue. To scream at him and scratch at his face. But Vladimir was close by and standing very still. To rant would be to give the game away. To give him the pleasure of knowing that she suspected. Because being confined to the room could only mean one thing. He knew. And he was happy in the knowledge. And the only reason that Dimitri Zharkov could be happy with such knowledge was if he had acted upon it. Avenged it. And a huge sadness seeped into her bones. She knew what Dimitri Zarkhov did to those who crossed him. Who took what was his. And with an awful certainty she knew that her email inbox would stay forever empty.

Nicholai had shaken Mickey and Tonto awake just after seven o'clock in the morning and it hadn't been an easy task. Half an hour later they emerged showered and feeling human enough to deal with bread and cheese and several cups of strong coffee. Then Mickey settled the bill with a random handful of twenty-pound notes, which left the receptionist looking rather bemused. Nicholai stepped in to do the calculation, and once he had written it all down the girl looked as if all her Christmases had come early.

"You are goodbye now I think. Make very nice match please."

"No problem love. We'll make the nicest match ever."

They were both fast asleep by the time they drove clear of the high-rise blocks on the edge of the city and for the next few hours they saw nothing of the Bulgarian countryside. Nicholai stopped for petrol a few miles short of the border and they stocked up on bread and cheese and two crates of beer.

"So. Sometimes this border he is OK. Other times not so much OK. Maybe we can be patient this time."

Being patient involved three hours of inching forward in the queues either side of the line and by the time they at last hit the road on the Turkish side it was already past one and they had made a healthy dent in the first tray of beers.

"So how long now Nicholai?"

"Now he is not far. Maybe two hours. Maybe three hours. Too close really."

"Sounds good enough." Mickey checked his watch and worked it out. Even if it took maybe three hours, they would still be at the ground for four o'clock, which was more than five hours in hand. Against all odds they were running smooth and on target.

Then the front tyre blew and Nicholai wrestled the taxi onto the verge.

"Is not problem. I have spare. We are ten minutes only."

But after ten minutes, the Bulgarian was sweating and cursing as he tried with all his might to loosen the wheel nuts. Then Mickey had a go. And then Tonto had a go. And two passing drivers who saw their red shirts stopped to have a go.

"They have made this one with machine. Too much hard. Not possible because of machine."

Nicholai gave the same story of the stupid young mechanic who had tightened the wheel nuts too hard to every car that stopped. It was past 2.30 when a van pulled in with a spider brace, which did the job. After that it was ten minutes like Nicholai had promised in the first place. The van driver dug around his memory for a few words of English before taking his leave. It took a while, but at last his face was a big smile.

"So. This Milan he too much die. Yes?"

They were back rolling for 2.45. Plus three at most. 5.45. No problems. It was still over three hours the right side of things. They cracked a couple more cans and continued south.

Dimitri didn't bring out his toys until they were onto the brandy.

"So. Now my friend I can show you these things. This is first." He placed a small box on the table. Eddie thought that it was not dissimilar in appearance to the ipods that his moronic sons spent their lives plugged into. It even had headphones. Dimitri did the demonstration.

"So you can make like this. Is nothing. Too much simple. Simple is good I think." He dropped the box into his breast pocket and fitted in the earphones. "You will hear bleep sound OK. When these thief are far away it is only small sound. No sound until you are maybe five kilometres. So now, there is no sound. They are further I think. As you make nearer, this sound he makes more loud. And then he is bigger louder and bigger louder until you are too much close. Then you will see these thief, OK?"

"OK."

"Then I think you can make with this one." He took a pen from the inside pocket of the jacket, which hung over the back of his chair. "So. I give one like this." He clicked the button at the top of the pen with his thumb and a nib emerged. He scribbled on his napkin. "Sure. Why not? Is pen, OK? You can write like this. But now you can see. This time I make two times. Two times and quick."

He depressed the button twice. Click. Click. And this time a small needle poked out instead of the nib. "You can make one time like this." He took a stab at some fresh air and then clicked the needle back inside the pen. "Only one time. One time makes these thief dead OK. You not need two and three times. Only one is good. And is finish. If you want, you can throw this one away. Find some drain. Is done. No more thief I think."

He passed the items over to Eddie. He placed the box in his pocket and had a few practice goes with the pen until he had mastered the quick double click that was required to reveal the needle.

"Thanks Dimitri. I won't forget this."

"Is nothing. We can do these things for friend. Now I think we can have more brandy."

"You there Lucy?"

It was the voice of her producer in her ear from London.

"Yes."

"Look, we're getting reports from the radio guys that it is complete chaos on the way to the stadium. It sounds as if the roads are like farm tracks. You best get along there now. We've got tonnes of stuff now from the square."

"OK. I'll keep you posted."

She was just about shaping a 'where the hell is Frank' thought when he popped out of a flag-waving clump of humanity and strode to her side.

"We're done. Any word?"

"No. It's still switched off."

"Shit."

"Anyway, we need to move now. London said that it is chaos all around the Stadium and they want some pictures."

"OK. Let's go."

One of the cameramen had engaged the services of a minibus-sized cab and they all jumped on board. For a hour or so the journey was slow but uneventful. There were plenty of buses and taxis packed with fans interspersed with the day to day traffic that clogged the narrow streets of the city.

Then the landscape started to change and everything started to feel a few notches poorer. Both Frank and Lucy had spent twenty years in the parts of town that locals would do their best to avoid. It was part of the human experience. Build a town because it has a bridge or a port or a coal mine. Let it grow and in time it will develop the right side of the tracks and the wrong side of the tracks. One side will be Kensington and one side will be Bethnal Green. Manhattan and Harlem. Every grinding slow kilometre now took them deeper into the wrong side of Istanbul's tracks. The magnificent views of the Golden Horn and Topkapi seemed light years away. Here was a place of row after row of crumbling high-rise blocks where the building control officers must have been on the take. There were grim looking industrial areas where health and safety didn't look like it had been invented yet. The pavements became mud tracks. Workshops for clapped-out cars. Mini-marts with gaudy signs and windows wrapped in thick mesh to stave off attack.

Now they were on a wide road that eased up a hill and on every lamppost a long, oblong banner hung down, to remind the cars and buses below that this was UEFA's 'Road to Istanbul'. By now the taxis and minivans and buses packed with fans seemed to make up all the traffic. The road had been built as a dual carriageway, but the yellow cabs dodged along four and five abreast.

The studio had been right. It was mayhem. But high spirited mayhem. Beer cans were being passed from window to window. She noticed that just about every driver had been furnished with a can and they were toasting all and sundry and filling the thick smoky air with the sound of blaring horns.

Lucy's initial impression about how the people of Istanbul felt about the red invasion from the United Kingdom was now confirmed. As the districts became poorer and more decayed, the clusters of well-wishers on the pavements became crowds. There were beaming children showing off the scarves and caps that had been passed to them from the windows of the queuing cabs. There were old women dressed from head to toe in black, with gummy smiles and wrinkly eyes that sparkled at the whole thing. Even the policemen were in on the act, grinning and giving the thumbs up.

Suddenly she felt tears welling. This was so much Mickey's world. She thought of all the lyrics from all his songs from the time when he was part of the motley group of bands who shouted in the face of the Thatcher storm. What she was seeing was the people from two great cities come together. More than that. People from poor cities. People who had decided to screw up the script and throw it in the bin. No doubt all these people had listened to those at the mosque who had warned that swarms of infidels were about to besmirch the city. The same infidels who wreaked death and destruction on the Muslim brothers a few hundred miles to the east in Iraq. And at the other end of the rainbow Bush and Blair and all their lapdog cronies had rallied every corner of the media to warn of the suicide bombing religious maniacs who infested all corners of the Middle East. And yet here thousands upon thousands of people had taken the words of hate and binned them. Their collective response was basically to say 'stuff that'.

This was a football thing. Not an oil thing. Not a Nike thing. Not a war on terror thing. Not a jihad thing. It was the same mass 'stuff that' emotion that she had felt in a small town hall in South Wales twenty-one years earlier. Then she had thought she was there to look and observe, but in the end she had sung with all the rest of them. Once again she was here to look and record. It was her job. But in her heart she was once again a part of it all. These were her people. They always would be. Bucking the trend and sticking two fingers up at the men from the boardrooms who tried to tell them what to do. These were the people from a city where the Murdoch Empire could barely sell a copy of the Sun sixteen years after they had written their sensationalised lies after Hillsborough. Rupert Murdoch grovelled to no man. In fact he summoned the leaders of the world to the foot of his throne to grovel to him. And yet so great was the wave of hatred that had swept out of Liverpool at the lies he had printed that he had sent numerous employees to go to the city and beg forgiveness. And every time the city had sent them packing. Stuff that. And still the Sun barely sold a copy.

What she was now a part of was similar in a way. Every person in every taxi had been drip-fed the same poisonous message by the media. The Muslims are the crazies. They're all Al-Quaida. Lunatics. Not to be trusted. Dangerous. And forty-five thousand Scousers had listened to all this and said 'stuff that'. Because this was a football thing. And if the citizens of Istanbul had made their decision to adopt the men in red, then the twelfth man was more than happy to pass a can of beer through the window and welcome them on board.

She could sense they were close now. Lines of police were stopping vehicles and checking tickets. The inspected cars were turning left at a petrol station down a road that looked like a cart track. When it was at last their turn they found that it probably HAD been a cart track a week or two earlier, but now it was covered in a fresh black covering of tarmac. The strip of smooth road was just about wide enough to fit the wheels of a single vehicle, but the cab drivers decided that one wheel was enough and went two abreast.

"Look Lucy. Over there."

She had been watching the endless yellow ribbon of cars as they jostled down to the bottom of a valley and then snaked up the narrow road on the far side. She had been wondering how many there were. It had to be hundreds. Maybe it was thousands. It was unbelievable. Now she followed the direction of her cameraman's pointing hand and there over the last ridge she saw the great grey bowl of the stadium perched on top of hundreds of acres of grassy nothingness. It was like being in some rather over the top arthouse film. Overhead the sky was battleship grey and the whole district was falling apart. And in the middle of it all was an expanse of rough ground with a brand new football stadium in the centre.

Crazy, crazy.

It took twenty minutes to reach the bottom of the valley and as they started to make their way up the far side she looked back to see that the road they had come down was still a fat yellow snake. Again she followed the direction of her cameraman's hand. There were soldiers half-hidden in the long dry grass of the hillside. Full battle dress, crouched down behind semi-automatic weapons, deployed in a skirmish line. And now they were level with the bored face of a white-haired shepherd who was looking on with bemusement, while around him his flock of twenty goats ignored the whole thing and got on with chewing mouthfuls of tired grass.

Crazy. Crazy. Crazy.

Now there were plenty of fans walking by them. The progress had slowed almost to a grinding halt and hundreds had decided to walk the last mile or so with crates of beer on their shoulders.

"Come on. Let's jump out and do some filming."

As the cameramen found a piece of flat ground to set up to get the best view of the scene, she reached into her bag and tried the phone again. She was so certain that there would be no answer that she was paying more attention to the view from the valley side than the ringing from the phone.

Ringing! Not switched off. Thank god . . .

"Yeah . . ."

"Mickey! It's me! Where are you?"

"Close. Listen. I'll ring you when I know a rendezvous. I've hardly any battery. Give me an hour or so. Traffic's shite . . ."

"MICKEY!!!"

But he had cut the conversation dead already to make sure his phone would have enough juice for the next conversation.

"What happened?"

Still Frank's voice was a sea of calm in the growing lunacy that was breaking out all around.

"Flat bastard battery. I couldn't tell him Frank! The silly sod cut me off to save his stupid battery. Christ. Only Mickey would have a flat battery . . ."

"What did he say?" She was nearly hysterical. Frank needed to get her back on the level. They were all going to need all their wits about them.

"Stupid, stupid, stupid . . ."

"Lucy!!" he put some snap into his voice that made the cameramen look up from fiddling with their lenses.

"He said he was saving enough battery so he could call once he had found a rendezvous point."

"You know where he was?"

"Close I think. He said there was tonnes of traffic."

"OK. All we can do is get there and wait. Keep it together Lucy." He reached for his own phone and dialed up Sir Hubert.

"Frank."

The old man's voice told him all he needed to know in two words. All he was dreading.

"Hello Frank." Flat. Beaten.

"What is it?"

"The locals have lost Tate and Dimitri."

"Tell me."

"They took a helicopter. Nobody knows where it landed. They aren't geared up for that kind of thing here. I expect they are probably at the stadium already. Where are you?"

"About a mile off. It's like the end of the world here. Christ knows how long it will take to get there. Lots are walking. Where are you?"

"At the stadium. Well, outside. I am with an officer who has a response team. I think you'd best get here as soon as you can Frank and find me. Have you managed to talk with your brother yet?"

"Lucy has. But she didn't get to tell him what was happening. He said his battery was about out. He said he needed to save it until he could tell her where to meet up."

"That isn't good Frank."

"I know it isn't. All we can do is hope to hell that he rings before Eddie finds him."

"And pray I think."

"Yeah. And pray. Look we'll get going now. We should be with you in an hour tops."

He snapped the phone shut and waited for Lucy to complete an interview with four hikers who carried a collective load of ninety-three cans of beer.

ISTANBUL – MAY 2005

"Lucy. We need to go now. We'll have to walk."

"Tell me."

"Sir Hubert's up at the ground with some sort of a local SWAT team. They lost Eddie. Him and Dimitri took a helicopter didn't they?"

His words seeped into her like rancid sludge from a nuclear reactor. And Mickey's words were again in her head. Mickey's superstition that had been proved right four times out of four. When Liverpool win the European Cup, Mickey and Lucy come together and Mickey McGuire's life goes down the toilet. Except this time it was worse than being flushed down the toilet. This wasn't about getting long term grounded by his mum and dad or locked in the cells for a night. This time it was about being made dead. Murdered. A permanent condition where there would never be another European Cup

"He's going to die isn't he Frank? He always talked about fate. This is what fate had in mind all along. My brother will kill him. Look about you Frank. That is why this place is like the end of the world. It IS the end of the world. He was right all along . . ."

He grabbed her shoulder and sank his fingers all the way down to the bone.

"Shut it Lucy. Mickey's dead when I see him laid on a slab. And that's not now. So now we walk up this bastard hill and we find the Bizzies. And we keep our shit together until there's no point. Now I don't want to give you a slap across the face but by Christ I will unless you shape up . . ."

"Is everything OK Lucy?"

Her cameraman had left his equipment and come across. There had been something about the tall stranger that Lucy had insisted on bringing along that had troubled him all along.

She clenched her teeth together and fought back the urge to scream with sheer blind anger and frustration and despair. "I'm fine. Really."

The words were aimed at the cameraman but Frank knew that they were really for him.

"OK. Let's go."

The irony was that to find Mickey all they would have had to do was to stand and wait. Two hours after reaching the outskirts of the city, Nicholai had at last navigated his way to the turn off onto the newly-laid tarmac strip down to the bottom of the valley. From the moment that they had been battered out of their takings outside the Berlin Club, Mickey had been in the grip of superstition. For a while his brain had convinced himself that this was the moment when the fates had at last decided to come over to his side.

But then a flurry of skinhead boots had put paid to any such complacency. From that moment in the alley, he and Tonto had been fighting fate for every last inch of the seventeen hundred and five miles from Anfield to Istanbul. Sometimes the feeling had been so strong that he felt completely doomed. This hit a peak when he had been convinced that they were about to die in the dark cutting outside Zedice. Other times he felt as if they had broken through some kind of force field and had got clear of the grasping hands of the gods.

And then something else would go wrong. When the tyre had blown and Nicholai couldn't change the wheel because a young mechanic had been over exuberant with his wheel nut machine, Mickey had once again been convinced that they were swimming into a remorseless tide. Then a lad had pulled over with a spider wrench and all seemed possible again.

Then they got lost. Then they were found again. And suddenly all around them were buses and minivans and taxis packed with fans clad in red. Slowly they were being sucked in. First it had been the Igor night in a dusty bar in a bullet-scarred Croatian village where they had been an army of two. Next had been the bar in Sofia under the red awnings by the dome-topped church and they had been an army of thirty. And now all of a sudden they were a part of an army that was fully massed. Thousand upon thousand upon thousand. Fans who had gone neck-deep into hock to get here. They had fallen out with wives and girlfriends and hawked possessions and ducked out of their jobs. Because in the end the only thing that remotely mattered at this brief moment in history, was getting onto the road to Istanbul. And now every lampost held a banner that told the army that the road was nearing its end.

Tonto was fully occupied in banter through the back window, passing out cans of Bulgarian beer to all who needed one.

"There's not many from Milan are there Mickey."

Nicholai was all charged up by the great invasion of a part of Istanbul that no passenger had ever wanted to visit.

"Look how all the people are so much happy. They all want this Liverpool I think." And as he waved to all those who had turned out on the pavements, Nicholai was a fully paid up Liverpudlian for the day. Then Mickey's heart jumped up the back of his throat and into his mouth as the screen on his fast-fading phone announced 'Lucy'.

"Yeah . . ."

"Mickey! It's me! Where are you?"

"Close. Listen. I'll ring you when I know a rendezvous. I've hardly any battery. Give me an hour or so. Traffic's shite . . ."

He killed the call fast and was relieved to see that the battery indicator still had a single bar of life left. They had reached the police lines now and a helmeted figure leaned down to talk with Nicholai. A fast conversation of Turkish and Bulgarian pidgin Turkish resulted in the driver turning to Mickey.

"So. This man say he need to see these ticket. You can show him I think."

Mickey's spirits hit the down side of the rollercoaster again. Always something. Just when you think you're nearly there another bastarding hurdle.

"Tell him there's a mate waiting with them up at the ground."

More fast banter. Nicholai was now a little troubled.

"This man, he say no. No tickets and no can go this road. I tell him, but he is not listen."

"Bollocks to it. In for a penny, in for a pound."

Mickey reached down into the holdall at his feet and pulled out a thick wedge of twenty-pound notes and held them towards the policeman whose eyes grew to the size of soup bowls.

"There you go whack. That good enough?"

A gloved hand reached in fast and the wad of cash disappeared from view as fast as a ferret down a drainpipe. The tough cop face became the beaming cop face.

"Go please. These Liverpool is best in football for sure."

He gave the roof of the cab a hearty wallop with his gloved hand and they eased into the slow moving yellow snake of cabs that wound through the valley to the stadium in the far distance.

"That's the ground isn't it Mickey?"

"That's it Tonto. Almost there now. Nothing to stop us now."

"Have you seen all the yellow taxis Mickey? There's thousands."

"And every one of them filled with reds."

"I'm glad we came Mickey. This is the best day ever."

"Let's hope so Tonto. Let's hope so."

Eddie and Dimtri had avoided the worst of the dramatic journey that the majority of the supporters were going through as they covered the last few miles to the stadium. Their helicopter had dropped them a few miles away and an air-conditioned Limo missed the worst of the traffic as they arrived at three o'clock as the majority of the multitude was starting to clear Taksim Square. Eddie had splashed out on a full corporate deal which not only included the best seats money could buy, but also use of a tented entertainment zone complete with trestle tables laden with an expansive buffet and white-teethed girls in smart uniforms serving champagne at $100 a go. Dimitri insisted that they celebrated their arrival straight away with a fast-guzzled bottle which he said couldn't hold a candle to the stuff they made in Georgia.

Eddie was about to make a suggestion that they should take a walk around the stadium and have a look round, but the Russian was already snapping his fingers and demanding more champagne. Dimitri was clearly in full Russian mode which Eddie knew meant that they both would get a pissed as rats. It was something he was still undecided on. His sensible head was giving a clear message that it would be a pretty good idea to make sure he had as clear a head as possible for what was about to happen. But another part of the brain found the idea of getting as drunk as possible to be more than acceptable.

He had sat quietly on the plane journey across Europe, staring out of the window and turning down the offer of the complimentary drinks his first class ticket entitled him to. The bottom line was that in the long course of his criminal career he had never actually killed anyone. Neither had his dad. Sure, he had battered plenty and scarred a few in his younger days when he had been building his reputation. But he had never actually switched off the lights. Not by his own hand. There had been three who had taken a bus into the great unknown on his orders. But he had never actually been there in person to do the deed.

He hadn't worried about whether or not he would have the bottle when the time came. Of course he would. But how would he feel at the moment he pressed home the needle? Would it be a surge of adrenalin? An instinctive joy at a moment of cold revenge. Or would he feel dirty? Would the moment be something that would deprive him of sleep in the years to come? So maybe it would be better to get hammered. And maybe Dimitri knew this. Maybe that was why he had waved over the brandies in the restaurant. Maybe that was why he was now bringing on more champagne. And maybe it was nothing but being paranoid. Eddie decided to go with the flow.

"Now we drink good OK. This is a day for much drink I think. You not worry about when you find these thief OK. I can give Anton this machine. He can listen when these thief are coming here. He can take you to them. All you have to do is make like this OK?"

Dimitri mimed a short stabbing motion whilst Anton allowed his eyes to flick around the merry crowd inside the tent. He took a sip of his coffee and seemed very still. Eddie was pleased that the Russian would operate the tracking machine. That was the only part that was complicated. Anton would take him to Mickey McGuire. Then he would kill him. Suddenly the whole thing was very simple.

It didn't take very long for Lucy to realise that the 'Fan Zone' that UEFA had laid on for the supporters was a complete disgrace. The cheapest tickets for the match were over £70 and in return UEFA had fenced in an area of loose black chippings about the size of two football pitches. It was just after five when they completed their hike in from the taxi queue and the area was filling up fast. She checked her face in a small mirror whilst a cameraman set up his gear. Then she switched her brain off from the terror that was only just under control and started doing interviews. The high spirits of the fans she talked with were indestructible. They said how all the food and drinks had sold out ages before. They said how there was an hour-long queue to buy a programme for a fiver. Overhead, the grey of the sky had darkened a shade and a cold breeze was blowing in over the bleak plateau that stretched out all around. But nobody seemed to care. Sure the place was the back end of nowhere and there was nothing to eat. Sure there were still JCBs trying to finish off work that should have been wrapped up months earlier. Sure it was weather for jeans and a decent coat and almost everyone was in T-shirts and shorts.

None of it mattered because this was the final. This was where Liverpool belonged. For some it was the fifth such occasion. For others it was what they had grown up with hearing about from dads and uncles and grandfathers. Now it was their turn. These would be their memories. Nothing mattered because wherever they looked they saw a sea of red.

"Hey love. Get your man to film that. Look."

A beaming supporter pointed to where hundreds had given up on their taxis and were marching the last mile. They were sweeping over the brow of the hill whilst a small boy sat among his rather skinny herd of cows.

"Bloody magic or what? Like that scene from 'Zulu' . . ."

And then he was gone. At the far end of the Fan Zone a band were doing cover versions of various songs of the Mersey. The floor was a sea of empty beer cans and every other supporter seemed to have a case on the shoulder. UEFA had announced that the Fan Zone would be an alcohol free area. They might as well have issued an edict that people were not allowed to wear red.

"As you can see, most of these fans have now made it to the end of their long road to Istanbul. What they have found is a place in the middle of nowhere that hasn't actually been finished yet. Thousands have given up waiting in the huge traffic jams and have decided to walk instead. The facilities to be honest are a complete disgrace. Already there is no food or drink left which considering what UEFA are charging for the tickets for this final just isn't good enough. But it seems like nothing could dent the spirits of all these amazing fans. I have to say that we have been here for more than an hour now and we have barely seen a Milan supporter. It is almost as if Anfield has come en masse to this very strange corner of Europe. All through this remarkable campaign we in the media have talked a lot about the passionate 'twelfth man' on the terraces that has shouted the team home. Well the twelfth man is very much here at the Ataturk Stadium. My best guess is that there must be over forty thousand twelfth men here. We are all getting ready for another of those Liverpool nights that will live in the memory for many years. All of these fans have played their part. Soon it will be down to the eleven men in the red shirts. This is Lucy Matthews. BBC News 24. Istanbul."

A few yards away, Frank was in deep conversation with the Chief Constable and a tough looking man in his early thirties who had been introduced as the leader of the strike team. The unit was made up of eight men in their early twenties, all of them in civilian clothing and clearly on edge. The world was slowly shrinking to just a few hundred square yards. When Mickey arrived, he would be almost bound to come to the Fan Zone. Then he would look for a rendezvous point. Nothing was all that obvious. There were a couple food stalls. There were great long lines of portable toilets. There was the stage. There was a big screen. And there were upwards of twenty thousand milling bodies.

All they could do was to wait for the call. Until then they were helpless. She once again forced down the feeling of hopelessness and started to distract her mind with more interviews.

"Nicholai, we're never going to make it at this rate. We haven't moved in twenty minutes."

The Bulgarian shook his head angrily. "These traffic too much bad. Is no good. Why they play this game in such crazy place? These road all too small."

"Look. Me and Tonto are going to walk now. You find somewhere to wait OK. I'll call you after the match and we'll find somewhere to meet, all right?"

"Is good. You can call. No problem. I will wait."

Mickey took two wads of his cash and offered them but Nicholai shook his head. "No please. You can pay when job he is finish. Not now. It can be later."

"You sure?"

"I am sure. You and Tonto are my friend. No problem. You can make this match now I think. Later you can call."

They shook hands and started on the walk along the line of gridlocked taxis towards the distant sounds of singing. They had driven seventeen hundred and three miles of the road. For the last two it would have to be Shanks's pony.

Eddie and Dimitri had left the corporate calm of the tent for the growing mayhem outside after the second bottle.

"Why they choose this place Eddie? He is not even finish yet! Look. Look at this one. Is like how things were in Russia in Communist days."

He had his foot on a newly-laid kerbstone which had never seen a drop of cement and could be rocked from side to side. Eddie

THE LONG AND WINDING
ROAD TO ISTANBUL

shrugged. He felt as if he were floating along and the scene all around him had a dream like quality. Ahead, the great crescent shape roof of the stadium loomed above them, black and foreboding with grey clouds beyond. A circular road took them around the stadium, past long ranks of TV trucks and areas fenced off for officials with passes. The AC Milan Fan Zone was sparsely populated and seemed very quiet somehow. There were queues now at the turnstiles as the gates had finally been opened.

Then they left the relative serenity of the Italian end of the ground behind them and made their way to the riotous sound that was pouring out of the Fan Zone at the north end of the stadium. They stood for a while and looked at the barely contained bedlam. In the centre of the zone a fifty-foot high pole rose up from the asphalt to provide lighting. At a level of ten feet there were down pointing spikes to discourage anyone who fancied a death or glory climb. Not surprisingly the pole had become an irresistible challenge and a bare-chested man of forty years, fifteen stone and a belly full of beer was giving it his best shot. The crowd that had gathered below was split into two camps. The larger camp cheered him on in his quest to get a Liverpool flag to the top. The second camp laughed and called him a fat tosser and in turn the climber paused to inform one member of the second camp in particular that when he got down he would kick his teeth down his throat. The barracker said yeah, like in your dreams pal, and made a private decision to leg it away into the anonymity of the mob before the climber was ten feet off the ground. At twenty feet the climber hit a leg reach that was beyond him and a second, much younger climber followed him up and collected the flag. Here was someone much better designed for the job and five minutes later he swung himself over the last parapet and waved the flag to the cheering crowd below.

"I think these English like to drink very much. Like we Russians. Is why we can be friends I think Eddie. Why we make nice business. I think maybe we can make some more champagne now. Is good?"

"Is great." Eddie turned to Anton who had stood watching the whole thing with a look of boredom. "Anything?"

"No. Nothing."

But halfway through bottle number three there was something. Only very, very quiet, but enough for Anton.

"So now he is here. Not close. But he is here."

Just a faint bleep when he listened in at one of the earphones. A soft sound. A nothing sound. The sound of a man entering the last minutes of his life. Welcome to Istanbul Mickey McGuire. Welcome to the last hour. Time to die. In the hotel room in Preston, Eddie had been so sure that the taste of revenge would be as sweet as candy. Now he wasn't so sure. He was about to kill to live up to a reputation that been thirty years in the making. And with the reputation had come the trappings. Big house in a street with trees where nobody carved their names in the bark. Umpteen cars. A stuck-up wife who had evolved into a mindless shopping-machine. Two sons who he had come to hate for their public school arrogance that had cost him endless thousands of pounds in extortionate fees. In theory, he had everything. In practice, he had nothing.

He mechanically poured champagne down. Glass after glass. Another bottle. Why the hell not? Always another bottle. Look at us. We're the men with money. That was why the pretty girl made sure she gave Dimitri's shoulder a good old rub with her tits as she poured. It was because he had paid for the last bottle with a five hundred Euro note and told her to keep the change. So of course she absolutely loved him. All of them did. They couldn't get enough of the two middle-aged drunk guys with the designer clothes and the fat wedges.

On his way across Europe he had felt really good about himself. Who would ever have thought it? Eddie Tate was on his way to the final and it would be First Class all the way. First Class on the plane. An air-conditioned Limo to the hotel. Five star hotel. Suite. Everything. Money, money and more money. A constant line of young waitresses whose smiles were always for sale. Tips and tips and tips. Tips that meant they wouldn't mind when you patted a seat in a restaurant for them to sit next to you. They wouldn't mind when you hung a drunken arm around their slender shoulders. They wouldn't even mind when your liver spotted hand wandered down to feel their tits. Of course they didn't mind because you were the kind of guy who would throw the hundred euro notes about like confetti at the end of the night. And the floor manager wouldn't mind either because there would be nice high-denomination notes for his breast pocket as well. And for the men like himself and Dimitri there was always another bottle of champagne and another pair of nineteen-year-old tits and another night of pretending that they actually belonged somewhere.

But they didn't. They were nomads, trailing first class around the world being met by false smiles and feeling false tits. Nobody wanted them. People grinned their crawling smiles and suffered them for the sake of a hundred-euro bill. Usually he cared not a jot. But tonight was different. Tonight was different because outside the corporate falseness of the tent were his people. Forty-something thousand of them. They had begged and borrowed their way to the end of the rainbow and they were apart from him. Once he had been one of them, but he had given up his season ticket. He had spent his adult life robbing them blind and getting their children addicted to smack so that he could throw the big tips and feel the tits of girls less than half his age. Outside the people of his city were meeting each other and hugging and shaking hands. Didn't know you were going to make it mate. Which way did you come? When did you get here? Want an ale or what? Friends. Mates. Neighbours. Real people with real lives from a real city. Not the fake everything for sale lie of the corporate tent. Outside were thousands from his city, but all he had was a Russian Mafia boss and his silent minder. Outside was his beloved baby sister, but she would rather die that speak to him. To share his bitter champagne. To join in his pretend world.

He waved the waitress and shouted for brandy. Then he gestured for another listen to the bleep. Louder now. Much louder. Soon it would be time to go. Time to kill. Time to build the great legend of Eddie Tate. Because that was what everyone expected of him.

"Jesus Tonto, would you look at that."

They had emerged over the last hill and before them the whole lunatic scene was spread out like some scene from a 1950's epic about the Roman Empire. The stadium looked starker and bleaker than ever in the fast darkening dusk. It stood out in the stark moonscape like an alien spaceship with its huge curved roof and sparkling floodlights. Below was a cast of teeming thousands packed like a zillion ants into the Fan Zone. By the time they reached it, the Zone resembled nothing like what the earnest UEFA officials must have intended when they came up with the concept. They had obviously been under the impression that the Liverpool fans would behave like proper Cub Scouts on a day out and be pathetically grateful for their long journey to be rewarded by the chance to kick footballs into bouncy castles and to listen to a few songs. The stage was in the process of being invaded. Figures with flags were clambering up and bouncing up and down to the horror of whichever official was in charge of the tannoy.

"NO!!! Liverpool fans . . . you have to leave the stage . . . please . . .this is dangerous . . . terrible danger . . . you must leave . . . NOW . . . !!"

Mickey clapped Tonto on the back. "Journey's end mate. We've made it. All we need now is a rendezvous point."

"What's that Mickey?"

"Somewhere to meet Lucy. A landmark."

"That stage is a landmark."

"Yeah. Looks as good as anything to me."

They started the slow process of forcing their way through the press of bodies to the stage, which by this time was home to upwards of five hundred flag waving fans.

"So my friend. Maybe it is time to go now. The sound he is loud I think."

Eddie drained his brandy glass and washed it down with a flute of champagne. Christ he was pissed. His legs almost didn't manage to take the stand up instruction from the brain.

"You coming?"

"No. I think I can stay here. Is very good here. I can wait I think."

The waitress had seemingly wangled a break and was now happily planted in the Russian's lap with the buttons of her blouse open enough for him to gaze down her cleavage from over her shoulder.

"Right. I'll be going then. Don't suppose I'll be long." His head was on the verge of spinning and he had to close his eyes for a moment to contain the rush. He carefully placed his hands on the edge of the table and leered at the waitress. "You give her one from me, OK Dimitri?"

"Sure. OK. Why not? You come soon. We make more drinking. Too much drinking!"

Too much drinking. Too much bloody everything. Too much. He was aware of the looks of hostility as be blundered his way out of the tent. Anton had a firm hand at his elbow. Guiding. Steering. Doing his job. Outside his clean-shaven face was all straight Slavic lines. Very calm. Very detached. Inside he was disgusted. This was where he had fallen. Years ago when he had passed the course to become a warrior of the Spetznatz, he had been a part of the elite force of a great Empire. Now everything had crumbled. Russia was a sick old cripple, riddled with corruption. And he spent his days watching over these pathetic middle-aged men as they pawed waitresses and counted their piles of cash. Now this one was on his way to kill and he had got drunk to the gates of oblivion because he hadn't the stomach for it. Anton remembered the murderous firefights his unit had been involved in with the Chechen fighters high in the snowy mountains of Central Asia. There had been something clean about that killing. It had been men fighting men. In the open. Above board. Eyes open. This wasn't any of those things. This was a sad old man staggering out to kill like a coward. And Anton would walk him all the way to his victim. Because it was his job. Because there were no longer any other jobs for men like him in the new Russia. And the bleeping was now loud in his ear.

"LIVERPOOL FANS . . . !!!! YOU HAVE TO LEAVE THE STAGE . . . !!!! THERE IS DANGER . . . !!!! PEOPLE MIGHT DIE!!!!!!"

It took Mickey and Tonto over ten minutes to reach the side of the stage. The desperate voice of the tannoy man was still beseeching immediate evacuation but nobody was taking the slightest bit of notice.

He pulled out his phone and was relieved to find the same one bar of power still in place. He dialled.

"Mickey! Is that you!"

He had to shout over the singing all around him.

"Yeah! I'm by the stage. Left hand side as you look at it . . . ."

Peep. Peep. Peep. He stared at the now blank screen.

"Oh bollocks. No battery."

"Is Lucy coming then Mickey?"

"I hope so. Christ. All I needed was another thirty seconds. Typical stupid bastard phone."

"Has she got the tickets Mickey?"

"Don't know. I never got the chance to ask. Keep an eye out for her."

By this time the tannoy man had beaten a retreat and the microphone was being used Karaoke style.

"Gerry Taylor!! Where are you, you stupid git. Meet me at the stage with the tickets . . ."
"TOMMY BENNET!! COME TO THE STAGE NOW OR I'LL BLOODY KILL YOU . . ."

Lucy stared at the face of her phone stupidly for a moment. Nothing. A square of empty space. Then she stared to almost hyperventilate.

"The stage. He's by the stage Frank. Get him Frank . . ."

"STOP!"

He was gripping her shoulder again. Hard. His eyes slammed into her. Then his words. "Tell me properly. Slowly. Now."

"The stage . . . the left hand side as you look at it . . ."

"Tell Hakan. Explain."

Then he was gone, six foot two of human battering ram, forcing a path through to the stage at the far side of the Fan Zone.

Lucy turned to the young officer who had watched Frank's fast departure with a look of mild surprise. It took all of her self-control to stop herself from gabbling.

"By . . . the . . . stage . . . Left . . . hand . . . side. . . ."

He gave a short nod of understanding and quickly briefed his men. Sir Hubert came close by Lucy.

"Come on. Come with me."

They followed the nine men of the SWAT team as best as they could.

Eddie was in a dream world. So many bodies. Millions of bodies. Bodies and sound. Great towering walls of sound that seamed to reach up into the dark sky above. He focused on the broad back of his Russian guide. He had the pen in his hand now. Gripped hard. His bones told him it would be soon. Very soon. He focused on keeping his feet. Not that he could fall. He was Eddie Tate. He couldn't fall. He was indestructible. A man apart. A man ready to make his first kill.

"See anything Mickey?"

"No. Not yet. Don't worry. Lucy'll find us. It's just dead packed everywhere . . ."

A face in a crowd. Big face. Familiar face. A face of the man that had once been the boy who had driven the car to the chemist shop. Close. Really close. Sweating. Slack eyes. Dead eyes. Eyes now fixed on him.

THE LONG AND WINDING
ROAD TO ISTANBUL

Eddie.

Christ.

Eddie Tate.

Here in Istanbul and it was Eddie Tate.

And he had stolen £400,000 from Eddie Tate.

And nobody did that. Not if they wanted to carry on breathing.

And he was here. Looking straight into his eyes. Five yards and closing. Liverpool win the European Cup and Lucy and Mickey come together and Mickey McGuire's life goes down the toilet.

Adrenalin made his brain race. Ridiculous maths. $2005 - 1977 = 28$. Twenty-eight years since the chemist shop. And that bus into town. And 'Close Encounters of the Third Kind'. And the first time he ever talked to Lucy. And the first time he ever kissed Lucy. And Tommy Smith had made it 2-1. Rome to Istanbul. And now he could see all the way into Eddie's terrible bleary eyes and he saw death. His death. He wanted his legs to run like Linford Christie but his legs were made out of stone. A yard now. And Eddie was raising his hand. A pen. Not a Stanley knife. A pen. The pen is more powerful that the sword, but Eddie was never much of a pen type of a guy.

And then Eddie wasn't there any more. Eddie was out of his line of sight. Where? Down. Someone had hit him in a head on charge. A big man. A familiar shape. Frank. It was Frank. But how?

His brain tried to find some order in the midst of the sound and the crush of bodies and the hurtling adrenalin.

Eddie Tate had been right there. Eddie Tate with cold death in his eyes. Then Frank had erupted through the crush of bodies like a cork from a champagne bottle. And he had felled Eddie with a flying tackle that would have graced any Rugby League match. And Eddie had been holding a pen. Why a pen?

There were more men now. Locals by the look of them. Pulling Frank to his feet. Pulling Eddie to his feet. And Eddie was vomiting now. It was all down his front and his eyes no longer had death in them. Now it was only fear. Pure naked terror as another spurt of brandy and champagne sprayed out of his mouth. Now his eyes were wide and fixed on Frank as firm hands pulled his hands behind his back and started to snap handcuffs into place.

And then Mickey crashed backwards into the stage as Lucy exploded from the crowd with even more velocity and clamped herself onto him like a limpet.

"You're all right Mickey. You'll all right Mickey. Oh Jesus bloody sodding Christ . . ."

Her tears were soaking his cheeks as she pushed her face in to his. What the hell was going on? The whole thing was being watched by many bemused faces all around them.

"MESSAGE HERE FOR JOSE MOURINHO . . . SINCE YOU'VE GOT NOTHING ON TONIGHT, COULD YOU TAPE EASTENDERS FOR ME . . ."

And he could feel Lucy's shoulders start to shake with laughter. She pulled her face back from his.

"Did you hear that?"

"What. The Mourinho thing?"

"Yes. The Mourinho thing."

"I heard it."

"Only bloody Scousers. Christ I love you Mickey McGuire."

And for the first time in well over twenty years she kissed him. And kept on kissing him until all the faces around them woke up to the fact that this was a major happy ending and started to cheer them both on.

Frank was catching his wind when he caught a glimpse of Anton who was moving discreetly away through the crowd with his phone to his ear. A hand on his shoulder. Sir Hubert.

"Are you OK?"

"Never better. Call your man can you? Get him to send in the lads at the hotel. I just saw Dimitri's lad walking away with a phone. The Chief made the call and was told that it would be done. Then he looked over to the sight of the BBC woman he saw most nights on the news involved in an end of movie snog that would have graced anything from fifties Hollywood. When it was at last over the crowd all around burst into a chorus of

"Are you watching . . . are you watching . . . ARE YOU WATCHING MAN - CHEST – ER . . . ARE YOU WATCHING MAN – CHEST – ER!!!'

THE LONG AND WINDING
ROAD TO ISTANBUL

He couldn't quite work out why it was so important that the good folk of the city at the other end of the East Lancs Road should be bearing witness to this romantic moment, but he really didn't care a great deal. Eddie Tate looked anything but a feared gangland enforcer as Hakan shoved him forward. The whole of his front was coated in sick and his hair was stuck in all directions. Frank's flying hit had left him winded and sucking in air like a fish. And then his watery eyes slowly focused on the face before him and a deep despair began to take over.

"Oh yes Eddie. Not a dream. Cold reality I'm afraid. And my god, are you ever nicked. You will be dreaming of a cell in Walton for every minute of the rest of your life . . ." At that moment he spotted the pen on the floor and he took a handkerchief from his pocket and picked it up. He then dropped it into a polythene evidence bag and sealed it.

"Hakan. Take this. You should have worn gloves Eddie. You really should have worn gloves. Oh, and by the way, I was never here. I am just a figment of your drunken imagination."

Dimitri had to ease the waitress off his lap to get the ringing phone out of his pocket.

"It's Anton. We have problems."

The Russian's head cleared in an instant. "Go on."

"Eddie didn't make the hit. He was about to when Frank suddenly appeared and took him down."

"Frank?"

"Yes. And he has seen me. Then there were cops. Plain clothes and tough looking. They've just cuffed Eddie."

"Have they got the pen?"

"Don't know. I couldn't see. It's crazy out here."

"Come straight back here."

"OK."

Dimitri took out a five hundred euro note and handed it to the waitress. "So now you can bye, bye. OK?"

It was more than OK. Five hundred Euro and she hadn't even had to suffer his hands inside her bra. He pushed his glass away and focused. This was stuff he was good at. Trained for. Frank was there. It could mean only one thing. Somehow they knew. And not just Frank. The Turkish police as well. Which meant he had to assume they knew where he was staying as well. The whole shooting match was blown sky high. All he could do now was to assume the worst and get out fast.

He speed dialled Vladimir who was back at base babysitting the girls.

Later, when she had been told the whole story, Ivana felt that her part in the drama had really been rather boring. The new bimbo was downstairs being beautified whilst she was under polite room arrest. She was sitting in front of the TV with Vladimir watching Sky's coverage of the build up to the final when there was a firm knock at the door. Vladimir checked that his gun moved freely in his shoulder holster then pulled on his jacket to hide it.

He opened the door to three uniformed Turkish policemen as his phone started to ring.

"Yes."

"You have one Ivana Petrovich here?"

The policeman was already looking over the Russian's shoulder at the woman in front of the TV. No options.

"Sure."

"She needs to come with us."

"Why?"

"You not need why. She can come. Bring bag."

Vladimir turned from the door and left the policemen waiting. He spoke in Russian. "You heard them. Pack a bag. I'll call Dimitri as soon as you're gone. I'm sure he'll sort it. Anything you need to tell me?"

"No. Nothing."

He gave her a level stare. Saw the lie in her eyes. But there was nothing he could do.

"Go on. Pack."

She threw some overnight things into a bag and left with the policemen with a sinking feeling. She was about to be blamed for something Dimitri was into. Blamed and in Turkey. She focused hard on keeping herself from any hysterics as they rode down the lift.

Vladimir checked the missed call. Dimitri. He returned it.

"It's Vladimir."

"We have problems. Police. You need to get out now. Get a car and head for Greece. Call me once you get to Athens. Bring the girls."

"Sir, I've just had the police here. That's why I couldn't get the phone. They've picked up Ivana."

"Why?"

"They didn't say. They just took her."

There was a pause as Dimitri digested this.

"Forget her. Just leave. Where is the other one?"

"The beauty salon."

"Leave her too. You'll be better alone. Call when you get to Athens."

"OK."

Vladimir was packed and out of the hotel in ten minutes. Like Ivana, he had no wish to become acquainted with a Turkish jail. The first taxi he flagged down was more than delighted to take him to the capital of Greece for $500 cash. Paid up front.

Hakan's men were discreet as they moved Eddie away from the teeming Fan Zone. They didn't want any potential flash point to develop if the supporters felt that one of their own was being rough-handled by the local police. Had Eddie fought and raged there could have been a few problems. But Eddie Tate was well past the fighting and raging stage. His head was spinning from all the alcohol and the world around him was a blurred mess of packed bodies and sound. He kept his head down, terribly conscious of the stinking vomit all over his front.

A van was waiting two hundred yards from the Fan Zone, which was now at last starting to empty out as the masses headed for the turnstiles. The police were not rough as they put him into the back. They were just businesslike.

Sir Hubert noted down a mobile number from Suliman and dialed. The phone was answered in unintelligible Turkish.

"Excuse me. You speak English?"

The voice at the other end had been told to expect the call.

"I can a little. You want talk to girl?"

"Yes please."

The policeman in the passenger seat passed his mobile over to Ivana who sat uncuffed and very confused in the back.

"There is one call here."

Sir Hubert passed the phone to Frank who was wiping away at the beer soaked dust that had covered his clothes when he went into Rugby League mode. Her voice was small. Frightened.

"Please? Who is this?"

"Francesco Sfortza."

"Frank. It is you?"

"Yeah. It's me. The other Francesco popped it five hundred years ago. Are you OK?"

"Me? I am OK. I think. I am in police car. They have taken me from hotel. I do not know why."

"Don't worry. I sorted it. They'll take you to a police station now. There's nothing to worry about. I'll be there soon to pick you up."

"You are coming?"

"I am coming."

"Where can we go then? What about Dimitri?"

"Don't worry about Dimitri. He's got other stuff on his mind right now. You know where we're going."

"I do?"

"Course you do. We talked about it. Cottage? Tuscany? Ring any bells?"

"I have no passport Frank. Dimitri has my passport."

"I thought he might. That's why I got you to do those photos in Liverpool. I've had one done for you."

"Is in my name this passport?"

"No."

"What is the name Frank?"

"Try a guess. At least at the first name."

She stared out of the window at the busy pavement filled with people living their lives amid the smell of cooking kebabs and fruit stalls. Two tears wandered down her cheeks. Of course she knew the name.

"Is Bianca I think."

"That's it. Bianca. I'll be there soon."

"I can wait I think."

"You've got no bloody choice darling. That's why I have you in police custody."

Sir Hubert took the phone back and pocketed it. "So Frank. I think that just about wraps things up. I can expect a dossier in the post can I?"

"You can. The Tate Empire, warts and all. Like I said, I'll give you all the cash and the locations of the stashes. I'll also give you a couple of the nutters. All the other guys, forget it. Most of them are just foot-soldiers. You'll have to catch them yourself."

"And do I get a forwarding address?"

"I don't think so Sir Hubert. I think we'll say our goodbyes now, don't you?"

The older man smiled and held out a hand, which was duly shaken. Frank remembered that the policeman still needed to get home.

"Are you going now?"

"Actually, not just yet. Suliman has arranged for me to watch the game with him in the police area. It would be a shame to miss the game. Now that I'm here and all that."

"I'll call Willie for you. Are you going straight to the airport after the match?"

"I am."

"OK. He'll be waiting."

"Thanks. Best of luck Frank."

"Yeah. And you."

When Lucy at last broke the great embrace to the acclaim of the watching crowd she immediately wrapped herself around an utterly bemused looking Tonto. He was a man who was pretty good at taking most things in his stride. But this was all weirder than normal. In fact he hadn't had such a bizarre time since the night in South Wales that had ended up with a year-and-a-half of prison. When she released him from the hug she kissed him on both cheeks.

"Have you any idea how glad I am to see you guys."

"You seem pretty happy Lucy."

A voice shouted from the crowd behind her.

"Is it just these two, or do we all get a go then?"

"In your dreams lads."

Tonto was now emerging from his state of shock and the cogs of his brain inexorably clunked round to the main issue of the moment.

"Have you got the tickets Lucy?"

"Course I have. You never thought I'd let you down did you?"

"No."

Mickey was nowhere close to coming to terms with all the drama. The pieces of the jigsaw were scattered all over the floor and he couldn't begin to work out where to start with it all. And then Frank was there.

"All right Mickey."

"All right Frank."

"You made it then?"

"Yeah. Look I'm sorry about the money and that . . ."

"No problem. You're here. It's all that matters. You're going to make a final at last. It's taken a while."

"Twenty-eight years. What the hell has just happened here Frank?"

"You'll find out all of it in time. Basically Eddie was trying to kill you and me and Lucy stopped him. He's finished now."

"But . . ."

"Seriously. Leave it for now. The lads are playing AC Milan in an hour's time. Just enjoy the match. All the rest can wait."

"Are you coming?"

Frank shook his head. "No. I've got someone to pick up."

Mickey smiled. "The Siberian bird?"

"The Siberian bird."

"Then what?"

Frank passed over a folded piece of paper. "This is a place I bought a while back. It's in Italy. Tuscany. My bolt hole. I'm taking Ivana. You'll come and see us, yeah? You and Lucy. And Tonto?"

"Course I'll come."

They stared at each other for a moment then Frank pulled him to him with his undamaged hand and they embraced.

"OK. I'm away. See you soon OK."

"Frank."

"Yeah?"

"When I get home I'm going to tell dad he's got to see you. I'm not taking no for an answer. You'll come will you?"

"Course I'll come."

"It's been a long time."

Frank smiled. "Twenty-eight years."

Frank left with Sir Hubert whilst Lucy watched with one arm around Mickey and one round Tonto.

"Who's the old boy with our Frank?"

"Maybe it's best you don't know."

"Ah come on Lucy, all this mystery stuff is driving me nuts . . ."

She cut him short with another kiss. Tonto waited patiently for her to finish.

"Are you sitting with us Lucy?"

She smiled. "If you seriously think I'm about to let either of you clowns out of my sight then you are completely unhinged."

Unhinged? This was a new one on Tonto. "Like a door you mean."

"Yes. Like a door."

Going into the stadium was like going into a different world. Outside everything had been bizarre and weird. The tiny roads gridlocked with yellow cabs. The snipers on the hillside. And goats. JCBs still trying to finish the place off three hours from kick off. A moonscape surrounded by blighted estates from an arthouse film about the end of the world. The great red human wave walking into the carnival chaos of the Fan Zone.

Inside it was like being in a football ground. Rather a fine football ground, but a football ground all the same. The ranks of the twelfth man seemed to pause to draw breath and collectively pinch themselves. This was reality. The European Cup final and they had made it and the clock was counting down to kick off.

"I'm starving Mickey." Said Tonto. "You want me to get you anything?"

"Three of whatever. Burgers, hotdogs, anything. Here you go."

He passed a handful of twenty pound notes.

"How much of my brother's money have you got left?"

Mickey took a nervous look at her face and was relieved to see a twinkle in her eyes.

"Enough for a bloody great holiday somewhere. You game?"

"I think I might be."

They sat for a while, arms around each other's shoulders, neither quite able to comprehend the fact that they were actually together. Their seats were level with the half way line and gave a panoramic view of the fast filling ground. It was becoming increasingly obvious that other than the banner-waving bank of fans behind the goal to their right, there were barely any Italians to be seen. All around the ground there were red shirts and scarves and banners. The Kop had come to know the Millennium Stadium in Cardiff as 'Anfield South'. Now the Ataturk Stadium was fast becoming 'Anfield Further South'.

"So. Come on Mr Expert. Are we going to win then?"

He gave a rueful grin and shook his head.

"No chance."

She drew back a little.

"That's not like you Mickey McGuire. Such pessimism?"

"Not pessimism. Fatalism. You know how it goes Lucy. Liverpool win the European Cup and Mickey McGuire's life goes down the toilet. Do I look like a man whose life is down the toilet? Or do I look like a man who has just found out that every day for the rest of his life is Christmas day. So no chance. The gods have done their bit. Mickey McGuire is in seventh heaven and the mighty Milan will cruise it 2-0. But there's always next year. That's one of the biggest plus points of not being dead in a Bosnian ditch."

"Am I to understand that you are actually suggesting that some things are more important than football?"

"Correct."

"Things like life and death?"

"Absolutely."

"So Bill Shankly was wrong?"

"Now hold on a minute, I wouldn't go that far. You see Bill was using an extended metaphor there. So he wasn't exactly wrong, just misunderstood."

"Because Bill Shankly couldn't possibly be wrong could he?"

"Course not. I reckon he's watching you know. Right now. Remember when he stood on the Kop that day?"

"I do."

"I reckon he's here right now. Somewhere in the middle of all this lot. No way he'd miss."

Tonto returned laden with hotdogs, which reminded all three of them of how hungry they were. The bread was older than most of the tarmac on the roads leading to the ground but it didn't seem to matter much. Tonto sprayed a cascade of crumbs from his mouth as he spoke. "Kewell's playing. Why do you think Kewell's playing Mickey?"

"Because it's written Tonto. Like everything is written. It's all part of the great plan."

"Like on the team sheet?"

UEFA managed to make up to some extent for the disgraceful paucity of the fan areas with an opening ceremony which involved a cast of hundreds including some bizarre looking ten foot high figures who seemed to float over the grass like something out of Star Wars.

THE LONG AND WINDING
ROAD TO ISTANBUL

And the noise built and built until twenty-two players emerged into the bright, shadowless light to contest the right to be the champions of Europe.

And at 9.45 p.m. local time, after thousands of miles of travel and hundreds of thousands of words both written and spoken, the game the world had waited on for three weeks at last kicked off.

The clock was still ten seconds shy of 9.46 when thirty-seven year old Paulo Maldini bounced a miss hit shot off the turf and into the top corner of the goal.

Milan 1 – Liverpool 0

Seventeen hundred and five miles and it was 1-0 after 50 seconds. All around them heads were held in hands. Surely not. But Mickey was a man in a cocoon of calm.

"Like I said. Written. There's no getting away from fate."

A guy in front spun round angrily. "Shut up will you, you pessimistic dickhead."

The next forty-five minutes unfolded out into a nightmare. Kaka. Shevchenko. Crespo. Two nil. Kaka. Crespo. Three nil. Milan were playing football from another planet.

"Told you. Know who Crespo has a contract with? Chelsea. He's only with this lot on loan. We play Chelsea for a hundred and eighty-six minutes and they can't score. But now one of theirs had got two. Like I said. Fate."

It was too much for the man in front. He was on his feet and trying to climb over his seat whilst his mates dragged him back.

"I've had enough of you . . . "

"You bloody dare." Lucy was on her feet like an angry cat and in the face of the would-be attacker.

The flashpoint calmed as fast as it had started. Mr Angry shrugged off the hands of his restrainers.

"Look. Sorry all right. I'm just pissed off that's all. I mean three bastard nil. Bollocks."

The half-time whistle blew and ten white shirted Italians strutted from the pitch to the rhythmic chanting of their band of fans that suddenly seemed much louder now. Eleven men in red left with heads down. And all was lost. All that was at stake was whether pride could be salvaged. Pride for the eleven men on the pitch that had defied the odds to get to Istanbul at all. And the twelfth man on the terraces that had done so much to make it happen. Behind the goal that had seen the ball three times in the first half, the Milan fans unfurled what must have been the biggest banner the world had seen since Hitler used to hold party shindigs in Nuremburg.

It was a thousand square feet worth of gauntlet in the face of the twelfth man and the twelfth man responded by raising their own colours high and singing the most defiant 'You'll never walk alone' there had ever been. The great Italian banner was slowly unfurled and silence fell over the Milan end. For a moment they stared around in bemusement at the forty-five thousand who drowned them in sound. Later the Liverpool players talked a lot about the moment. In the next-door dressing room they could hear the sound of the all-conquering Milan team loudly celebrating a famous victory that was already in the bag. Then they heard the sound of the twelfth man seeping down the concrete corridors and under the door.

And they said they knew that they really wouldn't have to walk alone. 3-0 mattered nothing. They wore red shirts. All of them. Eleven on the pitch. 45,000 off the pitch. It was a win, lose or draw moment. And from a song from the sixties came the first flickering light of hope in the red dressing room. And the first shreds of doubt in the white.

Shevchenko free kick. A tracer bullet. 4-0 a split second away. And Dudek saved it.

A Risse cross. A Gerrard header. And the ball beyond Milan's diving keeper. 3 -1.

A minute. A pass to Smicer. A shot. A Brazilian fingertip. A touch of the post.

3 – 2

"So what about your bloody fate now then!!"

Baying sound. Huge sound. Complete sound.

Through ball. Gerrard beyond the chasing Gattuso. Gerrard down. Referee pointing. Penalty. Who the hell has the bottle for it? Alonso the Spaniard. Cool as you like. Low and for the corner . . . saved . . . rebound . . . in.

Unbelievable. 3 -3. Every pundit in every paper and TV station had gone on and on and on about the mighty Milan defence which was the best in the business. And in six lunatic minutes they had let in three. It was something that just didn't happen. Not ever. Certainly not in a final. Certainly not in a European Cup Final. But it was happening

THE LONG AND WINDING
ROAD TO ISTANBUL

because the scoreboard said it was happening. It wasn't a dream. And hundreds of millions of viewers all over the planet realised that one of the greatest sporting dramas in history was unfolding in front of them. And those in the stadium itself knew that they were becoming a part of history. Their ticket stubs would become the evidence of the greatest 'I was there' of them all.

Lucy had completely lost it by this stage. She was on her feet with Tonto screaming until she felt like her throat was going to tear. Mickey was still lost in his own private zone. He stood with his hands in his pockets and a small smile of resignation. The gods were having their bit of fun. But in the end it was written.

For a while Liverpool knocked the ball around like gods as the Milan team tried to come to terms with what had happened. But as the clocked ticked on, the strength started to drain from the legs of the men in red and by the time the game moved into extra time they were hanging on against wave after wave of attacks. And then when a penalty shoot-out was almost inevitable, a cross came in from the left and the world's number one striker from the Ukraine arched his neck and headed the ball towards a storybook winner in the dying embers of the game.

But the storywriter hadn't quite seen it that way. The storywriter had decided that the son of a Polish coal miner should block the shot with a sensational save, leaving the world's greatest striker to win the game with a slammed shot on the rebound.

And still the storyteller didn't see it that way. The greatest striker in the world didn't miss hit his shot. Quite the opposite. He hammered it and the coal miner's son made a save that defied the laws of physics and gravity and everything else.

Then the whistle blew.

Penalties. Jamie Carragher was in the face of the coal miner's son. "See that Lucy. Jamie's telling him to do a Grobbelaarr. Remember. 1984 when Brucie clowned it in the final against Rome. I heard it on a radio when I was in the cell in Wales."

Lucy squeezed his hand, momentarily hurting at the memory. "Well you're not in Wales now. How are the fates now?"

He smiled. "Bloody awful. But at least we've seen the greatest game in bloody history. No shame in losing a match like this."

The man in front was too emotionally wrung out to be angry any more. He turned like a veteran of the Eastern Front.

"Look mate. For Christ's sake. Won't you just shut up. Tell him will you love."

Penalty number one. Serginho. Brazilian. Brazilians don't miss penalties. Not after all that football on the beach. The misty night air was thick with booing. And the Brazilian missed high wide and handsome as the coal miner's son jigged on the line like a disco dancing Silesian giraffe.

Penalty number two. Dietmar Hamman. A German with a Scouse accent. A stuttering run up. Then ice cool German efficiency. 1 – 0.

Penalty number three. Pirlo. Italian international. Not a man to miss. But he did miss.

Penalty number four. The fairy tale. Cisse. The man whose leg had been broken so badly five months earlier in Blackburn that the doctors had actually considered cutting it off. Now he was back. Mickey closed his eyes. Fate could be cruel. He hoped that it could be cruel to someone other than Cisse. But in his heart he knew that fate had no sentiment. He didn't watch as the Frenchman found the corner and stayed cool for twenty yards before going completely mental.

2 – 0. So fate had found a different kind of cruelty. It was going to take them to the very gates of the greatest victory in the history of everything. Because it was written. Like on a team sheet.

Penalty number five. Tommason. And the boos seemed to get even louder. He scored. So it starts, thought Mickey. The beginning of the end.

Penalty number six. John Arne Risse. The Norwegian with a jackhammer for a left foot. No doubt what he would do. He would hit the thing hard enough to break the keeper's hand if he got in the way. But he didn't. He placed his shot along the ground and perfect in the corner. And Dida stretched every inch of his massive frame and saved it.

2 – 1

Fate was clawing it back.

"Here we go. Now it starts."

Tonto shook his head. "No Mickey. Remember Rome in 1984. Stevie Nichol missed didn't he? He was a left back. And he had ginger hair. And we still won."

"He was Scottish."

Lucy was with Tonto on this one. "Bet he had Viking blood though."

THE LONG AND WINDING
ROAD TO ISTANBUL

Penalty number seven. Kaka. The Brazilian man of the match. Cool as ice. The ball smacked the back of the net. And Mickey could feel the fingers of fate working the dials. It was now just a matter of how it would happen.

Penalty number eight. Vladimir Smicer. A bloody shame. He was on his way out of Anfield at the end of the season. And this was the last game of the season. His last kick for the club was going to be a lifelong nightmare.

But it wasn't. It was a goal. And it was 3 -2. And all around him the hope was becoming horribly tangible.

Penalty number nine. Now Mickey could at least see what the gods had in mind. Bastards. The greatest striker in the world was marching up to the box like a man who knew that this time the coal miner's son wouldn't have a look in. Rumour had it that Chelsea were lining up a record smashing sixty million pound bid to take Andrei Shevchenko to Stamford Bridge. So he wasn't about to miss. He was about to score as if it were the easiest thing in the world. And it didn't matter how much everyone booed because he would score and that would leave Stevie Gerrard with the chance to crown his epic season with the winner.

Which he would miss.

Because when Liverpool won the European Cup Mickey McGuire's life went down the toilet. Always. Every time. Written.

The Ukranian strolled up to do the bidding of the gods.

And missed.

Missed.

A second's pause.

Then utter complete total bedlam.

And Lucy and Tonto were wrapped around his disbelieving body. And the man from the row in front who had climbed over his seat to join in the embrace. At last he took Mickey's face between his hands and screamed at him.

"Fate!! Bollocks to it!!"

And all of a sudden everyone was singing different songs at the same time whilst the players in red threw themselves on top of the coal miner's son who had become an Anfield legend.

And slowly one song took over from the others in their corner of the Ataturk Stadium.

"Are you watching . . . are you watching . . .ARE YOU WATCHING MAN - CHEST – ER . . .. ARE YOU WATCHING MAN – CHEST – ER!!!'

When Mickey and Lucy had entertained the crowd with their snog to end all snogs before the match there had in fact been no one from Manchester there to watch, despite the question asked by those who watched.

But now there were plenty in Manchester who were watching. These included two men of Jamaican descent who were watching the drama on tele in Moss Side. They heard the song and smiled. They were both City fans and they knew the Manchester the Scousers were singing about wasn't their Manchester. It was the other Manchester. Twenty-eight years earlier both men had sported rather fine Rastafarian hair. Now one had his grey locks trimmed short whilst the other had barely a wisp of hair left. Twenty years ago they had been purveyors of what many considered to be the finest grass in the North West. Then a spell of time at her Majesty's pleasure in Strangeways had changed their ways. Now they were both retired and had bus passes.

"You remember that Scouser? Cocky bugger. Promised to bring a tub of Valium and never showed."

"Yeah man. I remember. Eddie."

"That's it. Eddie. Wonder what 'appened to him?"

"And all of them blue Valium man."

They forgot about it as soon as they had said it, as the adverts were ending and they wanted to see the looks on the faces of the experts who had got the whole thing so horribly wrong.

And neither of them had the first clue about the chain of events they had set in motion by placing an order for a tub of Valium in May 1977.

And of course there was no reason why they should.

THE END

Other titles
by Mark Frankland

One Man's Meat
£5.99

The Cull
£5.99

Terrible Beauty
£6.99

Red Zone
£6.99

The Drums of Anfield
£4.99

Target One
£6.99

The Poisonous Past
£6.99

To order copies please complete the order for
at the back of the book or tel. 07770 443 483

All prices include P&P to customers in the UK

www.thecull.com

One Man's Meat by Mark Frankland

"Frankland turns crisis into drama"
Sunday Telegraph

November 1997 and British Farming
is being ripped apart by the BSE Crisis.
Vast areas of the countryside are facing devastation.
Finally one man decides that enough is enough.

Sir Alistair McIntyre, owner of the vast McIntyre
Holdings Corporation, makes the fateful decision to
save the Beef Industry. He hires a team of Mavericks
who claim to be able to solve any problem.
Their prize is massive. So is their task.

As their campaign gathers momentum
thousands of angry farmers at last start to fight back.
The story sweeps across the globe at breathtaking speed
from Argentina to Matabeleland,
from the windswept Scottish hills
to the shanty towns of Brazil,
from the Cabinet Room in Downing Street
to the Boardroom of a supermarket giant.

Every step of the way the team are sucked into ever
greater danger until their path inexorably leads them
to the lair of one of the most dangerous men on earth . . .

**To order a copy complete
the order form at the back of the book
or tel. 07770 443 483**

£5.99 (incl. P&P to customers in the UK)

www.thecull.com

The Cull by Mark Frankland

"Mark lifts the lid on Drug Town" **Sunday Post**

"Everyone who has lost a child to heroin will want to be Jack Sinclair. Tragic, thrilling, captivating." **Simon Houston, Daily Record**

Will Sinclair is dead. It seems as if he will be just another statistic. Another young man dead before he reaches twenty. Another Scottish junkie unlucky enough to shoot-up a bad bag of heroin. A few column-inches in the local paper. Ten seconds on the radio news. And then he will be added to the long, long list. Just another dead junkie.

But this time it is different. It is different because Jack Sinclair will not accept his son's loss with resigned grief. He refuses to forgive and forget. He was once Major Jack Sinclair of the Scots Guards. In three tours of Northern Ireland he learned all about fighting an unseen enemy. Then there were rules. Regulations. Restrictions. Red tape. His war against the drugs gangs who killed his son will be very different. This time the gloves are off. This time he has a free rein.

As Jack Sinclair lights his small fire, the story sweeps from the empty wilderness of the Galloway Forest to the war-torn streets of West Belfast, from the mean council estates of West Scotland to the Cabinet Room of 10 Downing Street. And the fire becomes an inferno.

"Like 'Trainspotting' before it, 'The Cull' takes the reader into the darkest corners of the Scottish drug world. Compelling. Harrowing. Always gripping. Nothing will stop you turning the pages."

**To order a copy complete
the order form at the back of the book
or tel. 07770 443 483**

£5.99 (incl. P&P to customers in the UK)

www.thecull.com

***Terrible Beauty* by Mark Frankland**

" Gripping and horribly realistic." **Glasgow Evening Times**

It is the story of the making of an outrage. An outrage which will be the greatest of them all. An outrage that will make Omagh and Enniskillen look like mere sideshows. An outrage that will blow the Good Friday Agreement into a million pieces.

It is the story of two men from West Belfast. It is the story of how their lives are swallowed up by the endless war of their peoples. Sean O'Neil travels the road of the IRA. For Davie Stanton it is the British Army and the UVF. Their journey carries them through thirty years of pain – Burntollet, the riots of 1969, the Battle of Ballymurphy, Internment, Bloody Sunday, Warrenpoint, The Hunger Strike, Loughgall.

Slowly their lives become intertwined. They become puppets in the dark game where their strings are pulled by the shadowy forces of the British Security Forces. And their destiny becomes one. In the end one man can no longer stand the Peace that he sees to be a lie. The Peace he sees a betrayal of his people. He plans an act so appalling that the fragile Peace will be shattered beyond repair. And there is only one man in the world who can stop him.

"A compelling read. Terrible Beauty is lovingly written, imbued with compassion, humanity, and great attention to detail. It will keep the reader entranced from the moment they pick it up." **An Phoblacht – Republican News**

"This book identifies the murky world of terrorism, it also shows how in more cases than not, an incident opens the path towards violence." **David Ervine – Leader of the Progressive Unionist Party**

"Frankland shows insight and authority about the perennial problems of the Province. It is also a rivetingly good read!" **Rt Hon Sir Robert Atkins MEP, Minister of State, Northern Ireland Office, 1992 – 1994**

£6.99 (incl. P&P to customers in the UK)

www.thecull.com

Red Zone by Mark Frankland

"An unrelenting pile driver of a read"

An asylum seeker goes berserk on the late night
streets of Sighthill. Three local teenagers are hacked
to death. The worst riot Glasgow has seen
in a generation rages through the night.

The Israeli Defence Forces stage a dawn raid
on a house in Gaza city. Mahmoud Bishawa,
the most notorious of all Palestinian fighters,
is taken into custody to await trial and execution.

Two events. By pure accident they happen within hours
of each other. Two events that are in no way related.
Two events in two cities thousands of miles apart.

It is the plan of one man which draws the two events
together. Khalil Bishawa will go to any lengths
to secure the freedom of his brother.

He brings the savagery of fifty years of fighting
between the Israelis and the Palestinians
to the towering blocks of the Sighthill Estate.

He takes the people of Glasgow into the Red Zone.

*"You watch the news and see the pictures from Gaza
and the West Bank and think it will never affect you.
You won't feel the same after you turn the last page."*

**To order a copy complete
the order form at the back of the book
or tel. 07770 443 483**

£6.99 (incl. P&P to customers in the UK)

www.thecull.com

The Drums of Anfield by **Mark Frankland**

*"A fantastic adventure book for all young
football lovers – even one as young as me!"*
Sir Tom Finney

Once in every generation a great new star emerges
into the world of football. Out of the slums of Sao Paulo
came Pele. Out of the bullet-scarred streets of Belfast
came Georgie Best. Out of the shanty towns of Buenos Aires
came Maradona. When Liverpool's veteran captain,
Tony Hobbes, suffers a crippling injury and receives a long
ban for violent conduct, he decides to take his son to Africa.

He expects to find lions and elephants amidst the Dark
Continent's endless wild plains. Instead, far away in the East
of Uganda under the shadow of the Mountains of the Moon,
he finds a boy called Simon Matembo. He knows that the
boy's talent is so huge that he could become the greatest
of them all. He knows that this boy can take Liverpool back
to the great days. But first he has to find a way to take him
back, and to do this he must overcome many huge challenges
from the tribe, the club, and even the forces of nature.

*"Anyone who loves football will love this book.
Football is about passion, unrelenting excitement
and, more than anything else, it is about dreams.
Exactly the same can be said about 'The Drums of Anfield'.*
Gerry Marsden, from 'Gerry and the Pacemakers'

"Genuinely hard to put down", **FourFourTwo Magazine**

**To order a copy complete the order form
at the back of the book or tel. 07770 443 483**

**£4.99 (incl. P&P to customers in the UK)
www.thecull.com**

Target One by Mark Frankland

'A head-spinning "Day of the Jackal" for the Twenty-First century. The pages almost turn themselves'

Roland McMillan is 95 years old and his doctors see little chance of him making it to 96. In 1926 he fled the desperate misery of his life in the mining town of Kirkonnel and emigrated to America. Over 79 years he has built up a colossal family fortune. Now it is time to tidy up his affairs.

McMillan's greatest treasure is his gallery of paintings which is reputed to be the most valuable and extensive private collection in the world. He has always known that one day he will bequeath it to the nation. The question he needs to resolve is which nation – Should it be Scotland, the land that bore him? Or should it be America, the land that made him?

His solution is an old-fashioned one. The fate of the McMillan collection is to be decided by a game of golf played by modern day gladiators. America's number one golfer will challenge Scotland's number one over Turnberry's majestic Ailsa course for the greatest prize in the history of sport.

George Albright the Third is one of the greatest sportsmen America has ever produced. A world figure. A sporting icon. The undisputed Number One in the world with a fortune fit for a king to his name. to his name. Archie Banks is an unknown. A hard-smoking, hard-drinking nobody from ttorious Sunnybank estate in Dumfries who is only his country's number one as a result of a fluky streak of results.

The twenty-first century version of David and Goliath catches the imagination of the world and sends the lives of both players into chaos. It is an event that everyone wants a piece of. Even the American President will be there to watch.

As the eyes of the world are fixed on the event, unwanted guests plan a dramatic intervention. When the news of the President's intentions reaches Al Quaida, they put in place a plan to assassinate their TARGET ONE.

**To order a copy complete the order form
at the back of the book or tel. 07770 443 483**

**£6.99 (incl. P&P to customers in the UK)
www.thecull.com**

The Poisonous Past by Mark Frankland

''This book is about why people take to the streets and throw stones. Like they did in the sixties. And the eighties. It's about how far some people will go when they get angry. And how far other people will go to stop them.'

South Yorkshire. 1984: Lenny Baxter and over 150 thousand coal miners take on the Conservative Govern-ment in a long awaited showdown. What starts as a strike is soon more like a war. Yorkshire becomes a near police state as the Government takes off the gloves and starts to fight dirty. And Lenny Baxter becomes the most hunted man in Britain.

Scotland. 2005: Once again Lenny goes to war. This time in a small Scottish town. And once again he finds the dark forces of the State deployed to meet him.

Lenny's journey spans the eras. From the burning sun of Orgreave to the killing fields of Iraq. From Reagan to Bush. From Thatcher to Blair. From the Cold War to the War on Terror.

From its shocking start to the nerve-shredding finale, The Poisonous Past takes the reader to the darkest corners of British life. It is a story from the places far away from the glossy image of Great Britain Plc. The sink estates, the baseball caps and hoodies. Discarded needles and burnt out cars. And the faceless man in anonymous offices whose job is to make sure the lid stays on . . .

"Here is a book that challenges our assumptions. The assumption that young people don't rebel any more. The assumption that their only icon is the Nike tick. The assumption that the Multinationals and the politicians they pay for will always win"

**To order a copy complete the order form
at the back of the book or tel. 07770 443 483**

**£6.99 (incl. P&P to customers in the UK)
www.thecull.com**

Order Form

Name ....

Address ....
....
....
....

Telephone ....

Email ....

Please send me .... **Copies of**

Please send me .... **Copies of**

I enclose a cheque for ....

**Please make cheques payable to:
'Glenmill Publishing'**

Return this form to:

**Glenmill Publishing
Glenmill
Dumfries
DG2 8PX**

Or Telephone   07770 443 483